One Good DRAGON DESERVES ANOTHER

From the author of *Nice Dragons Finish Last*

RACHEL AARON

ISBN: 1519249969
ISBN-13: 9781519249968

PROLOGUE

Svena, Terror of the Winter Sea, White Witch of the Three Sisters, and acting head of the world's oldest and still most powerful dragon clan, was awake before noon, and she wasn't happy about it. She was even less happy to be awake and *alone*, sulking in the middle of Ian's giant bed while she watched her young lover dress through narrowed, resentful eyes.

"I don't see why you have to leave," she said, brushing the sleep-tangled, ice blond hair out of her eyes. "Not even humans are awake at this beastly hour."

"On the contrary," Ian replied, tying his silk tie in the bedroom mirror. "Lots of highly successful humans are up and busy at six in the morning, which is why *I* am up at five." His reflection smiled teasingly at her. "That's the downside of young, ambitious dragons, darling. We still have to work."

Svena's scathing look let him know what she thought of *that*. As always, though, Ian just smirked, running a brush through his perfect black hair one last time before walking over to the bed. "Go back to sleep," he said, leaning down to kiss her. "You need all the rest you can get. We have the party tonight."

He said this like he was delivering the gravest of news, and Svena laughed. "But the invitation was *so* heartfelt. How could I dash your sweet baby brother's hopes by refusing? I'm a dragon, not an ogre."

Ian scoffed. "If Julius actually wrote that, he's even worse than I thought." He crossed his arms over his chest. "You know my mother—"

"Of course I know," Svena cut him off, snuggling back down into the pillows. "But that's the problem with *old,* ambitious dragons, darling. You are free to cut your own way to the top, but the Heartstriker isn't someone we can ignore, and I have my family to think of."

"You think of them too often," he said coldly. "Why must it all fall on you? Your sisters are perfectly capable of spinning their own plots. Or they would be, if they weren't so used to Estella telling them what to do, they've forgotten how to function without her."

"Perhaps," Svena said sleepily. "But at least *they* never woke me up before noon."

Ian heaved a long sigh, and then the bed dipped slightly as he reached down to stroke her long hair. "I'll come home early," he promised. "I want to take you somewhere before we have to go."

Svena's head shot up. "Where?" she asked, trying not to sound too excited.

Ian didn't answer, just winked at her as he stood and walked out of the bedroom. Only when the door shut behind him did Svena let her suspicious expression melt into a smile as she flopped back into the mountain of pillows.

Not that she would ever admit it, but things with Ian were going remarkably well. He managed the delicate balance of courtship with the adroitness of a dragon three times his age; showering her with just enough gifts and surprises to keep her interested, but never so many that it came across as trying too hard. He was also exceedingly easy on the eyes as both a human and a dragon. A shallow consideration to be sure, but one Svena found quite pleasing. Most astonishing of all, though, was how well they got along.

It wasn't affection; Svena barely felt *that* even for her sisters, but there was an ease of like minds between her and Ian that was surprisingly delightful. So much so that she often found herself granting him more access than she should, which would have to be curbed. A courtship this lovely deserved to be savored, not rushed, and after all the work she'd put into digging her clan out of the hole Estella had left it in when she'd vanished without a trace four weeks ago, Svena had earned some time to herself.

With that delightful thought, Svena rolled over, snuggling back into bed to catch another few hours of sleep before she was due to meet Katya for brunch and a status report. She'd just begun to drift off when she felt a cold, sharp twinge at the edge of her consciousness.

Svena sat bolt upright, holding her breath, but there was no mistake. Magic was rising in the room. *Very* familiar magic, and it was coming fast.

She sprang out of bed, trailing frost across the carpet behind her as she grabbed her dressing gown. She was still shoving her arms into the padded silk sleeves when the air in front of her closet began to warp and bulge before finally ripping apart entirely as a dragon tore its way into the world.

Svena jumped back with a curse. Not because of the dragon— given the magic, she'd expected nothing less—but because it was *black*. What should have been glistening white scales and transparent, frost-traced wings was hidden under thick layers of tarry, black residue, almost as though the dragon had been rolling in ash. The stuff didn't smell like any char Svena had ever encountered, but before she could get a better look, the dragon shifted and shrank until all that was left was its human shadow, naked and gasping on the ice-coated carpet.

"Estella!"

Svena ran to her sister's side, her hands shooting out to help her up before stopping short. Something was horribly wrong. Estella's normally snow-white hair and skin were as dirty as her dragon had been, and her fingers were bloody, as though she'd been digging through sharp stones. Worst of all, though, was what she clutched between them.

There were two objects. One, a beautiful golden ball the size of a large orange, was expected. Estella had never mastered the finer points of extraplanar travel, and she couldn't have found her way back to this dimension without the Kosmolabe. But while Svena was most definitely not pleased to see the golden troublemaker again, it was nothing compared to what was waiting in Estella's other hand.

At first glance, they looked like coiled lengths of black rope. On the second, she saw they were *chains*. Pencil thin, ink black chains were wrapped around Estella's hands and wrists, their tiny links glittering dully under the dimmed lights. The closest one twitched as Svena watched, curling around Estella's thumb like a thin, black tentacle.

"What is that?" she demanded, recoiling back from her oldest, and once dearest, sister. "What have you done, Estella?"

The seer didn't answer. She just pushed herself to her knees, looking around the penthouse apartment like she didn't know where she was. "How long was I gone?"

Svena winced. Her sister's voice was as rough as the rest of her. "Four weeks."

"Four weeks," Estella whispered, lifting a shaking, chained hand to her face. "It felt like centuries."

For a dangerous moment, the old sympathy came welling back, and then Svena remembered herself. "Maybe it should have been."

Estella's head snapped up, but Svena only gave her a cold look, rising from the floor to stare down at the dragon who'd nearly doomed their clan. She'd hoped to have more time before it came to this, but it didn't matter. Svena was prepared, and it was best to settle things now, quickly, before Estella had a chance to recover.

"You should not have returned."

"And you should not speak to me that way," Estella said, lifting her chin. "I will give you a chance to take it back."

"I don't need your chances," Svena growled. "I'm not your pawn any more."

Estella opened her mouth to argue, but Svena didn't give her a chance. "While you were gone, I convened our sisters. Eleven daughters of the Three Sisters, all together in one place for the first time since our mothers went to sleep, and for once in our lives, we were able to come to a consensus. You are no longer welcome among us."

She stopped there, waiting for the shock, but she should have known better. Estella was a seer. She didn't even look surprised. "That's not something you get to decide," she said haughtily. "Our mothers—"

"Our mothers have been asleep for over a thousand years," Svena reminded her. "But if they woke today, they would be disgusted by how you've managed things in their absence. You are forever saying that we are the daughters of gods, but your endless, petty grudge against the Heartstriker and her seer has brought us closer to destruction than any other disaster in our history, *including* the loss of magic. Your selfishness put us all at risk, endangered Katya, and diminished our standing as a clan. That is incompetence, Estella, and we are no longer willing to tolerate it." She bared her teeth. "Your rule is over, Northern Star. It is our consensus that your mind has finally been eaten by the seer's madness, leaving you incapable of guiding our clan any further. From here on, *I* lead the Daughters of the Three Sisters, and you will follow, or you will be banished."

By the time she finished, Estella was shaking with rage, her hands curling into fists on the frosted carpet as magic began to rise. Svena called hers as well, ready to finish this. She was no longer afraid of the future. Estella was not the wise, savvy leader she'd once been, the dragon Svena had always looked up to. This filthy creature was nothing but a shadow, and Svena was younger, stronger. She would win. But as she summoned the ice to her hands, shaping the cold magic into a blast that would send Estella through the penthouse window, the seer suddenly slumped.

"I knew you would do this," she said sadly, lowering her hands as she sat back down on the floor. "Your future vanished from my sight a long time ago, but I didn't need to see to know. You have always been ambitious, Svena. It was inevitable that you would turn on me."

"Congratulations, then," Svena said mockingly. "You were right one last time."

"Not this time," the seer said, shaking her head. "I will not fight you, little sister."

Svena paused, confused. "Then you will bow?"

"No," Estella said with a crooked smile. "You will."

And then her arm shot out.

Svena dodged automatically, throwing up a barrier of razor sharp ice, but it didn't help. The moment Estella's arm extended, one of the black lengths of chain leapt from it, curving impossibly in mid-flight to slide over the barrier and wrap around Svena's throat. But while she saw the black chain hit, the metal had no weight against her skin, and when her frantic hands shot up to tear it away, there was nothing. Nothing at all.

"*What did you do?*" she roared, grabbing frantically at her bare neck.

"I fixed you," Estella said sweetly. "Don't worry, love. I'm going to fix everything."

The words fell soft as snow, and when they were done, the invisible thing around Svena's neck wrenched tight. She sank to the ground, choking as she clawed at whatever it was Estella had thrown, but like before, there was nothing to feel, not even magic. Her throat was simply closing, cutting her off, not from air, but from the world. It was like she was being squeezed out of her own body, and as she fought helplessly on the floor, Estella knelt beside her, reaching down to brush Svena's hair out of her face as she had when they were young.

"Go back to how it was," she whispered. "Come back to me."

That was the last thing Svena heard before everything ended.

• • •

Two thousand miles away, in the heart of the mountain that rose like a thorn from the center of the vast expanse of New Mexico desert that now belonged exclusively to Bethesda the Heartstriker, in a cave stuffed to bursting with treasure and trash collected in equal measure, Brohomir, Great Seer of the Heartstrikers, fell out of his hammock.

He landed on his feet only by habit, shaking his head in an attempt to clear the horrible dream. Sadly, this too was only habit. He already knew what he'd felt was no dream.

It was a problem.

Bob turned away from his hammock with a scowl, clambering over piles of antique chessboards, watering cans, crowns, ancient artifacts, and hubcaps in his rush to get to the corkboard propped up on top of the unpainted, sideways door that served as his desk. His *actual* desk was currently being used as a stand for the massive bird habitat he'd installed for his pigeon.

His sudden fall must have woken her, because she came fluttering over to perch on the shoulder of his threadbare t-shirt, her talons picking tiny holes in the design that wouldn't be suitably ironic for at least another decade. For once, though, Bob didn't notice. He was too busy digging through the massive layers of pink and yellow sticky notes that covered the corkboard like overlapping scales, looking briefly at each one before tossing it on the ground.

"No," he muttered. "No, no, no, no—AH!"

He clutched the neon orange slip of paper like a winning lotto ticket and turned to the bird on his shoulder. "Darling," he said sweetly. "I'm afraid I'm going to have to ask you to do some flying."

The pigeon tilted its head, blinking its beady eyes with a questioning coo.

"Yes, far," Bob said, showing her the paper. "As far as it gets, I'm afraid."

The pigeon cooed again, and Bob sighed, walking over to grab the tin of butter cookies lying on top of a dusty pile of VHS tapes. He cracked the lid and picked out a sugary square. The bird perked up immediately, hopping onto his open hand. When she'd pecked the bribe to crumbs, Bob stroked her rainbow-feathered neck with a gentle finger. "Now, please? It's kind of important."

The pigeon bobbed her head and took off, beating her wings hard as she worked her way up through the heavy air to the tiny window at the top of the artificial cavern. Bob watched her until she was out of sight, and then he slapped the lid back on the cookie tin, tossed it on his desk, and, since he clearly wasn't going to get another chance to do so any time soon, went back to bed.

CHAPTER ONE

In a dark corner of the DFZ Underground where the touristy, old Detroit kitsch of lower downtown collided with the clapboard factory neighborhoods, in the top floor walk-up of a crumbling apartment building so poorly constructed, it had to lean on the nearby skyway pillar to stay upright, Julius, youngest son of Bethesda the Heartstriker and greatest failure of the Heartstriker dragon clan, was engaged in a standoff.

He stood with his back to the water-damaged drywall, his green eyes locked on the shadowy kitchen, where another pair of eyes—these round, reflective, and traffic-cone orange—watched him from the dark. Below the eyes, a massive jaw was open in a threat display, showing off twin rows of short, shark-like teeth with a growl that sounded like a miniature chainsaw. It wasn't nearly the scariest wall of teeth Julius had faced, but he knew from unfortunate personal experience that whatever those fangs lacked in size, they made up for in sheer power. A tank badger could bite through steel if it got mad enough, and this one seemed to be well on its way, stomping its stubby, long-clawed paws on the stained linoleum as it paced back and forth, looking for a way past the dragon's guard.

He was not going to find it.

The moment the badger's pacing brought it into range, Julius attacked, sweeping in with his catchpole. The long, carbon-fiber rod flexed like a fishing pole as Julius tipped it sideways, deftly slipping the steel wire loop at the end over the tank badger's armored head. The moment the noose was in position, he turned the pole again to cinch the loop tight, trapping the animal in a choke at the end of the stick.

"Gotcha!" he cried, bracing with his arms out to keep the thrashing badger at the end of the pole as far from his body as possible. He was reaching back with his foot to slide the warded cage into position when a *second* tank badger jumped out of the broken cabinet above the fridge to land on top of the first, biting through the steel wire that Julius had looped over its neck like so much taffy floss.

"Oh come *on*," Julius cried, yanking back his now useless catchpole as both tank badgers turned to growl at him, their squat, heavy bodies blocking the kitchen doorway in a wall of armored muscle and sheer orneriness. "I thought you guys were supposed to be territorial."

The badgers snarled in unison, snapping their powerful jaws. Julius bared his own teeth in reply, trying to remind them who the bigger predator was around here, but he might as well have been growling at one of his siblings for all the good it did. Tank badgers were immune to poison, most magic, and their armored hides were tough enough to stop bullets. They were also fireproof, which meant they cared about dragons only slightly more than they cared about humans, which was not at all. Plus, there were two of them now, which was one more than Julius was prepared to deal with.

"Marci!" he called, keeping his eyes on the badgers as he tossed the broken catchpole away. "How's it going?"

There was a long, frustrated silence before she called back. "Could be better."

That was not the answer he'd hoped for. "Better how?" he asked, risking a look away from the badgers just long enough to dart his eyes back to the living room where Marci was standing over their client, a young man whose prone body was overshadowed by the ghostly apparition of a tank badger the size of a car.

"It's not *my* fault," she growled, scowling into the glowing spellwork circles she'd drawn all over the cheap parquet floor. "This should have taken ten minutes, but this stupid curse is so buggy and poorly made, it's actually almost impossible to remove. It's like whoever did it went all the way around the circle of incompetence and ended up at accidental brilliance."

"I keep telling you, it's not a curse," the client croaked, his pale face covered in a sheen of nervous sweat that only got worse every time one of the tank badgers made a noise. "It's a love spell."

A love spell that attracted male tank badgers looking to mate sounded like a curse to Julius, but he kept his mouth shut. There was no point in antagonizing the client, especially since Marci was doing such a good job of it on her own.

"It's a scam, that's what it is," she said, flaring her spellwork as she fed more magic into her circles. "You got yourself tricked into paying for a summoning by some idiot, no-license shaman, and now you've got a female tank badger spirit sitting on your head like you're her new den. You're lucky attracting randy males is all she's doing."

"So get rid of her," he gasped.

"I'm trying!" Marci snapped. "But it's kind of hard to undo spellwork when you have it permanently attached to your body." She stabbed her finger down as she said this, pointing straight at the crude and obviously brand new spellwork tattoo encircling the client's bicep. "Seriously, dude, what were you *thinking*? Why would you get spellwork *tattooed* when you don't even know what it *does*?"

The man began to look panicked. "Just get it off!"

"Too late for that," she said, rolling up her sleeves. "It looks like the spell's already gotten cozy with your magic, which means it's going to take more than physical removal of the ink to get it out." Marci shook her head. "Nothing for it. We're going to have to burn her down."

The man began to sweat harder. "Burn down? That doesn't sound good. Are you sure you're qualified for this?"

"Burning down a spirit just means Marci's going to siphon off magic until it's small enough to banish," Julius explained, slipping into his unofficial job of team peacekeeper. "Just relax. I've seen her do this plenty of times, and I assure you it's perfectly safe."

Marci rolled her eyes at that last bit. Fortunately, the client wasn't looking. "Just hurry up," he rasped, closing his eyes. "She's crushing me."

Like it could hear them talking about it, the giant female tank badger spirit hissed and crouched down harder over its prey. The noise caught the attention of both males, and they barked in reply, their stubby, club-like tails bashing holes in the kitchen floor in their excitement.

"Can you keep the hordes at bay for a few more minutes?" Marci asked, looking at Julius. "I'm going to try and finish this in one swoop."

"I'll do my best," he promised, unclasping the industrial strength cattle prod from his belt. The voltage was calibrated to stun a buffalo, which meant it'd be enough for one of the badgers. The other was another story, but from the intent way they were staring at the female spirit, Julius knew he was just going to have to wing it. Now that they outnumbered him, any hesitation the badgers might have had was gone. They were going to get to the female, and they were ready to go through him to do it. So, before the beasts could shuffle out of the kitchen to flank him, Julius jumped straight at the bigger one, leaping through the air to shove the cattle prod's electrode deep into the gap below its armored jaw.

The animal's squeal went off like a siren, piercing his ears as the tank badger's body went stiff from the shock. It fell over a second later, too stunned to even breathe. The shock wouldn't last long, though, so Julius didn't waste time. He'd already whirled around, dropping the prod, which took five seconds to rebuild its charge, to grab the warded cage he'd hauled up five flights of steps back when they'd thought they'd only have to deal with one tank badger, and not a moment too soon. He'd barely closed his fingers around the cage's spellworked metal tines when the second badger launched itself at his head.

For such a squat, heavy animal, the tank badger was impressively fast, but here, at last, Julius had the advantage. Moving with supernatural quickness, he planted his feet and spun, positioning the cage in front of him. By the time the tank badger saw what was waiting, it was much too late. It was already in the air, and there was nothing it could do but squeal as it flew into the open cage like a ball into a goal. The impact when it crashed into the back was still enough to nearly take Julius off his feet, but he caught himself just in time, bracing against the doorway as he locked the cage door in place, shutting all one hundred pounds of furious tank badger behind an inch-thick grid of spelled metal.

And just like that, one threat was eliminated. The caged badger snarled and snapped, but the slits between the bars were too small to get its nose through, much less teeth around. Feeling satisfied that it was caged for now, Julius turned back to face the larger badger, who was already shaking off the cattle prod's stun, hissing like a cat as it rolled to its feet. He was trying to figure out what he was going to do about that since they'd only brought one cage when a bowling ball-sized blast of swirling air flew over his shoulder and slammed into the badger's face, knocking it head-over-claws back into the kitchen.

It hopped back up almost immediately, shaking off the magic like it was nothing, but when it turned around to growl at Julius again, its orange eyes no longer had the crazed gleam. The poor thing actually looked more confused than anything else, its pointy snout snuffing in the dark. Then, almost as though it had done the math and decided this whole mess was no longer worth the bother, the badger turned and fled, jumping through the shattered kitchen window and rattling away down the rickety metal fire escape.

Julius waited a few seconds to make sure it was really gone before looking over his shoulder to see Marci standing behind him with her arm out and her bracelet shining like a flood light. "Thanks."

She beamed at him. "Glad I could get the assist." Her bracelet snuffed out, and she shook her hand like it stung. "Man, those bastards are tough. That blast should have sent it flying into Ohio."

"I'm just glad it decided discretion was the better part of valor," Julius said, grinning back. "I take it you're finished, then?"

5

"Yep," Marci said, stepping aside to reveal their client, who was no longer being crushed under the shimmering image of a spirit. More telling to Julius, he also no longer reeked of female tank badger. This was a huge improvement for everyone, but especially for the badger in the cage, who was already noticeably calmer.

"Is it gone?" the client whispered.

"Not really, but she's banished for now," Marci said, reaching down to help him up.

The man looked bewildered. "What does that mean?"

"Well, a spirit can never truly be destroyed," Marci explained. "I drained enough of her magic to temporarily disperse her, but so long as there are tank badgers and magic, she'll always come back, and so long as you have that summoning spell tattooed on your arm, she'll come looking for you."

"So if I get it removed, she won't be?" he asked hopefully.

Marci nodded, her eyes sharp. "Next time, sir, I'd suggest you stick to qualified, licensed mages like myself for your spells, especially permanent ones." She flicked her wrist, and a business card appeared in her hand. "Our rates are very reasonable, and as you see, we get the job done right."

By the time she finished, the young man was gaping at her, but Julius could only smile. That was his Marci—she never missed a chance. Fortunately, the client was too happy to notice he was being hustled. Despite all the panicked complaining he'd done earlier, he was now staring at Marci and Julius like they were his own personal guardian angels. "Thank you," he said, voice shaking. "You saved my life."

"It was our pleasure," Julius said proudly, and he meant it. *Oh, how he meant it.*

Technically, their business was magical animal removal. This being the DFZ, though, the scope of the jobs that came in was much larger. In the month since he and Marci had gone into business together, they'd done everything from banishments to home warding to clearing out an entire warehouse overrun with sentient snails. They'd seen some pretty crazy stuff, but while tank badgers were definitely too high up on the danger scale for Julius's comfort, jobs like today's were actually his favorites. Clients were always happy when you did a good job for a fair price, but when you saved someone from a monster in their home, they treated you like a hero. That was an incredible feeling for a dragon who'd been able to count on one hand the number of times he'd been thanked just four weeks ago, and Julius couldn't keep the stupid grin off his face as he reached down to hoist the snarling cage containing the remaining badger onto his shoulder.

A mistake he didn't realize until it was too late.

"Wow," the man said, his eyes going wide. "You're a *lot* stronger than you look."

"He works out," Marci covered quickly. "Necessity of the job. Speaking of." She whipped out her phone. "We've got a dangerous animal removal plus a banishment. Would you like to add on a ward as well? You know, just in case?"

The client began to sputter, and Julius took his chance to flee down the stairs so he wouldn't have to hear her taking the man for all he was worth. He didn't begrudge Marci her mercenary nature— it was the main thing that had kept them afloat since they'd started this business together—he just didn't like to listen to it. All that up-selling felt…rude.

That was a terribly undraconic thought, but Julius let it roll off with a shrug. He didn't care about stuff like that anymore. Ever since he'd left Jessica's apartment the night they'd rescued Katya and foiled Estella's plots, he'd barely thought about other dragons. Other than Ian's occasional check-ins, he hadn't talked to one either. Even his mother hadn't called. It was like he'd fallen off the face of the dragon world, which was why—despite crazy animals jumping at his head nearly every day—the last four weeks had been the happiest of Julius's life. He had nothing he'd been raised to think was important: no wealth, no power, not even a proper lair, plus he was still sealed, but he couldn't care less. For the first time ever, he was living without constantly looking over his shoulder or worrying about when he'd be attacked. It wasn't much by dragon standards, but to Julius, it was paradise, and definitely worth risking some tank badger bites for.

Like it knew what he was thinking about, the badger in the cage chose that moment to try and bite his fingers where they held the cage handle, whining when it couldn't get through. Julius held the cage a little farther away as he took the rusted cement stairs down two at a time to the street where Marci had parked her car.

Technically, it was their car now, though Julius could never look at the rusted out, mustard yellow sedan without thinking of Marci. They could have bought a car ten years younger for what the old rust bucket had cost to fix, but the car had belonged to her father, and Marci was noticeably happier when she was in it, which, to Julius, made the repairs worth every penny. He'd still sprung for a few upgrades, though, like a better autonav and a ventilated, expanded trunk big enough to fit cages like the one he had now. He was strapping the metal box into place when he heard Marci's footsteps on the stairs behind him.

"How'd we do?" he asked, closing the trunk.

"Medium," she said, still tapping on her phone. "I couldn't sell him on the ward, but he did tip. I think you impressed him with that cage catch. We'll have to conjure another two calls before next Wednesday if we want to actually get into the black this month, but we won't starve for now, so that's something."

"We're not going to starve period," Julius assured her, walking around to the driver's door. "Speaking of, let's go get some dinner. It's nearly sundown."

"How can you tell?" Marci asked, looking up at the unchanging, cave-like dark of the DFZ Underground.

"Because I'm hungry," he said, plopping into his seat. "Come on. It's Friday night. Let's find a nice empty lot to dump Mr. Snarls where he won't bother anyone, and then we'll go for pizza."

He looked up to see if that appealed to her, but Marci was still standing beside the car. "You know," she said quietly, leaning down to look at him through the open door. "The bounty for an intact, living tank badger is currently listed at over two thousand bucks."

Julius dropped his eyes.

"They're pretty dangerous nuisances," she went on. "And two thousand bucks *would* go a long way toward filling the hole in our budget…"

She trailed off, her voice painfully hopeful, but Julius couldn't say a word. It wasn't that he didn't agree with what she was saying. Turning the animals they caught in for Algonquin's animal control bounty had actually been his plan to start with. But that was back at the beginning, when he'd assumed every job would be like the lampreys: nasty, aggressive, violent menaces that needed to be put down for everyone's benefit. Once they'd actually started going out on calls, though, he'd quickly realized that most of the animals they got hired to deal with weren't like that at all. Even the tank badgers weren't normally aggressive toward people. They were just animals doing their best to survive in the shadow of the enormous human city that had popped up like a mushroom on top of them, and as an illegal magical creature trying to make his own way in the DFZ, the thought of turning them in to be killed for Algonquin's bounty hit a little too close to home. It must have shown on his face, too, because Marci let out a long sigh.

"Never mind," she said, flopping into her seat. "Forget I said anything."

Julius started the car. "I'm sorry."

"It's okay," she assured him quickly. "Really. I just wanted to ask."

It *wasn't* okay. Julius was all too aware of the money his bleeding heart had cost them. Without the added cash from bounties, the fees from their removal jobs were barely enough to cover expenses. Things had gotten better when Marci had started selling her spell-work services, but Julius was painfully aware that this wasn't the life she'd signed up for when she'd agreed to come work with him. Happy as he was to be free of his family, the money issue was one of the two giant problems that kept Julius's current life from actually being perfect. Even so.

"Things are getting better," he assured her. "Word's spreading, our name's getting around. We'll keep taking more jobs until we don't have the time to do them all, and then we'll raise our rates. It'll all work out."

"I know, I know," Marci said, buckling in. "Like I said, no big deal. But can we stop by the house and change before we go for food? No offense, but you kind of smell like a badger."

Julius looked down at the padded tactical suit he wore for work. The thick fabric was meant to protect him from the bites and stings and other unpleasantness they got into on a daily basis, but it also had an unfortunate habit of sucking up every odor it came in contact with, and tank badgers definitely had a strong odor.

"Of course," he said, blushing as he gripped the wheel and gave the command for the autodrive to pull them out into the street. "Home first."

Marci smiled and leaned back in her seat, propping her knees on the dashboard as she balanced her massively over-packed shoulder bag on her lap and started digging through the pockets, re-organizing her already meticulous collection of casting materials. Due to the bag's size, this move bumped her leg into Julius's arm where it rested on the console between the seats. It was a tiny touch, barely more than a brush, but he felt it all the way to his toes. It took all his self-control not to shiver, and he looked away at once, hiding his flushed face behind a sudden feigned interest in the old car's battery system.

This was his *other* giant problem. He'd always thought Marci was cute, but since they'd started living together, the attraction had gone from exciting to downright debilitating. He could keep a lid on it when they were working and there were plenty of distractions, but at times like this, when they were sitting close together in the car or on the couch at home, his awareness of her went from constant to hyper. Even a tiny touch like the one just now was enough to unsettle him for hours, and given how much they were together, this meant Julius was unsettled pretty much all the time.

When he thought about it, which he did way too much, he completely understood what was happening. Marci was beautiful, strong, talented, and smart. She was also the only girl he'd ever spent real time with face-to-face instead of online. Add in every-thing they'd been through together and Julius would've been con-cerned if he *didn't* get a massive crush on her. But while he knew exactly what was going on and why, he didn't have any idea what to do about it.

He knew what he *wanted* to do. And given the number of times he'd caught her staring, he was pretty sure Marci felt the same, at least a little. But even assuming he could overcome his shy-ness enough to actually act on his feelings, Julius didn't dare. He *couldn't*. Marci was the most important person in his life: his trusted ally, insanely competent business partner, and best friend all rolled into one. Their relationship was the first he'd ever had that wasn't built on debts, fear, or obligation, which also made it the one thing in Julius's life that he absolutely, positively, could-not-under-any-cir-cumstances afford to mess up. If he tried anything—a confession, a kiss, even a misconstrued look—their friendship as it was would end.

That was a risk Julius couldn't take. He was already happier right now than he'd ever been in his life. He was free of his family, doing work he enjoyed with his best friend for people who thanked him. Even his mother's seal didn't bother him much anymore. If he could just figure out how to solve their revenue issue, life in the DFZ would be perfect. It was close enough already. But while a proper dragon wouldn't stop until he had everything, Julius had never been one of those, and he wasn't about to risk what he had in a greedy grab for more.

This was the same conclusion Julius had come to every day over the last few weeks, but wise and prudent as he knew his logic was, it didn't do him much good at the moment. No matter how many times he told himself it was all a hopeless pipe dream, nothing could dampen the thudding of his heart that came from being in close proximity to Marci. It didn't help that she looked ridiculously adorable today in her brightly colored jacket and zippered skirt. He couldn't actually remember seeing her wear that skirt before, but she wore it well, and the purple tights she had on underneath it were some of his favorites. The way they hugged her legs so perfectly all the way up to—

He jerked his eyes back to the road, cheeks burning. The heat only got worse when Marci leaned closer, snapping her fingers in front of his face. "Earth to Julius. You okay?"

"Fine," he said much too quickly. "I'm fine. Let's go home."

Marci frowned, but she didn't press as Julius began madly fiddling with the autodrive's GPS, drawing a path manually along the grid of streets back to their house.

Thankfully, they didn't have far to go. In a move that'd surprised everyone, Ian hadn't just made good on his deal to find Julius a building as payment for his part in finding Katya, he'd done so spectacularly. The house he'd given Julius was just across the old interstate from the river in a fading neighborhood that had once been called Mexican Town. These days, it was an industrial crossroads where the haphazardly expanded Fisher Freeway fed traffic up from the Underground to the skyways for access to the New Ambassador Bridge, which was still the only road connecting Detroit to Canada. The resulting traffic jam had nearly wiped out what the flood had left of the old neighborhood, but a few classic old houses still hung on amid the forest of highway on-ramps and support columns. Ian's property was one of these: a classic brick three-story, pre-flood house with arched windows, a big porch, Gothic accents, and what must have once been a very nice, treed-in yard.

The trees had all withered and died years ago when the skyways cut them off from the sun, and the yard was now little more than a gravel lot, but it was still an epic amount of room by DFZ standards. Even better, being surrounded by a spiraling maze of traffic ramps meant their house was almost completely cut off from the rest of the city. The only way in was through a tiny, unmarked access road that ran underneath an on-ramp, and the house itself was hidden inside the eye of the hurricane of ramps, bridges, and support structures that funneled commuters up from the Underground to the elevated Upper City. True, it was dark even by Underground standards, and being directly inside one of the busiest traffic exchanges in the city meant the roar of cars was constant, but the house and surrounding lot were big, private, in good repair, and, best of all, *safe*.

That was the most important factor when you were a dragon living in a city where you were considered prey. Marci had been a harder sell. She'd wanted a little bit of daylight, but she'd jumped on board once Julius showed her the giant, open attic with its peaked windows and marvelously pointed ceiling that he'd set aside to be her lab. After that, Marci had pretty much moved in on the spot.

Not that they'd had much to move, of course. At that point in time, everything they'd owned had fit on their backs. But the DFZ was a great place for secondhand anything. Now, one month of bargain hunting later, their hidden house was almost homey, the lit windows winking at them brightly in the dark as they drove under the ramp and pulled to a stop next to the front porch.

"I'm going to run upstairs and take a quick shower," Marci said, hopping out of the car. "I swear I smell more like a badger than you do."

Julius was opening his mouth to tell her she smelled fine when Marci froze. The change set him on instant alert, and he jumped out of the car. "What's wrong?"

Marci's eyes were wide as she turned and pointed at the flat stretch of gravel that had once been a side yard. "There's a freaking limo over there!"

He whirled around. Sure enough, though, she was right. A huge, black, heavily armored limousine was parked in the shadows right beside their house.

"Maybe it's a rich client?" Marci whispered, looking at him accusingly. "Did you give our address to someone big and not tell me?"

Julius shook his head, breathing deep through his nose. Now that he was outside the car, something in the air smelled off. Between the badger in the trunk and the reek of the highways overhead, he couldn't pick out what it was exactly, but it set his whole body on high alert, which meant it wasn't a good smell. He was still trying to sort it out when Marci turned and ran up the steps to the front door.

"What are you doing?" he hissed, running after her.

"What do you think I'm doing?" she hissed back, frantically fitting her key into the deadbolt. "There's an unknown car in our secret base! I'm going to get my big guns."

Julius hadn't realized Marci had things in her attic lab that would qualify as "big guns." When she opened the door, though, he forgot all about it. The moment the insulating seal cracked, the tiny wisp of teasing scent he'd been worrying over became overwhelming. It was the smell of his childhood, an unmistakable mix of blood and gold and fire. It was so out of place here, though, Julius couldn't do anything but stand and stare stupidly as Marci shoved the front door open to reveal the dragon sitting in their living room.

For a shocked moment, nobody said a word, not even Marci, and then the dragon smiled. "Now Julius," she said, her voice a thousand times sweeter and more terrifying than it ever could be over the phone. "Is that any way to greet your mother?"

And just like that, all of Julius's happiness vanished in a puff of smoke.

● ● ●

"What are you waiting for?" Bethesda said, her human fingers curling like claws as she pointed at the folding chair in front of the couch. "Sit."

Julius almost sat right there on the floor. He hadn't actually seen his mother since the night she'd kicked him out, and as always after an extended absence, the first sight of Bethesda the Heartstriker hit him like a punch.

It was a disconcerting thing to notice about your own mother, but Bethesda the Heartstriker was mesmerizingly beautiful. All dragons were pleasing to look at in their human guise. That was the entire point: to be so beautiful, actual humans fell at their feet. But Bethesda's beauty had always been in a class by itself, and she knew exactly how to use it.

Today, for example. She was wearing a super short, electric-blue cocktail dress that set off her black hair and dark complexion so perfectly, there had to be some sort of advanced color calculation going on behind it. Her eyes, the original Heartstriker green, were thickly lined in the fashionable new Egyptian style, a heavy counterpoint to the overt sexuality of her razor precise red lips. Her hair followed the Egyptian trend as well, falling in a perfectly straight, ink-black curtain over her shoulders and down her bare back. Gold flashed at her ears, throat, wrists, and anywhere else that would hold it, including her shoes, which looked to be little more than diamonds and gold chains knotted around her perfectly pedicured toes. The combined effect was classic Bethesda: dazzling, unspeakably expensive, and just past the edge of good taste. Her most striking accessory of all, however, was the dragon leaning on the wall behind her.

He was *massive*, six-foot-six easy with shoulders that took a lot of creative tailoring to fit into human-sized clothes. Between his giant build and the massive Fang of the Heartstriker positioned prominently at his side, the dragon strongly reminded Julius of Justin, though the truth was the other way around. Julius might have spent his life avoiding the upper alphabet members of his family, but even he knew that the dragon standing guard behind his mother was none other than Conrad, First Blade of Bethesda, Champion of the Heartstrikers, and the last surviving member of C-clutch aside from Chelsie herself. He was also Justin's idol, and if they looked alike, it was because Justin copied everything Conrad did, from his military-short haircut to his preference for motorcycle boots to the way they both wore their swords low on their right hip, despite the fact that Justin was not left-handed.

But terrifying as it was to have his mother and her champion appear unexpectedly in his living room, Bethesda's fancy get-up and Conrad's presence actually gave Julius hope. His mother would never waste this kind of display on a disciplinary visit to an underperforming child. He was probably just a stop on their way to somewhere more important, and he was scrambling to think of what he could say to make sure it stayed that way when a high-pitched squeak went off right next to his ear.

"Oh my *God*, you're *Bethesda the Heartstriker!*"

In the shock of seeing his mother, Julius had completely forgotten about Marci. She was still beside him, staring at the head of the Heartstriker clan with eyes wider than he'd known a human's could go.

"I've wanted to meet you forever!" she cried. "You look just like you do on TV!"

Her excitement was met with stony silence as Bethesda's eyes narrowed to dangerous green slits before flicking back to her youngest son. "Is this *your* human?"

"Yes!" Marci proclaimed happily, producing a business card from her sleeve with a flick of her hand as she charged forward. "I'm Marci Novalli, Julius's mage and business partner. We're—"

"Why is it talking to me?"

The chill in her voice would have stopped most mortals cold, but this was Marci. She rolled right over the warning with barely a pause for breath.

"I'll only be a moment. I just have a few—"

"Still talking," Bethesda said sweetly. "Conrad?"

Conrad pushed off the wall with a sigh, dropping his hand to his sword. But while he didn't actually seem ready to draw, the threat alone was enough to finally knock Julius out of his shock.

He lurched into motion, grabbing Marci and dragging her behind him before Conrad's hand finished tightening. "I'm very sorry," he said, holding Marci in place as he bowed low before his mother. "It's my fault. She's new, she doesn't know—"

"So teach her," Bethesda snapped, running her fingers through her perfect hair. "Really, Julius. If you're going to keep a pet, the least you can do is teach it some manners."

"Yes, Mother," he whispered, tightening his grip on Marci's arm in an attempt to make her understand just how much danger she was in.

A wasted attempt, it turned out.

"I meant no disrespect," Marci said, squirming against Julius's hold. "I just have so many questions! You were old and powerful before the magic vanished, right? If I could just get a few seconds of your time—"

"*Marci!*"

She jumped at his tone, but Julius didn't even look at her. "Get out."

"But—"

"*Now.*"

Marci froze in shock, her whole body going still. Julius was a bit shocked himself. He'd never heard his voice sound so menacing and, well, draconic. But it was the only way he could think of to make Marci stop talking and go. And she had to go. Right now. Before his mother's infamous temper turned her into a pile of ash.

"I'm sorry," she said, softly now. "I was just—"

"Hush, child," Bethesda said, her voice switching from terrifying to honey sweet again as she gloried in Julius's discomfort. "Can't you see you're embarrassing him? Surely you know my son doesn't need any help on *that* score. Now run along. Clan business is no place for chattering humans."

For one long moment, Julius thought the hurt on Marci's face would actually kill him. Then, without a word, she turned and fled, running up the stairs toward her workshop. He was still staring at the place where she'd been when his mother heaved an exasperated sigh.

"*Mortals.* They're *so* dramatic. But I must say I was impressed with how you handled her. For a moment there, I could almost imagine you were one of my other, less embarrassing children."

She paused expectantly, a cruel smile on her red lips, but Julius was in no mood for his mother's games. He wasn't even that scared anymore. He just wanted her to leave so he could go upstairs and apologize to Marci. "Why are you here?"

"Watch your tone," Bethesda said sharply, rising from the couch to loom over him. "Do you even know how lucky you are that I've deigned to visit your little..." Her voice faded as she looked around the sparsely furnished room. "What is it you're doing here again?"

"Running a business," Julius replied, standing a little taller. "We're called New Horizons Magical Solutions, and—"

"*That's* what you're calling it?"

When he nodded, she laughed. "What? Were you trying to stand out in the listings by having the longest name, or were you trying to make a clever acronym and got confused?"

Julius scowled. It *was* a bit of a silly name, but he liked it. It was fitting, because even after he'd messed up on the killing-animals-for-the-bounty end of things, New Horizons had remained exactly that: a new horizon for his life. A promise for a better future. But his mother would respect that kind of sentimentality even less than a harebrained scheme to game the business listings, so he decided to just move on.

"We're a magical animal control company," he explained patiently. "It's a booming business here in the DFZ. We've haven't even been operating for a month, and already—"

"So you're a rat catcher."

Julius couldn't exactly argue with that since he'd just gotten back from a job catching what were essentially giant magical rodents, but he didn't appreciate her tone. "It's a major industry!"

"Still waiting to hear why I should care," Bethesda said, looking down to examine her knife-sharp, gold painted nails with a dangerously bored expression.

Julius clamped his jaw shut, forcing the growl back down his throat before it got him into trouble. "With all due respect, Mother, it's only been a month. If you'd given me more time before checking in, I would have had something more impressive to show you."

"Show me?" she scoffed. "*Really*, Julius? Did you *really* think I'd risk setting foot in Algonquin's little playground to hear your humdrum tales of small business success?"

Well, not when she put it like that. "But," he said, confused. "If you're not here to check on me, why *are* you here?"

As always, Bethesda let him dangle for a moment before saying, "I'm taking you to a party."

He couldn't have heard that right. "A what?"

"A party," she repeated. "A social event in a private home. A get-together."

"I know what a party is," Julius said. "But why would you want to take *me?*"

"Because it suits me," she replied, her voice growing dangerously sharp. "And if you want to be unsealed this decade, you'll stop asking stupid questions and do as you're told."

The word "unsealed" had barely left her lips before the block she'd placed at the root of Julius's power started to clench up. It was only moderately painful, nothing like when she'd actually put the seal on him, but it made him extremely aware of how cramped and uncomfortable he was in this shape. His wings, which he normally didn't even think about, suddenly ached to uncurl, and his tail prickled like a limb that'd fallen asleep. Even his feathers were itching, making him want to roll around on the ground. Bethesda must have known it, too, because her smile only grew crueler. "Any more comments you'd like to add?"

"No, Mother," he said softly, lowering his head.

"Good boy," she cooed. "Now let's go. This detour has taken far too long already."

She and Conrad were already halfway out of the room before Julius realized she meant *right now.* "Wait!" he cried, looking down in a panic at his padded work clothes, which still reeked of tank badger. "At least give me a moment to change."

"Why?" Bethesda said, sweeping down the short hall toward the kitchen. "No one expects anything of you, so why should we pretend? It's not like you have something nicer to wear."

Julius did not, in fact, have anything in his closet at the moment that wasn't second-hand jeans and t-shirts, but that didn't make her assessment sting any less. "I can still—"

His mother growled deep in her throat, an inhuman noise that vibrated through the floor and set his hair on end. After that, Julius didn't say another word. He simply lowered his head and scurried after her, ducking through the kitchen and out the back door Conrad held open into the gravel alley behind the house where Bethesda's limo was waiting.

CHAPTER TWO

A nd this was how, an hour later, Julius found himself flying over the Great Plains in his mother's private sub-orbital jet.

Under different circumstances, this wouldn't have been so bad. Like everything else she owned, Bethesda's private jet was luxurious to the point of absurdity. It didn't even have seats, just couches and lounges strewn across a cabin that looked more like a flying living room. But it was hard to enjoy the luxury when he didn't know where they were going, or why Bethesda had decided to take *him*. His mother wasn't helping, either. She hadn't actually said a word to him since they'd left the house.

This wasn't to say she'd been silent. His mother had talked the whole time, just not to him. Instead, she'd been lounging on her throne-like couch, using her phone and smart mic to have multiple, simultaneous conversations with at least a dozen of his brothers and sisters, switching seamlessly between each call so each dragon thought she was talking only to them.

As a small and unimportant cog in the Heartstriker machine, Julius had heard of his mother's legendary ability to multitask, but this was the first time he'd witnessed it himself. At least now he understood how one dragon managed to keep a hold on so many plots, though it did make him wonder just how many other family members she'd had on hold all the times she'd called to threaten him.

Since Bethesda seemed to have temporarily forgotten he existed, Julius took the opportunity to message Marci, both to let her know he'd be gone for a while and to apologize for what had happened earlier. Seconds after he hit send, though, the text bounced back with an error message that the number he was trying to reach was not receiving calls. He tried again, just in case, but again, the text bounced back, making it clear this was not a technical failure. Marci's phone was getting his messages just fine. She just didn't want to talk. At least, not to him.

This realization sent Julius slumping down into the overstuffed leather sofa that passed for a rear seat on Bethesda's mansion of a plane. Really, though, he had no one to blame for this situation but himself. He should have seen this coming, should have been prepared, but *no*. He'd stupidly let himself believe he was free, that a few weeks of no dragons somehow meant he'd escaped them forever. What a joke. His mother had swept into his house in the DFZ just as easily as she used to barge into his room back at Heartstriker Mountain. His victories last month might have won him a bit of leeway, but when push came to shove, nothing had really changed. He was still a pawn, a tool, and unless he was willing to stand up to Bethesda and challenge that (and accept the swift death that would follow), he might as well get used to it.

It shouldn't have been hard. After all, until last month, his whole life had revolved around keeping his mouth shut, his head down, and his opinions to himself. But for a failure who'd had a sweet taste of freedom, going back was proving to be a surprisingly bitter pill to swallow. Fortunately for him, his survival instincts were picking up the slack, burying his simmering anger under a self-protective mask of meek submission as the plane began its final descent into the arid wastes of the New Mexico desert.

In hindsight, their destination should have been obvious. There was only one place in the world a dragon with as many enemies as Bethesda could safely attend a party, and that was in her own territory. But knowing they were going home only made Julius's sense of impending doom worse, especially when Heartstriker Mountain itself came into view on the horizon.

Tall enough to blot out the setting sun, Bethesda's fortress rose from the flat desert like a dragon fang. Once a petrified seabed, most of the natural rock had been dug out ages ago to make way for the numerous expansions needed to house a clan as large as Heartstriker. But while the base of the mountain looked like a military base with its air strip, helipad, and human town crouching in its shadow like a feudal village around a castle, the thorn-like peak was every inch the classic dragon mount with a rugged, natural surface and numerous dragon-sized caves open to the night air for easy landings. At the moment, it even had a full flight of rainbow-feathered serpents circling in the sky above it, their green eyes keeping constant watch on the surrounding desert. Julius was pressing his face against the window to try and see who was on patrol when his mother abruptly hung up all her calls and turned her own green gaze on him.

"I expect you to be on your absolute best behavior," she said, tapping her nails on the leather arm of her massive, throne-like chair. "It's not often a dragon like you gets to mix with a crowd like this. Fortunately, tonight should be a very simple visit for you. Just keep your mouth shut and try not to look so nice."

Julius glanced down at the shabby clothes she hadn't given him a chance to change out of. "But you said—

"Not *that*," Bethesda snapped irritably. "This." She smiled wide, her eyes growing distant and happy in a way that made her look totally different, almost kind, before her face went back to its usual cruel, dangerous beauty. "*Nice.*"

"Got it," Julius said with a sigh.

"Good," she said, pulling a compact mirror out of her gold-beaded clutch purse to check her still flawless makeup. "If things go the way I expect, I won't even need you, but you can still mess things up if you act too Julius-y, so don't."

"I'll do my best," he promised. "Though it'd probably be easier if you just told me what I'm not supposed to act like myself for."

His mother flashed him a knife-sharp glare. "Don't get cute. You might have wiggled your way off my To Kill list for the time being, but that can change at a moment's notice."

He dropped his head at once. "Yes, Mother."

"That's better," Bethesda said, closing her mirror with a snap. "And, as you'd already know if you paid *any* attention to current events, tonight's the night we cement our new friendly relations with the Daughters of the Three Sisters."

Julius nearly choked. He managed to hide it under a cough at his mother's dirty look, but still... *friendly relations?* With the *Daughters of the Three Sisters?*

That couldn't be right. The Three Sisters had been their clan's greatest enemies since forever. Estella had been openly trying to murder them all just last month. He'd heard from Katya that Ian and Svena were doing well, but there was no way a few weeks of progress could overturn centuries of hatred.

"I can hear you thinking," his mother said, her voice a teasing sing-song. "Have you finally figured out why you're here, then?"

He flinched at being put on the spot, and Bethesda rolled her eyes. "Come *on*, Julius," she said, snapping her fingers impatiently in front of his face. "For all your other failings, you've never been stupid. Do you think I brought you along tonight for the pleasure of your company?"

"No," he started. "But—"

"Then use your brain," she growled. "Why would I burden myself with you? What is the *one thing* you have that I could possibly want?"

By the time she finished, Julius was sweating bullets. Fortunately, when she put it like that, the answer was pretty obvious. "Katya of the Three Sisters owes me a life debt?"

Bethesda smiled, making his chest heave in relief. "See?" she said. "Was that so hard?" She leaned back in her throne-like lounge, smiling out the port-hole window at the setting sun. "This is the night of our victory, Julius. With the Northern Star run off to lick her wounds in another plane of existence and the Three Old Hags still asleep, we've never had a better chance to bring the remaining ice snakes to heel. Svena and her baby sister have already been invited. All you have to do is stand around and be a reminder of what they owe us."

She said this like she was doing him a favor, but his mother's words left a sinking feeling in Julius's stomach. He had no idea how she was actually planning to leverage Katya's life debt, but he didn't like the idea one bit. He doubted Katya would return the sentiment, but in his mind at least, she was his friend, and friends didn't use each other. Not that Bethesda would care. She'd just ripped Julius out of his home and walked all over his mage just so he could serve as a sign post. Fortunately for him, his mother seemed to be over-looking a vital point.

"You've invited them," he said nervously. "But will they accept? The Three Sisters have hated us since before the Heartstrikers were a clan. I know we've got a life debt now, and I'm sure Ian's been working on her, but I can't imagine Svena would be trusting enough to accept a party invitation from her ancient enemy at our home fortress?"

"Of course she's not," Bethesda said sweetly. "That's why I made sure the invitations she and Katya received came from *you*."

Julius blinked. "Me?"

His mother grinned wide, showing a line of sharp, blindingly white teeth. "Brilliant, isn't it? The White Witch has always been a suspicious snake. She'd never accept an invitation from me, but who could suspect our very own Nice Dragon of laying traps?" She chuckled. "Of course, once they accepted, I had to go out of my way to make sure you'd actually *be* here, but that's a minor inconve-nience. Putting up with you for a few hours is a small price to pay for such a victory, don't you think?"

The plane touched down as she finished, letting Julius hide his horror under the guise of bracing against the landing bump. If he hadn't been so terrified for them, he would have been flattered that Svena and Katya trusted him enough to be lured into something like this. But while part of him couldn't believe his mother would use his good name like that, the rest of him wondered why he was surprised by anything his mother did anymore. Bethesda had never met a circumstance she couldn't exploit to her advantage, and now she'd pulled him into it, too.

Just the thought made him sick. He spent the rest of the landing desperately trying to think of some way he could warn Katya and her sister without it being blatant treason against his clan. He was still working on it when the plane finally rolled to a stop, and his mother rose gracefully to her feet.

"Don't look like that, darling," she scolded as Conrad hopped up to open the exterior door. "This is the most use you've been to me in years. You should be happy, especially since you don't actually have to do anything. In fact, if you behave yourself tonight and this all works out like it should, I *might* just be happy enough to unseal you. Wouldn't that be lovely?"

She paused there, waiting for his answer, but Julius said nothing. What was there to say? If he agreed, he'd condone the use of his good reputation to trap those who trusted him. If he didn't, she'd accuse him of being ungrateful, revoke the offer, and use him anyway. That was how his mother worked: by leaving you no option but to dance to her tune and thank her for the opportunity.

When he didn't answer, Bethesda's smile fell. "You truly are a miserable excuse for a dragon," she said, turning away. "I give you opportunity after opportunity, but do you take it?"

He took a breath to defend himself, but his mother cut him off. "Do yourself a favor, Julius," she said as she started down the stairs the human crew had just finished rolling into position. "Keep that mouth shut. When we get to the party, find a corner and stand in it until I tell you to do otherwise. Can you manage that?"

"Yes, Mother," he said quietly, following her down the stairs to the tarmac where Frieda, the Heartstriker who served as his mother's secretary, was already waiting to walk them into the mountain.

Given how much he'd hated living here, Julius didn't even want to look at the place again. Before he could think of dragging his feet, though, a voice behind him growled, "Move."

Julius looked up with a start to see Conrad standing on the stairs behind him, his massive arms crossed over his inhumanly wide chest. He looked pointedly at the doors on the other side of the airstrip, and Julius got the hint, scurrying after his mother like a mouse.

His terrifying brother followed right on his heels, bringing up the rear as they left the jet to the human crew and stepped through the automatic, sound-proofed doors into the massive complex that was Heartstriker Mountain.

It looked the same as always. Julius wasn't sure what else he'd expected. He'd only been gone a month. Given how much his life had changed in the last four weeks, though, coming back to the same spotless green carpet, overly ornate gold light fixtures, and arched stone hallway full of human servants all scrambling to bow to Bethesda as she passed felt oddly surreal. The fortress didn't even feel like home anymore, an uncomfortable realization given that, up until a few weeks ago, this was the only home he'd ever known. He was still trying to decide how to feel about that when his mother marched them past the multiple elevators leading to the various family floors and into the special, gilded elevator at the far end that connected the public base of the mountain with her private lair at the peak.

Julius stopped with a gulp. He'd lived his whole life in Heartstriker Mountain, but he'd only taken this elevator a handful of times, and only when he was in deep, deep trouble. There was no other reason a dragon like him would be invited up to Bethesda's throne room or treasury. Considering clan parties were always thrown in the grand ballroom on the first floor, he was surprised they were going there now. Perhaps Bethesda was just going up to her rooms to change? If so, then he might be able to duck back down to his old room to grab something as well. He was sure he had something that could pass as formal wear in his old closet. Assuming, of course, Bob had been kidding when he'd said he'd sold everything.

When he mentioned going back to his room to his mother, though, Bethesda just scoffed. "Don't be stupid," she said, yanking him into the elevator without looking up from the tablet Frieda was holding for her to read. "This is an intimate gathering of the Heartstriker elite, not a cattle call. The ballroom is for the masses. *We're* going to the throne room." Her reflection in the elevator's golden mirrored doors smirked at him. "Now do you understand what an honor it is to be included?"

Julius muttered something about it being an honor, indeed, but inside he was fighting down panic. Any party hosted by his mother was a terrifying ordeal, but the Heartstriker gatherings he'd been forced to attend growing up had always been big enough for him to count on hiding in the crowd. A small, elite party was another matter entirely. Julius didn't even have a strategy for something like that, and there was no time to think of one. The swift, silent elevator had already rushed them to the mountain's peak, the great doors opening to reveal a stone hallway big enough to drive a tank down.

As the home of a young, modern clan who'd come into their power during the magical drought, most of Heartstriker Mountain had been designed to a human scale. Here, though, in the place that was the top of Heartstriker in all ways, things were built for dragons. Just stepping out of the elevator made Julius feel like an insignificant speck, but, as always when entering his mother's lair, what really got him were the heads.

The giant stone tunnel that ran from the elevator to the throne room's enormous double doors a hundred feet away was lined with severed dragon heads. They hung in a grid from floor to ceiling, each one a grisly trophy from the clans the Heartstriker had destroyed during her rapid rise to power, mounted on a custom mahogany plaque the size of a car. Since Bethesda's first conquests had been in the Americas, most of the skulls were feathered, including those from her two older brothers, but there were plenty of scaled heads from the European clans, fish-like heads from the Sea Serpents who ruled the Pacific, even two narrow, snake-like skulls from the Asian clans, and these were just the intact ones she liked to show off. Bethesda had even more trophies stored in her treasury, but the entry hall was reserved for the most impressive specimens, the defeated dragons big and famous enough to serve as a proper reminder of just who lived here, and what she was capable of.

Julius *hated* walking down this hall. Even knowing the severed heads were stuffed and their eyes were glass, he swore he could feel the dead dragons watching him and plotting revenge. His mother, on the other hand, loved it. She'd rushed them all the way from the plane to the elevator. Now, though, she took her time, smiling up at each head like she was greeting old friends. But creepy as it was to stroll through a postmortem gallery of your enemies, Julius was actually grateful for the slow pace. It gave him time to adjust to the growing scent of dragons coming from the doors at the end.

Since his mother had come to pick him up herself, Julius had hoped he'd have some time to prepare himself before the others arrived, but leave it to Bethesda to be fashionably late to her own party. He didn't have the experience needed to separate all the individual scents floating down the hall, but there were definitely a *lot* of dragons already waiting on the other side of the doors at the end of the hall. Nothing like the massive gatherings of Heartstrikers that showed up for his mother's annual birthday celebration, of course, but still more than Julius wanted to deal with in an enclosed space.

Just thinking about standing in that predatory crowd made him twitchy, but it was way too late to run. Conrad had already walked ahead of them to grab both of the massive door handles, looking over his shoulder at their mother for a signal. After taking a moment to pull herself to her maximum height, Bethesda nodded, and Conrad pushed the heavy, dragon-sized wooden doors open with a single shove to reveal Bethesda's enormous, gilded throne room, which was packed nearly to the walls with the most terrifying crowd Julius had ever seen.

When he was a young dragon, his sister Flora, who'd been in charge of the new Heartstriker's education, had shown J-clutch a scale model of the solar system. Years later, Julius could still remember how tiny and insignificant he'd felt coming face to face with the reality of interstellar distance, and it was the same feeling he had now. Even with his mother standing between him and the throne room, Julius could feel the force of the crowd's attention like a pressure zone as every dragon in the room turned to look at Bethesda's grand entrance.

Apparently, "small, elite gathering" was a relative term. There were so many deadly, beautiful faces turned toward them, Julius couldn't begin to count them all, but one glance was enough for him to know to his bones that he was the smallest thing in this room by a power of ten. Bethesda, of course, took their notice as her due. Regal as a queen, she lifted her chin, surveying the well-dressed crowd like she was trying to decide if it met her minimum requirements.

Like all her displays of power, it went on forever. Since Julius was trapped up there at her side, this meant *he* had to stand and be stared at forever, which was rapidly becoming a problem. Being the focus of this much draconic attention would have been the stuff of nightmares under any circumstances, but for some reason, the fear was hitting him even harder than he'd anticipated, weakening his knees even as it jacked up his body with the desperate need to flee.

It was this place, he realized, reaching up furtively to wipe the nervous sweat off his brow. Just looking at the gilded cave-turned-palace that was the Heartstriker's seat of power brought back a lifetime of bad memories. It was here that he'd first had to prove to his mother that he could fly, jumping off the massive, open balcony at the room's far end while Bethesda watched. He'd nearly crashed, too. Not because he was a bad flier—flying was actually the one part of being a dragon Julius had never had trouble with—but because his mother's critical glare had made him trip all over himself. The throne room was also where she'd first singled him out for being a failure, calling him up to stand beside her on top of her throne in front of all his siblings so he could see the view he'd never earn. But bad as the old memories were, he had a sharper, far more recent reason to hate this place, because the throne room was where Bethesda had sealed his dragon form.

That was a night he never wanted to remember, but it was impossible not to think about it when he was standing on the threshold of the place where it had happened. Everywhere he looked—the massive throne on its dais, the walls set with gold and gemstone mosaics depicting his mother in all her feathered glory, the smooth stone floor with its numerous, tell-tale dark stains—reminded him viscerally of what he didn't want to think about. Even just standing here in the doorway beside his mother, he could almost feel her claws in his flesh again as she dragged him up here from his room, but he couldn't get away. He couldn't even turn. So Julius did the only thing he *could* do. He looked up, staring determinedly over the heads of the terrifying crowd.

Since he'd always had his head down in his mother's presence, the roof was the only part of her throne room that didn't trigger flashbacks of events he'd rather not revisit. But even this wasn't a completely safe strategy, because looking up meant that Julius was now staring straight at what he used to consider the scariest part of his mother's trappings of power: the massive, bus-sized skull that hung suspended from the domed ceiling by enchanted chains.

Unlike the preserved, taxidermy dragon heads they'd walked past on their way here, this one was nothing but bleached bone. But despite its shabbiness, the huge skull was Bethesda's greatest trophy, because it was the head of her father, the Quetzalcoatl, the ancient dragon whose death by her hand had earned Bethesda the title of Heartstriker. It also looked different than the last time he'd seen it.

At least that was enough to shock Julius out of his fear. The Quetzalcoatl's skull was the Heartstrikers' most priceless family heirloom. His mother didn't allow it to be dusted, let alone messed with, but something was definitely different. He was staring harder, trying to put his finger on what, when a dragon broke from the crowd to approach the still preening Bethesda.

Not surprisingly given the purpose of this party, it was Ian. The dragon looked as impeccable as always in his slim-cut tux, but his expression was uncharacteristically nervous as he bowed low over Bethesda's hand. "Mother."

"Darling," she cooed back, eying Ian like a rancher would her prized bull. "Where is your date?"

There was only one "date" Ian could possibly bring tonight, but Julius didn't smell Svena, or any daughter of the Three Sisters, in the crowd, which explained why Ian's face was now the color of his white tie. "She's running a little late," he said, his voice impressively smooth, considering.

Bethesda's smile fell. "Late?"

The word came out like a dagger, making Julius flinch, and he wasn't even the one it was aimed at. But Ian was the dragon's dragon, and he took it with barely a grimace. "I'm given to understand she had some difficulties with her sister," he said calmly. "She will be here soon."

"She'd better be," Bethesda growled, turning away with a sweep of her shiny black hair. "Since we're being made to wait, I'm going to make my rounds," she announced. "Ian, you're with me. Julius, go find a corner and stand in it. When Svena deigns to grace us with her presence, return to my side. Otherwise, I don't want to see so much as a—"

Bethesda's voice cut off like a falling knife. Her body went still at the same time, freezing in place like someone had hit pause. At this point, Julius would have said it was impossible for him to be on higher alert than he already was, but apparently the sight of his mother freezing in her tracks was enough to jack his survival instincts to new heights. Time actually seemed to slow as his eyes flew over the crowded room, scanning the beautiful faces for the threat that could make Bethesda the Heartstriker stop in her tracks. In hindsight, he needn't have bothered. Picking out the dragon who'd made Bethesda freeze was as easy as following his mother's death glare.

In the far corner of the room, a dragoness in a crimson red dress was lounging against the mosaic-tiled wall, drinking what appeared to be a pint glass filled to the brim with whiskey. When she noticed Bethesda glaring, the dragoness lifted her glass like a salute. The whole interaction couldn't have taken more than five seconds, but by the time she'd lowered her cup again, Bethesda had dismissed her existence completely, shoving her arm into Ian's and marching into the crowd, her golden heels clicking angrily on the stone. Back on the steps, Julius was still trying to figure out what he'd just witnessed when a hand the size of a dinner plate landed on his shoulder.

"Move."

The terrifying order made him forget all about the strange dragoness. He jumped, whirling around to see Conrad glaring down at him like he was daring Julius to disobey. Not wanting to lose the joint Conrad currently had a death grip on, Julius put his head down and obeyed, letting his hulk of a brother steer him along the wall until they reached the throne room's inside corner. When they got there, Conrad took hold of both his shoulders and set Julius bodily against the wall and ordered, "Stay."

"I'm not a dog," Julius muttered, earning himself another deadly glare. "Right," he amended, dropping his eyes. "Staying."

Conrad nodded and turned away, resting his hand on the hilt of his massive sword as he walked back through the crowd toward Bethesda. But while it was amusing to watch the other dragons scurry out of Conrad's way, with his scary brother gone, Julius realized he was now alone. Alone, in a giant room full of the cruelest, most ruthless dragons in his family, many of whom were now looking at him like he might be entertaining.

He squeezed himself into the corner, putting his back to two walls at once as he hunched his shoulders in an effort to look as inconspicuous as possible. Blending into the background was a defense he'd learned early in his life. Dragons exploited weakness as a matter of principle, but if you could get them to overlook you entirely, you had a chance. To that end, Julius focused on staying small, staying back, and most importantly, avoiding eye contact. Since the room was packed, this once again meant looking up, which, since it took up most of the ceiling, brought him right back to his grandfather's skull.

Given the unspeakable, life-scarring things that usually happened in his mother's throne room, he'd never actually gotten a chance to just stand and stare at what was left of the Quetzalcoatl, which was probably why he'd never noticed just how much the skull's triangular, viper-like shape and curving front fangs resembled his own. Or, rather, Julius resembled him since the Quetzalcoatl was the original. As someone who'd always thought of his grandfather as more of a myth than an actual, historical figure, though, it was eye opening to see the physical proof that he actually was related to one of the most powerful dragons who'd ever lived, but he still couldn't shake the feeling that something was different. No matter how hard he stared, though, he couldn't place it. He was about to dismiss the whole thing as paranoia when it finally hit him.

The Quetzalcoatl's skull had an extra fang in its mouth.

His eyebrows flew up in surprise. Being so firmly at the bottom, Julius didn't know much about the treasures of his clan, but *every* Heartstriker was taught how the clan's greatest weapons, the five swords that made up the Fangs of the Heartstriker, had originally been *actual* fangs, as in *teeth*. Only one—the sixth—had been left in the Quetzalcoatl's skull, supposedly as proof of the legendary weapons' origins, though Julius didn't buy that for a second. If the teeth really did become the Fangs of the Heartstriker, then there was no way Bethesda would leave one just hanging around as decoration if she had any other choice. Whatever the real reason was, though, the fact remained that Quetzalcoatl's skull had had only one fang in its mouth for as long as Julius could remember. Now, there were two. The front two, specifically, curving from the skull's top jaw like a pair of viper fangs.

Careful not to draw attention, Julius inched away from the wall to get a better look. Sure enough, the new tooth looked as natural and deeply embedded as the old one, but that couldn't be right. There was no way a thousand-year-dead skull could just grow another tooth, so either his mother had decided after centuries to give her father dentures, or one of the Fangs of the Heartstriker wielders had died, and their sword had been returned to the skull to wait for its next carrier.

Both ideas were ridiculous. As his mother had pointed out, Julius wasn't exactly up on Heartstriker current events, but there was no *way* he could've missed the death of a Fang. They were the biggest, baddest dragons in the clan, the closest thing Heartstriker had to lieutenants under Bethesda herself. But even as he was writing the idea off as absurd, it suddenly hit him that he hadn't talked to Justin since the Pit.

Julius froze, heart pounding. No, that couldn't be it. Justin was Mother's baby. Chelsie could make his life miserable, but Bethesda would never let anything permanent happen…right?

He bit his lip, scrambling to think of someone, *anyone* else who might have lost a Fang in the last month. Conrad still had his, clearly, and though Julius didn't see Chelsie in the crowd, he'd bet money she was fine. But other than the two Cs and Justin, Julius realized with a start that he didn't actually know who had the final two Fangs.

That was just absurd. The Fangs were famous. Justin had never shut up about the stupid things. But no matter how hard Julius thought, he couldn't name more than three, which was a red flag that the identities of the final two Fangs were most likely yet another family secret he wasn't important enough to know. But while that was annoying, it also meant that the new tooth in the Quetzalcoatl's head *could* be one of the secret Fangs, which would mean Justin was just fine! But…if that was the case, why wasn't Justin here?

Julius glanced back at the crowd, sniffing the air, just in case, but it didn't change what he already knew. The party for Svena was a Who's Who of Heartstriker. Just in his immediate vicinity, Julius saw David Heartstriker, the six-term Senator from New Mexico and only dragon ever elected to the US Congress, talking with Edmund, the Heartstriker's official liaison to China, and at least three other Heartstrikers that, while Julius didn't know their names by sight, were all obviously Es or higher. But though an event like this practically demanded the presence of a Knight of the Mountain, Julius couldn't see or smell any trace of his brother, and the more he thought about that, the more worried he became. He was about to try just calling Justin and asking when someone grabbed him from the side.

Julius yelped in surprise, arms flailing to catch his balance as his unknown assailant yanked him back into the corner.

"Stop that pathetic noise," Ian growled, glancing over his shoulder. "Do you want to draw everyone's attention?"

"Maybe if you wouldn't sneak up on me, it wouldn't be an issue," Julius hissed back, clinging to the wall as he tried to calm his hammering heart. "Aren't you supposed to be with Mother?"

"I left her with a gaggle of Gs," he said flippantly. "Ambitious ones. That should keep her busy for at least five minutes, and I needed to talk to you alone."

Julius paled. "Alone?"

"It's not my first choice, either," Ian said, his neon green eyes sharp and worried. "But these are desperate times. Have you talked to Katya?"

"Not today," Julius said, confused and more than a little worried. "Why? Isn't she with Svena?"

"Do you think I'd stoop to asking you if I knew that?" Ian snapped, glancing over his shoulder again at Bethesda, who was standing in the center of a group of nearly identical-looking dragonesses. "Seeing how Mother used your name to tie this entire mess together, I assumed you'd already tried to call and apologize or some other nonsense, but it seems you can't even manage that."

Julius looked down, suddenly ashamed. Not because of his brother's insult, but because warning Katya hadn't even occurred to him until Ian said it. "I'll call her right now."

"It's too late for that. This entire situation is a fiasco." Ian raised his hand, pinching his fingers together in the air just in front of Julius's nose. "I was this close to convincing Svena to throw in with me on her own," he growled. "*This close*, Julius. Then Mother got impatient and decided to throw this monstrosity of a party, and now I'm high and dry without a prayer." He bared his teeth. "If Svena walks into this mess thinking I was involved, all the work I've put into building her trust will be utterly ruined!"

For the first time in his life, Julius felt real sympathy for his brother. He might not be playing anywhere near Ian's level, but he knew what it felt like to have Bethesda stomp all over your plans. "So why don't *you* call and warn her?"

"You think I haven't tried?" Ian said, looking more worried than ever. "I was planning to take her to lunch on a yacht this afternoon precisely so we could have a mechanical failure that would excuse our not showing up tonight, but she wasn't at the apartment when she said she'd be, and she hasn't answered her phone all day."

"Maybe she was busy with her family?" Julius suggested. "I'm sure there's a perfectly reasonable—"

"No, there's not," Ian said sharply. "I know Svena. She's organized to a fault. If she says she's going to be somewhere, she'll either be there, or she'll do something to make sure you know that her absence is on purpose to put you in her place. She never just *doesn't show up*." He sighed, running a hand through his dark hair with what seemed to be real worry. "I don't know if something else is wrong or if she got wind of this ridiculousness early and has already cut ties. I was hoping you, with your absurd knack for ingratiating yourself to larger dragons, would have had better luck, but you haven't even tried yet." He glared at Julius in supreme disappointment. "It appears you're even less bold than I gave you credit for."

"I didn't know this was happening until fifteen minutes ago!" Julius said frantically. "And when I did find out, Mother was *right there*. What was I supposed to do?"

At the mention of Bethesda, both dragons looked her direction to see their mother coldly detaching herself from her clinging daughters. "I have to go," Ian growled. "Thanks for nothing."

"Wait!" Julius said, grabbing his brother's perfectly tailored sleeve. "Do you know why there are two fangs in grandfather's skull?"

Ian's eyebrows shot up in surprise. "Why do you care?"

An honest answer to that would reveal more of himself than Julius was willing to show a cut-throat dragon like Ian, so he went with a half-truth instead. "I'm just curious, and you know everything that goes on."

His brother rolled his eyes at the obvious flattery, but to Julius's great surprise, he answered. "Mother took Justin's Fang."

Julius gasped, and Ian shook his head in disgust. "How can you possibly be surprised by this? Your idiot brother turned into a dragon *inside* the DFZ Underground. What did you think was going to happen?"

"But," Julius said. "He's Bethesda's favorite."

"Bethesda's favor is fickle and doesn't extend to morons who make her look bad," Ian reminded him, yanking his sleeve out of Julius's grasp with a haughty look.

Julius cringed. It wasn't that Ian's words had actually surprised him, just that he'd been really *really* hoping they weren't true. True, Justin had broken some pretty big rules when he'd turned into a dragon in the Pit, but he'd done it to save them, and Katya. Julius might have the life debt, but Katya wouldn't have been alive to grant it if Justin hadn't done what he'd done. And sure, maybe he'd gone too far, but being a Knight and wielding the Fang of the Heartstriker was Justin's entire *life*. It was his great dream, the goal he'd worked their entire childhood to achieve. Taking that away, especially for something that had actually helped the clan, just felt unnecessarily cruel. "I hope he's not taking it too badly."

"Justin?" Ian scoffed. "Don't be stupid. He's taking it exactly as badly as you'd expect. But that's none of our business, and we have far more important things to worry about than Mr. Ex-Fifth Blade's hurt feelings." He glanced back at Bethesda, who was now glaring at them from across the crowd. "I have to go deal with her," he said quickly. "Call Katya and let me know the instant you find anything."

"But you just said not to bother," Julius reminded him.

"I know," Ian said as he strode off. "But you're a sentimental fool who'll do it anyway, so I might as well get something out of it."

Now that was just uncalled for, but as much as Julius wanted to do nothing just to spite him, Ian was right. Worried as he was about Justin, he'd lost his Fang a month ago. Katya's crisis, on the other hand, was going down *right now*. As her friend and part of the reason this was happening at all, it was Julius's duty to warn her as soon as possible. But when he dug his phone out and hit her number, the call instantly came back as disconnected.

He tried two more times with the same result, and a cold weight started to form in his stomach. Logically, he knew there were plenty of perfectly benign reasons why Katya's number would be disconnected, but none of them could chase away the feeling that something was very, very wrong. When Ross, Katya's crocodile shaman boyfriend, *also* failed to pick up, the feeling became dead certainty.

Julius hunched over his phone, pulling up his contacts as he counted out his strategies. Now that he was sure something was wrong, there were plenty of other contacts he could call to try and find out what. Unfortunately, his talk with Ian had drawn some curious stares, undermining his plan to stay beneath the room's notice. The general population of Heartstriker might not yet know about his connection to Katya, but Ian was the dragon of the hour. If he'd come over to talk to Julius, others would follow soon enough to find out why.

Just the possibility of that kind of attention was threatening enough to overcome even his fear of Conrad. The clan champion could give orders all he liked. Julius wasn't going to stand around and let himself be cornered. So, sucking in all his courage, he composed his face in what he hoped was a purposeful look and set off across the throne room to find a place where he could make his phone calls without being watched by a peanut gallery of predators.

He had several options. Despite (or perhaps because of) its size and grandeur, the Heartstriker throne room had several hidden hallways branching off it to connect the enormous room with other parts of the mountain's upper infrastructure. Unfortunately, being the obvious out-of-the-way places meant that all of the side halls were already full of dragons gossiping in secret. In the end, the only place connected to the throne room that wasn't infested with Heartstrikers was the balcony.

Jutting out a good thirty feet from the side of Heartstriker Mountain, the throne room balcony served more as a landing pad than anywhere you'd actually want to stand. There was no railing, no windbreak, no consideration of any sort for those who couldn't fly. Just a half-moon disk of smooth, reinforced rock and the night wind howling up from the desert below. But terrifying as it was to stand on the edge of what was essentially a cliff several hundred feet in the air, the balcony—with its strong winds and dusty air—was fashion suicide for the perfectly coiffed and dressed dragons. That made it the safest spot in the throne room by Julius's standards, especially once he found the spot where the balcony edge over-lapped the side of the mountain, creating a hidden nook where—if you flattened yourself against the rock—no one inside the throne room could see you without risking walking into the wind.

Given the obvious money spent on hair and make-up for the crowd behind him, this was as close as Julius was ever going to get to actual privacy, and he collapsed against the stone with a sigh of relief. The mountain's face was digging sharply into his back and the night wind was blasting and cold, but none of that mattered. The ledge was still by far the most comfortable place Julius had found since the moment he'd walked in to see his mother sitting on his couch. He was pulling out his phone again to call one of Ross's shaman circle buddies and ask if she knew anything when an unfamiliar scent drifted by on the wind.

Julius clenched his fists with a curse. Seriously, could he not get five minutes to himself in this stupid mountain? Was that too much to ask? He didn't even know what the scent *was*, but after a night of nasty surprises, he wasn't taking any chances. He just pressed his back harder into the mountain and breathed deep, sorting through the expected scents of desert and dragon for the one that didn't belong.

And that was where things got weird, because even though Julius found the scent again easily, he still had no idea what he was smelling. He wasn't even sure how to describe it. The best he could say was that it smelled very strongly of nothing. He was trying to decide what that meant, exactly, when someone laughed above him

Julius jumped like he'd been shot, almost falling off the mountain. He caught himself at the last second, grabbing the wall behind him and craning his head back to see a dragoness he didn't recognize perched on a tiny irregularity in the stone mountainside directly above him. She waved when she saw him looking and hopped down, taking the eight-foot drop like it was nothing, but it wasn't until she landed beside him on the narrow ledge that Julius realized he *did* actually recognize her.

It was the dragoness in the red dress. The one who'd made his mother freeze.

Sweat began to bead on his neck. The strange dragoness was as tall as Bethesda with the same imposing, statuesque build, but that was where the similarities stopped. Where his mother was painfully fashionable, this dragoness's knee-length, crimson A-line dress was at least a century out of date. Likewise, her hair was almost comically bad: a nest of wildly uneven black braids that looked like she'd done them herself in the dark. But while all of this was a clear sign that he was dealing with a very odd dragon indeed, what really got him was the fact that her eyes were a light hazel brown.

This wasn't to say they weren't beautiful. She was a dragon in her human guise; *everything* about her was beautiful. But in a supposedly exclusive Heartstriker gathering, the lack of the iconic green eyes was as good as a billboard that she didn't belong. Julius was thrashing his brain to figure out who in the world she could be when the dragoness suddenly laughed.

"Easy, Tiger," she said, leaning against the wall beside him. "I'm not going to turn you in. I'm out here hiding myself."

That was probably the one thing Julius hadn't been worried about, though it was surprisingly thoughtful of her to say. Still, the thought of hiding out with a strange dragon Bethesda apparently hated wasn't exactly comforting, especially since his mother *had* to know they were out here. He wasn't actually sure why Bethesda hadn't done something about that already. She didn't normally tolerate interlopers on her mountain. He was trying to think of a way to just ask the dragon what was going on without being unforgivably rude when the dragon turned to dig down into the ancient, burn-marked leather bag she carried slung over her shoulder.

"Here," she said, holding something out.

He looked down in surprise to see a dented metal flask in her outstretched hand. "What is that?"

"A drink," she replied with a grin. "You look like you could use one."

Julius had never seen the point of drinking. Dragon metabolism wasn't compatible with alcohol unless you were willing to down barrels of the stuff, and surely no one drank liquor for the taste. He definitely didn't feel like drinking something out of a metal flask from a stranger. On the other hand, though, refusing a gift was a terrible insult, and the open flask didn't smell like anything bad. Well, anything worse than liquor.

In the end, Julius decided he'd better take it. Strange as she looked, the dragoness was the only one who hadn't started a conversation by insulting or demeaning him tonight. It would be a shame to insult her. Plus, given the way his mother had reacted, she was probably pretty powerful. Way too far above him to bother with poison in any case, especially when she could just punch him off the mountain. So, before he could chicken out, Julius took the flask with a nod of thanks. Keeping his eyes on hers, he lifted it to his mouth for a tiny sip…and nearly choked.

"What *is* that?" he sputtered, wiping his tongue on the back of his hand in a futile effort to stop the burning.

It took several seconds for the dragoness to stop laughing long enough to answer. "Whiskey cut with hydra venom," she said finally, wiping her eyes. "My own recipe." She started giggling again. "The look on your face…"

Julius watched in horror as she took the flask back and tipped it up to her own mouth for a long swig, drinking several swallows before lowering it with a satisfied sigh. "So," she said conversationally, tucking the flask back into her leather sack. "Which one are you?"

That would have been a strange question anywhere else, but Julius was far below most dragons' notice, and Bethesda had a *lot* of children. "I'm Julius."

"*Julius?*" she repeated, eyes going wide. "We're on *J* now?"

"Yes," he said slowly, trying to feel out if that was a joke or not. He'd never expect any dragon, family or otherwise, to know his name, but which clutch Bethesda was on was public knowledge. The dragon, however, looked truly flummoxed.

"No wonder you look so little," she said, still gawking at him. "What are you, fifteen?"

"I'm twenty-four," Julius said, trying not to sound defensive.

The dragoness shrugged. "Same difference. You're adorable, whatever you are." Her hand shot out to ruffle his hair. "I always forget how *cute* you little whelps can be. Do you still have your baby fluff?"

"I lost that on my first molt." *Fifteen years ago*, he added to himself as he dodged out from under her hand. "But thank you."

She stared at him blankly. "What?"

"Thank you," he said again, pronouncing it clearly this time just in case English wasn't her strongest language. There was always the chance she really was surprised by his thanks since it wasn't something dragons said often, but he was far more inclined to believe she was toying with him. He was trying to think up a safe, polite way to get away from this conversation and into a better hiding spot when her face lit up.

"Wait, I know who you are!" she cried. "You're the one Brohomir was going on about. The nice one."

The mention of Bob's name made Julius pause, and the dragoness clapped her hands in delight. "I knew it! No one else would be so polite for no reason. Go on, then. Do it."

He blinked. "Do what?"

"Say something nice."

Now he *knew* she was messing with him. Still, if Bob was involved, there was a chance this might be important, so Julius sucked it up and played along. "Um, thank you for sharing your drink with me. It's not really my taste, but I appreciate the offer."

"Oh, you're *good*," she said, giving him a wink. "Tugging at my heartstrings with your adorable baby face and building up camaraderie while still making it sound all sincere and humble." She whistled. "Very pro."

Julius frowned. When she put it that way, he sounded horribly manipulative. "But I wasn't—"

"I *know*," she said. "That's what makes it work." She smiled again. "Well, if you're going to have manners, I suppose I need them too." She stuck out her hand. "Pleased to meet you, baby J. I'm your sister, Amelia."

Julius's breath caught so fast he almost choked. "Amelia?" he squeaked out. "*A*-melia?"

She nodded.

"B-but," he sputtered. "Your eyes. I mean—"

"It throws everyone," his sister said with a shrug. "Let's just say Mother hadn't quite gotten the hang of the whole egg-laying-factory thing yet with our set. She was only ninety-nine when I hatched, you know."

He did know, but knowing and actually meeting a dragon from Bethesda's first clutch were two very different things. "You're the oldest daughter of Bethesda," he said, eyes wide. "The last surviving A."

"Heir to the Heartstrikers," she continued for him. "The Planeswalker, Clan Magus, and Consort to the Concept of Mountains." She sighed. "Just between us, though, that last one's a wash. The Concept of Mountains and I broke up two years ago. He just wasn't going anywhere."

From anyone else, Julius would have thought that was a joke. Amelia looked serious, though, so he played it straight. "I'm sorry to hear that."

"It was inevitable," she said. "Have you ever tried having a relationship with a conceptual entity who exists simultaneously on multiple planes? Communication issues doesn't even *begin* to cover it."

She said all this casually, but Julius could only stare at her in wonder. "So there really *are* higher planes?"

Amelia nodded. "Higher, lower, outer, side to side, though the term 'plane' isn't really accurate. The other realms aren't flat, two-dimensional fields. They're independent realities that bump up against our own. Think of it like a bunch of balloons caught together in a net. Some are as large as our own, others are smaller than this balcony, but each one has its own boundaries, rules, and magic. Plus, they're infinite as far as anyone knows, which means you never run out of new places to visit."

"So you've been to other worlds?"

"That would be the Planeswalker part of my name-tag," she said proudly. "Honestly, though, getting in is the easy part. Anyone with enough power and leverage can brute force their way into another plane. Navigating safely once you're inside, though? *Veeeeeery* tricky. You never know if you're going to open a portal into a world of liquid methane or the surface of someone else's sun, not to mention you can lose your home reality forever if you don't take care to leave a good path back."

"Or have a Kosmolabe," Julius said excitedly. "My mage always said hers could be used to navigate the outer planes."

Amelia went very still. "Your mage has a Kosmolabe?"

Julius bit his tongue. That had been a stupid, *stupid* thing to say. Talking to Amelia had been so easy, he'd let himself forget what she was: a powerful dragon who, thanks to him, had just discovered something she wanted.

"Had," he said quickly. "She *had* one, but only for a few days before it was lost."

Amelia gave him a skeptical look. "That's too bad," she said slowly, looking down at the dark desert. "Kosmolabes are incredibly useful, and, from what I can tell, unique to human sorcery. Anyone can use them, but their creation seems to hinge on the human ability to push magic around. I should know, too. I spent the better part of a century trying to fix a broken one." She turned back to him. "So do you still have this mage?"

Julius was sorely tempted to lie. Friendly as she seemed, he didn't like his eldest sister's interest in Marci one bit. Dragons, especially old ones, tended to view humans like pets you could just trade around. But lying to an ancient, extremely magical dragon was a bad, bad idea. In the end, he decided to stick to the truth, albeit through the worst possible interpretation.

"She still works for me, yes, but she's very young," he said apologetically. "She got the Kosmolabe by accident and lost it just as quickly. I'm afraid she wouldn't be much use to you."

His sister looked horribly disappointed, and Julius fought the urge to take it all back, if only so Marci would never find out he'd ruined her chance to meet an ancient dragon mage. *Sorry, Marci.*

"More's the pity," Amelia said with a sigh. "I love humans. They're so much more open-minded than dragons. I was delighted when I heard they finally got their magic back. The last time I was here, it looked like things would be locked up *forever.*"

He couldn't have heard that right. "You've been out in other planes since before the meteor hit and brought back magic?"

Amelia nodded. "I actually wasn't planning on coming home for another half-century, but Brohomir's pigeon said it was *dreadfully* important, so here I am."

Well, Julius thought, at least that explained why he'd never seen Amelia before. She'd been outside this realm of existence since before he was *born.* He was still trying to wrap his brain around that when he realized what else she'd said. "Wait, Bob's pigeon can *talk?*"

"Of course she can talk," Amelia said, glancing over her shoulder at the glow of the throne room behind them. "Though she didn't say anything about how *boring* it would be. From what I can tell, this whole party's nothing but an elaborate mouse trap for the White Witch." She snorted. "Talk about a waste of time. Why anyone would want to do anything with Ice Queen Svena is beyond me. She's obnoxious."

Julius blinked in surprise. "You know Svena?"

"Nearly lost my tail to her three hundred years ago," Amelia huffed. "Of course, I'd already taken off one of her wings at the time. I'd have had the other one, too, if she hadn't kicked me into that mountain." She chuckled wistfully, lost in the memory. "Really, though, you can pretty much count on every dragon over a thousand knowing each other at least by name. That's the part about immortality they don't tell you: live long enough, and attrition makes your pool of acquaintances pretty shallow. Svena and I have a special bond, though. We've been the only two dragon mages worth the title since Imotella the Undying made her name hilariously ironic in the 1400s."

"But," Julius said, confused. "I thought the Three Sisters had been our enemies forever?"

"Oh, we try to kill each other whenever we can," Amelia said. "But that doesn't mean we're uncivil about it. Sometimes it's fun to call a temporary truce and go out drinking. We're the only two dragons left who know enough to actually appreciate each other's work. Besides, when you've kicked around as long as we have, the difference between an ancient enemy and an old friend is just a matter of perspective."

That struck Julius as incredibly sad. He had aberrant views about friendship for a dragon, though, and he didn't want to insult his sister, so he kept his mouth shut. He was about to ask Amelia what kind of work she and Svena did when his sister's head suddenly whipped around.

"Speak of the devil," she muttered.

Julius didn't have to ask what she meant. He'd felt the cold wind, too. Considering they were literally standing on the edge of a mountain at night, that was hardly out of the ordinary, but this wasn't just a chilly breeze. It was an arctic one, biting cold and wet with hints of glacial ice, and it was coming from *inside* the throne room.

"What's going on?" he whispered.

"You'll see in a second," Amelia replied, walking off the ledge and back into the throne room like she was striding into battle. "Heads up, Buttercup. We've got company."

Before Julius could ask what that was supposed to mean, the throne room doors flew open with a bang as the icy breeze grew into a gale. The wind was so strong, it almost blew Julius off the balcony, and the cold was even worse. In seconds, the temperature had gone from pleasant fall evening to chest freezer, turning their breaths into crinkly puffs of frost. Ice was actually spreading across the floor in front of the doors, covering the stone steps that led down to the throne room in a mosaic of frost that thickened as Julius watched. There were icicles, too, growing rapidly in long, perfectly clear spears that hung like teeth from the doorway's arch. They were nearly to the floor when the howling wind stopped as suddenly as it had begun, leaving the throne room silent and still as a winter night.

And it was in that silence that the white dragons appeared.

CHAPTER THREE

Before this moment, Julius would have sworn it was impossible for dragons to simply appear out of thin air. Now, he was forced to revise his opinion, because there was no other explanation for what had just happened. Since he'd never seen anything like this before, he could only assume it very powerful magic. Considering which dragons had just appeared in the icy doorway, though, magic wasn't an issue.

There were three of them—all female, all pale as snow, and all dressed head to toe in unrelenting white. Julius recognized the two in the back instantly: Katya, looking even more terrified than she had when he'd confronted her in the diner, and Svena, cool as always with frost trailing from her fingers as she let her magic fade. He did not, however, recognize the tall, willowy, snowy-haired dragoness standing at the front of the group, but given how the other two were obviously under her command, it was easy enough to guess.

"My, my," Estella said, looking over the crowded throne room with a smile as cold as the ice at her feet. "Such a turnout. One would almost think I was expected, but I know *that* isn't true."

Her gaze landed on Bethesda as she finished, but the Heartstriker just turned up her nose. "My seer has better things to do than predict something as regular as your arrogance, Northern Star," she said haughtily, walking out of the crowd. "But I don't believe you were invited to this gathering."

"You're right," Estella said. "I don't need to scrounge for invitations to affairs of this...quality. But I had business to discuss with you, Heartstriker, and my sister was happy to extend the invitation."

Svena did not look happy at all. If anything, she looked ready to bury the whole room in an avalanche of ice. Conrad stepped forward in answer, hand ready on the hilt of his Fang. A heartbeat later, Chelsie appeared beside him. Julius hadn't even known she was here until she stepped into position on Bethesda's left, hand resting on her own sword, which was incongruously strapped over what would otherwise have been a very nice black pants suit.

The two Cs weren't alone, either. All around the room, Heartstrikers were reaching for weapons. But then, just when open war seemed inevitable, Estella raised her hands in surrender.

"Call off your dogs," she ordered. "Our clans have their differences, but *we* would never be so vulgar as to spill blood as guests in your home."

"Then why are you wasting my time?" Bethesda snarled. "You said you had business with me. Speak it or go. I have no more patience for your dramatics."

"You would be the expert in *that* department," Estella said, but then, before the Heartstriker could take offense, the seer turned and laid her hand on Svena's shoulder. "It seems my dear sister has become inexplicably fond of your whelp of a son. Naturally, this came as quite a shock to me. We are the daughters of gods, above you in every way, but even I can no longer deny what I see in our shared futures." She heaved a heavy sigh, like this was the worst thing that could happen, and turned back to Bethesda. "It seems that an alliance between the greatest dragon clan and the largest has finally become inevitable. Therefore, I have come to you in peace to discuss terms for a mating flight between Svena, Second Daughter of the Three Sisters, and Ian Heartstriker, to take place as soon as possible."

Stunned silence filled the room. Bethesda's jaw was actually hanging open for several seconds, and then her face split into a Grinch-like grin. "Is that so?" she said, the words practically oozing with smug satisfaction. "I'm always open to securing a new alliance, but this is no place for such delicate negotiations. Why don't we stop putting on a show for the crowd and go discuss the details of this contract in private?"

"As you like," Estella said, descending gracefully down the icy steps. The crowd parted in front of her, creating a path straight to Bethesda. Svena followed a second later, but Katya stayed behind, hovering in the icy doorway like she wanted to bolt right back through it.

That struck Julius as very strange, but everyone else seemed to be too busy watching Estella and Svena to care. When the two dragons reached her at last, Bethesda's smile grew even wider as she turned and took Ian's arm. Knowing what he did about his brother's plans, Julius was probably the only one who saw him flinch, but Ian had always been a perfect dragon, and now was no exception. If he had any doubts, he hid them instantly, nodding regally to Svena like this has been their goal all along.

"Come," Bethesda said, leading the way around her massive throne to the doorway in the wall behind it which led to her private apartments. "I already have a mating flight contract prepared in my study. What a stroke of luck."

Luck nothing, Julius thought with a scowl. That contract was the entire point of this trap of a party. But while that should have been the biggest warning in the world, Estella and Svena didn't say a word. They just fell into step behind her, leaving Conrad and Chelsie to bring up the rear as the heads of the world's two most powerful dragon clans disappeared into Bethesda's lair.

• • •

The moment they were out of sight, the throne room erupted into whispered conversation as the speculation began. But while the rest of his family seemed to be falling over themselves in their rush to divide up the spoils of the Three Sisters' apparent surrender, Julius was making a beeline for Katya.

"Hold up."

He paused and looked over his shoulder to find Amelia glaring at him. "What are you doing?"

"Going to talk to a friend."

Even as he said it, Julius didn't actually think it would work. Estella was a seer, and talking to Katya was the most obvious move. There was no way she hadn't planned for this, but Julius had to do *something*. His mother had set this whole thing up using his name. Katya deserved an explanation for that at least, and though it had never felt like much of one, this was still his family. He couldn't just stand by while Estella did…whatever it was she was here to do. Talking to Katya was literally the least he could do, and he was about to start pushing his way through the crowd when Amelia grabbed his arm. "Let me give you some advice."

"Can it wait?" he asked, trying not to sound frustrated.

"No," she said, looking down at him with a strange expression. "You're a cute kid, Julius, so here's a survival tip, from one Heartstriker to another: don't get involved."

"But I have to," he said. "Mother's—"

"Bethesda's going to do what Bethesda's going to do," Amelia said bitterly. "And that's what's best for her. Not for you or for me or for the clan. Her. The sooner you understand that, the happier you'll be."

Julius had never had a problem understanding that, but his sister was wrong. "It's because she's like that that the rest of us have to do what we can," he said angrily. "We can't count on her to save us."

Amelia shook her head. "You need to focus on saving yourself. Or is that seal on your magic just for decoration?"

He winced. "You noticed?"

"Hard not to," his sister said with a shrug. "Mother's work, I'm guessing?"

Julius nodded, and Amelia's expression darkened. "Look," she said with a sigh. "I don't know what's going on, and I really don't care, but you're barking up the wrong mountain if you think sticking your neck out for the Heartstriker will get her to unseal you. Once Bethesda's got her claws in, they never come out."

"I know that," he said. "But I'm not doing this for her. There's a lot more dragons than just Bethesda who'll be hurt if Estella strikes. You're safe because you can just go to another plane, but the rest of us are stuck here." Like Katya, like himself, like Bob and Chelsie and Ian and Justin and everyone else in his family he didn't want to die. Not to mention that, if he didn't do anything, and things *did* go bad, he'd never be able to forgive himself.

"I appreciate your advice," he said, smiling at his sister. "You're the only one who's treated me like I had a brain tonight, but I can't let this go. I don't know if it'll do any good, but if I have a chance to figure out what's going on, I need to at least try."

Amelia stared at him for a long moment, and then she shook her head. "You're an odd little bird, Julius Heartstriker. I'm beginning to see why Bob picked you."

Julius wished she'd tell him, but it was too late. His sister was already turning away. "Do as you like," she said. "Personally, I'm going to get while the getting's good. If you're still alive later, maybe I'll drop by and meet your mage. Sound like fun?"

It sounded like trouble, but Julius didn't want to insult his sister any more than he already had. And besides, for a dragon like Amelia, "later" might be in twenty years. "Sure," he said. "See you then."

She waved over her shoulder as she walked back out onto the balcony, presumably to fly away, but Julius didn't have time to wait around and see. He was already plunging into the crowd toward Katya.

Given how many whispering Heartstrikers were staring her down, Julius had fully expected Katya to bolt. By the time he got close enough to catch her attention, though, she was still in the frozen doorway, sticking to the ice like a lifeline. Her blue eyes lit up when she spotted him coming toward her, but Julius shook his head rapidly, pointing instead to the discreet door that led to the toilets.

When she nodded, he turned back around and started slipping his way through the whispering crowd in the same direction.

Like all places meant to be accessed by dragons, the hall leading to the toilets was richly decorated in a lavish display of Bethesda's wealth. In this particular instance, it was her collection of antique textiles, including several historically significant Mesoamerican wall-hangings and carpets, which Bethesda kept unprotected on her walls and floor, because nothing said "I have money to burn" like walking over an irreplaceable historical artifact on your way to the restroom.

Since Katya had to give a whole room the slip, Julius fully expected to have to wait, but by the time he'd weaved his way through the crowd and down the hall, she was already there, sitting on the black leather ottoman that marked the discreet entrance to the ladies' room. She jumped up the moment she saw him, grabbing his hand and yanking him into the alcove behind a 13th century Mayan serape before he could even say hello.

"What's going on?" he whispered, pushing the heavy wool hanging away from his face so he could see her. "Are you okay?"

Katya put her finger to her lips and stuck her head back out into the hall, looking up and down its entire length as she breathed deep through her nose. She must not have scented anything, though, because she ducked back in behind the hanging a second later. "I don't know," she said frantically. "I didn't even know Estella was back until she blasted her way into our bedroom this morning. She nearly killed Ross."

Julius winced in sympathy. Ross was Katya's beloved human mage. "Is he okay?"

"I'm not sure," Katya said. "Estella took my phone. She won't let me contact anyone, and she won't say why. She doesn't even talk to me unless she's ordering me around, and worse, Svena's *helping* her."

She said that like it was unthinkable, but Julius didn't understand. "Don't they usually work together?"

Katya shook her head. "Not anymore. Svena's made a lot of changes to the Daughters of the Three Sisters. If you'd asked me yesterday, I'd have sworn she'd die before she let Estella rule her again, but now—" Katya's voice broke as she grabbed his hands. "Something's *wrong* with her, Julius!"

"I believe you," he said, clutching her fingers reassuringly. "Ian mentioned she was acting strange as well, but do you have any idea why? Is there some kind of blackmail or threat Estella could be holding over her to make Svena go along with her plan?"

"Nothing that could make her act like this. She won't even talk to me." Katya bared her teeth. "Estella must have done something, trapped her in a spell. Whatever it is, I'll kill her for it. No one hurts my sister!"

The raw fury in her voice surprised him. When she'd been on the run, Katya had been…not meek, exactly, but wary. She was like a wounded animal: ready to fight if she had to, but more interested in running away. Now, though, Katya looked ready to charge in and start ripping things apart for Svena, which was kind of touching. No one in Julius's family felt that way about him. But while he was sure Katya would give it a good try, there was no way she could beat a seer. At least, not directly.

"We'll figure this out together," he promised. "First, though, we need to find out what Estella's actually after. Can you tell me about this mating flight?"

"I found out about it when you did," Katya said angrily. "Svena and I knew this party was a trap the moment we read your invitation. We were still planning to accept—I think Svena wanted to show your mother that she couldn't be manipulated—but never in a million years would I have guessed that Estella would want to come here. She *hates* the Heartstriker."

"Could it all be a ploy just to get close to Bethesda?" Julius asked. "Mother's well protected, but offering her the mating flight she's been obsessing over for months would be a surefire way to get her to the negotiating table and into striking range."

"I thought about that, too," Katya said. "But you don't have to be a seer to know that wouldn't work. Svena's amazing, but even she can't beat a throne room full of Heartstrikers. Attacking now would be suicide for all of us, but I don't know what else Estella could want."

Julius didn't either, but her words made him remember something Bob had said. "Do you think she could be going mad?"

That was a terrible thing to say about someone's sister, but he didn't know how else to phrase it, and Katya didn't look surprised in any case. "It's possible," she said sadly. "All seers lose their minds in time, and Estella is the oldest of us all. But she doesn't *seem* mad. Just the opposite, she's been more driven and alert today than I've seen her be in ages. Svena's the one acting strange. Normally, ordering her to do something is the fastest way to make her do the exact opposite, but she's followed everything Estella's said today like an obedient doll. It's creepy. Sometimes, she looks at me, and I don't even recognize—"

Her voice cut off with a gasp. For a heartbeat, Julius couldn't understand what was wrong, and then he felt it. An icy wind was blowing down the hallway, chilling him to the bone.

"Go ahead."

Even though he knew it was coming, the soft, cold voice still made Julius jump. He came down with a thump, peeking out from behind the wall hanging to find Estella standing in the hall directly in front of them.

"Go ahead, Katya," she said again. "I've already found you conspiring with the enemy, why not finish the job? It's not like I haven't already foreseen what you're going to do."

"I—" Katya stammered. "I was only—"

Estella silenced her with a wave of her hand. "Save your excuses. If you're delusional enough to think you can betray me, do it now and be done. Otherwise, go back and wait until you're called."

Katya's hands tightened to fists, and for a moment, Julius thought Estella had pushed her too far. But then, without a word, Katya turned and fled, racing back down the hall toward the party.

Julius watched her go with growing dread. He hadn't wanted her to stay and suffer her sister's wrath, but now that she was gone, he was alone with Estella.

"Don't move."

Julius hadn't moved since he'd spotted her, but he froze again anyway, not even daring to breathe as he met the eyes of the seer whose plans he, Bob, Justin, and Marci had ruined so thoroughly four weeks ago. He'd never actually seen Estella before tonight, and never up close until now. But while she was every bit as beautiful and terrifying as one would expect from the oldest daughter of the Three Sisters, what struck Julius the most was how sickly she looked.

Even under the heavy white gown that covered her from her shoulders to the tips of her fingers and down to the floor, it was obvious Estella was grossly underweight. Her cheeks were so hollow, the bones stood out like blades, and her eyes were ringed with dark circles. But what would have signaled weakness in a lesser dragon only made Estella look more deadly as she studied him, her ice-blue gaze boring into his until Julius was forced to lower his head.

"So," she said at last, her voice as cold and distant as a snow-topped mountain. "You're the one he's set against me."

She reached out as she spoke, and Julius couldn't hide his flinch as her icy fingers landed on his face. Normally, he would have said Estella wouldn't dare kill him with so many Heartstrikers around, but that was before Katya had told him she might be mad. As her hand dipped down to trace a sharp nail over his windpipe, Julius believed it, but he had no idea what to do. Running from a dragon only made it want to chase you, but staying was feeling like a worse idea every second. Estella wasn't even looking at his face anymore. She was just staring at his throat like she wanted to rip it out, her fingers spreading to dig into the soft flesh on either side of his windpipe, and Julius squeezed his eyes shut with a whimper. Why couldn't Chelsie be waiting behind him *now?*

But then, just when he'd decided to take his chances and run, he heard whistling in the distance. Someone was coming down the hall, whistling a happy, jaunty tune Julius didn't recognize. He couldn't see who it was with Estella blocking him, but even with her back to the hall, the seer must have known, because her face broke into her cruelest smile yet.

"I was beginning to think you wouldn't come."

She turned as she spoke, loosening her grip on Julius's neck just a fraction as Bob stepped into view.

Julius's relief was so intense it hurt. He had no idea how or when his oldest brother had arrived, but he'd never been happier to see someone in his life. It didn't even matter that the seer looked like he'd just rolled out of bed in his ratty, red terrycloth bathrobe, cat-print pajama bottoms, and bare feet. He was *here*, and that was what counted.

Or, at least, Julius hoped that was what counted. Bob had yet to actually look at them. He was still whistling and staring at his relic of a phone, tapping the worn keys with his thumbs, seemingly oblivious to the near-strangulation happening in front of him.

Finally, after several long, awkward seconds, Bob finished his message and slid his phone into his bathrobe pocket. "Fashionably late, I admit," he said, tossing his long, sleep-tangled black hair over his shoulder. "But in my defense, I didn't expect you to be done quite so soon. Formal mating contracts usually take more than ten minutes to draw up."

"Not if one of the parties says yes to everything," Estella replied. "But then, your mother always has been eager to please."

"Insulting my mother's virtue?" Bob said, eyes going wide. "I have *never* heard that one before. Now," he put out his hand, "if you're done with my baby brother, I'd like him back. This is his first party, and I don't want to put him off the exercise forever."

Estella gave Julius a shove. A hard one. If he hadn't spent the last month dodging all kinds of dangerous animals, he would have bounced off the wall and gone sprawling on the dark wooden floor. As it was, he caught himself at the last second, scrambling away from Estella into the shelter of Bob's shadow. When he looked up again, the seer was staring at his brother with a hard, triumphant smile. "Well?"

Bob stared at her blankly. "Well what?"

"Aren't you going to ask what I'm doing?"

He shrugged. "Why should I? You're going to tell me whether I want to know or not. That's the whole reason we're here, isn't it? Unless I'm grossly misreading the situation." He glanced down at Julius. "Should I not have interrupted?"

Julius shook his head rapidly, and Bob turned back to Estella, who seemed to be nearing the end of her patience.

"I forgot how tiresome you can be when you're covering up your insecurities," she said, lifting her chin haughtily. "The game is over, Brohomir. I've won."

Bob's smile turned into a smirk. "Are we talking about the same game? Because 'winning' isn't the word I'd use to describe your situation."

"Then you've just proven how little you really know," she snapped. "You might be a prodigy of a seer, little Heartstriker, but I was orchestrating the downfall of empires before your mother was even born. I warned you a lifetime ago not to challenge me, but you never could learn to listen."

"And you never could learn not to brag," Bob said. "It's very poor sportsmanship, and highly susceptible to ironic quotation when we reach your inevitable—"

"*Enough!*" Estella roared, sending a ripple of frost across the floor. "No more jokes, Brohomir. No more games. The future has been bought and paid for, and you have no place in it."

For the first time since he'd arrived, Bob's expression grew serious. "The future is never set, Estella," he said firmly. "Not until it happens."

"This is," she promised. "I know. I've seen it. I'm so sure, in fact, I'll even tell you."

Bob sighed. "Tell me what?"

"Everything," Estella said, spreading her arms wide. "I'll answer all the questions I know are burning a hole in that devious mind of yours—why I offered this mating flight, what I'm going to do to your favorite sister, how I'll destroy your clan piece by piece. I'll even tell you your own fate, the parts you *haven't* already seen. I'll tell you everything you want to know, and all you have to do is ask me the right way."

Bob arched an eyebrow. "And what way would that be?"

Estella raised her arm, slipping her hand out of her voluminous sleeve to extend one slender finger down toward the ground. "Kneel," she commanded. "Kneel at my feet and *beg*. Beg to know what you are too blind to see, and I will tell you everything."

Bob took a deep breath, his eyes darting from Estella to the floor in front of her. He stared at the spot for so long, Julius began to worry he might actually do it. But then, like the sun coming out from behind a cloud, Bob's smile returned.

"Sorry," he said brightly. "But I only beg on alternate Thursdays."

"Then you can stand there and wait for death," Estella snarled, snatching her arm back to her side. "Either way, I win. I *always* win, Brohomir. Remember that." Her eyes flicked to Julius. "If you attempt to contact Katya again, I'll kill her."

That came out of nowhere, but Julius was used to being threatened, and he stopped his flinch in time. Not that it mattered. Estella didn't even wait to see if her parting shot got through. She was already marching down the hall, leaving nothing but the smell of winter and a trail of frosted footprints behind her.

• • •

"Well," Bob said, nudging the fragile fronds of melting frost with his big toe. "That went better than expected."

"What were you expecting if *that* was better?" Julius said, rubbing his neck. "She almost took my head off."

"Ah, but she *didn't*. You're not even bleeding." Bob winked. "She must like you."

That wasn't even worth replying to, so Julius just moved on. "We have to warn someone."

"We have to do no such thing," Bob said. "Estella loves bragging as much as the next dragon, but she doesn't go around dramatically telling others her business for no reason. She's trying to manage us, feeding us just enough information to make us react in a way that moves her plan forward. It's not even a proper seer trick. Mother does it all the time. But then, Estella never did have much in the way of imagination."

"Well, we have to do *something*," Julius said. "She just told us to our faces that this whole mating flight is a plot to destroy our clan!"

Bob rolled his eyes. "Newsflash, Julius. Someone is *always* trying to destroy our clan. We're always on the brink of some disaster or another, and yet we always pull through. It's almost as though we have someone in the know. A brilliant, handsome, vigilant dragon with the vision to see what's coming and the daring to do what must be done."

He struck a dramatic pose as he finished, and Julius sighed. "If that's the case, why are you only getting here now? You're too late to do anything."

"I wasn't *late*," Bob said, insulted. "I made a *dramatic entrance*. I also happened to be *asleep*. I do still have to do that on occasion."

Fair enough, but, "Why did you go to sleep if you knew this was coming?"

Bob's eyes narrowed. "You know, I think I preferred it when you were deathly afraid of me. Far less back talk."

The apology was already on Julius's lips before he realized what his brother was doing. "You're changing the subject!" he cried. "You *didn't* see this coming, did you?"

Bob's answer was an angry look. Not comically or dramatically angry, either. *Really* angry. The sight sent a chill up Julius's spine, but just as he was wondering if he'd finally said too much, Bob flopped down on the ottoman where Katya had been waiting, patting the cushion for Julius to sit next to him.

"It's not as simple as she makes it sound," he said as Julius joined him. "It's the nature of seers to get in each other's way. I've never been able to see Estella's movements any more than she can see mine, but lately the larger future has been…" He frowned, searching for the right word. "Difficult," he said at last. "It's not blindness.

I can still look down the stream of possible futures and see what decisions will lead to the desired results, but lately, threads have been disappearing."

That didn't sound good. "What do you mean 'disappearing'?"

"Exactly what it sounds like," Bob said. "Every decision we make creates possible futures, even if we never actually get to act on it. Usually, these branching lines of possibility end only when the individual making the decisions that create them dies, but this time…they just aren't there anymore." He blew out a frustrated breath. "I don't know how else to describe it, and frankly I'm only telling you in the hope that saying it aloud will help it make a little more sense. Svena's future was the first to go. I couldn't even see for sure if Estella would be here tonight until I spotted one of your possible futures ending as a stain on Mother's antique rug. Given all the bonding we've done recently, I felt I should do something about that." He glanced over. "You're welcome, by the way."

"Thank you," Julius said belatedly. "But it's interesting you mention Svena. Katya and Ian both said she was acting strange."

"She shouldn't be acting at all," Bob growled. "I just told you, the future is built from decisions, and from what I can see, Svena's not making any of those at all. Or, at least, she's not making them for herself. That's a very dangerous development for the most powerful dragon mage on the planet, which is why I called in Amelia. She's the only dragon alive who can toe-to-toe it with the White Witch, and given Estella's hatred of all things us, I thought that was important."

Julius swallowed. "Do you really think it'll come to that?"

"Who knows?" the seer said with a shrug. "I'm still not sure all that drama earlier wasn't a decoy, something big and shiny to keep us looking at one hand while she stabs us with the other."

He mimed stabbing motions in the air, and Julius shook his head. "Surely it won't come to that. Whatever Estella is trying to pull off, they're still just three dragons, and Katya doesn't even want to fight. There are over a hundred Heartstrikers all together, and we've got you. Whatever she's done to Svena, it can't be enough to beat those odds."

"Your vote of confidence touches my heart," Bob said. "But if there's a single truth I've learned about this business, it's never trust a seer. They're liars to the core who never show you a move unless they want you to counter it."

"I see," Julius said. "And does that assessment include yourself?"

Bob gave him an enigmatic smile. "What do you think?"

Julius took a moment to consider that. "I think you're too invested in our clan to let it fall," he said at last. "And I think you hate losing too much to let Estella win anything."

His brother flashed him a wide smile. "That's an impressive bit of social insight for a dragon who claims not to be manipulative," he said, standing up. "But as much as I'd love to stay and live down to your expectations, I have to move on. Schemes to foil, plots to thwart, naps to resume, you know how it is. You, however, should get back to the party. Mother's going to want to see you in—" he looked at his bare wrist "—two minutes, and you *don't* want her to come looking for you."

That went without saying. "What does she want from me?"

"You'll find out in one minute, fifty-eight seconds," Bob replied, jogging down the hall away from the party toward the interior of the mountain. His pigeon joined him halfway, fluttering off its perch on one of the hanging tapestries to land on his shoulder. That was all Julius saw before the seer vanished around the corner. Even so, he stood there a moment longer, staring at the place where his brother had been and debating the wisdom of just bailing back down to his old room. In the end, though, disobeying a seer's advice on top of everything else that had happened tonight felt too much like inviting disaster, and so, with a heavy sigh, Julius turned and began trudging back to see what his mother wanted.

• • •

By the time he got back to the throne room, the party was in full swing. Estella must have left immediately after her encounter with Bob, because Heartstriker was once again the only scent in the room, and everyone seemed to be celebrating. Bethesda was perched on her throne at the top of the raised dais, holding court while Chelsie and Conrad flanked her feet like a pair of guard dogs. Neither C looked happy about this arrangement, but their mother was almost cackling in delight. Even the sight of Julius didn't seem to bring her down. Quite the opposite. She waved him over the moment she spotted him, motioning for her other, more highly ranked children to step aside.

"The diplomat returns unscathed," she cooed. "I can't tell you how many reports I've gotten about you sneaking off with Katya. Gold star for initiative! So let's hear it. What did the Failure of the Three Sisters have to say?"

The last thing Julius wanted to do was repeat what Katya had told him in confidence to his mother. Fortunately for him, there was little Bethesda would care about to report. "She knows nothing," he said honestly. "Estella came back this morning and scooped her up, but otherwise hasn't told her anything."

"Is that so?" His mother pursed her lips and turned to Ian, who was standing beside her with a look of polite interest so attentive it had to be faked. "What do you think?"

"It makes sense," he said. "Svena dotes on Katya, but anyone with eyes can see she's the weak link of the clan, and highly prone to running. Of course they wouldn't tell her anything important."

"Pity," Bethesda said. "But I suppose it makes no difference. Whatever plot Estella is hatching, the mating contract between our clans is signed in blood. Even seers can't wiggle out of that. I don't care if the world is burning, Ian *will* fly a mating flight with the White Witch Sunday evening if I have to throw her into the air myself."

She said that last part like she was looking forward to it. Julius, however, had gotten hung up on the bit before it. "Sunday?" he said, horrified. "As in the day after tomorrow Sunday?"

"What other Sunday would I be talking about?" his mother said, tossing her hair. "I'm not giving them time to figure out how to betray me."

The dragons around her made agreeing sounds, but Julius couldn't believe his ears. "What about us?" he asked. "That's no time at all! I mean, when something is so obviously a trap, surely *we* need time to—"

"Oh, Julius, don't be dense," Bethesda scoffed. "*Everything* between dragons is a trap. But what you and Estella both fail to grasp is that it doesn't matter. Today, tomorrow, or a week from now makes no difference at all. So long as the flight takes place over Heartstriker territory, I've already won. The Northern Star can twist her plots however she likes, but nothing changes the fact that she will be in *my* mountain, which is protected by *my* seer and *my* dragons and *my* military grade security systems." Her smile turned bloodthirsty. "Given all that, you could say Estella's walking into *my* trap. But do you want to know the best part, Julius?"

He wasn't sure he had the stomach for it, but she was going to tell him anyway, so he nodded.

"The best part comes after," Bethesda whispered, leaning down to grin at him. "Once Estella's dead, caught in the very trap she laid for me, Svena will become head of the Three Sisters in truth, and everyone will know that *I* was the one who put her there. I'll destroy my ancient enemy, earn their new clan head's life debt, *and* get my mating flight all in one fell swoop. If that's not a reason to celebrate, I don't know what is."

Julius hadn't actually considered the situation from that angle. But even with his mother's obvious confidence, he still couldn't bring himself to believe that walking into a trap, even when you were *sure* yours was better, was a good idea. He didn't see how *any* of this was good, period, but from the conversations going on around him, it was clear the rest of the clan thought Bethesda had just clinched the deal of the century, and that made him angrier than anything. Logically, he knew it was foolish to pit his own opinion against dragons with centuries more experience in this sort of thing, but this kind of premature victory celebration felt arrogant even by dragon standards. No matter how tight that contract was, Estella was still a seer. Like Bob said, she never showed a move unless she wanted you to counter it. How could Bethesda and the others possibly be this confident?

But infuriating as it was, there was nothing he could do, and it wasn't like this behavior was a new development. Bethesda's behavior tonight was just more of the same arrogant, aggressive, winner-take-all thinking that had made her the Heartstriker in the first place. She'd built her empire by taking seemingly hopeless opportunities and making them work by whatever means necessary. For all he knew, Sunday night would be no different. Tonight, though, Julius was done. He'd done his duty as a good son and voiced his warning. If his mother wanted to ignore it, that was her decision. Right now, he had more important matters on his plate.

"Where's Justin?"

His voice cut through the buzz of conversation, and Bethesda cast him a cutting look. "What?"

"Where is Justin?" Julius said again, forcing himself to meet her eyes. "I already heard you took his Fang. I just want to know where he is so I can talk to him."

"Talk to him?" Bethesda laughed aloud. "What good will *that* do?"

Julius began to sweat. He was more than used to being mocked by this point, but the way she said that made him feel like he was missing something. "I just thought he might be upset and—"

"Please," his mother scoffed. "Who do you think he is, you? Justin's a *dragon*, darling. A proper one. He doesn't get upset. He gets even."

Now Julius *really* felt like he was missing something. "What does that mean?"

"It means that when Chelsie confiscates his sword for breaking the rules, he doesn't waste time moping around," she said proudly. "He immediately starts scheming on a plan to convince me that he deserves it back."

With those words, everything came together with chilling clarity. "So he's just out there alone?" Julius asked, voice shaking. "Plotting to impress you?"

"Yes," his mother replied. "Personally, I can't wait. Justin can be a thick-headed idiot, but when it comes to audacity, he never disappoints." She pressed a hand against her chest. "My genes at work, clearly."

The other dragons chuckled at that, but Julius had no time to waste. The idea of his brother alone with the loss of his sword was bad enough, but the thought of him trying to pull off a stunt big enough to impress Bethesda on his own was absolutely terrifying. "Where is he?"

"I haven't been keeping track," Bethesda said with shrug. "He's hardly relevant at the moment, and I don't want to spoil the surprise when he finally does burst back onto the scene."

Julius couldn't believe his ears. "So you don't know where he is?"

Her eyes narrowed. "Watch your tone."

He shut his mouth at once, and, after a moment, Bethesda relaxed. "If you're *so* concerned, you can ask Chelsie," she said casually. "It's her job to know what you're all up to."

That was not the answer Julius was hoping for, but it was better than nothing and most likely all he was going to get. From her bored look, Bethesda was clearly done with him, so Julius took his chance to slip out of the crowd of better, more ambitious dragons competing for the Heartstriker's attention and set off in search of his sister.

He didn't actually have high hopes of finding her. He'd seen her when Estella showed up, so he knew she was in the mountain, but Chelsie was called Bethesda's Shade for a reason, and it wasn't because she was easy to find. Sure enough, despite searching the throne room and its adjacent hallways for almost twenty minutes, Julius ended up back by the restrooms where he and Katya had spoken with nothing to show for his efforts.

He sank onto the ottoman with a tired sigh, pulling out his phone to book a commercial flight back to the DFZ since he obviously wasn't going to be getting a ride back home from his mother tonight. He was trying to decide between flying out of Albuquerque or Las Vegas when a dry voice whispered in his ear.

"I understand you're looking for me?"

Julius almost had a heart attack. He jumped a good foot off his seat, clutching his chest as he looked up to see Chelsie looming over him. "Do you *have* to do that?"

She gave him a cutting look. "I wasn't *trying* to scare you," she said. "You're just critically bad at paying attention to your surroundings. Get better and this won't be a problem."

Easy for her to say. By this point in the night, though, Julius was numb to dragons criticizing him. He was just happy he didn't have to keep searching for her. "Mother said you knew where Justin was?"

"Justin?" Chelsie frowned. "Why do you care?"

"Maybe because he's my *brother*?" Julius said, exasperated. Seriously, why did no one understand this? "I'm worried about him, okay?"

"Don't waste your worry on that idiot," Chelsie said bitterly. "I warned him, just like I warned you. He knew exactly what would happen if he messed up in the DFZ, but he did it anyway, so I took his sword."

"But isn't that a little harsh?" Julius asked, wringing his hands. "I mean, yeah, he broke the rules, but he also—"

"There is no *also*," she growled. "Rules are rules, Julius. Contrary to what some dragons might think, they're not made to be broken. And for the record, I took Justin's sword because it's the only thing he cares about enough to actually be a punishment. I was planning to let him stew on it for a few months in the hopes that he'd have an epiphany and decide to stop acting like a moron, but then Mother filled his head with all that nonsense about earning his blade back, so now he's off doing that." She looked Julius up and down. "I don't think he'd appreciate your assistance."

He probably wouldn't, but, "It's my fault he was in the Pit to begin with," Julius said firmly. "The only reason he got into trouble was because he was helping me. I want to return the favor."

She snorted. "You want to get in trouble?"

"That's not what I meant," he said quickly. "I just want to know where he is so I can offer my help if he wants it. Please, Chelsie."

By the time he finished, his sister looked even more coldly disdainful than usual. "It's not my policy to give out information for free," she said suspiciously. "Especially not to whelps who'll only use it to make my life harder. But it just so happens that I was planning to have a talk with you tonight as well."

Julius stopped his cringe at the last second. "Really? Why?"

She leaned down, dropping her voice to a whisper. "Earlier tonight, Bob and Estella talked. I know you were there, and I know you heard, so I want you to tell me exactly what was said. Give me that, and I'll tell you where your brother is."

That wasn't an unreasonable request at all. In fact, Julius was incredibly relieved to find someone besides himself who was willing to take this Estella stuff seriously. He didn't like *how* she'd asked. Trading information like this about family members felt slimy, especially since he'd have gladly told her whatever she wanted about Bob and Estella without the bargaining. But explaining all of that would just further confirm Chelsie's low opinion of him, and it was far too late for this nonsense, so Julius just sucked it up and told her, repeating Bob and Estella's conversation as best he could remember.

By the time he finished, his sister looked even grimmer than usual. "I don't like it," she muttered. "The trap you can see is never the real one."

Julius could have hugged her for that. "That's what *I* said!" he cried. "Can you please talk some sense into Mother?"

"If I could do *that*, life would be very different," Chelsie grumbled, pulling out her phone. "Our problem is that Estella knew exactly how to bait her trap. Bethesda's always resented the Three Sisters for looking down on her. Now she has a chance to destroy the clan that made her feel inferior and get her mating flight at the same time. That's an offer she can't refuse, and if we're going to get through it alive, we're going to have to be prepared."

Julius winced. "How do you prepare for a seer?"

"That's not your concern," Chelsie said coldly, tapping the air above her phone. "Here."

His phone beeped in his pocket, and Julius pulled it out to see a series of messages from a number he didn't recognize. "What's this?"

"Clearance to take the second jet back to the DFZ."

Julius couldn't believe his ears. "You're sending me home?"

"You shouldn't have been here in the first place," she snapped. "I don't know why Bob keeps dragging you into situations like this, but you're way too short for this ride, and I don't have time to baby-sit you while Mother turns the mountain upside down."

He opened his mouth to argue, but Chelsie cut him off. "You want to be helpful?" she asked. "Take the out when it's offered. Go home to your mage and your little animal control business and leave the plotting to the dragons who can handle it."

Julius lowered his head. His sister was right, he *was* too short for this ride. He'd wanted to go home since he got here, and now he had a chance to do just that, and on a private plane no less. He should be delighted by this turn of events, but the way Chelsie had offered it made him feel...useless. Lower than low. Plus, there was still the matter of Justin.

"I told you what you wanted," he said, standing up from his seat. "Now, where's my brother?"

Chelsie folded her arms over her chest with an inscrutable look. "Why do you think I'm sending you to back to Detroit?"

The *why?* was already on his lips before Julius read between the lines. "He's in the DFZ?"

She nodded. "I don't know what he's doing there since I can't follow idiot plans, but I don't have to explain why Justin heading back into Algonquin's territory would raise warning bells. I was actually planning to go retrieve him tonight, but then this Estella nonsense happened, and now I've got more pressing issues than your brother's stubbornness. But if you want to go and bash your head against that brick wall, be my guest."

"I will, thank you," he said with a smile. "But, um, could you give me something a little more specific? The DFZ's a pretty big place."

Chelsie's lips quirked like he'd just told a joke. "You run a business hunting down nuisance animals in the city, don't you?" she said, turning away. "Figure it out."

Julius gaped at her. "A dragon's different from a tank badger!" he cried, but it was too late. Chelsie was already walking back toward the party, moving down the hall in long, purposeful strides.

"Not my problem anymore," she called over her shoulder. "You wanted Justin? You got him. Now go home, Julius."

He took a step after her, but stopped again almost immediately. There was no point in arguing further. She was already gone in any case, vanishing into the crowded throne room like the shade she was supposed to be. So, with nothing left to do, Julius turned and started down the hall in the other direction, opening an unmarked door that led to the hidden service area to beg one of his mother's employees to smuggle him out.

This was where decades of sneaking around Heartstriker Mountain came in handy. Unlike most of his family, Julius had always made it a point to maintain friendly relations with the employees who kept the stronghold ticking. Barely ten minutes after Chelsie had left him, he'd convinced his mother's manager to let him use the service elevator back down to the public levels. Ten minutes after *that*, he was safely aboard his mother's second, far less luxurious high-speed jet getting his final clearance for the flight back to Detroit. All in all, it was a pretty fantastic change of fortune, but eager as Julius was to get away from his mother's madhouse, he was having trouble concentrating. It was now almost midnight, and Marci *still* wasn't answering his calls.

That was enough to send him into a panic. He hadn't been too worried by her silence earlier—scratch that, he'd been obsessively worried, but he'd known why she wasn't talking to him, so he hadn't been *scared*. Now, though, Julius was petrified. It was nine o'clock in New Mexico, which meant he'd been gone for a little over five hours. It didn't matter how mad Marci was, there was no way she'd ignore his calls for that long. Not unless she was in trouble. Or hurt. Or worse.

That was a horrible realization to have when you were trapped in a plane, but there was nothing Julius could do. He'd already called, texted, and pinged her though every social media account she had a dozen times each. At this point, the only option he had was to wait until he was back in Detroit and go after her personally. Until then, though, he was stuck, and so, rather than sit and grip the chair white-knuckled all the way home, Julius distracted himself by staring out the window into the dark, silently rehearsing what he would say to Marci when he finally found her.

CHAPTER FOUR

The DFZ is a surprisingly small place when you don't want to go home.

Marci stared glumly through the windshield, watching the red river of taillights move sluggishly down the eight lanes of the Underground's last functional highway. Normally, she avoided the congested mess that was the I-94 at all costs, but the highway was the only direct route between the southern and northern halves of the DFZ that didn't require paying skyway tolls, and it wasn't like she was in a hurry. She'd already released their poor, confused tank badger in an abandoned lot by the border of Algonquin's Reclamation Land. Now, other than a vague plan to head uptown and check out what was new at the discount magical supply warehouses, Marci had nothing.

It probably wouldn't even be worth the trip. Reagents from big box stores were always of dubious quality. But wandering aimlessly through aisles stacked with pre-made spells and bins of slightly broken casting chalk still sounded better than going home.

Not that the distance could stop her from thinking about it.

Marci dropped her head to the car's control dash with a *thunk*. Of all the embarrassing things she'd done in her life, tonight had to be some kind of record. She'd had Bethesda the Heartstriker, a creature of myth from before the disappearance of magic, *in her living room,* and she'd screwed it up. She'd made a fool of herself in front of everyone, and then Julius had yelled and sent her away like she was a child bothering the adults.

That was the part that had stung the most. Marci didn't blame Julius snapping—she *had* been going overboard—but she'd never felt the distance between them more pointedly than at that moment. Living with him, it was easy to forget—not that Julius was a dragon, Marci never forgot that—but that he was part of a world that considered her disposable, beneath consideration. Tonight, though, she'd had a sharp reminder, and like all reality checks, it hurt. To a girl who'd just started to hope that maybe she and Julius could be something more than business partners, it hurt a *lot*.

Marci shook her head with a frustrated sigh. She had to snap out of this. It was stupid to be upset. This was all her fault, anyway. She'd let herself get comfortable over her month with Julius and forgotten the standard she was trying to measure up to. Well, one look at Bethesda had solved *that*. No mortal could come close to the supernatural beauty dragons took for granted, and this was assuming Julius even liked humans in that way. Since she'd only ever seen him as a human, it was too easy to forget that the Julius she knew and loved was only a disguise. It wasn't his real face, it probably wasn't even the one he preferred, and it was foolish for Marci to just assume that he had a human standard of beauty. Or that he'd choose her even if he did.

That toxic thought threatened to send her right back down into the pit, but really, what else could she expect? She'd *always* known Julius was out of her league, and she had no right to cry foul when reality kept being reality. But just as Marci was reaching new depths of feeling sorry for herself, her phone chimed in her pocket.

The sound made her flinch. She'd set the thing to reject all, the modern equivalent of locking herself in her room. But while that super-mature decision kept her from having to face the outside world, it didn't apply to her internal alarms. It was too late in the evening for any of her work notifications, though, which meant this was her *other* alarm. The one she'd been putting off for a week.

Her first impulse was to send it away again. She wasn't normally a procrastinator, but some things were just too much to face with anything less than her best, which she was definitely not tonight.

That said, though, she'd been putting this off for a long time, and it wasn't like she was actually doing anything right now…

Like it could sense her indecision, the alarm chimed again, vibrating in her pocket. Marci grabbed it violently, stabbing her finger through the projected AR notice to kill the annoying sound, but the blinking red warning remained. She stared at it for several long seconds, and then she tossed the phone into the empty seat beside her with a curse, reaching over with her other hand to change the autonav's destination, because why not? Misery loved company, so why not pile everything together? It wasn't like tonight could get any worse.

That was a self-destructive line of thought and she knew it, but this really did need to be taken care of, and it wasn't like she had to go far. By sheer coincidence, her aimless pity driving had already taken her into the right part of town. Barely ten minutes later, she was at her destination, pulling into the underground deck below the massive, five-story complex that was the downtown branch of the DFZ 24-Hour Private Postal Service.

Even at this time of night, the place was packed. She had to drive nearly to the bottom of the deck before she found a parking spot, and the stairs up to the lobby were a highway of humanity. Crowded as it was, though, the Private Postal Service existed specifically to allow people to pick up packages without giving their name, so even though the crowd on the stairs was packed in shoulder to shoulder, no one said a word. That suited Marci just fine, and she dutifully avoided eye contact as she hurried up the cement stairs into what looked like a multilevel warehouse stacked floor to ceiling with aisle after aisle of locked metal post office boxes.

Her pick-up number was for the fourth floor. The crowd thinned as she climbed, and by the time she actually found her box amid the endless rows of identical metal squares, Marci was alone. She still looked over her shoulder before punching the single use code the coroner's office had sent her almost two weeks ago into the number pad. Her hands were shaking so badly, it took her two tries before the light turned green, and the metal door opened with a *click* to reveal a plain, shoebox-sized cardboard container marked only with a barcode and a name printed in stark, Unicode font.

Aldo Giovanni Novalli

The letters grew blurry as she looked at them, and Marci closed her eyes. "Stop it," she hissed, covering her face with her hands. "Don't cry. Don't you dare…"

But there was no stopping it, not this time. She'd held on for so long, but the sight of her father's ashes sealed up by some government mortician and mailed to her because she was too broke and scared to go back to Las Vegas for an actual funeral was the very last straw. She couldn't fight it if she tried, so she didn't. She just slumped over, sliding down the cold metal wall of pay-by-delivery mailboxes as she started to cry in big, ugly sobs.

She cried for her father, who'd deserved so much better than to be shot and left in the desert like trash. She cried because Bixby was already dead, and she couldn't kill him again. She cried because she'd never get to tell her daddy she'd met a dragon, or show him the DFZ. He'd always wanted to come here, and now he had. In a box. Not even a proper urn, but a stupid cardboard box. She hadn't even gotten to say goodbye.

That set Marci off all over again. Behind her, she heard the soft scrape of footsteps as other people came in to check their mail only to turn around again when they saw the crazy lady sobbing over a package, but mortifying as it was, she couldn't stop. All the emotions and fears and regrets she'd been putting off since the night she'd fled her house were finally coming due, and she had no choice but to keep going until, at last, she'd cried herself dry.

When she looked up again, she was sitting on the floor. The narrow aisles of mailboxes were deathly silent around her, probably because she'd scared off all the other customers. That was fine with her. Marci had always hated crying, but crying in front of others was the worst. Ironic, too, because her father had always encouraged her to cry. He'd claimed that tears were how you let go of the things that hurt too much to keep, but Marci didn't feel like she'd let go of anything. She was still miserable, and her father was still dead, along with everything he'd wanted for her. She'd dropped out of school, first because she was running from Bixby, and then because working with a dragon in the DFZ had been so much more appealing than going home to Vegas where she'd be constantly reminded of her dad. She'd rationalized the situation by telling herself that if she just stuck with Julius, she was bound to meet a dragon who could teach her ten times what her professors knew. Then, tonight, she had, and she'd screwed that up, too.

That set her off all over again. But just as Marci was curling back into a ball for sobs round two, something cold and soft bumped into her back.

Her head snapped up in alarm, and she looked over just in time to see Ghost jump through the wall of boxes. He landed on the cement floor beside her, giving his fluffy, semi-transparent body a shake before turning to greet her with a slow blink of his glowing blue eyes.

It was a sign of just how miserable her life had become that this scrap of affection from her undead cat actually made Marci feel better. "Hello to you, too," she croaked, holding out her hand. "Where have you been?"

Ghost meowed silently, bumping his head against her hand. Marci smiled back, ignoring the grave-like chill of his fur as she scratched behind his ears. "You know, for a bound spirit, you sure do vanish a lot. Where do you go, anyway? Undead mouse hunting?"

Instead of answering, Ghost butted his head demandingly against her scratching hand, causing his transparent ears to pass right through her fingers. A few weeks ago, that would have creeped her out. Now, Marci thought it was kind of cute.

"Well, wherever you went, I'm glad your day seems to have gone better than mine," she said sadly. "Not that that would be hard. I'm pretty sure you didn't humiliate yourself in front of the most powerful dragon in the Americas." He bumped her hand again, and Marci obediently scratched harder, closing her eyes against the institutional white glare of the post office's high-efficiency halogen lamps. "Why am I such an idiot, Ghost?"

It was supposed to be a rhetorical question, but the semi-transparent cat purred in her mind.

Human.

"Tell me about it," she grumbled, pulling her cold-stiffened fingers back to tap on the cardboard box containing all that was left of her dad. "I'm just full of reminders of my mortality today. It's not like I mind being human, but…I wish they wouldn't treat me like I was worthless, you know? It's not our fault we die, or that we lost all our knowledge of magic. There *was* no magic for a thousand years. Now that it's back, we're having to reinvent everything from scratch, and it's so freaking pointless. Look at my dad. He was part of the first generation of mages, and they had no idea what they were doing. There was no one to teach them, and that's just so stupid when you think about the fact that there are *immortal creatures* waddling around who could explain everything if they could stop looking down their snouts for three seconds and answer some basic questions!"

Her hands were clenched into fists by the time she finished. She hadn't even realized how angry she was about this until it all came spilling out. The more she thought about it, though, the angrier she got.

"It's just so wasteful!" she cried. "My Theoretical Thaumaturgy professor back at UNLV was the best in his field. Not because he was anything special, but because *there was no one else.* We've only had magic for sixty years. That's not enough time to develop any sort of real understanding. We still don't know why magic works or where it comes from, we don't even know why there are spirits. Maybe we did once, but if that information existed, it's long gone. Now we're back to fumbling around in the dark for whatever we can find, and all the spirits and dragons are sitting around watching us with their fingers on the light switch, but they won't flip it on because they're all a bunch of stingy, egotistical *bastards!*"

She turned to give Ghost an *Am I right?* look, but the cat was cleaning his paws, utterly uninterested.

Marci flopped back against the wall of PO boxes with a sigh. Served her right for ranting at a cat, she guessed, but it had still felt good. Anything was better than crying like a baby over things she couldn't change.

"I just wish I could make them talk," she said wistfully. "There are legends of ancient wizards who shot dragons out of the skies like clay pigeons, but there's no evidence that the pre-drought mages were more powerful than us. The only difference between then and now is knowledge. If we got that again, not even Bethesda the Heartstriker could look down on us."

Now *there* was a satisfying thought. Too bad it was a pipe dream. If there was one thing the immortals of the world seemed to actually agree on, it was that humans should be kept in the dark. Marci supposed that made sense when you considered the whole 'shooting dragons out of the skies like skeet' thing, but it still sucked. But what could she do? Nothing. For all she knew, Bethesda wasn't even bringing Julius back.

"Come on," she said, pushing herself up. "Other people need to use their boxes, and I think I've done enough crying for one night. I need to get Daddy home and into a proper urn."

She tucked the cardboard box containing her father into her shoulder bag and started down the hall. But when she looked back to make sure Ghost was following, that cat was just sitting there, staring at her with unblinking eyes.

Want to know?

"Excuse me?"

Magic, he said in her mind. *Power. Do you want it?*

Marci shifted uneasily. That was one of the most complete sentences she'd ever heard Ghost speak, which would have been great if it hadn't sounded so much like a deal with the devil. "Of course I want to know about magic," she said cautiously. "And who doesn't want power? But—"

I have, Ghost said casually. *Can share.*

Okay, now he was just making fun of her. "Likely story. We're directly connected, remember? If you had power, I think I'd know."

Can share. Ghost said again, ignoring her sarcasm. *Help me.*

And then he vanished back into the wall.

"Wait!" Marci cried, slamming her hand against the postbox he'd just passed through. "Where are you—"

Follow, Ghost purred in her mind. *Downstairs. Quickly.*

Marci swore under her breath and bolted for the stairs, blowing past a pair of curious, off-duty Algonquin security officers who'd clearly been eavesdropping from the next aisle over. Her cheeks burned at the thought of someone overhearing her emotional breakdown, but she didn't have time to stop or anything she could say to explain, so she just kept going, taking the stairs down two at a time until she spotted Ghost sitting on the ground floor landing.

He stayed still just long enough for her to catch up before slipping through the fire exit.

Follow.

"But I'll set off the alarm," she panted.

Ghost's voice grew irritated. *Hurry.*

Marci was not about to get fined for what was probably a wild goose chase, but she couldn't let Ghost go, either. In the end, she compromised, running through the lobby to the post office's front door and then around the building until she reached the back alley where the emergency fire door let out.

Like most places in the DFZ Underground, the area around the post office was a confusing patchwork of money and abject poverty. The buildings facing the main streets were as bright and jangly as the tourist traps she'd led Julius past the night they met. Once you stepped away from the high traffic areas, though, the lights faded after only a few feet, giving way to an interior network of narrow, pitch black alleys lined with tiny shops and massage parlors that served a seedier, much more desperate segment of the population.

As a whole, the back alley slums of the DFZ weren't quite as bad as the movies made them out to be, but a few could be worse. From what Marci could see of the tiny crack of an alley that ran behind the massive, windowless post office, Ghost had led her right into one of the latter. "What are you doing?" she hissed, sucking magic out of the moist, polluted air into her bracelets as she hurried after her glowing cat. "Are you *trying* to get me mugged?"

Ghost didn't answer. He just kept going, trotting around a corner into a second, even smaller crevice between buildings that looked like the sort of place where people got stabbed for their organs. With a last, longing glance at the bright, crowded street behind her, Marci followed, using her glowing bracelets as a lantern as she picked her way around potholes that could have swallowed a full-grown cow.

In the end, the only nice thing she could say about it was that she didn't have to go far. Barely thirty feet after it began, the tiny alley dead-ended into the back of a run-down convenience store. Ghost was waiting for her on the edge of one of the shop's rusted dumpsters, his tail lashing back and forth as he waited for Marci to join him.

"Okay," she said when she'd finally made it safely around all the pot holes and mysterious black puddles to the end of dumpster alley. "I'm here. Now, will you *please* tell me what's going on?"

Ghost gave her the cat equivalent of an extremely unamused glare and tapped his paw down on the dumpster's closed lid. *Help.*

Marci blinked in surprise. In the month since she'd bound him, Ghost had never asked her for anything. She wasn't even aware he had things he needed help with. But he was pawing the dumpster lid with increasing urgency, and so she grabbed it with her finger tips, touching as little of the filthy metal as possible as she flipped it open. Naturally, the lid passed right through Ghost, leaving him standing in the empty air above the dumpster's open bin. But before Marci could ask why he hadn't just phased through the thing in the first place, she saw what was inside, illuminated by Ghost's soft, white light.

She jumped back with a yelp, slapping her hands over her mouth. There was a *person* lying in the trash at the bottom of the dumpster. Almost as soon as that thought crossed her mind, though, her brain rejected it. The curled over shape was far too still for a person, which meant she'd just discovered a *corpse*.

That was infinitely worse. Marci edged forward again, peeking over the dumpster's edge to make absolutely certain she wasn't seeing things. Sadly, she wasn't. Between the glowing spellwork on her bracelets and Ghost's pale light, she could clearly make out the body of a teenage boy. A *very* thin teenage boy with ribs clearly visible where his filthy, oversized shirt hung down from his slender neck. Malnourished as he obviously was, though, hunger wasn't what had killed him. The cause of death was a wound on the top of his head—a long, caved-in gash that matched the sharp metal support bar that ran across the dumpster's base.

As soon as she saw that, Marci's fear turned to overwhelming sadness. "Poor kid," she whispered. "He must have been looking for food and fallen in, or fainted."

Either way, it was a tragedy, and not an uncommon one. People slipped through the cracks all the time in the DFZ. Stuff like this didn't even make the news. Still. "We need to report this."

Why? Ghost looked down at the boy. *Still dead.*

"That's not the point," Marci said angrily. "He has family somewhere, people who care about him. They'll want to know."

No. No one.

"How do you know that?"

The cat looked back up at her. *Calls to me. Help.*

"What do you mean, calls to you?" Marci asked. "Was he a mage or—"

Not mage, Ghost said firmly. *Dead.* His eyes flicked to her glowing bracelets. *Give.*

Before she could ask what he meant by that, Ghost pulled on the connection between them, his cold presence reaching in to tug on the magic she'd gathered for self-protection.

"No way," Marci said, grabbing the magic tight. "You're not getting a drop until you tell me what you're doing."

Ghost flicked his tail. *Helping. You help, I help. Together, power.*

Marci glared at him suspiciously. Then again, though, if anyone could help the dead, it would probably be a death spirit. Ghost was so creepy sometimes it was easy to think of him as evil, but everything Marci had learned about spirits suggested they didn't function along simple lines of morality. Or, at least, not human morality.

They were more like forces of nature, and naturally speaking, death was just another part of life. Not that she felt that way at the moment, clutching the box that held her father's ashes, but Ghost was looking at her desperately now, and it wasn't like he could make the boy's situation worse.

"You won't hurt him?"

She knew how silly that question sounded even before the words were out of her mouth, but she couldn't help herself. He might be dead, but he'd still been human. Thankfully, Ghost answered her straight. *No*, he said solemnly. *Help*. He tugged on the gathered magic again. *Help*.

Marci blew out a long breath. Then, slowly, she unclenched her mental fist. "All right," she said. "But just a—"

She didn't get to finish. The moment she let go, Ghost snatched the magic she'd pushed out to her bracelets and yanked it back. As always, the power burned coming back in, but it only hurt for a second before Ghost sucked it down, drinking the magic into himself and leaving only the bitter cold of the grave behind.

She was half-frozen by the time he finished. Ghost, on the other hand, was glowing brighter than ever. He dropped into the dumpster, landing on the boy's chest as magic began to hum the air. Not her magic, either, but something else. Something dark and heavy. Marci was trying to get a better feel for it when Ghost threw back his head in a silent yowl, and the entire alley began to move.

All around them, shadows began to creep inward. When they entered the circle of Ghost's blue-white light, though, she saw they weren't shadows at all. They were cats. Hungry strays, their eyes shining with Ghost's reflected light, poured out of the dark alley and into the dumpster. It was just like when they'd come for Oslo when he'd attacked her and Julius at her house last month. Back then, she'd been delighted. This time, all Marci felt was horror.

"What did you do?" she cried, jumping away from the tide of cats running past her legs. "You said you were going to *help* him! How is being eaten by cats helpful?"

Ghost looked surprised by her outburst. *It is helpful to the cats.*

Marci supposed that was true, but she was too busy staring at Ghost to say so. The spirit had jumped back up on the edge of the dumpster as he'd spoken, and while his light was dimmer than it had been when he'd taken her magic, it was still much brighter than usual. His voice in her head was stronger, too, the words louder and clearer than she'd ever heard them.

He was forgotten, Ghost said, swishing his tail, which was slightly less transparent than before. *Now his flesh returns to the cycle while his soul is remembered.* He gave her a slow blink. *Very helpful, yes?*

Marci didn't answer. Instead, she turned to face her spirit. The one she was now very certain was *not* a death spirit for cats.

"What are you?"

Ghost gave her a Cheshire Cat smile. *Names are expensive. Make me more, and I'll tell you mine. We can be very powerful together.*

He leaned on their link as he said this, and Marci realized she could feel him much more strongly than before. Whatever had just happened, it had changed something fundamental in their bond, and she wasn't sure if that was a good thing or a bad one.

"All right," she said, crossing her arms tight to ward off the cold shiver that had just run down her spine. "This is officially too creepy. I'm not doing anything else until I know more about…whatever this is." She pointed at the cats that were still jumping into the dumpster.

I told you already, Ghost said irritably. *He called, I helped.*

"But why?" she said. "How does a dead body call, and why you? And how did you even know he was back here? Can you explain that?"

Ghost shifted uncomfortably. *No.*

She scowled. "Why not?"

The cat's expression turned belligerent. But then, just when Marci was about to start grilling him again, he said, *I don't know.*

"How do you not know?"

Because I don't, he grumbled, looking away. *I don't know how I do these things or why, just that I have to. I don't know my name, either.*

That struck Marci as incredibly sad. "How don't you know your own name?"

Ghost flicked his ears. *Like I said, names are expensive. When I woke, I had nothing. Just cats and death. Then you.* He looked up. *I thought you could help me, so I accepted your binding. But you won't help.*

"I never said that," Marci said quickly. "I'm completely willing to help you with whatever you need. I just want to know what's going on first, maybe run a few tests. Once I'm convinced I'm not going to be doing something I'll regret, we'll take it from there. Is that an acceptable compromise?"

Sufficient, Ghost said, hopping down from the dumpster. *But not right now.* He yawned. *Tired.*

"Then why don't you go home and get some sleep?" she said, trying not to sound too eager. Her fingers were already itching to start researching what could cause a spirit to make such an obvious jump in intelligence, or at least talkativeness, and that would be a lot less awkward if he wasn't looking over her shoulder. Fortunately, Ghost didn't seem to mind being sent away. He was already fading, taking his light with him. *Un*fortunately, this left Marci alone, in the dark, with the cats.

The sound of their eating was even worse now that she couldn't see. Trying not to gag, Marci stumbled away, tripping over the uneven pavement as she rushed out of the alley. She didn't slow down until she was back in the underground parking deck. Even then, she was so happy to finally be back somewhere with light and no dead bodies, she didn't even notice the man in the navy blue Algonquin security uniform waiting by her car until he said her name.

"Marci Novalli?"

She looked up just in time for the black bag to slide over her head.

• • •

By the time Julius landed at the private airport on the Canadian side of the Detroit river, the only place that aircraft registered to dragon clans could touch down near the DFZ, it was almost one in the morning. Thankfully, the auto-cabs ran twenty-four hours a day. Fifteen minutes after leaving the airport, Julius was pulling up to his house.

His dark, obviously empty house.

He ordered the cab to wait and jumped out, racing across the conspicuously empty driveway and up the front stairs. The second he opened the door, though, his nose confirmed what he already knew. Marci wasn't here, and hadn't been for some time. Five minutes of searching revealed she hadn't left a note, either, and her phone was still in ignore mode, which meant Julius still had no idea where she was and no way to contact her.

Julius being Julius, this sent him immediately to the worst-case scenarios: she'd left him forever, she'd been in a wreck, she'd been kidnapped, she was dead. Logically, of course, he knew he was overreacting. Marci was a grown woman and a ridiculously competent mage. Why would she sit at home alone? She was probably out having a night to herself, blowing off steam after the horrible things his mother had said. But even though he knew he was being ridiculous, he couldn't seem to *stop*. The idea that Marci was out there and angry with him and he couldn't talk to her to fix the problem was more than Julius could take on a normal day. After everything else that had happened tonight, it was nearly enough to break him. Marci was his best friend, the spot of sanity in the storm that was his family. If she left, he'd have *no one*.

Also, he'd been counting on her magic to help find Justin.

Just thinking that made Julius feel like the worst kind of user, but he really did need her help. The DFZ was a massive area, over five hundred square miles, and that wasn't counting the extra landmass added by the double layer of the skyways. He supposed he could hire his hacker again to trace Justin's phone like he'd done with Katya, but seeing how Justin hadn't answered a single one of Julius's multiple calls, he wasn't sure his brother even had his phone on him. But even if he found Justin tonight, though, it wouldn't change the fact that Marci was gone.

ONE GOOD DRAGON DESERVES ANOTHER

That thought was enough to make his knees buckle. He sat down hard on the floor, burying his head in his shaking hands. It wasn't until he started feeling like he was actually going to throw up, though, that Julius realized he needed to get a grip.

Yes, he'd had a terrible, stressful night, and yes, something was probably horribly wrong with Marci, but freaking out was only making things worse. Now more than ever, he needed to dig down and find the calm, plotting dragon that had to be in him somewhere. It wasn't impossible. He'd found Katya when all seemed lost, surely he could find his brother and his best friend.

That line of thought didn't do much to relax the terrible choking panic inside him, but it *did* get him up off the floor. He was psyching himself up to think of a brilliant plan when he noticed a strange glow coming from the living room.

After everything that had happened tonight, it would be just his luck to find *another* dragon waiting on his couch. But fate must have finally decided to throw him a bone, because the source of the strange glow wasn't draconic or monstrous or any of the other horrible things his brain could imagine. It was Marci's cat.

It said something about your state of mind when discovering a ghost cat sleeping on your couch was the high point of your evening. "Ghost!" Julius cried, rushing over to pet the spirit's icy fur. "Thank goodness! Where's Marci?"

The cat didn't answer. This wasn't actually a surprise—Ghost *never* talked to him—but he'd at least hoped the spirit would wake up. No dice. No matter how much he poked or yelled, the cat refused to open his eyes. He just rolled over onto his back, his transparent feet kicking slightly as he dreamed. But while this wasn't the reaction Julius had hoped for, the spirit's presence alone was a huge relief. He didn't know the specifics of Ghost and Marci's relationship, but there was no way the spirit would be here sleeping if she was dead or in danger, right?

That bit of logic did more to soothe Julius's panic than anything else. He still wasn't convinced Marci was okay, but he was reasonably sure she wasn't hurt or in an emergency. Unfortunately, that was more than Julius could say for his brother, which meant finding Justin was now his first priority. He just hoped he wasn't already too late. Chelsie hadn't mentioned how long he'd been in the DFZ, but an angry Justin with something to prove was a recipe for disaster anywhere. With no magic or phone trace to rely on, though, he wasn't sure where to begin. Even if he limited his search to the Underground, the DFZ was way too big. If he didn't want this to take weeks, he was going to have to come up with something to narrow the search area. With that in mind, the question became: if he were Justin, where would he go?

Julius sat down on the couch beside Ghost, staring at the cracks in the ceiling as he tried to remember if Justin had ever suffered a blow like this before, and how he'd dealt with it. He couldn't remember anything specific. In fact, until this point, what he'd seen of his brother's life had been almost suspiciously serendipitous. Still, given what he knew of his brother, Julius had the feeling that an upset Justin would go somewhere private to lick his wounds. Somewhere with no humans or dragons, but not so far that he couldn't come back when he inevitably got lonely. Somewhere with food.

The last one gave him an idea. He pulled out his phone and typed in a search for pizza delivery places in the DFZ. This turned up thousands of results, so he shrank his search to only the local chain Justin had ordered from when he'd stayed in the Heartstriker family safehouse. The first four locations had nothing, and the fifth wouldn't answer his questions, but the clerk working the phones at the sixth shop was all too ready to complain about the strange customer who called five times a day and ordered more pizzas than any one person could possibly eat.

"He's a machine," the man groaned. "He calls when we open and then every three hours until we close, and he doesn't even get the same pizzas! If he was consistent we could bake ahead, but every order's different, and it's been going on for *three days*."

"I'm sorry," Julius said with real sincerity. "I don't suppose you could tell me where the orders are coming from? I wouldn't normally ask, but he's my brother, and I'm worried about him."

The clerk gasped, and then there was a rustling sound as he muffled the phone with his hand to shout, "*Hey!* This guy knows the bottomless pit!"

A chorus of voices cheered in the background, and then the clerk said, "We'll give you his address, man, no problem, just make him stop calling. Corporate doesn't allow us to refuse his orders, but dude lives in the middle of nowhere and orders a hundred pizzas a day, no joke. Plus, he doesn't tip."

"I'm *very* sorry about him," Julius said again, pulling up his bank account. "How much does he owe you?"

It took a few minutes for all the cooks and drivers to figure out how much Justin had stiffed them in tips over the last three days. The number they ended up with still sounded low to Julius, especially given what they'd put up with, so he doubled it, transferring the money as soon as they told him where to send it.

"Thanks a million, man," the clerk said, his voice so bright Julius knew he had to be grinning from ear to ear. "You're, like, our best friend now. Just sent the deets to your number, and if you ever need a pizza on the house, just let us know."

"I will," Julius said, grinning when the address for Justin's pizza pick-up appeared on his phone. "Thank you."

The clerk thanked him several more times before Julius finally got him off the phone so he could send Justin's location to his still-waiting cab.

• • •

The party at Heartstriker Mountain was still in full swing when Conrad, First Blade of Bethesda and Champion of the Heartstrikers, left his mother happily toying with her more ambitious children and went back to his room. As the highest ranking warrior in the clan, it wasn't much of a walk. His apartment—a lavish, seven-room setup complete with his own take-off balcony overlooking the mountain's northern face—was located just below Bethesda's own. He shut his door and locked it twice before walking into his armaments room to set his Fang on its stand. He was still unhooking the massive blade from his belt when he felt a familiar presence behind him.

"What are you still doing here?" he asked, not even bothering to look as his sister stepped out of the shadows. "I'd have thought you'd be after Justin by now."

"I was planning to," Chelsie said, walking over to stand beside him. "But I got some unexpected help in that quarter. Well-timed, too, since it seems that, for once, Justin isn't our biggest disaster."

"I assume you're referring to Estella," Conrad said, locking his sword into its custom stand.

She nodded. "What do you intend to do about her?"

"At the moment?" He crossed his arms as he turned to face her. "Nothing."

"Are you kidding?"

"No," Conrad said calmly. "But you're overreacting. Estella is not a threat. Bob defeated her long ago. These dramatics are nothing but a final, failing attempt at relevancy."

Chelsie looked at him like he was crazy. "She's still a seer."

"A desperate one."

"That's even worse," she snapped. "This isn't the time to get cocky. Estella's always hated us, but she's never been foolish enough to set foot in Heartstriker Mountain until tonight. Something fundamental has changed."

"Good," Conrad said, grinning. "Our clan's been too long without a war. The younger clutches don't even know what it means to fight like dragons. They fawn at Bethesda's feet, playing her games and stabbing each other in the back for a scrap of her favor. We could use a good battle to thin out the ranks, and it's not like we're in danger of actually losing. We're the largest dragon clan in the world, the strongest of the strong. Even if the Three Sisters woke tomorrow, what could they do? Heartstriker is over a hundred drag-ons strong, and our mountain is a fortress of modern weapons and magic. I'd like to see them try and attack us."

"They're not going to charge the mountain," Chelsie said irrita-bly. "If Estella strikes, she's going to go for Bethesda."

"Which means she'll have to get through both you and me," Conrad said with a shrug. "Even less likely to work."

His sister was already opening her mouth for her next argu-ment, but Conrad cut her off. "It doesn't matter what Estella does," he growled. "Even if she did manage to actually succeed in killing Mother, that's not a loss for us."

Chelsie went very still. "What do you mean?"

He flashed her a knowing look. "Surely you saw who was stand-ing out on the balcony tonight?"

"You can't be serious," she said, rolling her eyes. "Amelia's a drunk."

"And the top dragon mage in the world," he reminded her. "That's the sort of power we should be cultivating here, not send-ing off to the planes. It's a waste to go without one of our best just because Bethesda is terrified of having an heir who might actually be able to defeat her."

Chelsie scowled. "That's a dangerous thing for a champion to say."

He shrugged. "It's because I'm champion that I can say it. My sword and my loyalty belong to Heartstriker. I support whatever brings strength and power to the clan."

"And to you, of course."

"Naturally," Conrad said. "I still don't believe any plan of Estella's will succeed, but *if* it did, there's no point in pretending we'd be heartbroken over a change of leadership, or have you learned to enjoy being Bethesda's dog?"

Chelsie's eyes flashed with a hint of the old fury before she turned away. "You're my last full brother, so I'm going to forget I heard that. I just came to tell you that Mother's ordered us to pre-pare the clan for war."

"Already done," Conrad said. "I told you, I've been waiting for a chance like this for centuries. Tonight was the last time those ice snakes will leave this mountain alive."

She nodded and vanished, just disappeared into thin air in front of him. Normally, she saved that trick for when her target's back was turned, but Conrad knew all of his sister's secrets, so pretense was unnecessary. He was about to set the wards and head to bed when a breeze blew in from his open balcony, its air heavy with the scent of the frozen northern sea.

Conrad's lips peeled back into a feral grin. "I knew you ice sisters were desperate," he growled, grabbing his sword off the rack as he turned to face the White Witch, who was now standing on the edge of his balcony. "But I didn't know you were stupid."

He paused there, waiting for her to say the usual rot about how he was dead and so forth, but the dragoness didn't speak. She just stood there, her striking blue eyes as cold and empty as sea ice. As an intimidation tactic, it worked better than Conrad liked to admit, but he was the Champion of the greatest dragon clan in the world, and it took more than creepy silence to make him flinch.

"What?" he taunted, positioning his sword for the strike that would take off her head. "No final words?"

"She has nothing to say to a son of the broodmare," growled a voice behind him. "And neither do I."

Conrad's eyes went wide. He spun, lashing out with his Fang at the second dragon, the one he'd only now realized was standing behind him. But for all his speed, all his training, Conrad barely managed a half-turn before Estella's hands shot out to wrap a black chain around his neck.

That was the last thing he saw before the world went dark.

• • •

Far below, in the backseat of Svena's sleek, armored sedan, which was currently hidden by magic to look like just another stretch of desert, Katya, youngest and most disappointing daughter of the

Three Sisters, sat with her face pressed against the bulletproof window, staring up at the balcony where her sisters were beginning their attack on the Heartstriker Champion.

No, she thought angrily, she had only one sister here. Despite the familiar face, there was no way the silent puppet who obeyed Estella's orders without question was actually Svena. But while Katya was now certain her sister was not herself, it didn't change her situation. Whatever that thing beside Estella actually was, it still had Svena's power and knowledge. Katya, on the other hand, had nothing. No money, no weapons, not even a phone. She couldn't even get a moment to herself to think up a strategy. Other than the brief chance she'd stolen to run to Julius, Estella hadn't let her out of her sight.

Unless, of course, you counted right now.

Katya licked her lips. This far down, there was no way Estella could see her, and while the car was locked and sealed with magic, it was nothing compared to the protections she'd slipped through all the times she'd run away from her mothers' fortress. It would be so simple: a quick kick to break the lock and then freedom. But though Katya could see the whole escape like it had already happened, she didn't move.

Part of her was mortified. What sort of dragon was she to let a chance like this, perhaps her *last* chance, slip by? But the rest of her, the parts that valued survival over pride, knew that every time she'd run, Estella had caught her. Every time she'd escaped, the seer had always been waiting at the end. This time, though, Katya didn't think her sister would be satisfied with simply returning her to her prison in their mothers' glacier. This time, Estella would kill her.

That was enough to dampen even Katya's instinct to run. But just as she decided that her odds of surviving were better if she stayed put and played along, something thumped against the car's rear windshield.

Katya jumped, hand flying to her mouth to stifle her surprised yelp. When she whirled around, though, it was just a bird. A pigeon, to be precise, fluttering against the window like it was trying to get in.

Shaking her head, Katya slapped her hand against the glass to scare the stupid thing away, but the bird wouldn't go. It just flapped harder, cooing loudly. She was about to bare her true nature and give it a real scare when she saw the bird had something in its claws.

Before she could see what it was, the bird flew away, abandoning its catch on the trunk of the car. Now that there was no longer a pigeon flapping around on top, Katya could see it wasn't a mouse or some other garbage, but an elegantly folded piece of paper. With her name on it.

Katya went very still, ears straining. Other than the fading flap of the pigeon's wings and the ceaseless desert wind, though, she didn't hear a thing. Both of her sisters were still dealing with Conrad, and the Heartstrikers were all inside their mountain, leaving the desert empty, but not for much longer. If she was going take a risk, it had to be now.

Heart pounding, Katya reached out, transforming her hand just a fraction until she had enough claw to pop the rear door lock. It broke with a soft *crack*, and then her arm snaked back, her fingers returning to their human shape as she snatched the paper off the trunk where the pigeon had dropped it. The moment the note was in her fingers, she darted back into the car, curling herself into a ball in the far corner of the backseat as she spread the folded paper flat over her knees to read the scribbled handwriting in the bright moonlight.

From a friend, it said. *Don't be late.*

Below this, someone had printed out a small map to an address in the DFZ, but that was it. There was no signature, no instructions, no additional information of any kind.

Clutching the note in her hands, Katya glanced up through the window at Conrad's empty balcony, and then back over her shoulder at the door she'd already broken. Beyond it, the empty desert sky beckoned, and Katya inched closer, breathing the fresh air deep into her lungs as she hovered on the threshold.

At this point, it was no longer a question if she would run. The door was already broken, and there was no way to fix it before

Estella and Svena returned. They'd know she'd disobeyed, which meant she was already committed. But there was a world of difference between mere fleeing and a planned escape, and with Estella on a rampage, Katya was going to have to plan this very carefully indeed. Since her enemy was a seer, getting caught was pretty much a foregone conclusion. With that in mind, the challenge wasn't avoiding her sister, but surviving the confrontation when Estella cornered her.

Fighting her was out of the question. Not even Svena had been able to do that. What Katya really needed in this situation was insurance, something Estella valued more than Katya's life that she could hold over the seer when things inevitably went bad. She was trying to think of what when her eyes landed on the golden orb of the Kosmolabe, carefully nestled in the cup holder between the front two seats.

A wicked smile spread over Katya's face. She made no sound, used no magic, but when Estella and Svena finally returned to the car, the Kosmolabe was no longer in it, and their youngest sister was nowhere to be found.

CHAPTER FIVE

When the guy at the pizza place said Justin lived in the middle of nowhere, Julius had assumed he was speaking hyperbolically. When he reached the address, though, Julius realized the man had been telling the plain truth.

Apparently, Justin had been living, or at least eating, at the end of the abandoned strip of land that ran between Algonquin's Reclamation Land and the industrial parks of the DFZ's southwest. The intersection where the automated cab dropped him was within sight of the border at 8 Mile Road, even farther from the city than Marci's hoarded cat house had been. There, at least, the neighborhood had still been semi-inhabited. Out here, there was nothing, just overgrown grass, collapsed houses, and magic. Wild, thick, unfriendly magic that hung in the night air like humidity, warding off even the most daring and desperate squatters.

Just climbing out of the cab was enough to make Julius's hair stand on end. If it wasn't for the fact that he could smell Justin nearby, he would have climbed right back in. But he'd come out here on a mission, so he ordered the car to wait and set off down the cracked road in search of his brother.

If it wasn't for the creepy magic, this would have almost been pleasant. The September night air was cool without being cold, and the empty lots were quiet and still. Other than the occasional flood-light on the chain fence that separated Reclamation Land from the rest of the urban wilderness, there were no lights anywhere, but compared to the cave-like dark of the Underground, the night itself was almost bright, especially now that the moon was rising. But even with the quiet and the natural light to help him, it still took Julius almost five minutes before he finally spotted his brother crouching on the toppled steeple of an old church like some kind of post-apocalyptic Batman.

"Were you going to say something eventually?" he called, walking out into the middle of the cracked street.

His brother's eyes flashed neon-green in the dark, and then he turned away. "Get lost."

Julius shook his head and started circling the church's crumbling walls. "How did you even get up there?" *Please don't say flew.*

"I jumped. I'm not stupid."

Considering he was currently sulking in a magic-soaked wilderness on a roof that was in sight of the border of a private domain claimed by a spirit who'd sworn to kill every one of their kind, Julius wasn't so sure he agreed with that assessment at the moment. But his brother clearly wasn't coming down any time soon, so he started making his way up, using the rotting window sills and cracks in the brick walls as handholds until, at last, he hauled himself onto the roof.

"Good grief, Justin," he sighed, looking around at the filthy nest of old soda bottles and discarded pizza boxes. "What are you doing up here?"

"What's it to you?" his brother sneered, hunching his shoulders. "How'd you find me, anyway? You suck at tracking."

"But I know your eating habits," Julius said, nudging a grease-stained, waterlogged breadstick box off the roof's edge so he could sit down. "And I wanted to make sure you were okay, which you're clearly *not.*"

"I don't recall asking your opinion," Justin said bitterly. "Didn't I just tell you to go away?"

Julius ignored him, taking a seat on the opposite side of the roof as he tried to think of the best way to deal with this. Obviously, the first step was to get Justin away from this landfill of a roof. Also, get him a shower, because the dragon was *filthy.* His t-shirt and jeans were caked with old grime, and there was blood on his boots. His blood or someone else's, Julius wasn't sure, but it looked awful. All of him did.

"Justin," Julius said firmly. "I know why you're out here."

His brother snorted. "I doubt that."

"I saw your sword in grandfather's skull."

Justin went very still, and then he turned on his brother with a look of pure poison. "What were *you* doing in the throne room?"

"Mother made me go to the party for Svena," Julius explained. "She picked me up earlier this evening and—"

"Bethesda the Heartstriker came to the DFZ to pick *you* up?"

Julius nodded, unable to tell if his brother was furious or disbelieving or both. Either way, he looked like he was about to explode. "Well," he growled at last. "Good for you. Guess you're a real big shot now."

Julius began to sweat. This was backfiring rapidly. "It's not like that," he said quickly. "I was only there because of the Katya life debt thing."

"Yeah? Well, I wasn't even *invited*," Justin snarled, hands clenching into fists. "Who put his neck on the line to rescue the Three Sisters' baby in the first place, huh? *Me.* There wouldn't even be a life debt if I hadn't dragoned-up and saved all your hides. But how was I repaid? By getting snatched out of the sky!"

"I know," Julius said earnestly. "Believe me, no one appreciates what you did that night more than I do. But..."

He faded off, trying desperately to think of the best way to say this, because it was complicated. There was no denying Justin had saved all their lives the night he'd turned into a dragon and blazed through Algonquin's Underground. On the other hand, though, Julius also didn't blame Chelsie for doing her job, especially since, given the sirens they'd heard on the way out, she'd probably saved Justin's life by getting him out. But there was no way to explain that to his brother when Justin was in a rage. He'd probably just accuse Julius of being on Chelsie's side, or worse, of pitying him.

In the end, there was only one thing Julius could say without any quantifying statements. Fortunately, he also had the feeling it was the one thing his brother needed to hear. "She was wrong to take your sword."

Justin's eyes shot up in surprise, and then he looked away. "You have no idea," he growled, fists tightening. "That Fang is *mine.*"

"I know," Julius said quickly. "And I also know you're eager to get it back, but—"

"You don't know anything," his brother snapped. "You've never held a Fang of the Heartstriker. Do you think it's just some normal sword? No. They're ancient dragon magic, the kind we don't get anymore. Each one is different, and they don't let just anyone use them. You have to be chosen, like I was." He bared his teeth. "That sword picked *me*! She had no right to take it."

"That's what I just said," Julius reminded him. "Look, I know you're upset, and you have every right to be, but this isn't the end of the world."

"Who said it was?"

Julius gave him a flat look. "You did. Maybe not in so many words, but just *look* at yourself, Justin. You're living like a hobo up here."

Justin turned away with a growl, but Julius just stood up and walked over to lay a gentle hand on his shoulder. "It's going to be okay," he said quietly. "You're more than your sword, Justin. I know you're angry and hurting right now, but—"

"Is *that* what you think this is about?" Justin said, smacking Julius's hand away with a look that was equal parts amused and insulted. "You think I'm out here *sulking*?"

That was *exactly* what Julius thought, but apparently he was wrong, because his brother was cracking up.

"Why else would you be all the way out here?" Julius demanded, his face heating as Justin doubled over. "We're in the middle of nowhere!"

"On the contrary," Justin said, pointing out into the dark. "I'm right where I want to be."

Julius frowned and turned, but he still didn't understand. There was just as much nothing where Justin was pointing as anywhere else out here. Just more of the same overgrown lots, broken streets, caved-in houses, and the endless barrier of the Reclamation Land fence running off into the—

"Oh no."

"Oh *yes*," Justin said, breaking into a sharp-toothed grin as he rose to stand beside his brother. "Reclamation Land, Algonquin's secret base inside the DFZ. That's what's leaking all the crazy magic we're sitting in out here, but no one knows why. No dragon has ever been past that fence."

"With good reason!" Julius cried. "You're talking about Algonquin's *private property*. She doesn't even let in her humans unless they've signed so many NDAs they can't place an order at a restaurant without consulting their contracts."

"All the more reason to find out what's inside," Justin said with a shrug. "No one makes that big a fuss unless they're hiding something."

He walked to the edge of the roof, green eyes gleaming as he stared at the floodlit fence in the distance. "I've been watching that border for three days now, tracking patrols and getting an idea of their security." He reached into his pocket, pulling out a grubby piece of paper covered in numbers and notes. "I've almost got their whole system cracked. Once I know what to expect, I'm going in there to dig out whatever it is Algonquin's hiding, and when I get it, I'm taking it straight back to Mother."

He glanced back at Julius, his face flushed with anticipation. "Can you imagine a better prize? Thanks to me, Heartstriker will have information no other dragon in the world has access to. Even if we don't use it ourselves, there are other clans with interests in the DFZ who'll pay through the nose for even a hint at Algonquin's long-term plans. That's *power*, Julius, and once I present it to Mother, it won't matter how much Chelsie gripes. She'll *have* to give me my sword back." He smirked. "What do you think? Brilliant, huh?"

Julius could only stare in amazement. Honestly, it was a much better plan than he'd expected from Justin, who, though an excellently ruthless and aggressive dragon, had never been what you'd call tactical. He was on the nose about their mother's reaction, too. Bethesda would go absolutely *nuts* if she got her hands on Algonquin's secrets. But while Julius was quite impressed with his brother's plan, there was one vitally important element Justin was overlooking.

"It's a daring strategy," he admitted. "But how are you going to do it? Even if you can sneak your way into Reclamation Land, it's not like Algonquin's going to let you have a look around and walk back out."

"You're assuming she'll be able to catch me," Justin said, lifting his chin. "I'm not exactly a soft target. Even if she did manage to corner me, I'm not afraid of Algonquin."

Julius gaped at his brother in horror. "Are you out of your *mind?*" he cried. "This isn't some low-ranking dragon we're talking about. This is *Algonquin*, the *Lady of the Lakes*! Spirits who used to be worshiped as gods come to the DFZ to work for *her*. And let's not forget her private army that she uses to kill dragons, or the fact that she keeps a sea monster the size of a cruise ship for a *pet*. *Everyone* is afraid of Algonquin!"

"Exactly," Justin growled. "And that's the problem. Algonquin comes in, takes a city, declares her hatred for dragonkind, and every clan in the world freaks out, even ours. Why else do you think Chelsie was able to get away with taking my sword? It's because they're all scared witless of a stupid lake spirit, even Mother. But I'm different. I'm not afraid, because unlike the rest of you, I actually remember what it means to be a dragon. We're the top of the pyramid, the biggest monsters on the board. We run from nothing."

"You should run from this," Julius cried, frustrated. "This isn't some chest pounding competition, Justin! You could actually die here."

"You say that like it's a reason to quit," his brother said with a sneer. "But that sort of defeatist attitude is exactly why you're a failure, Julius." He turned to glare at the fence again. "I'm actually hoping Algonquin sends her anti-dragon team after me, because then I'll get to burn them all alive and prove that Chelsie was wrong when she snatched me out of the sky 'for my safety.' I'm going to show them all that I don't need Bethesda's Shade following me around like a nanny. I don't need help from anyone, and when this is over, the whole clan will know it." ·

He bared his teeth as he finished, but Julius just turned away, defeated. He'd rushed out here to stop his brother from doing something crazy in his despair over the loss of his sword. Now, he was wondering why he'd even thought that was an option. His insane brother wasn't depressed without his sword. He was more reckless, pig-headed, and Justin-y than ever. Julius had a better chance of stopping a speeding freight train with his hands than of convincing his brother not to charge face-first into Algonquin, but that still didn't mean he could leave Justin to his fate. No matter how crazy or aggressive he got, Julius owed Justin his life multiple times over, including for the incident last month that had started all of this in the first place. He had to do something, protect his brother somehow, and so, with all sensible paths blocked, Julius did what he always did when Justin needed to be corralled for his own good.

He changed the subject.

"I see you've really thought this through," he said, lowering his eyes in a show of submission. "Unfortunately, we've got more immediate problems than Algonquin. Remember how I said I was at that party? Well, it didn't go as planned. That's why I came to find you, actually, because just a few hours ago, Estella of the Three Sisters declared war on our clan."

Justin's eyes went wide. "What?"

"Well, technically she offered us a mating flight," Julius explained. "But everyone can see it's a trap. Mother's already preparing the others, but since I'm holding the life debt between our clans, and I obviously can't protect myself against other dragons, she sent me to find you in the hopes you could watch over me."

That was a whopper of a lie wrapped in several mostly truths, but it was also what Justin most wanted to hear. Julius had learned years ago that nothing got his brother moving like a mission that made him feel singled out and important, and it worked like a charm now. He could actually see Justin fighting to keep the smile off his face while he pretended to think it over.

"I'm not inclined to take a job without my sword," he said at last. "But you *are* pretty pathetic when it comes to combat, so I guess I'll do you a favor and keep you alive."

A prouder, better dragon would have been insulted by that, but Julius had never been that dragon. His pride was a small, flexible thing, easily pushed aside for better causes, like getting his stupid brother off this roof.

"I'm happy you'll be watching out for me," he replied, shaking Justin's hand. "For now, though, let's go back to my house. It's in the DFZ, but it's pretty defensible, and we can order something that's not pizza."

Justin's eyes lit up at the word defensible, and even more at the mention of food. "Let's go then," he said, hopping off the roof like the two-story drop was nothing.

Julius happily climbed down after him. Just getting his brother away from Algonquin's fence helped assuage any lingering guilt Julius felt about his lie, and who knew? He might actually need Justin's help before this Estella business was over. For now, though, he just wanted to get them both back to the house where, hopefully, Marci would be waiting for them.

That was a happy thought indeed, and Julius hopped the final few feet down to the ground, motioning for Justin to follow him back to the cab.

• • •

There must have been something in that bag.

Marci opened her eyes with a groan, followed by a self-recriminating curse. The last thing she remembered was getting caught off-guard in the parking deck like an *idiot*. But though she'd have sworn she'd only been out for a few seconds, it must have been much longer, because she was now in a completely new building, strapped to a metal chair in the center of a dirty cinderblock room with a reinforced door, a single bulb on a string above her head, and a metal drain set into the floor at her feet.

Bile rose in her throat. She'd seen these kinds of movies. Nothing good ever happened when you woke up in a room with a drain. Worse still, her bracelets were gone, as was her bag, the chalk in her jacket pocket, and the backup casting marker she kept inside her left boot. She couldn't even reach Ghost, though whether that was because she was being blocked or he was just too sound asleep to answer, Marci had no idea.

Well, she thought bitterly, wiggling against her restraints, at least whoever had brought her here was taking her seriously. That was a small comfort after what'd happened with Bethesda, but Marci was still in a real bind. Now that her eyes were adjusting to the glare, she could see that the cinderblock walls of her cell weren't actually dirty like she'd first assumed. They were written on.

Someone had covered the inside of the cell from floor to ceiling with line after line of spellwork. The painstaking black markings were clearly the work of a Thaumaturge—no Shaman would be so precise—but of a type Marci didn't recognize. Her best guess was that it was one of the proprietary languages corp mages used to keep people from hacking their spells. Given how much spellwork was going on here, though, whatever this thing did had to be crazy complicated. She was trying to figure out which of the symbols were the variables when the door to her cell cracked open, and a small, middle-aged woman wearing the navy uniform of the Algonquin Corporate Security Forces slipped inside.

"What's going on?" Marci demanded, sitting up as straight as she could. "This might be the DFZ, but I still have rights. This is an unwarranted arrest."

She hadn't really expected that to go anywhere. Sure enough, the other mage ignored her, pulling a penlight out her pocket, which she used to check Marci's eyes.

Marci glared into the light. "I want a lawyer."

The woman arched an eyebrow as she clicked off her penlight and turned around to hit a small button beside the door. Marci had already opened her mouth to launch into a new slew of demands, but she never got a chance. The moment the woman pressed the button, a strange sound had started outside. It was distractingly familiar, a low pitched, rhythmic thumping, almost like someone was riding a horse at full gallop down a dirt road, which, of course, made zero sense. You were more likely to see a unicorn than an actual horse in the DFZ. The sound was so distinct, though, she couldn't actually imagine what else it might be until the woman opened the door, proving that Marci's first instinct was both right and terribly, terribly wrong.

She'd been busy staring at the spellwork on the walls when the woman came in, so Marci hadn't actually gotten a look at what was on the other side of the door until this moment. Since they were in a room, she'd just assumed they were also in a building, but again, she was wrong. There was no hallway or building or even a roof beyond that door. Only forest. An honest-to-god, moss carpeted, sun dappled, fairy-tale-style old-growth forest that started just across the door's threshold like the cement room had simply been air-dropped into the wilderness.

Naturally given how crazy that was, Marci's first instinct was that had it to be an illusion. An extremely good one since she could smell the rotting leaves and wet dirt from here, but an illusion all the same. But while there was a *lot* of magic on the other side of the door, it didn't feel like a spell. It was just power, a dense bank of loose magic sliding between the trees like mist, and in the middle of it was a man on a horse.

No, Marci thought with a sharp shake of her head. The thing outside the door *looked* like a man on a horse, but no horse had ever been that big or reflective. It actually sparkled in the hazy sunlight like it was made of glass, but even that wasn't quite right, because it was clearly moving. Water, she realized at last. It was water, an amalgam of crashing waves put together in the shape of a horse. Likewise, the man on its back wasn't actually a man at all.

It was a spirit.

Or, at least, she *assumed* it was a spirit. With the notable exception of Ghost, Marci's experience with spirits was limited to ones like the tank badger they'd banished this afternoon: the small, stupid, animistic spirits you ran into in normal life. She'd certainly never seen one this large, or humanoid, but while the spirit's shape resembled a large, burly, Viking-warrior sort of man, his skin was a dark, stormy, and definitely inhuman blue. Likewise, his long hair, full beard, and bushy eyebrows were dark green sea kelp, while the armor he wore from his neck to his toes was made of scallop shells with their scallops still inside. But remarkable as all that was, what really made Marci stare was the enormous driftwood spear the spirit held in his right hand.

From inside the room, it was hard to tell scale, but going from the relative height of the trees around him, the spirit's weapon was easily as long as a telephone pole. But while it looked like nothing more than a glorified pointy stick, the runes scratched into its handle radiated a cold, crushing power that sliced through the ambient magic of the forest like ice water down your back. Marci wasn't sure what those runes did exactly, but the old, dark stains on the spear's tip made her think it wasn't something she wanted to mess with.

Thankfully, the spirit set his weapon down when he dismounted, propping it up against one of the massive trees. Seeing him disarm almost made her feel more comfortable. That was, until the spirit stepped inside, ducking his head to fit through the human-sized door the security woman held open for him.

Marci shrank down in her chair. The spirit had looked big standing outside, but being in the same room with him was like being trapped in a closet with a grizzly. It wasn't just his size—though being stuck in a small room with a man whose head brushed the eight-foot ceiling was definitely intimidating—it was also his presence, a chilling, heavy aura that filled the room until Marci felt like she was drowning. With all that, it took every ounce of her pride just to lift her head enough to look him in the face. She was working up the courage to repeat her demand for a lawyer when the spirit suddenly spoke, his voice booming and grinding through the small room like breaking sea ice that just happened to be forming words.

"Servant of the dragon," he rumbled. "You have been restrained by order of Algonquin, Lady of the Great Lakes and ruler of this land. By her mercy alone, your life has been temporarily spared so that you may tell us everything you know about your master."

And that was when Marci knew she was screwed.

"I don't know what you're talking about," she stalled frantically. "I was just trying to check my mail."

The spirit's scowl deepened. "You are a very bad liar."

Marci began to sweat. "I am not—"

"I can hear your heart pounding like a trapped animal," he said over her. "You are afraid, as you should be, and lies flow as a result." He turned around, beckoning to the Algonquin Corp. mage, who was still in the room. "It seems we must take precautions to prevent further indiscretions."

The mage nodded, placing her hands on the spellwork covered wall. The moment she touched it, Marci felt a flare of magic, and the writing lit up as the spell activated. Pressure clamped down on her head at the same time. It wasn't painful, just uncomfortable, like someone had tied a string around the front portion of her brain, and Marci's fear turned to righteous indignation.

"Did you just cast a *lie detector* on me?"

"No," the spirit said, nodding at the glowing spellwork surrounding them. "This is a truth teller. So long as it is active, you will be physically unable to speak anything but the truth within this room."

Marci's eyes shot wide. Lie detector spells were internal magic that monitored your body for heart rate changes and other physiological signs of deceit. They were highly invasive, which was why they were regulated in every country that cared about personal privacy, but not actually dangerous. Truth tellers, on the other hand, were close enough to true mind control that they'd been outlawed everywhere. Marci had never even seen one in person, and she didn't like being inside one now.

"You can't do this!" she snarled, trying her best to sound threatening. "Mind-altering spells were forbidden by the Stockholm Magic Treaty of 2045. Even Algonquin is bound by international law!"

"Not in this place," the spirit said, glaring down at her with black, glinting eyes. "Foolish mortal, where do you think you are?" He nodded back over his shoulder at the closed door that led to the strange forest. "This is Reclamation Land. Here, there is no rule but ours."

For the second time in as many minutes, Marci felt like the floor had just been kicked out from under her. Reclamation Land was Algonquin's private sanctuary, a whole quarter of the DFZ fenced off from the rest of the city for spirit use only. She'd never even heard of an outsider getting in, probably because, if they did make it inside, they never left again, which meant she was screwed. The knowledge must have shown on her face, too, because for the first time since he'd appeared, the spirit smiled.

"I'm pleased to see you understand," he said, holding out a massive hand. Behind him, the human mage jumped and reached into the official looking document bag on her shoulder to pull out a manila folder. A real, paper one. Marci hadn't even realized they still made those things, but the spirit just took it as a matter of course and flipped the file open.

"Marcivale Caroline Novalli," he read. "Formerly of Las Vegas, Nevada." He glanced up. "This is you."

It wasn't a question, but she nodded anyway. "I go by Marci."

His response to that was a cold glare she felt to her bones. "As is the proper way of things, I will now state my name so that you may know the fate you face. I am Vann Jeger, Lord of the Black Narrows, spirit of the Geirangerfjord, and the Death of Dragons."

Marci didn't know what a Geirangerfjord was, but the last part was definitely not good. "You're one of Algonquin's dragon hunters."

"I am her *only* hunter," Vann Jeger corrected. "Or, at least, the only one that matters." He flashed her a cruel smile, turning to hand her file back to his assistant. "We know you are a servant of the dragon who appeared over the Pit last month. You will now tell us where that dragon is hiding."

Marci held her breath, waiting for the inevitable "or die," but the spirit didn't bother with an ultimatum. Apparently, he wasn't even going to give her that choice. Marci supposed she could take it herself, but despite the catastrophic turn her life had just taken, she wasn't actually ready to die tonight. But when she started to say she didn't know what he was talking about, her tongue seized up before she could open her mouth.

She stopped, puzzled. The words were there, clear in her mind, but she couldn't actually make the sounds. It was like there was a clamp holding her tongue in place. Apparently, the truth teller spell worked by physically preventing spoken lies rather than actually keeping her from thinking them. But while the curious Thaumaturge in her found the highly specific nature of the spell's limitation fascinating, the rest of her was already working on a way around it.

There *had* to be one. Truth was subjective, and spells, no matter how sophisticated, were still just sets of instructions. Even a big, expensive construction like this one wasn't actually intelligent, or all-knowing. In order to identify what was lie and what was fact, the magic had to be checking her answers against some kind of reference, most likely her own mind, which meant if *she* knew something was a lie, the spell would, too.

That should have put her in a real bind. Instead, Marci had to bite her lip to keep herself from grinning. *Gotcha.*

"I don't serve any dragon," she said, looking the giant spirit straight in the face. "And I never have."

Vann Jeger's scowl darkened, forcing Marci to bite her lip to keep from laughing aloud. It had worked! So long as she considered something to be true, the spell did, too, and Julius had gone through great pains to make sure Marci knew she wasn't his servant. Second, the dragon Vann Jeger was talking about was *Justin*, not Julius, and Marci hadn't even served him pizza. Given these two facts, what she'd said was technically true, and if the spell was going to let her skate by on technicalities, then she could do this all night. But while Marci was finally feeling like she'd found a glimmer of hope, Vann Jeger looked more dangerous than ever.

"You speak around the rules," he growled, leaning down until he was in her face. "You are clever to have figured out the truth teller's weakness so fast, but I would not continue this game. I am not in a benevolent mood."

"I'm not exactly peachy myself," she said, glaring right back. "Being kidnapped and interrogated kind of puts a crimp in your evening. What made you think I serve a dragon, anyway?"

Again, the technicality skated easily around the truth teller's restrictions, and Marci gave herself a mental high five. But while the question was mostly meant to stall, she was actually curious how they'd found her. She and Julius had been living in the DFZ for a month now without so much as a peep. Something must have tipped them off tonight, and Marci's money was on Bethesda. The haughty dragon clearly cared nothing for subtlety. She'd probably led Algonquin's hunter right to—

Her anger cut off like a switch when Vann Jeger reached back again for his mage to hand him something from her bag. This time, though, it wasn't an antique case file. It was a gun. A large, horrifyingly familiar revolver sealed inside a plastic evidence bag.

"During our investigation of the Pit event, we discovered the body of a human male," the spirit said casually. "He was missing his right hand, but the forensics team reported that the actual cause of death was the gunshot wounds inflicted by this weapon."

He waved the bagged gun in front of her face, and Marci began to tremble.

"After running his dental records, the victim's identity came back as one Eugene Phillip Bixby, also of Las Vegas, Nevada," Vann Jeger went on. "The fingerprints on the gun's grip, however, match the ones on your State of Nevada magic license. Our investigation also discovered that the Clark County Coroner's Office recently mailed you the unclaimed remains of a family member to a forwarding address at the downtown branch of the DFZ Private Post Office. From there, all we had to do was watch and wait."

He paused to let that sink in, but Marci wasn't sure she could sink any lower. Her memories of the Pit were a chaotic mess, but while she clearly recalled shooting Bixby, she couldn't actually remember what she'd done with the gun afterward. Apparently, she'd left it on the ground for anyone to find like an absolute moron, and now Algonquin's private cops had her prints on a murder weapon. Then, as if all that wasn't enough, they'd set a trap using her dad's ashes as bait, and like a blind idiot, she'd walked right in.

Marci slumped forward, squeezing her eyes tight. Forget embarrassing herself in front of Bethesda, *this* was the screw-up that trumped all others. It was also likely her last. Murder charges were serious business anywhere, but the court system in the DFZ didn't work like the one in the US. Here, there was no guarantee of a fair trial or a jury of her peers. All criminal cases were settled privately through binding arbitration, and they didn't send you to jail, either. If you were found guilty, you went to Algonquin, and you never came back.

"I see you've finally comprehended the severity of your situation," Vann Jeger said, handing the bagged gun back to the uniformed mage. "But hope is not yet lost. The Lady of the Lakes cares nothing for the death of a human criminal. All we want is the dragon. If you cooperate, and your actions result in a successful kill, Algonquin is willing to wipe your record clean."

Marci's head shot up before she could stop herself, and the dragon hunter smiled a cold, inhuman smile. "That's right," he said quietly. "You can continue your life, Marcivale Caroline Novalli, and all it will cost you is your cooperation in ending the dragon who keeps you prisoner. A very generous offer, don't you agree?"

If Julius had been a normal dragon, Marci probably would have. But he wasn't, and now she didn't know what to do. The spirit hadn't said what would happen if she *didn't* help, but it wasn't hard to guess. The stakes were pretty clear: get booked for murder, or betray the only person left in the world who actually cared about her. Both were unthinkable, so Marci did the only thing she *could* think of.

She stalled.

"Why do you want him so bad, anyway?" she asked, giving the spirit a look she hoped he'd interpret as earnest. "The dragon didn't do anything except burn a bunch of magic eaters who normally feed on spirits. If you look at it that way, he actually did Algonquin a favor. It's not like he was flying around flaming the skyways, and I don't believe for a second that Algonquin cares about a few scorch marks in a place as wrecked as the Pit. So why go through all this trouble? You're obviously a great and powerful spirit. Surely you've got better things to do with your time than chase down a little dragon who isn't hurting anyone?"

She was legitimately curious, and the questions flowed by the truth teller without so much as a tinge, but Vann Jeger just shook his head. "You are human," he said, clearly disappointed, like Marci's humanity was a personal failing. "Dragons have always been irresistible to your kind. Why else do you think they assume your shape? Their beautiful faces are lies, tools designed to trick and seduce you into doing their bidding, and do you know why?"

"No," Marci said innocently, perfectly happy to play her part to the hilt so long as it bought her more time. "Why?"

"Because they are not predators," he said bitterly. "They are *parasites.*"

Vann Jeger folded his giant hand into a fist and pressed it against his armored chest. "I remember when they came to this world. It was not so long ago by our reckoning, but still before your frail, death-bound species discovered how to record your history for the next generation. To you, dragons have always been here, but we are the souls of the land. We remember a time when there was naught in this world but the Earth and those who came from it. When the dragons arrived as conquerors, we fought them. Thousands of years, we fought, and we were slowly winning, for though the dragons were strong, we could not die. We are the land itself, and so long as the land persists, we shall always rise again. But then, one day, the magic of the land faded without warning, and we faded with it, trapped in a sleep not even the greatest of us could wake from."

His lips peeled back, revealing a mouth full of blunt, yellow teeth. "With no power left to cull them, the parasites spread unchecked," he rumbled. "When we woke at last, there was not a government in the world that wasn't infested. Even here, in Algonquin's own city, the serpents plot and scheme, hiding in the shadows and using humans as their pawns. Just look at yourself. It is clear you are enamored with the dragon and seek even now to save him, despite the fact that you are nothing to him."

"I'm not *enamored*," Marci scoffed, though the only way the words made it past the truth spell was when she kept Justin's face firmly in her mind. "And I *don't* serve a dragon. You keep implying that I'm lying, but you guys were the ones who put me in this stupid truth box to begin with, so listen to the words that are coming out of my mouth. Yes, I was in the Pit that night for personal reasons, and yes, I saw a dragon, but I don't know where he is or how to find him, and that's the plain truth. Just admit you've got the wrong mage and we can forget this ever happened."

For a moment, that *almost* seemed to work. Vann Jeger's scowl *almost* looked skeptical, and then he doubled down again, crossing his arms over his chest. "Then I suppose all we caught was a murderer," he said casually, holding out his hand in front of him. "I've never been one for trials. I prefer to handle justice in the old way, and since I've already seen the evidence, we can get this over with right now."

Magic condensed in his hand as he spoke, flowing into his fingers like water in a current. It lasted only a moment, and when it finished, a sword winked into existence above Vann Jeger's empty hand. It was much shorter than his spear, though still longer than Marci's arm. She was wondering how he'd pulled it out of seemingly thin air when Vann Jeger flipped the blade and leaned down to press the sharpened edge against her neck.

"Do you feel that?" he asked softly, his deep voice sinking to a rumbling whisper as he pushed the cold metal against her throat. "That is death. *Your* death. One more inch, and all that is you—all you have ever known or accomplished, all that you've loved and fought for—will be nothing but red on the floor. There will be no songs sung for you, no rites read. You will be forgotten utterly. Lost to the flow of time, as all mortal souls eventually are, unless…"

Marci knew the answer already, but she asked anyway, if only to keep the sword against her throat instead of in it. "Unless?"

Vann Jeger smirked. "You know your choice. If you wish to continue what is left of your short life, you will tell me where the dragon is. If you want to keep taking me for a fool, I will kill you and find him anyway. It's all the same to me."

With each word he spoke, the blade at her throat crept closer, and Marci shut her eyes. She had to do something. This was all her fault. Her careless revenge against Bixby had come back around full steam, and now her choices were get run over or throw Julius onto the tracks instead. Both were intolerable, but she couldn't stall forever. What she needed was a clever trick, some way to look like she was betraying Julius without actually doing so. Unfortunately, strokes of genius like that weren't exactly dial-on-demand, but while Marci didn't have a brilliant plan on tap, she *did* have a crazy one, and with a sword at her neck, that was good enough.

"Okay," she blurted out, opening her eyes. "I give up. I'll give you what you want, just get that thing away from me."

Vann Jeger looked deeply skeptical, but he backed the sword up until it was no longer touching her skin. "You will tell me where to find the dragon?"

"I wasn't lying before," she reminded him. "I really don't know where he is." At least, not right now, anyway.

The spirit scowled. "But you know how to contact him?"

"I do," she said reluctantly. "But it won't work. Dragons like the one who burned up the Pit aren't exactly the come-when-you-call type."

Again, she held Justin's face in her mind as she spoke. Thankfully, Vann Jeger seemed too happy to be finally getting some progress to notice her side-stepping.

"Dragons who keep mortals often prize them," he said, eying her thoughtfully. "Doubly so for mages. What if we cut something off and let him hear your screams? Would that bring him running?"

Marci winced, curling her fingers protectively into fists. Screams of pain would get Julius for sure, but technically they were still talking about Justin here, and thinking back to some of the horrible things he'd said the last time they were together, it wasn't too hard for Marci to think the worst of Mr. Angry Dragon.

"No," she said. "If I called him in pain, he wouldn't come. To him, I'm just a human, which ranks slightly below a dog. Plus, even if I could somehow convince him to walk into a trap, this dragon has the most amazing sense of smell you've ever encountered. He'll pick up anything you lay down from a mile away and abandon me without a second look back, so if you were hoping to use me as bait, you're in for a major let-down."

Vann Jeger bared his yellow teeth in a snarl. "Do not presume to tell me how to conduct my hunt."

"I'm sure you know all about how to hunt dragons," Marci said quickly. "But I know best how to handle *my* dragon. I'm not saying I won't help you nab him, I'm just saying we're going to have to be really extra careful about it."

The hunter sneered. "And why is that?"

"Because he's *big*, for one," Marci said, remembering Justin's forty-foot body lit up with green fire in the blackness above the Pit. "This isn't some urbane, boardroom dragon we're talking about. He's huge, powerful, bad-tempered, and fast with his fire. You have no idea the collateral damage he could cause if you piss him off in the wrong setting. He wouldn't think twice about bringing down a skyway or two if he thought it would help him win."

All of these things were absolutely true about Justin, and they flowed easily past the truth teller, causing Vann Jeger to look at her with a new eye. "Very well," he said grudgingly. "How would you suggest we trap the beast?"

Marci swallowed, heart hammering. Here went nothing.

"Let me go," she said. "Give me a few weeks to wiggle back into the dragon's good graces, and I'll come up with a tale that will convince him to come with me to the location of your choice. All you have to do is give me a place and a time and I'll get him there, and then you can hunt him to your heart's content."

"Absurd," Vann Jeger growled. "You want weeks to lure a dragon I'm already closing in on?"

"But you're *not*," Marci said. "That's what I'm trying to tell you. You might have caught me, but my dragon's dug in deep. I don't even know if he's in the DFZ anymore. But if you'll just give me some time, I guarantee I can get you his head on a platter."

"What assurance do I have that you will not warn the dragon and flee?" the spirit asked, his black eyes narrowing. "You are beholden to a dragon and bargaining for your life. Your word is worthless."

"Not dying seems like a pretty strong incentive to me," she said. "Though if you wanted something more concrete, I could—"

Her voice turned into a gasp as the spirit pressed his sword back into her neck. "What if I kill you now?" he asked, calm as ever. "He might not respond to your pain, but all dragons are possessive. If he's as reckless as you claim, it shouldn't be too hard to draw him into a confrontation by killing his property."

"Maybe," Marci croaked. "But there's only one of me. Like you said before, if you kill me now, it's over. Do you really want to cut off your options so early in the game?"

Vann Jeger shrugged. "It's a calculated risk. You might be in earnest now, but human minds change with the wind. If I let you go, I might not get a chance like this again."

Marci looked him straight in the eyes. "What if I made sure you did?"

The spirit arched a green eyebrow. "Explain."

"Your mage," she said, glancing pointedly at the human woman who'd activated the truth teller spell. "She's police trained, right? That means she knows binding curses."

The mage cast a worried glance at Vann Jeger. When he nodded, she said, "Yes."

"Well, there you go," Marci said, smiling wide. "If you're so worried I'm going to double-cross you and run away with the dragon before you can catch him, then I invite you to curse me. A good binding curse will lock me inside the DFZ for a year at least. That way, if I don't deliver, all you have to do is hunt me down again and we'll be right back where we started."

She had lots more things to add about how this was a no-lose scenario and he'd be a fool not to take it, but Marci forced herself to stop there. If she looked too eager to get cursed, she'd tip her hand, and that would ruin everything. Vann Jeger might have a formal file on her, but what he probably didn't know was that before she'd come to the DFZ, Marci and her father had been professional curse *breakers*. Even a police-grade binding curse was little more than the magical equivalent of a car boot for her. She'd have that sucker cracked in thirty minutes, tops, and then all she had to do was find Julius and get the two of them out of town.

Just the thought of her upcoming clean escape was enough to make Marci grin, but she didn't dare crack even a hint of a smile. If Vann Jeger suspected anything, this whole plan could blow up in her face. Instead, she focused on looking nervous, not exactly a challenge in the current situation, and waited, staring at the dragon hunter until, at last, he nodded.

"You suggest an acceptable scenario, mortal," he said, stroking his seaweed-green beard. "I have not fought a true dragon on open ground since before the magic vanished. To do so again would be… pleasing." He breathed deep, savoring the idea. "Most pleasing."

"Then it's settled," Marci said, trying not to sound as relieved as she felt. "Just give me a week, and—"

"You will have one day."

Marci gaped at him. "*One?* How in the world—"

"Tomorrow night," he continued, talking right over her. "At sunset, in the open fields that mark the edge of the Lady's lands. I can think of no better place for challenge."

Marci could think of plenty, but one day was better than nothing. If she told Julius tonight, they could be on a plane anywhere in the world by tomorrow morning, and then all of this would be just a bad memory. "Sounds like a plan," she said, looking at the mage and spreading her arms as much as the restraints allowed. "Bind away."

The woman looked at her like she was crazy, but Vann Jeger nodded sharply. "Do it," he ordered. "A Sword of Damocles on her neck, marked for sunset tomorrow."

The mage nodded and started forward. Marci, however, lurched like she'd just gotten kicked in the teeth.

"A *what?*" she cried, yanking against the straps. "No, no, *no!* We had a deal! You were going to *bind* me, not *kill* me!"

The dragon hunter laughed, a horrible, deep-water sound. "Foolish mortal. Did you really think I'd agree to a curse you could break?"

Marci stared at him in horror, but the more she thought about it, the more she realized Vann Jeger had played her even as she tried to play him. Technically, the Sword of Damocles *was* a binding curse: a spell that would bind her to a place and a promise. In this case, the DFZ and her pledge to bring the dragon to a place of the spirit's choosing at sunset tomorrow. Unlike every other binding curse, though, the Sword of Damocles required the cursed party's full participation. It was designed to be the ultimate vow: an oath made in good faith, written in magic on the victim's skin. If you were true to your word, nothing would happen, but if you broke your promise, the sword would fall wherever the spell was written. By writing the curse on her neck, Vann Jeger was ensuring that Marci would lose her head if she didn't deliver.

That left her even worse off than she'd been when this started, but what could she do? Accuse the spirit of taking away her chance to cheat? She'd already told him she'd get the dragon. Backing out now would be the same as admitting she'd always intended to betray him, which he was almost certainly counting on given the blood-thirsty gleam in his eyes.

Well, she wasn't going to give him the satisfaction. Marci fixed him with a surly look and tilted her head, baring her neck. "Do it, then," she said through clenched teeth. "I'm ready."

The fact that the words made it out of her mouth meant that they were true, which was kind of a shock. Marci hadn't realized she was so ready to die. But then again, maybe she wasn't. Just because she'd never heard of anyone breaking a Sword of Damocles didn't mean it was *actually* impossible, but the fact that Vann Jeger thought it was meant he'd probably leave her alone once it was done. That was a better chance than she'd had at the beginning, and if the sword *did* cut off her head tomorrow, she wouldn't be any more dead than she'd be if she tried to back out now. Either way, Marci was ready, and she clung to that truth like a rock as the mage ordered her to lower her shields.

Marci obeyed with a shudder, dropping her passive protections one by one until her magic was wide open and raw. When she was bare, the mage reached into her bag and pulled out a heavy silver needle, the same kind blood mages used for human rituals. The fact that an Algonquin Corporate mage would have such a sinister tool just lying around in her bag was slightly horrifying, but Marci didn't have time to think about it. She was too busy trying not to panic as the woman retrieved a glass vial and turned to Vann Jeger.

For a moment, Marci couldn't think why, and then the spirit made a fist, digging his claws into the flesh of his palm. It happened so quickly, the mage almost didn't get the vial in place fast enough to catch the black, watery blood before it dripped onto the ground. Even sitting several feet away, Marci could feel the cold, deep power of that blood, and while she knew perfectly well that the source of a magical material had no impact on the end spell, she still cringed when the mage dipped the tip of the silver needle into the black liquid.

"This might sting a bit," the woman warned, tapping the excess blood off on the edge of the glass before she leaned over Marci's neck and jabbed the needle home.

It hurt like nothing else ever had. With her defenses down, the mage wasn't just poking her skin. She was poking *inside* Marci's magic. Each stab was so cold it burned, and even when the silver needle pulled out, the spirit's blood remained, a drop of stinging salt water in each wound. It went on forever, but every time Marci wanted to break down and beg for them to stop, she remembered what was at stake. If she bailed on this, she'd either be killed or hauled off for murder. If she vanished, Julius would come looking for her, making himself a sitting duck. Marci couldn't let that happen. Not to Julius, not to her, and certainly not over a stupid needle. So she closed her eyes and pushed through, breathing in long, ragged gasps until, at last, the stabbing stopped.

"Done," the mage said, wiping the beaded sweat from her forehead. "It's done."

Marci collapsed into the chair, wishing with all her might that they'd undo her hands so she could clutch her neck and cry. "Let me see."

The mage took her phone out of her pocket and held up its shiny surface for Marci to use as a mirror.

Well, she thought bitterly, at least it didn't look at bad as it felt. On the left side of her neck, halfway between her jaw and her collar bone, a two-inch-long, solid black sword stood out like a brand against her bloody skin. Along the top of the sword's edge were two strings of numbers, geographic coordinates for the location of the fight, and a time stamp for the precise moment of sunset tomorrow. That took care of the where and when, but what really made her wince was the line below the sword, where the corporate mage had transcribed Marci's own words in neat, professional cursive.

Hunt him to your heart's content.

She was still reading when the mage reached in to pat the area clean with a square of sterile gauze. But even when her blood was gone, the curse remained, the black mark painting a clear line where the magical sword would fall if she went back on her word. Just thinking about it made Marci grimace, and the mage didn't look happy either as she bound the wound with a clean bandage. The only one who did look pleased by all of this was Vann Jeger, who was grinning like he'd just won the lottery.

"You have given me a great gift, mortal," he rumbled, laying a cold, heavy hand on Marci's shoulder. "A true battle, after so many years." He beamed at her. "It will be a thing of beauty. You will see, for you will be there, or you will be dead."

"Thanks for the reminder," Marci muttered, swallowing against her bitter anger. She had to get out of here. When the spirit looked at her like that, she swore she could feel his cold blood stirring under the cursed mark. "Not that I haven't had a great time and all, but if you actually want your fight, you have to let me go. A day's not much time to bring a dragon around, and I need to get to work."

"Done," the hunter said, motioning again to his mage, who was still cleaning up. She nodded and dropped what she was doing, reaching into her pocket to pull out a black bag.

"Oh no," Marci groaned. "Not that thing again."

"It's the only way for those not sworn to our cause to leave this place alive," Vann Jeger said with a shrug. "Would you like to reconsider my offer to kill you?"

Marci sighed and lowered her head.

"I see your anger, little mortal," Vann Jeger said as the mage began to ease the black cloth gently over her scalp. "You think me a villain, but you are deceived. It is the dragon who is to blame. His kind has beguiled yours from the moment they appeared, living off the fruits of your labor while giving nothing in return but sorrow and death. You think that you are different, that your dragon will not betray you, but so has every mortal they've ensnared. When I kill your master, you will see at last that I was right, and if you wish then to join our cause, I will take you to Algonquin myself. You are clever and brave for a mortal, and skilled in magic. The Lady always has need for ones such as you."

He paused, clearly expecting gratitude for that condescending job offer. When Marci didn't reply, he said, "Bag her."

The mage yanked the cloth down, cutting off the world behind a wall of black. When it came back again seconds later, Marci opened her eyes with a gasp to find herself sitting in her car in the Post Office parking deck.

She burst into motion, running her hands over her body, but other than the bandage at her neck, everything was as it should be. Her bag with her dad's ashes, her bracelets, even her chalk and emergency markers were all back in their normal places. Her phone was there, too, sitting on the passenger seat right where she'd dropped it before she'd gone in. She grabbed the device with trembling fingers, dismissing the Do Not Disturb block to see a wall of missed calls and messages from Julius.

Under any other circumstances, that obvious show of concern would have made Marci giddy. Now, staring at a phone Algonquin's goons had had access to for who knew how long in a car that was almost certainly bugged, all she felt was a cold stab of fear.

Striving to look as normal as possible, Marci opened her door a fraction and leaned down, shoving her phone directly beneath her front tire. When it was wedged into place, she yanked herself back inside and closed her eyes, focusing hard on her connection with Ghost.

It was a lot more difficult than she'd expected. She'd called for Ghost several times before, but she'd never actually tried to talk to him across distance. She wasn't at all sure it was working this time, but finally, after several mental pokes, she felt him stir.

Find Julius, she thought, forming each word like an object in her mind before sending it down their connection. *Tell him I'll meet him at the house. Also, tell him to clean out my closet.*

If Ghost found any of that odd, he didn't say anything. Marci wasn't even sure he'd gotten the message, but she had no time to try again. She'd already been here too long, and the van in the row behind her had been idling with its engine running since she'd woken up.

Marci eyed it suspiciously in her mirror. It could be just her paranoia, or it could be a tail. Either way, they were going for a ride.

With a last, bitter smile at her reflection, Marci set her autonav in the opposite direction of home and backed out, crushing her compromised phone under her tire in the process. Sure enough, the idling van rolled out as soon as she hit the exit ramp, following her through the pay gate and out into the street. After that, Marci didn't even bother watching. She just grabbed her casting markers out of her bag and got to work, crouching down in her seat as she began drawing a magical circle onto the car's dash.

CHAPTER SIX

Marci was not at the house when they returned.

Julius kept it together, calmly sending his brother upstairs to take a shower and change before going for his phone. But while Marci's phone seemed to be off lockdown, she *still* wasn't answering. Even more alarming, the cellular triangulation app—which Marci herself had installed on both their phones for just such an emergency—didn't seem to be working, either. Now that she was no longer blocking him, Julius should have been able to use the cell towers to pin her location down to within a thousand meters, but every time he tried, all he got was an error. If it wasn't for the fact that Ghost was still on the couch, he'd have thought Marci was dead in a ditch for sure.

Then again, maybe Ghost's presence here didn't mean anything at all? Julius still knew almost nothing about the actual mechanics of how human mages bound spirits. They'd all gone to sleep when the magic had vanished a thousand years ago. What if they went back to sleep when their master died, too?

That thought made his blood run cold. By the time Justin—washed and dressed in Julius's loosest pair of sweat pants—stomped back down the stairs, Julius was deep in the spirit forums, looking up everything he could find on what happened to bound spirits when their human died.

"Would you stop acting like a nervous hen?" Justin said, plopping down on the couch beside Ghost, who *still* hadn't moved.

124

"What should I act like?" Julius snapped. "It's almost three in the morning, and Marci's still missing."

"Three a.m.'s nothing on a Friday night in the DFZ," his brother replied with a shrug. "She probably went to a club or something. Unlike you, *some* people enjoy doing things besides staying at home and staring at their phones like old ladies."

Julius grit his teeth. It was a dark day indeed when Justin was the reasonable one.

"Besides," his brother continued. "If you're *so* worried, why are you still here? She's your human. You want her home, go out there and drag her back."

"She's not a lost dog," Julius snapped. "And it's not that simple."

"Why not?" Justin demanded.

"Because she might not want to come home!"

Julius hadn't meant to say that. Like most fundamentally true things, though, it had slipped out on its own, making Justin roll his eyes in disgust. "Is that what this is about?"

"No," Julius said, and then he sighed. "Maybe. I don't know." He walked over and sank down opposite his brother on the couch's one remaining free cushion. "I was pretty mean to her tonight, and now that she's missing, I can't help wondering if maybe it's on purpose?"

"That's stupid," Justin scoffed. "We're dragons. Whether they love or fear us, humans can't stay away. Even you can't mess that up. She's probably just off sulking somewhere. Though I suppose she could be dead. Mortals kick over at the drop of a hat, after all."

Julius buried his head in his hands. "Not helping, Justin."

"Can I help it if you make everything complicated?" his brother snapped. "You're the one who always insists on treating your humans like they're equals. If you want her to act like a pet, then slap a collar on her neck and be done with it, but you can't give her freedom and then freak out when she uses it."

Julius sighed. It *did* sound pretty ridiculous when he put it like that, but though he'd arrived at it from the completely wrong angle, Justin was right. He was being an idiot. If Marci was out this late without calling, then she was probably in real trouble that had nothing to do with Julius's insecurities. He'd apologize to her later. Right now, though, he was going to find her. He was turning to ask his brother for help when something icy pressed into his leg.

Julius looked down with a start. Ghost, who'd been dead asleep between them on the couch the last time he'd looked, was now sitting straight up with his paw on Julius's thigh and his ears pressed flat back against his head.

"What's it doing?" Justin asked.

"I don't know," Julius said, leaning down to look at the spirit on his level. "What is it, Ghost?"

The cat's eyes narrowed at the Lassie-esque question, and Julius bit his tongue. He was about to try again with something less insulting when the spirit's voice whispered in his head.

She's coming home.

The rush of relief that followed those words was so intense, it was almost painful. "Really?" he cried, jumping off the couch.

The spirit blinked at him, which he assumed meant yes. *You are to clean out her closet.*

Julius's soaring hopes skidded to a confused halt. "Her closet? Why?"

The spirit looked away, clearly insulted, and Julius scrambled to backtrack. "I'm sorry. I'll do whatever she needs me to. Is there anything else?"

He certainly hoped there wasn't, because Ghost was already losing interest, fading into the air like sunlight behind a cloud. A few seconds later, he was gone completely, leaving Julius staring at the now empty cushion beside his brother, who looked appalled.

"Did you just apologize to a *cat?*" he cried. "Because that's a new low, Julius. Even for you."

Julius was too excited to be insulted. "Marci's coming home!"

"I told you it'd work itself out," Justin said, getting off the couch to follow Julius as he sprinted up the stairs to the second floor. "So where was she?"

"I don't know yet," Julius said as he threw open the door to Marci's room. "But I have to clear out her closet."

Justin stopped. "Seriously?"

"I wouldn't make something like that up," he said, smiling. "But if Ghost told me to do it, I'm guessing it's important." And right now, he'd gladly tear down the whole house and rebuild it from scratch if it would bring Marci home even a minute sooner. "Come give me a hand."

Justin rolled his eyes so high it must have hurt, but eventually he came over, grudgingly helping Julius move the massive collection of clothes, notebooks, and various magical materials out of Marci's closet to reveal the spellwork hidden underneath.

• • •

Thirty minutes later, Julius was starting to worry Ghost had played him for a fool.

He and Justin had cleaned Marci's entire closet, uncovering the intricate circles of spellwork that, in hindsight, Julius should have been expecting from the beginning. But while the magical markings explained the mysterious cleaning spree, it didn't explain why Marci *still* wasn't back, or why she had yet to answer her phone. Julius had actually given up calling by this point, settling for sitting on the porch like—as Justin repeatedly informed him—a dog waiting for its master. Fortunately, Julius had also given up being insulted. He just wanted Marci to come home so he could stop feeling this way.

"She's not coming," Justin said as they crossed the half-hour mark. "Face it. You got stood up via cat."

Julius was opening his mouth to tell him to shut up when he saw a flash of light in the dark. "Really?" he said instead, breaking into a grin. "Then what's that?"

Justin's head snapped around just in time as the car pulled around the corner into their hidden drive. "You got her a pickup?"

"What are you talking about?" Julius said, jumping to his feet to go meet her.

Rather than answer, his brother just pointed at the approaching headlights, and Julius's hopes began to crumple, because he was right. The car coming down the gravel road was not Marci's sedan, but a beat up, rust-colored pickup truck that looked like it had been driven straight off a construction site. Likewise, the human sitting in the driver's seat was most definitely *not* Marci. It was an old man wearing a backwards cap, his bearded face blank and bored as he steered his truck toward the house.

"Ooooh," Justin said, smirking. "I get it now."

"Get what?" Julius said, his shoulders slumping even further when he spotted the lettering on the truck's door. "That's just one of the skyway maintenance contractors. They come in every—"

"Have you completely forgotten how to be a dragon?" Justin growled, cuffing him across the back of the head. "Use your nose, moron."

Julius didn't understand, but he did as he was told, sucking in the air through his nose until his breath hitched. Marci's scent was there! It was faint and buried by smells of cement and oil and dirt, but now that he'd caught it, Julius realized hers was the only fresh human scent in the area. It was coming closer, too, moving with the truck as the vehicle creaked to a stop in front of the house.

It was moments like these when a lifetime spent looking over his shoulder really came in handy. Even though Julius wanted nothing more than to run down and grab her, hugging someone while they were in disguise totally defeated the purpose, and even in his excitement, Julius knew better. He did jump down to get her door, though, holding it open as the old man who smelled like Marci climbed down, did a double-take at Justin, and then hurried up the steps into the house.

Once they were all inside, Julius locked the door and put his back against it, heart pounding as he stared at Marci's transformed face. "What is going on?"

"I'll tell you in a moment," she said in a stranger's deep, masculine voice, which was pretty unnerving. He'd never seen her use an illusion this thick. If it wasn't for his nose, he would never have known the man going around his living room and closing all the blinds was Marci at all.

"Did you get my message?" she asked.

"I did," Julius said. "Your closet is clear, but I don't understand—"

She grabbed his hand before he could finish and yanked him toward the stairs. When Justin started to follow, though, she ordered, "No."

"Excuse me?" the dragon growled.

Marci didn't respond, just looked at Julius, who sighed. "Give us five minutes."

You'd have thought he was asking Justin to betray the clan. But while he looked seriously pissed, he stopped trying to follow them up the stairs, leaving Julius and Marci alone as she led the way down the hall to her bedroom and straight into her newly emptied closet. The moment they were both inside, she kicked the door shut, plunging them into darkness for a split second before the spellwork lit up.

Circles of spellwork flared all around them, filling the closet like a camera flash before fading to a warm yellow glow only slightly brighter than a candle. But while the flash and fade was in line with most of Marci's spells, what got Julius's attention was that the sounds had faded, too. The moment the spellwork had lit up, all exterior noises—the creak of the house, the dull roar of the cars overhead, Justin's impatient pacing on the floor below—had vanished, leaving the closet in deep, unnatural silence. He still could hear his own breaths, and Marci's, but nothing else. "What is this?"

"My isolation booth," she said, standing up. "I was testing a theory for a ward against sound. Think of it like you're standing inside a pair of noise-canceling headphones."

"I'd say it works pretty well," Julius said, rubbing his ears in an attempt to get used to the deafening quiet. "But Marci, what is going on? Why didn't you answer my calls? And why did you come here disguised like a…"

His voice trailed off as Marci's illusion evaporated, revealing her real face, which looked like she was about to cry. "Oh, Julius," she said, her voice breaking. "I messed up. I messed up so bad."

"Messed up what?" he said frantically. "And what happened to your neck?"

Marci's neck was swathed in bandages. He didn't think she was actively bleeding, but she had been not too long ago. "I knew something was wrong," he said, curling his shaking hands into fists. "Marci, what is going on?"

She dropped her eyes to the floor. "After you left, I went downtown to pick up my dad's ashes. I know we're supposed to be hiding, but I thought I was clear since I didn't use our address. When I came out, though, Vann Jeger was waiting for me."

Julius froze. "Vann Jeger?" he whispered at last. "*The* Vann Jeger? As in Algonquin's hunter?"

She nodded, and Julius's stomach clenched. He might not be a proper dragon, but even he knew of Vann Jeger. He was a monster from ancient dragon history—the spirit who hunted the hunters— and the rumors about him had only gotten worse since he'd joined Algonquin shortly after she'd claimed Detroit. But though Vann Jeger was famous for killing dragons, he generally stayed away from humans. Or, at least, that was what Julius had heard. "Did he hurt you?"

"No," Marci said, and Julius sighed in relief. "But…"

"But?"

"I told him," she said, her eyes locked on the ground. "About you."

Julius tensed, and Marci's head shot up. "Not voluntarily, I swear! And I didn't tell him much. Not your name or your clan or anything big like that. I wouldn't have said a word, but he had my prints on the gun I used to shoot Bixby. He was going to book me for murder unless I told him about the dragon. I tried to lie, but they had me in a truth teller. I got around it a little, but…" She looked down again, covering her face with her hands. "I betrayed you."

"Marci, no," Julius said, moving closer. The closet was so small, there wasn't far to go, but any space at all felt like too much right now. "It's my fault there was a hunter in the first place. You did absolutely nothing wrong. I'm amazed you got away."

"But I didn't," she said, reaching up to tug down the bandage on her neck. She did this like she was revealing some kind of horrible truth, but Julius had no idea what he was looking at.

"They drew a sword on your neck?"

"It's a curse," she said bitterly. "A big one, called the Sword of Damocles."

Julius winced. He didn't know most curses from croutons, but the Sword of Damocles was famous. You saw it in movies all the time, especially crime dramas. It was supposed to be a mutually unbreakable pact, which, now that he thought about it, didn't make sense in the current situation. "How did they put it on you?" he asked, confused. "I thought the whole deal with the Sword of Damocles was that both parties had to be willing for it to work?"

It was an honest question, but Marci looked like he'd just kicked her. "Vann Jeger was going to turn me over to Algonquin if I didn't tell him where you were," she said, shaking. "I tried getting around the question, but he had a sword to my throat, so I stalled by telling them I needed time to lure you into a trap. I told them to put a binding curse on me to keep me in the city, so they'd know it wasn't a trick. My plan was to break the curse, grab you, and run before they knew what was up, but I miscalculated." She put her fingers on the black tattoo. "This was the only curse he'd accept. If I turned it down, I'd basically be admitting I was planning to betray him. I *had* to let him do it, and now, if I don't keep my promise to bring you to him at sundown, it's going to cut off my head."

Her voice was cracking by the end, and Julius couldn't stand it. "It's okay," he said, reaching out to gently grab her shoulders. "You bought us time. That's great! It means we can still figure this out."

"No, we can't," she said, pushing his hands away. "I was *stupid*. I should have known they wouldn't give me something I could break. I should have left my dad in Nevada. I should have remembered the stupid gun! You'd think I'd be better at destroying evidence after all the cop shows I've watched, but *no*. Apparently I'm one of those incompetent murderers who gets caught the first time!" She slid down the closet wall with a hopeless, angry sound. "Your mother was right," she muttered as she reached the floor. "I really am a bumbling, foolish human, aren't I?"

"Absolutely not," Julius said, squatting down as well so he could look her in the face. "Listen to me, Marci. You are the cleverest person I know. What my mother said was wrong then and it's wrong now. You're not my human or my pet or anything like that. You're my best friend and ally who tried everything she could think of to save me from a dragon hunter. That's *huge*. Thanks to your quick thinking, we have time to plan. Now we just have to use it to figure out a way to break your curse."

He actually thought she'd been brilliant, not to mention brave. Any of his family would have sold him out to Vann Jeger in a heartbeat, but Marci had protected him, even tried to con an ancient spirit while he'd had a sword at her *neck*. Julius didn't have words for what that kind of loyalty meant to him, and he wasn't about to waste a second of the time she'd bought second-guessing how she might have done it better. But while he was ready to get to work, Marci looked like she'd already given up.

"The curse can't be broken," she said bitterly. "Or, at least, I've never heard of anyone breaking a Sword of Damocles, and I don't want to gamble your life on my being the first." She shook her head with a bitter sigh. "You need to leave."

Julius shook his head. "I'm not leaving you."

"This isn't open to discussion," she said firmly. "I screwed up, okay? I know that, but there's no reason both of us should have to pay for my mistakes."

"*Your* mistakes?" he cried. "Marci, you were captured by a *dragon hunter*. Last I checked, you aren't a dragon. How can this possibly be your fault?"

"Doesn't matter," she said, banishing his words with an angry stab of her hand. "And we're wasting time arguing. I already wasted too much ditching my car."

"Your car?" he said, confused. "So that truck outside isn't an illusion?"

"My sedan was too compromised," she explained quickly. "Same for my phone and bag and everything else. If I didn't want to lead Vann Jeger right back here, my only option was to dump everything. I couldn't replace my phone, obviously, but I stole a new ride—"

He gasped. "You *stole* a car?"

"*That's* what you're upset about?" she cried. "Like Grand Theft Auto matters next to the freaking *murder charge!*"

"Sorry," he said with a wince. "You're right. I was just surprised."

"Well, fat lot of good it did in the end," she grumbled. "I might have stopped Vann Jeger from following me home, but you and your brother still need to leave. Right now."

"No." Julius said.

Marci scowled. "But—"

"*No,*" he said again. "No buts. I don't care what's happening, I am *never* going to run away and leave you to die. *Ever.* Under any circumstances."

He kept his voice calm and firm, trying his best to prove to her that he was deadly seriously about this. Rather than looking reassured, though, Marci looked more upset than ever. "Can't you stop it for one second?"

Julius frowned. "Stop what?"

She looked down at the ground. "Being so nice."

He had no idea what she was talking about, but Marci wouldn't even look at him.

"Do you know how hard it was for me to accept this?" she said quietly. "It's not like I want to die, but unless I can figure out how to break an unbreakable curse in the next few hours, it's a done deal. Those aren't odds I'd bet my own life on, and I'm definitely not betting yours. You're the only reason I have a life to lose to begin with. If you hadn't saved me last month, I'd be a trophy on Bixby's wall."

"That's not true," he said quickly. "I—"

"It *is* true," she said stubbornly. "I'd made peace with the fact that it was time for me to return the favor, but now you're here being understanding and saying we can make it and getting my hopes up and…" She cut off with a ragged breath. "It's not fair, Julius! I'm trying do the right thing here and take responsibility for my mistakes, and you're making it *harder*."

"Good!" he cried angrily. "It should be impossible."

She glowered and opened her mouth to argue, but Julius didn't give her a chance. "I don't want you to be responsible and do the right thing. I want you to *stay alive*. I don't even care why any of this happened. All that matters to me is how we're going to get out of it, the *both* of us. Because I'm never going to leave you to deal with something like this on your own. Not to save my life. Not for any reason. Okay?"

He set his jaw as he finished, ready to take on her next argument the moment it came, but Marci just sighed. "Okay."

Julius blinked in surprise. "Really?"

She nodded, cheeks flushing. "I know I should put up more of a fight after all that, but…I *really* don't want to die."

"That makes two of us," he said, smiling as he helped her up. "Honestly, though, I'm still getting over the relief of having you home in one piece."

Her eyes went wide. "You were worried about me?"

"Of *course* I worried about you," he said, confused how this could even be a question. "I…"

She nodded, waiting, but Julius couldn't continue. He didn't even know if there was language to describe how painfully happy he was that Marci was back safely, or how much what she'd done tonight meant to him. After a lifetime of being a failure, the shame of the Heartstrikers, the most worthless piece on the board, the idea that she, a human, had stood against something like Vann Jeger to protect him—*him*, the very worst dragon—was more than Julius could articulate. Just thinking about it did things to his insides, shifting priorities and assumptions around like landmasses in an earthquake, and when it was over, the world looked very different.

The closet, for example. When she'd first pulled him in, he'd been too worried to think about anything but what was going on. Now, the thing that struck him most was how small the space was. Even standing on opposite sides, he and Marci were almost chest to chest. He could actually feel the heat of her body radiating across the inches that separated them, tempting him to lean even closer.

This afternoon, that exact temptation had been enough to send him into his usual lecture about how this was all a Very Bad Idea. Now, though, Julius was having a hard time seeing the point. It wasn't that he didn't care about their friendship anymore—he cared more than ever—but the future was no longer something he could take for granted. There were no guaranteed years of partnership waiting to be irrevocably ruined by a single impulsive moment. There was only now, and now was very short. Short and precious, the sort of thing that shouldn't be squandered.

With that, his heart started hammering harder than ever. This time, though, Julius didn't try to calm it. Slowly, carefully, giving her plenty of time to back out, he reached down to rest his hands on Marci's shoulders.

Her breaths stopped when he touched her, but she didn't push away like she'd done before. She moved closer, stepping in until their bodies were touching and Julius could feel her heart racing as fast as his own as he leaned down. Marci rose up on her toes at the same time, lifting up to meet him halfway. She didn't have far to go, Julius wasn't that tall, but it still seemed to take forever. And then, just when he could feel her soft breath against his lips and the kiss he'd wanted for so long finally seemed on the verge of being inevitable, the closet door behind him flew open.

For a baffled moment, Julius just stood there, frozen by the sudden blaze of light and roar of returning sound, and then a hard hand grabbed his shoulder and yanked him backwards. The next second was spent flailing in free fall before his training finally kicked in, spinning him around into a crouch right in front of his scowling brother.

"*This* is what you made me wait for?"

"*Justin!*" Julius shouted, his face burning. "What are you doing?"

"You said five minutes," Justin growled. "I normally give people in closets seven, but I'm not in a giving mood tonight. Now." He turned and fixed Marci with a killing stare. "Start explaining."

"I don't have to explain anything to you!" she shouted, her cheeks flushed with embarrassed fury. "Why are you even here?"

"I invited him to stay with us," Julius explained quickly.

"Not that a dragon needs a mortal's permission to do anything," Justin added, giving Marci a superior look

She flashed him a killing glare of her own, and Julius sighed. Marci barely tolerated his brother under the best of circumstances, which definitely did not include right now. It didn't help that Justin seemed to be going out of his way to be even more of an arrogant jerk than usual. Clearly, if Julius wanted any peace tonight, he was going to have to make it himself.

"Justin, back down," he said calmly. "We have an emergency."

The dragon rolled his eyes. "Is that what the kids are calling it these days?"

"Would you lay off?" Marci yelled. "Do you even know what kind of day I've had?"

"*No!*" Justin shouted back. "That's what I'm trying to find out!"

"*Guys,*" Julius said, stepping into the middle before either of them did something he'd regret. When no one tried to punch or shoot a fireball past him, he turned to Justin. "Marci was late because she was captured by Vann Jeger."

He paused there, because that was what you did after a bomb drop, but his brother didn't look scared at all. Quite the opposite. He looked delighted, his eyes flashing with excitement as he motioned for Julius to continue.

With a sinking feeling, Julius obliged, quickly repeating the parts of the story he knew and encouraging Marci to fill in what he didn't. Since she clearly didn't want to share any of this with Justin, it was a struggle, but Marci had always been a stickler for accuracy. In the end, she told him the whole thing plus some extra bits that hadn't made it into the version she'd given Julius, like how Vann Jeger was specifically hunting the dragon from the Pit.

Hearing that made Julius more nervous than ever. Justin, however, looked like a kid who'd just woken up to an unexpected Christmas morning. "So let me get this straight. You," he pointed at Marci, "are going to be short one head unless you bring Vann Jeger a dragon by sundown tomorrow, which, since we're now well into the AMs, actually means tonight, right?"

"Yes," Marci said after taking a moment to work her way through that convoluted sentence. She tapped the bandage over her mark. "The mage wrote the exact time as seven-thirty-eight p.m. on Saturday, September the sixteenth."

Julius paled as he checked his phone. "That's only seventeen hours away."

"So it is," Justin agreed. "Where's the problem, again?"

Julius stared at him. "Is that a joke?"

"You're a joke if you think so," Justin said, grinning. "Didn't you hear your human? She just said the curse compels her to bring a dragon to Vann Jeger, but she didn't say anything about that dragon having to do anything. Sounds to me like all we have to do is show up and the thing's broken."

"Technically, maybe," Marci admitted. "But I don't think Vann Jeger's going to let us just walk up, wave, and leave."

"Of course not," Justin scoffed, crossing his arms over his chest with a look of absolute superiority. "That's why you two lightweights are going to focus on getting in and getting out while *I* take on the dragon hunter."

Stunned silence followed that pronouncement. Then, because someone had to, Julius asked the obvious question.

"Are you insane?"

"Are *you*?" Justin snapped. "Because I'm offering to solve your problem, here. For free, I might add."

"Have you been listening to *anything* we've said?" Julius cried. "We're talking about *Vann Jeger*, the *Death of Dragons*. He didn't give himself that name, you know! I'm pretty sure he's killed three of our siblings already."

"Four," Justin corrected. "But I'm not afraid of Vann Jeger."

Julius had already had this conversation with his brother once tonight without success, but this was too important to let slide. "I'm not trying to downplay your battle prowess," he said diplomatically. "But let's be realistic here. Vann Jeger is the spirit of a fjord that was formed over multiple ice ages. He also leads a private army of anti-dragon equipped humans with Algonquin herself on call for backup. Bethesda herself couldn't win a fight like that."

Justin scoffed. "You *clearly* don't know what our mother is capable of."

"But I do know *you*," Julius said. "If you had your Fang, maybe you'd have a chance, but without it—"

"But I won't get my Fang back if I don't do this!" Justin cried. "Don't you see? This is my *chance*. Forget sneaking into Reclamation Land. If I can take Vann Jeger's head, I'll be famous! They'll *have* to give me my sword back."

He finished with a grin, clearly waiting for someone to congratulate him on his daring, but Julius was speechless. "*That's* what this is about?" he ground out at last. "Your stupid *sword?*"

Justin looked insulted. "The Fifth Fang of the Heartstriker is not a stupid—"

"We're not playing around here, Justin!" Julius yelled. "Marci could die if we screw this up! I could die, you could die. This isn't the sort of thing you can joke about!"

"Who's joking?" Justin growled, stabbing his finger into Julius's chest. "I came here because you needed protection from the Three Sisters, *not* because I was giving up on my sword! *Nothing* is going to stop me from reclaiming what is mine. Now I've found a way to do just that *and* save your human at the same time, and all you can do is complain? This is a win-win situation for us, Julius! Aren't those the ones you like?"

"Not if you die!" Julius cried.

"I'm not going to die!" his brother yelled back. "I've been a Knight of the Heartstrikers for seven years. I know what I'm doing, and I'm telling you, I can beat Vann Jeger, because even though he's everything you just said, he's also a spirit who's *thousands of miles from home.* Since you spent our tactics classes reading your dumb Fantasy novels, you probably don't know what that means. Lucky for you, *I* remember that spirits get weaker the farther they get from their source of power." He lifted his chin with a cocky grin. "Vann Jeger might be the big fish back home in Norway, but out here, he's just another sack of water."

"That is true," Marci said skeptically. "But if he's so easy to beat, why hasn't anyone else killed him? And how are you even going to take his head if he's made of water?"

"I don't know," Justin growled. "But you're pretty mouthy for a mortal who had to come running to us for protection, so why don't you show some respect and shut your—"

"*Enough!*" Julius snarled, baring his teeth. "That's *enough,* Justin."

Justin didn't look like he'd had anywhere near enough. Neither did Marci, whose bracelets were shining in a way that never meant anything good. Clearly, tempers were running way too high to get anything done at the moment. It was time to defuse the situation, and the quickest way to defuse anything was to get Justin out of it.

"We've all had a long night," he said, keeping his voice down and his posture submissive as he turned to face his brother. "If we're going to battle an ancient spirit, we all need our rest. Justin, why don't you take my room? Down the hall, first door on your left. Meanwhile, I'll stay up and work on the curse angle with Marci."

His brother shot him a poisonous look. But while he clearly knew that he was being managed, Justin never had been able to resist a surrender. "This isn't over," he said, glaring at both of them. "When I wake up, we're going to make a plan of attack. A *real* one, so you'd better bring your A-game. I don't want to hear some stupid nonsense about how we should *talk* to Vann Jeger or anything like that. Understood?"

"Understood," Julius said dutifully. "Goodnight, Justin."

His brother lifted his head proudly and stomped out into the hall. A few seconds later, Julius heard his bedroom door slam, followed by the tell-tale clunks and crashes of someone angrily getting undressed. But while Julius wasn't optimistic about the fate of his bedroom furniture, at least it didn't look like his brother was going to be rushing off to his death immediately. He was taking comfort in small mercies when Marci walked to her bedroom door and closed it with a frown.

"I'll be honest," she said, turning to face him again. "I only followed about half of that. What happened to Justin's sword?"

Julius sighed. "Chelsie took it away because of what happened in the Pit. He lost his position as a knight, too, so you could say he's sore about it."

"More like throwing a tantrum."

"You don't know the half of it," Julius replied tiredly, reaching up to rub his aching head. "I know he doesn't deserve sympathy with the way he's behaving, but if you could cut him some slack, I'd really appreciate it. He's had some big falls since you last saw him."

He'd hoped that explanation would help smooth down any ruffled feathers, but Marci's frown only deepened. "Not to meddle in your family business, but I don't think you're doing him any favors thinking like that. I know being compassionate is, like, your thing, but it is possible to be *too* nice. Justin's a grown man. Well, grown dragon, but he still has to face reality, and the reality is that if he goes up against Vann Jeger, he's going to die."

"I know," Julius said with a frustrated sigh. "But he won't listen tonight."

"He won't listen tomorrow, either."

"I don't know what else to do," he snapped. "I can't stop him."

"So call someone who can," she said. "Chelsie can clearly manage him."

Julius shook his head so fast it hurt. "He'd *never* forgive me if I called Chelsie."

"Then what about your mother?" Marci asked. "He's her favorite, right? Doesn't she care that he'll die?"

"He's her favorite precisely *because* he does stuff like this," Julius said bitterly. "Mother values audacity and ambition over everything else. I swear, sometimes I think she'd rather he die doing something stupidly dramatic than live to see his hundredth birthday."

And now that he thought about it, that made him angrier than anything. Justin was so strong and fierce, it was easy to forget that they were the same age. Like him, Justin was only twenty-four, a baby by dragon standards, and painfully desperate to prove himself. Marci was right about him needing to live in reality, but how could he do that when everyone else, especially his mother, acted like he was a dragon twenty times his age? The only one who didn't was Chelsie, and Justin hated her for it. He'd probably hate Julius, too, if he knew what he was thinking, but for once, Julius didn't care.

"I'll stop him," he growled, clenching his fists. "I put it off once today, but never again. I'm not going to lose my brother or you, because none of us are going anywhere near Vann Jeger."

"Sounds great," Marci said. "How are you planning to accomplish that?"

Julius shrugged. "I thought we'd start with the curse. That's the lever forcing us into this mess. If we can break it, we can run and avoid everything."

"Works for me," she said, smiling. "I'm still not sure it's possible to break a Sword of Damocles, but impending death *is* the mother of invention. I've actually got some ideas already for—"

The door to Marci's room banged open again, making them both jump. By the time Julius landed, his brother was on top of him, shoving both him and Marci to the floor.

"Ow!" Julius yelped as Justin slammed him into the hardwood floor. "What are you—"

"Shut up," Justin growled, glaring at the ceiling. "And stay down. We've got incoming."

"Incoming *what?*" Marci hissed.

Julius was about to ask the same thing when a wind strong enough to rattle the windows swept over the house, followed by the unmistakable *thud* of a dragon landing on their roof.

CHAPTER SEVEN

The house was still shaking when Julius scrambled back to his feet. "Did I not *just say* to stay down?" Justin hissed, grabbing for him.

Julius dodged him without thinking, focusing on the familiar scent in the air as he raced for the stairs, feet barely touching the ground. He cleared both flights in a single jump, landing with a scramble as he lunged for the front door, yanking it open just in time to be blown back again as the enormous, pure white dragon hopped off the roof to land directly in front of him, her wings creating dust storms with every flap.

"HOLY—"

Marci's shout echoed down the stairs, but it was instantly drowned out by the thunder of Justin's feet as he charged toward his brother. "Get back inside *now*!"

Again, Julius ignored him, his eyes wide with wonder. He'd heard stories of the daughters of the Three Sisters, but nothing could have prepared him for the real thing. Though only two thirds the size of Justin, the white dragon was a jaw-dropping blend of ethereal beauty and coldly efficient predator. Even covered in grime from her flight through the city, her white scales and frosted wings sparkled like fresh snow in the dim glare of their porch light. Cold, pale smoke curled from behind the white, razor-sharp wall of her teeth, and her eyes were the vivid, electric blue of sea ice. Even Justin couldn't seem to find his voice again in the face of such striking, terrifying beauty, which was why no one said a word until the dragon changed a few moments later, collapsing in on herself like an ice sculpture melting in the sun until she was just Katya again.

A completely naked Katya, shivering on her knees with her hands clutched tight against her chest like she was trying to hold herself together, or trying to hold onto something. He was still staring dumbly when Marci whistled.

"Wow," she said. "I guess that answers the question of where your clothes go."

Julius jumped and dropped his eyes at once, cheeks flaming. Justin, of course, kept staring, earning himself a sharp elbow in the ribs from his brother, which he didn't seem to feel. Julius ignored him after that, ducking back inside to grab his raincoat from their coat closet before running down the stairs to throw it over Katya's shoulders.

She clutched the long, plastic coat with a nod of thanks, pulling it around her body like a cape as she rose shakily to her feet. "I'm sorry to burst in on you like this," she said quietly, her normally soft Russian accent thicker than ever. "I didn't know this was your home."

"It's fine," Julius said quickly. "You're always welcome."

"Unless you were followed," Justin growled.

Katya looked offended. "Who do you think I am?"

"No sirens, no problem," Julius shooting his brother a *not now* look before offering his hand to Katya, who seemed to be having trouble staying upright. "How far did you fly?"

"From your mountain."

His jaw fell open. "You flew over a thousand miles *tonight*? Like, since the party?"

She shrugged. "I've always been a good flier."

Julius would have said amazing. A flight that long would have taken him days. But then, from the hunted look in her eyes, he didn't think Katya had done it for fun.

"Let's get you inside before someone sees," he said, guiding her toward the stairs. When he tried to take her up them, though, a big, Justin-sized roadblock stepped into their path.

"What do you think you're doing?"

"Helping," Julius said with a scowl. "She's not our enemy."

"Did the definition of 'enemy' change while I was in the shower?" Justin shouted, stabbing his finger at Katya's face. "You told me not an hour ago that her clan just declared war on us, and that Mother wanted me here to protect you and your life debt. Now a daughter of the Three Sisters literally lands on your doorstep, and you want to *help* her?"

"Yes," Julius said, exasperated. "Katya's the one who owes me the life debt you're protecting, remember? Now move over and let her in before we end up with more dragon hunters on our tail."

Katya's eyes widened. "Dragon hunters?"

"Long story," Julius looking over his shoulder. "But, I have to ask, did anyone see you coming in?"

"Absolutely not," she said proudly, giving Justin an icy look. "Contrary to what some might think, it's not hard to slip by Algonquin's defenses, and you don't escape as many times as I have without getting very good at flying without being seen."

"How did you even know where to fly?" Justin snapped, turning back to Julius. "Do you just give your address to everyone, now?"

"I already told you, I didn't know this was his home," she said, opening her clutched hand to reveal a crumpled square of dirty paper. "A pigeon gave me this."

Justin snapped his mouth shut while Julius did a double-take. "A pigeon?"

Katya nodded, and the Heartstrikers exchanged a look.

"Fine," Justin growled. "We'll hear what she has to say. But remember, this is *your* idea."

Julius sighed and glanced back at Katya, who was shifting uncomfortably under his cheap raincoat. "We should probably get you into some real clothes before we do anything serious," he said, guiding her into the house. "Marci? Do you have something she could borrow?"

"Sure," Marci said, watching Katya with a mix of awe and intense curiosity. "This way."

Clutching the plastic coat shut with one hand, Katya followed her upstairs. Julius locked the door and walked over to join his brother, who was still glaring up the stairs after them like he expected a fireball at any second.

"What's the plan?"

"I don't know," Julius admitted tiredly. "Talk to her, I guess?"

"Talking isn't a plan," his brother said with a sneer. "I say we take her hostage."

"Okay, first, Estella tried to kill Katya herself just last month, so I don't think that'll work," Julius said. "Second, Katya's my friend, and friends don't take friends hostage. Third, Bob's the one who sent her here. He doesn't do things without reason."

"He does things for no reason all the time!" Justin said. "Remember three years ago when he sent us all used hubcaps for our birthday?"

"This is different," Julius said quickly. "I'm not saying we're going to rush out and do whatever she wants, I just want to talk to her and see what's going on."

He thought that was all pretty reasonable, but his brother still looked dangerously growly, so Julius decided to use his big gun. "I'll buy us dinner."

Like always, Justin perked up at the mention of food. As ploys went, it was an expensive one—his brother was a bottomless pit even by Heartstriker standards—but all dragons were at their most peaceable while eating. Katya was probably starving as well after a flight like that, and Julius hadn't eaten since lunch yesterday. A meal would smooth this process out for everyone, but getting enough to feed three dragons and a human was no easy task. Fortunately, Julius had a good relationship with the rapid-delivery Vietnamese place on the other side of the on-ramps. Ten minutes after he placed the order, a delivery driver showed up with enough food to feed a small army. Justin was already claiming multiple bags for himself when Katya and Marci finally came back downstairs.

Katya must have taken a shower, because her blond hair was damp and all the dirt from her flight was gone. That alone made her look infinitely less bedraggled, and while the six inch height difference between her and Marci should have made her look ridiculous in her borrowed clothes, Katya carried it off with typical draconic grace. If Julius hadn't known for a fact that Marci's UNLV Thaumaturgy Casting Team t-shirt normally fell past her hips, he would have assumed it had always been meant to be a crop top from the elegant way Katya wore it, sitting down at their shabby, delivery-bag covered kitchen table like she was taking her place at a banquet.

Since it was usually only Marci and Julius, they only had two chairs. Since their guest had already take one, Julius gave Marci the other and hopped up to sit on the kitchen counter. Justin, as usual, chose to stand, looming in the corner and scowling at Katya over his box of spring rolls like he was one excuse away from eating her as well. When Julius tried to signal him to take the aggression down a notch, he blew out a line of smoke, and Julius gave up with a sigh.

"Please excuse my brother."

"What is there to excuse?" Katya said with a sad shrug. "I am an enemy of your clan seeking shelter in your home. If the situation was reversed, my sisters would be acting far worse."

If their situation was reversed, Julius was pretty sure he'd be dead. "So," he said nervously. "What brings you here? Not that I'm not happy to see you again, of course."

She flashed him a feeble smile. "As much as I enjoy your company, I didn't set a new record for flying cross country just to visit. I'm here because, a few hours ago, Estella and Svena attacked the Heartstriker Champion."

"*What?*"

Justin's yell made everyone except Katya jump, but when Julius whirled around, his brother looked more insulted than angry. "She's lying," he snarled. "There's no way any of her puny sisters could beat Conrad."

"Svena was toppling clans centuries before your overgrown brother was even *born!*" Katya said fiercely, drawing herself up in righteous fury.

"I don't care if she was toppling gods," Justin replied. "Conrad is the top fighter in our clan, *and* he has the strongest Fang of the Heartstriker. He is undefeatable!"

Katya bared her teeth at him. "Do you think I flew all this way to lie?"

Justin bared his as well, taking a menacing step forward before Julius could jump between them. "Easy," he said, putting up his hands. "Justin, calm down. Katya, I believe you, but what my brother says is also true." Or, he assumed so. He didn't actually know the Heartstriker rankings of who was strongest or who had the best sword, but Justin definitely would, which was proof enough for him. "Why don't you explain what happened so we can understand. Was there a fight?"

"I don't know," Katya said, frowning at the table. "It happened after we left the party. Estella had us wait in the desert, and then she ordered Svena to teleport the two of them to Conrad's balcony. I don't know what happened from there. The pigeon appeared shortly after, and it was the first time they'd left me alone, so..."

"So you took your chance and ran," Julius said.

She nodded, but Justin rolled his eyes. "If you didn't stick around to see the end, how do you know they won? Conrad probably wiped the floor with them."

Katya shot him an icy look. "Two on one? Estella is a seer, and she's stronger than ever. Your brother didn't have a chance."

"Yeah, right," Justin said. "Sorry to rain on your fantasy, but I think we'd have heard if Conrad died to your sisters. Stuff like that gets around fast."

That was actually a very good point. Conrad getting killed by another clan inside Heartstriker Mountain would be *huge* news, but Katya was shaking her head. "They wouldn't have killed him," she said confidently. "Estella has a plan. I don't know what it is, obviously, but she's setting up the board for something big."

"Seers always are," Julius said tiredly, pulling out his phone. "Let me call Bob."

He tapped through his messages until he found the last one Bob had sent. He didn't actually think it would work—the seer could be amazingly chatty when he wanted to be, but getting hold of him when *you* needed something was nigh impossible—but telling any other Heartstriker about Katya would put her in even more danger. He had to say *something*, though, so he typed up a long report about the supposed attack on Conrad and Katya's warning and dutifully hit send…and immediately got a reply.

> *Thank you for contacting Everyone's Favorite Heartstriker! Alas, all of our seers are busy at the moment. Fortunately for you, I already know what you're calling about. Rest assured that Your Concern will be addressed in the order in which it was received. Assuming I care and/or remember.*
>
> *Hearts and kisses, your infallible brother,*
> *Bob*

"I don't know what else I expected," Julius said, shoving his phone back into his pocket with a sigh. "But I suppose it doesn't matter."

"*Doesn't matter?*" Justin roared. "Her sisters attacked our clan! I don't know what game Bob is playing, but I say you can't trust a thing they say. The ice snakes have *always* hated us."

"Estella has," Katya said quickly. "But Svena is different. From the moment she took over the clan, she's been working to make peace with Heartstriker."

Julius blinked. "Really?"

"Of course," she said, lifting her chin. "We are proud, not stupid. None of my sisters like your clan, but it's suicide to try and fight the Heartstrikers now. You outnumber us ten to one. Svena understands this. Why else do you think she's stayed with Ian so long? Or agreed to go to the party in the first place? I shouldn't be telling you this, but this last month while Estella was away, Svena was trying to rally the rest of our sisters against her. She was succeeding, too. We'd actually managed to get almost all of them on our side before Estella came back and did…whatever it was she did."

"I'm sorry," Marci said, breaking her silence. "I'm out of the loop, here. What did Estella do to Svena?"

"I don't know," Katya growled. "But that *thing* is not Svena. My sister would *never* take orders like that!"

Given what he'd seen of Svena during the fracas last month, Julius didn't doubt that for a second. He also didn't doubt Katya's story about her sister's plans to form an alliance with Heartstriker. Playing on Bethesda's obsession with a mating flight to broker peace between their clans was exactly the sort of savvy politics he'd expect from a dragon like Svena. Likewise, ruining that fit right in with what he knew of Estella, who, as they'd discovered last month, seemed to hate Heartstriker to the point of cutting off her nose to spite her face. The only thing Julius *didn't* understand about Katya's story was, "What about your other sisters?"

Katya looked up. "What?"

"There are twelve daughters of the Three Sisters, right?" he said. "You, Estella, and Svena are accounted for, but where are the rest? If you're the youngest, then your sisters must all be all-powerful, ancient dragons, so why aren't they here helping you save your clan?"

By the time he finished, Katya's expression was the bitterest he'd ever seen it. "No one fears change like old dragons," she growled. "My family is not like yours. We were once the greatest in the world, the magic-born children of the three most powerful, most ancient dragons to survive the trip from our original home."

"Original home?" Marci interrupted. "What original home?"

"Dragons aren't originally from here," Julius explained quickly. "We came to this world as conquerors from another plane ten thousand years ago."

Her eyes went round. "Ten *thousand* years? So the Three Sisters are *ten thousand* years old?"

"Older," Katya said. "That's why they have to sleep. Dragons who were born on this world are attuned to its magic. They were able to survive the magical drought by simply retreating into their more efficient human forms, but my mothers have no such thing."

She looked at Julius. "It was the same with your grandfather, the Quetzalcoatl. He was only able to stay awake through the disappearance of magic by harvesting human sacrifices. He was still greatly weakened, though, which was the only reason your mother was able to kill him."

That wasn't how Bethesda told the story, but it made a grim sort of logic. Julius knew all about his grandfather's love of human sacrifices, of course, but he'd always assumed the Quetzalcoatl just liked killing people on altars. If he'd been using them as a way to harvest magic when nothing else was available, though, that made a lot more sense. It also meant he was directly descended from one of the most prolific blood mages in history. But when he glanced at Marci to see how she'd taken this grisly revelation about his family's history, she was staring into her carton of rice like it contained the mysteries of the universe.

"Back to the important stuff," Justin said, crossing his arms as he glared at Katya, "You're saying that the rest of your clan, the vaunted Daughters of the Three Sisters, are so stuck up and stuck in their ways, they won't get off their butts even to save their own hides?"

Julius winced at his brother's bluntness, but to his amazement, Katya didn't look offended. She was actually nodding. "More or less," she said. "But you have to understand, Estella's run our lives according to her visions since we were hatched. It doesn't matter what plans we make, she knows what we're going to do before we do it. My sisters were barely willing to risk siding with Svena while Estella was on another plane. Now that she's back, they won't even show their faces. No one knows better than us that you can't beat a seer."

By the time she finished, Katya sounded utterly defeated, but Julius was less convinced. "Are you sure that Estella's unbeatable?"

"Of course," Katya said. "She's still a seer."

"But she's not the only one on the board," Julius said, pointing at the crumpled up piece of paper with his address that Katya was still clutching in her hand. "If she was actually watching you all the time, there's no way Bob's pigeon would be able to bring you notes, and definitely no way you'd be able to run all the way up here to talk to us."

"Unless this is part of Estella's plan, too," Marci pointed out.

"If we go around thinking everything is a seer plot, we'll never be able to do anything," Julius argued, turning back to Katya. "You told me back at the mountain that Estella was different. Is it possible that she's not as in control as she used to be?"

"Maybe," Katya said with a thoughtful frown. "It's obvious she still sees the future, but defeating Brohomir is all she talks about. It's like she's let her grudge against your clan completely consume all of her other ambitions."

Julius had noticed that himself when he'd watched Estella lord her knowledge over Bob in the hallway. At the time, her obvious obsession had terrified him. Now, though, it gave him an idea.

"Just because she's still capable of seeing everything doesn't mean she's looking," he said quickly. "Dragons who let themselves get hyper-focused on a single goal can fall prey to tunnel vision. I bet Estella's no different. In the hallway, she claimed the future was bought and paid for and that nothing could change it. I don't actually know what she meant by that, but if she's really that confident, she's probably not keeping as close an eye on things as she should."

"But what does that matter?" Katya said sadly. "Even if you're right, and she's not paying attention to the details, she still knows how everything ends. I see what you're saying, but if there's any lesson I've learned in my life, it's that you can't escape Estella. The best you can hope for is to enjoy the run before she catches you."

"But this *isn't* Estella," Julius said. "You said so yourself—she's not the dragon she used to be. How do you know you can't beat her now if you won't try?"

"Because I *have* tried!" she cried. "Do you think I stayed locked in my mothers' glacier all those years out of choice? It doesn't matter how clever I am or how far I run, Estella always gets me in the end, because she's *already seen where I'll be*. That's still true. Even if she is deteriorating, one month doesn't change centuries."

"Then I guess you're screwed," Justin said. "Sucks to be you."

"*Justin!*" Julius hissed, but Katya looked more depressed than ever.

"He's right," she said miserably. "For all I know, my escape tonight is just Estella's way of getting rid of me. Even if I did actually manage to get free, what would it matter? I'm the magic-stunted failure of my clan." She glanced at Julius. "Could you stop Brohomir if our situations were reversed?"

"Not alone," Julius admitted. "But I wouldn't try alone, and neither should you." He moved closer, walking around the table and crouching down until he could see Katya's lowered face. "You're not alone," he said quietly. "And you're not a failure."

Katya glowered. "Don't try to nice your way out of this. It's insulting."

"I'm not trying to nice my way out," he said. "I'm telling the truth, and the truth is that you're wrong. Yes, you're the youngest of your clan, and yes, you don't have the famous Three Sisters' command of magic, but that doesn't change the part where you're still a clever, ancient dragon strong enough to fly all the way to the DFZ from New Mexico faster than a jet *and* savvy enough to slip past Algonquin's defenses. Those aren't the actions of a failure. And if a dragon like you is the bottom of your clan, then I also think you're giving your sisters far too little credit. I mean, have you even tried to contact them?"

"No," Katya admitted, looking away. "But they won't listen."

"Then *make* them," Julius said firmly. "This isn't something they can afford to ignore. We don't know what's going on with Svena, but it doesn't take a seer to see that if Estella isn't stopped, she's going to take you all down with her. You might not be able to take Estella on your own, but the Daughters of the Three Sisters are some of the most feared and powerful dragons in the world. If you worked together, even a seer wouldn't stand a chance."

"And I'm just supposed to tell them that?" Katya scoffed "This isn't a novel, Julius. I can't just go to sisters who've despised and looked down on me as weak our entire lives and *ask* them for help.

They'd laugh in my face, assuming they'd see me at all. Worst case, they'd give me back to Estella to curry favor, because they know as well as I do that the seer always wins."

"But she *doesn't*," Julius cried. "And you're the proof! She tried to kill you just last month, and she failed so hard she had to run to another dimension. That's a pretty compelling argument that Estella's not the infallible force she used to be. I'm not saying it'll be an easy sell, but aside from you, Estella, and Svena, there are still nine Daughters of the Three Sisters out there. Surely *one* of them will listen."

Katya sighed and sat back in her chair. "Assuming you're right," she said grudgingly. "How would I reach them? A conversation like this can't be had over the phone. Some of my sisters don't even *have* phones. If I'm going to convince them, I'm going to have to go to each one myself, which is impossible since Estella can still see every decision I make. Wherever I go, she'll just be waiting there to pick me up the moment I arrive."

"Then we'll just have to send you in a way she can't see."

Katya turned to him in confusion, but Julius was already searching through his phone. "Estella can see *your* decisions," he said, pulling a whole cluster of travel booking services into the glowing field of his AR. "But I'm Bob's brother, which means she can't see *mine*. Give me five cities you want to go to, and I'll pick one at random and buy the ticket. We'll do it all by flight numbers, that way you won't even have to know where you're going until you're actually boarding the plane."

Julius was pretty proud of that plan, but Katya was staring at him like he'd just suggested they go to the moon. "*Why?*"

"Because you don't make any decisions this way," he explained. "I mean, obviously you'll know where you're going once you get to the airport, but all the actual choices will be mine instead of yours, which means there should be no way for Estella to look into your future and see what you're up to until it's too late."

"No, I understand that part," she said. "I meant, why are you doing this for *me*? I'm not even your clan. Doing this puts you directly into Estella's line of fire. Why would you take that risk for me?"

"Because you're my friend," Julius said without hesitation. "And because it's the right thing to do. I've been bullied by more than my fair share of dragons, but Estella's stolen your entire *life*. I don't want her to get away with that. Also, I really do think this will work. Whatever Estella's planning, the most likely time for her to do it will be at the mating flight tomorrow night. My mother thinks so, too, which is why she's planning a trap for that same—"

"*Julius!*" Justin roared. "Don't tell her that!"

"Why not?" he said. "Katya's not dumb. Attacking while Estella is guaranteed to be on her home turf is obviously Bethesda's best move. Estella has to know that, too, and I'm betting she already has a counter plan in place for every one of Bethesda's traps. But what she'd never expect is for the Heartstriker to have help from the other Daughters of the Three Sisters."

"Wait," Katya said, eyes wide. "You want *me* to go to my *sisters* and convince them to help Bethesda the Broodmare take on Estella?"

"Pretty much," Julius said with a grin. "It's the next logical step. Svena wanted peace between our clans, but she was in a bad position to push for it while Estella was in hiding since, without your own seer to balance things, the Heartstriker clan's size advantage gave Bethesda the power in any negotiation. *But,* if your family comes in at the last second to rescue her, my mother will owe all of you her life. That's a much more even starting point for a negotiation between our clans. If you can convince your sisters to help us, there's a good chance we can stop Estella, save my clan, save Svena, *and* get a fair peace treaty all in one swoop. That's a win-win for everyone."

"Everyone except Estella," Katya said. She wasn't smiling yet, but there was a hardness in her voice that Julius liked a lot more than the defeat he'd heard earlier. "You do realize this is an extreme long shot? Even if I could convince one or more of my sisters to show up at the mating flight, there's zero chance I could get them to attack. And if things start looking bad for the Heartstriker, they might even join in and help Estella take Bethesda down just to prove they were on her side all along."

Justin was growling by the time Katya finished, but Julius refused to let him ruin this. "That's not going to happen," he said firmly. "I don't know your sisters like you do, but I've never met a dragon who would attack an outside threat before punishing a traitor, and a traitor is exactly what Estella became when she turned on you and Svena. If your sisters could see what you've seen, do you think they'd side with Estella?"

Katya shook her head.

"Then you have to try," Julius finished. "Even if you get out there, and they say no, it's not like your situation with Estella can get worse."

"Things can *always* get worse," Katya said bitterly. "But if I can save Svena, it's worth it. She's the one who's protected me from the others since I was small. I owe it to her to help now, before Estella drags us all down forever."

Julius grinned. "So you'll let me get you a flight?"

She nodded, her face growing determined. "I will, and I swear on all three of my mothers that I will repay you. No one can offer two life debts, but—"

"You don't owe me a thing," Julius said firmly. "Like I said, you're my friend, and doing this helps us as much as it helps you. I won't accept a debt."

Katya shook her head wildly. "No! I can't let it be so uneven. I already owe you my life, and that was before I ran to you. The debt between us—"

"Is all in your head," he finished with a smile. "I told you back in the diner: I don't play dragon power games. I'm helping you because it's right, I want to, it could very well prevent a war, and it makes me happy. End of story. Now," he glanced down as his phone. "Where do you want to fly?"

Katya didn't answer for a long time. She just sat there, staring, and then she ducked her head. "Thank you," she whispered, furtively wiping her eyes.

Julius answered just as quietly. "You're welcome," he said, stepping back to lean on the counter again, giving Katya her space until, at last, she began naming cities.

Fifteen minutes later, Katya's flight was booked and she was on her way out the door. Julius had also gotten her a cab and some money to cover food and other expenses. It was more than he could really afford, especially given what he'd spent this month already, but helping Katya was more important than money, and he'd made sure to take it out of his personal account so Marci wouldn't suffer. Marci herself had already gone up to her attic workshop to get started on the curse, and Justin had refused to take part in any of this, which meant Julius and Katya were alone when the auto-cab arrived to take her to the airport.

"I know you won't accept it," Katya said as the tiny, automated car pulled up. "But I swear I will repay you."

"You don't have to—"

"I do," she said sternly, looking him up and down. "You are a very nice dragon, Julius Heartstriker, but you are still a dragon. You hide your cunning under the guise of kindness because it differentiates you from those who tried to crush you, but tonight proved that you are every bit as clever and conniving as any Heartstriker, and I am proud to call you my ally." She smiled. "That being true, though, you said yourself that alliances should always be fair and equal, which is why, assuming I get out of this alive, I'm going to repay you whether you like it or not."

She put her hand out as she finished, and Julius, unsure what else to say, took it. "You *really* don't have to."

Katya laughed. "And *you* really have to learn to stop throwing away people's gratitude." She released him and climbed into the cab. "I'll call you if I get news. Good luck."

"You, too," he said, stepping back as the little taxi took off into the night. He was watching the last glimmer of its taillights vanish around the bend when something behind him growled.

"I can't believe you did that."

Julius sighed. "Did what?" he asked, turning to face his brother, who was waiting on the porch.

"Any of it," Justin said, arms crossed over his chest. "You told her Bethesda's plan, gave her advice on how to tear down our negotiating position for a treaty, and then you financed her escape." He bared his teeth. "You've betrayed the clan so many times tonight, I don't even know where I'm going to start when I call Mother."

"Tell her whatever you want," Julius said. "Just don't forget to mention that Bob was the one who sent Katya here in the first place."

"Don't hide behind him," his brother growled. "Bob's motives have always been questionable, but he didn't tell you to blabber clan business to the enemy's *sister*."

"At least we're doing something!" Julius cried. "From what I saw at the mountain, Mother's acting like this whole seer business is a done deal already. She doesn't even seem to care that she's walking into a trap."

"Of course not," Justin said. "When someone attacks you, you don't sit around fretting and wringing your hands. You attack them back without hesitation. It's called audacity. If you want to win, you have to be willing to go for it, even if that means eating some losses."

"*Losses?*" Julius cried. "Justin, you're talking about *us*. When Mother takes losses, *we're* what she loses. Not pawns, not assets. Us, her *children*, and it's wrong. We're individuals with our own goals and feelings. We're not pieces to be thrown away."

Justin rolled his eyes. "Now you're just being dramatic."

"Oh yeah?" Julius said. "How would you like it if she threw *you* away?"

"We both know she won't throw *me* away. I'm too good."

He said this like it was undeniable fact, and Julius bet that, to Justin, it was. He also bet it was what every other self-important Heartstriker thought right before Bethesda maneuvered them into position. Too bad his brother had a vested interest in never understanding that. Bethesda was the source of all his importance: the head of his clan, the queen to his knight. He'd be loyal to her right up to the moment she stuck his head on a spit. Being at the bottom of the clan, Julius had grown up with a very different view, and having already avoided being his mother's fall guy once before, he was dead-set determined to never let himself, or anyone else, be put in that position ever again.

"Well, I'm not waiting around to get used again," Julius growled. "Conrad's already paid the price for Mother not taking this seriously. If we don't want to—"

"Funny thing, about that," Justin interrupted, folding his arms over his chest. "I just got off the phone with Frieda back at the mountain, and she says Conrad's fine." He gave Julius a superior look. "Looks like your *friend* lied to you about that one. Wanna try again?"

That didn't add up to Julius. Why would Katya have lied about the attack? But while he was sure something funny was going on, he was too angry to even contemplate what that might be. He loved Justin, he really did, but his brother could be a world-class jerk sometimes. He certainly seemed to be going for a record today, and with everything else falling apart around his ears, Julius had officially had enough.

"You know what? I don't even care!" he yelled. "You're always going on about how I should be a dragon and stand up for myself, but all of that starts with refusing to be a pawn!"

"You didn't stand up for yourself!" Justin yelled. "You told an outsider secret information to help her engineer a situation where Bethesda is forced into a life debt with another clan! That's not refusing to be a pawn. That's just selling out your *family* to the *enemy*."

"When are you going to get it through your head that Katya's not our enemy?" Julius cried. "She's fighting against Estella just like us. That makes her our *ally*, and we need those more than ever." He clenched his fists. "The clan is my family as much as it is yours. I want to keep it safe just like you do, but that doesn't mean I'm going to sit around protecting Mother's secrets while she decides which one of us she wants to throw under the bus. And you *know* she'll do just that, because it's *what she always does!* If she goes ahead with her plan to trap Estella, who knows how many of us will go down with it? At least my way doesn't call for losses except for Bethesda's pride, which we can both agree is no loss at all."

"Oh, please," Justin sneered. "Would you get over yourself already? You're not some special snowflake, Julius. We're in a clan war here. Dragons are going to die, that's just how it is. It's not Mother's job to save our lives. It's her job to *win*—surviving to enjoy the victory is our responsibility."

"Maybe it shouldn't be," Julius growled. "Maybe, and I know this sounds crazy, but just *maybe* if we worked together and helped each other instead of always going every dragon for himself, we wouldn't get into these kind of doomed, eat-or-be-eaten situations in the first place!"

"Spoken like a true failure," Justin said, shaking his head. "But maybe if *you* got better at not dying, you wouldn't need all that help all the time."

Julius's shoulders slumped. "I don't even know why I'm talking about this with you," he grumbled, stomping into the house. "You tell Mother whatever you want. I'm going upstairs to help Marci try to keep us all from getting killed by Vann Jeger."

"Why bother?" Justin yelled after him. "I already told you I've got it."

"Then feel free to go to sleep," Julius yelled back.

He felt guilty as soon as the words left his lips. He'd just promised Marci he was going to stand up to his brother and tell him he wasn't going to be facing Vann Jeger, but he was so *sick* of fighting. It wasn't like Justin would listen, anyway. He'd just call Julius weak again and do whatever he wanted anyway. At this point, his best shot at saving his brother was to help Marci break her curse and avoid fighting Vann Jeger at all. Maybe then Justin would actually survive to see Julius and Katya's plan work. Not that the ungrateful jerk deserved it.

That angry thought just made him feel depressed, but Julius didn't have time to mope about it. His family crisis with Justin was going to have to get in line behind all the others, because right now, he had to make good on his promise to Marci. With that, he put the conversation with his brother determinedly out of his mind and started up the steps, climbing them two at a time toward Marci's lab to offer his help however he could.

CHAPTER EIGHT

W hat was left of the night passed in a haze.

Marci worked like a machine, using up every casting marker and stick of chalk in her workshop as she went through spells one after another after another trying to crack the curse. She tried dusts and powders from her stockpile. She drew spellwork on her skin, on Julius's skin, and even around where Ghost was sleeping on his bed in the corner. At one point, she actually made a perfect double of herself using a circle written in her own blood—a technique she later admitted she'd gotten from a blood mage forum—to try and trick the Sword of Damocles into jumping over. But no matter what she tried, the black sword on her neck didn't budge, and with each failure, Marci's expression grew more bitterly determined until she seemed to be plowing through spellwork on sheer stubbornness.

If things had been less dire, it would have been an amazing thing to watch. Julius had never known human magic could be cast in so many ways. As promised, he helped wherever he could, fetching things down off of high shelves and keeping her stocked with coffee. He would have liked to do more, but a month wasn't enough to pick up even the basics of the incredibly complicated world of Thaumaturgic magic. Mostly, he acted as her battery, letting her siphon magic off of him once her own stockpiled reagents ran dry.

After what had happened with Bixby's goons, Marci had never asked to use his magic again. Given how uncomfortable that first time was, Julius had been happy to leave it at that. Now, though, things were too dire for him to be squeamish, but in a rare stroke of luck, Marci's pull on his magic didn't feel nearly as bad this time around. Not being in a rage and facing down a horde of gunmen, she was almost dainty about it, taking his magic in tiny sips over the course of multiple hours. But even with her extra care, the cumulative draw took its toll.

By the time the darkness under the skyways began to shift from the neon-lit night black to the sooty, almost-black of morning, Julius felt like he'd run twelve marathons in a row. Every muscle in his body throbbed, and he could barely smell anymore. He tried to soldier on—this was life or death, after all—but when Marci scrubbed out her latest failed circle and began to draw three more, Julius reached his end.

"I'm sorry," he said, flopping down on the hard futon couch under the low spot where the sloping attic roof met the wall. "That's all I've got."

"Oh my God," Marci said, dropping her chalk to hurry over. "Are you okay? You look terrible."

"It's not that bad," he lied. "I just need to rest a bit."

Marci didn't buy it for a second. "Why didn't you tell me I was taking too much earlier?"

"Wanted to help," he panted, closing his eyes. "I got you into this. Least I could do."

The couch creaked as Marci sat down beside him. "That's no call to kill yourself over it," she muttered angrily, taking his hands and rubbing his cold fingers between her warm ones, which would have felt amazing if only he'd been well enough to appreciate it. "I should have kept better track, but I got so wrapped up in my work I didn't notice. Not that it did any good."

He cracked his eyes open again. "The day's still young. We've only been at this for..." he trailed off, frowning. "What time is it?"

"Nine in the morning," she replied. "So about four and a half hours. But I'm not sure how much more I can do. I've already tried every curse breaking trick my dad and I knew, plus everything I learned in school, *plus* everything I could find online, but I might as well have gone out for a crazy, last-night-alive bender for all I've got to show for it."

"Sorry," Julius said again.

"It's not you," she said quickly. "You could be a never-ending fount and it wouldn't matter. This is a problem of leverage, not power."

He looked at her questioningly, and she reached up to touch the no-longer-bandaged black mark on her neck. "By putting the curse under all my protections, literally *in* my magic, the police mage left nothing for a counter-curse to grab onto," she explained. "Most curses are designed like bear traps. The magic clamps onto the victim, which means getting it off is just a matter of shoving enough power inside again to force it back open. But the Sword of Damocles is different. It's like someone hammered a headless nail deep into what makes me a mage. It doesn't matter how hard I pull when there's nothing to grab on to. So far, the only way I can see to get it out is to rip my own magic apart, which would kill me even faster than losing my head." She sighed and glanced over at the cat bed in the corner. "I thought about asking Ghost to try pushing on it from the inside, but he's still sleeping, and I'm pretty sure our bond doesn't work like that, anyway."

"He's been sleeping a lot," Julius said, follow her gaze to the transparent, curled up cat. "Is something wrong?"

A shadow passed over Marci's face, but then she shook her head. "Nothing I know of."

That was a lie, but Julius didn't have the energy to press. He'd figure it out later. Right now, all he wanted was to eat every scrap of food in the house and sleep for the rest of his life. But when he looked over to ask Marci if she wanted anything from the kitchen, she was sitting hunched over with her face buried in her hands.

"Are you okay?" he asked, knowing how stupid that sounded but unable to think of anything else to say.

"Not really," she muttered. "I know it's a waste of time to get depressed—crying over spilled magic and all—but I just feel like it's already over."

"It's not over," he assured her. "We're not dead yet."

"We're as good as," she said, turning her head to peer up at him through red rimmed eyes. "It isn't like I'm not used to failing. I fail all the time—see the last twelve hours—but magic is different. It's the one thing I was always really, *really* good at. Even knowing the Sword of Damocles was supposed to be unbreakable, I thought I could crack it. I thought I was different, but now…"

She trailed off with a miserable sigh. "I've never had a spell I couldn't master," she said softly. "But I'm starting to think this one really is my Waterloo. I know I should keep trying anyway, but I've burned up every magical material in the house, including you, and I'm no closer to breaking it now than I was when I started." She slumped lower on the futon. "I don't know what to do."

Julius didn't either. "We'll figure it out," he said anyway.

"Or die trying," Marci said sullenly.

He was about to tell her that was no way to think when the back of his neck began to prickle. Marci went stiff at the same time, her head snapping up. "What the—"

Her words made him jump. He was the one with supernatural senses, and he hadn't heard or smelled anything. Sure enough, though, when he turned his head to follow hers, a dragoness was standing on the stairs, smiling at them over the rim of what looked like a two-gallon mimosa.

"I hope I'm not interrupting anything," Amelia said, though the blatant innuendo in her tone suggested otherwise.

Julius was too shocked to answer. His oldest sister, heir to his family and possibly the greatest dragon mage alive, was *in his house,* and he hadn't even smelled her coming. He supposed he could have blamed that on being exhausted, but Amelia was obviously not even trying to be stealthy. She was actually more outlandishly dressed than she'd been last night, wearing a cherry-red tank top, ancient ripped jeans, and chunky wedge flip-flops that hadn't been in style for a century. Her long black hair was pulled back in a messy pony tail, and her hazel eyes, always jarring in her clearly Heartstriker-featured face, were painfully smug as they drifted past him to lock on Marci with a broad smile.

"Who are you?" Marci demanded, shooting to her feet. "How did you get in here?"

"Easy, Sparky," Amelia said, grinning wider. "It takes more than a locked door and a few wards to keep me out. Besides," she pointed at Julius, "*he* invited me to come meet his human."

After what had happened with Bethesda, Julius didn't know how Marci would respond to that, but she just pulled herself straighter. "That's me," she said proudly. "But you still haven't said who *you* are."

"Don't you see the family resemblance?" Amelia asked, pointing at her face. "I'm his sister."

"He has a lot of those," Marci said, looking her up and down. "Are you Chelsie?"

Amelia's eyes went wide, and then she burst out laughing. "Me?" she whooped. "Miss Killjoy? Do I look like a humorless killing machine?"

Hearing Amelia talk that way about Chelsie raised every hair on Julius's body. He didn't even wait for her to finish laughing before he launched into a self-defensive round of proper introductions. "Marci," he said quickly, hopping to his feet. "This is Amelia, my oldest sister. Amelia, this is Marci Novalli, my mage and partner."

By the time he finished, Marci's eyes were as wide as eggs. "Amelia?" she said. "*A*-melia? But...doesn't that mean..."

"It means everything you fear and more, pet," Amelia said, her boisterous laughter cutting off as quickly as it had started. "But I promise I don't bite unless you ask. I just dropped by because I heard you had a Kosmolabe."

Marci opened her mouth, but Amelia beat her to it. "I already know you don't have it anymore," she said, strolling over to run her hand over the multiple rubbed out chalk circles on Marci's casting table. "Just tell me whatever you can about where and how you lost it, and I'll be on my—"

She cut off so suddenly, Julius thought maybe she'd hurt herself on the residual magic, but Amelia wasn't looking at the spellwork. She was staring at Marci's desk in the corner. Specifically, she was staring at the cat bed beside it where Ghost was still sleeping, his body curled into a furry, glowing ball.

"What is that?"

"My cat," Marci said defensively, stepping over to stand between Ghost and the dragon. "And Heartstriker or no, I'm not telling you anything about my Kosmolabe until you tell me why you want to know."

Any other time, Julius would have been both proud of Marci for standing up to a dragon as obviously dangerous as Amelia and terrified of what would happen because of it. Right now, though, all he felt was confusion, because Amelia didn't look angry at all. She didn't even seem to care that a human was talking back to her. She just pointed at Ghost and asked, in a trembling voice. "That's *your* spirit?"

"Yes," Marci said, crossing her arms over her chest. "Now, would you please—"

Amelia stepped in before she could finish, stopping right in front of Marci with a smile so genuine and friendly, she didn't even look like a dragon anymore. "I think we got off on the wrong foot," she said brightly. "Let's try this again. Hello, I'm Amelia the Planeswalker, and I am absolutely delighted to meet you,...?"

"Marci," Marci prompted.

"Marci," Amelia said, eyes sparkling. "May I pet your cat?"

By this point, Marci had gone from the usual healthy suspicion that came from having a dragon suddenly appear in your house to looking flat-out ready to fight. Julius wasn't far behind her. He had no idea what had caused his oldest sister to flip into best friend mode, but he didn't like it one bit. "What are you doing, Amelia?" he asked, walking over to stand beside Marci.

"What are *you* doing, Baby-J, asking such silly questions?" Amelia said, never letting up on her smile. "And I was talking to Marci, not you."

That made Julius more alarmed than ever, but Marci actually looked slightly mollified. "I suppose you can pet him," she said, turning around to scoop Ghost up off his pillow. "But I'll warn you. He's cold."

"Cold," Amelia whispered, placing her shaking hand on Ghost's back. "So he is." It didn't seem possible, but her smile got even wider. "Magnificent. Absolutely magnificent."

"Thank you," Marci said, giving the dragon an odd look as she clutched her sleeping spirit back against her chest. "Now, about the Kosmolabe—"

"Forget it," Amelia said, waving her hand dismissively. "It's just a long running side project. It can run a bit longer. We've got more important issues on our hands." Her light brown eyes flicked up. "Or necks, in your case."

Marci flinched, and Amelia's smile grew pointed. "Having a dragon hunter problem, are we?"

"How do you know about that?" Julius demanded.

Amelia rolled her eyes. "You have a human with a Sword of Damocles on her neck that reeks of Vann Jeger's magic. It doesn't exactly take Sherlock Holmes levels of deduction to guess what that's about. Though I am curious what you're planning to do."

Marci and Julius both dropped their eyes to the ground, and Amelia smirked. "Thought so," she said. "Up curse creek without a paddle, I see, but don't feel singled out. Targeting humans was always VJ's opening move. He almost got me that way once." She sighed. "I guess some things don't change."

Julius gaped. "*You* fought Vann Jeger?"

"Of course not," she said. "Why else do you think I'm still here? I did lose the human, though. Real pity, too. He was one of my best." She smiled at Marci, who'd gone very pale. "Not that that's going to happen to you, of course."

"So you know how to break the curse?" she asked, her voice so hopeful it hurt.

Amelia shook her head. "Nope. It's absolutely impossible. The Sword of Damocles curse is perfect in its simplicity. Once it gets in, nothing can stop it from fulfilling its purpose."

Marci looked instantly crestfallen, though not as much as Julius had feared. "Well," she said with a grim smile. "At least I know it isn't just me."

"Not at all," Amelia said. "But just because we can't break it doesn't mean it's going to kill you."

"How does that work?" Julius asked.

"Just because we can't crack the sword on her neck doesn't mean it has to fall," his sister said. "There are still conditions attached, right?"

Marci nodded. "I have to meet Vann Jeger tonight with a dragon."

"Well, there's your answer," Amelia said with a tip of her giant drink. "We'll show up, kick Vann Jeger to the curb, and wham, bam, your problem's solved. Thanks, Amelia!"

She finished with a grin, but Julius couldn't believe what he was hearing. "You can't be serious."

Amelia arched an eyebrow. "Can't I?"

"You *just said* you let your human die rather than fight him," he reminded her. "And it's not like Vann Jeger's working alone here. He's Algonquin's Hunter now, the Death of Dragons! Fighting him directly is suicide."

He was getting mighty sick of explaining that, but Amelia just looked down on him with an expression so haughty, even Julius, who got looked down on all the time, was impressed.

"Who do you think I am?"

Julius swallowed. "I know you're strong, but—"

"Strong?" Amelia scoffed. "You're not old enough to comprehend the word." She set down her drink, and the room seemed to grow heavy. He actually thought she'd cast a spell until he realized he didn't smell any power but Marci's. The pressure he felt wasn't magic. It was Amelia herself as she turned the full weight of her predatory attention on him.

"Do not confuse me with the rest of our scrabbling clan," she said quietly. "While those snakes coiled and plotted in Bethesda's shadow, hoping to catch a scrap of her power, I left and found my own. I am the Planeswalker, the last great dragon mage, unequaled in this world or any other. If I appear before him tonight, it is Vann Jeger who will be afraid."

169

From another dragon, Julius would have dismissed that as sheer bravado, but given the power Amelia could apparently turn on like a switch, he wasn't so sure. But while he was reeling from just how badly he'd miscalculated a potential threat, Marci grabbed on to another part of his sister's speech entirely.

"Dragon mage?"

Amelia smiled. "Didn't he tell you? I'm kind of a big deal." She turned back to Julius. "As to your question earlier, I didn't fight Vann Jeger in my youth because he was on his fjord then, and I wasn't stupid. But he's a long way from home out here, and I am older than I look." She smirked. "Age in dragons equals strength, but spirits never grow no matter how long they live. They are eternally limited by the land that birthed them, while I am limited by nothing but my own ability to survive. And, as my status as the last A proves, I'm *very* good at surviving."

She paused to let that sink in, taking a long sip of her drink before adding, "I'd be happy to use my phenomenal powers to crush Vann Jeger into a watery pulp. Provided, of course, you can pay my price."

Julius grit his teeth. He should have known that was coming. Dragons did nothing for free. Amelia had them over a barrel, too. She knew they couldn't possibly fight Vann Jeger, which was why she'd just made such a big deal that she could. Now, the only question left was, "What do you want?"

Amelia laughed. "From you? Nothing. You're adorable, Baby-J, but not very interesting. Your human, on the other hand, has much to offer, so I'll be dealing exclusively with her from now on, say over breakfast?"

This question was directed solely at Marci, who was staring at Amelia like the dragon was Santa Claus and a winning lottery ticket rolled into one. Before she could say what she was clearly going to say, though, Julius grabbed her arm and pulled her into the corner.

"What are you doing?" he whispered, putting his back to Amelia, who wasn't even pretending not to listen. "You can't trust her. She's a dragon."

"*You're* a dragon," Marci pointed out.

"That's different," Julius hissed, growing more afraid by the second. "We're talking about a serious power, here."

"But that's exactly what we need!" she whispered excitedly. "If breaking the curse is off the table, then our only other option is to find someone big enough to take on Vann Jeger. Plus, she's a dragon mage!" Her voice squeaked. "A *dragon mage*, Julius! One who worked with humans before the magic vanished!"

"I think you mean *owned* humans," he growled, but Marci wasn't listening.

"Just think of how much she must know!" she said, almost levitating with delight. "I blew it with Bethesda yesterday, but this could be my second chance, not to mention our only chance on the Vann Jeger front. I know you think she's dangerous, but—"

"I don't think, I *know*," Julius said. "You can't trust a word she says. For all we know, she planned this from the beginning."

Marci gave him a deeply skeptical look. "Are you implying she's responsible for Vann Jeger? Because that's ridiculous. She didn't even care about me until she saw Ghost."

"I don't like that, either," he grumbled. "And I'm not implying anything. I'm just saying dragons can't be trusted until you know what they're planning, and even then you can't be sure."

"I don't care if she's planning to eat me for dinner," Marci said, crossing her arms over her chest. "This is too good a chance on too many levels for us to possibly pass up. And it's not like she can kidnap me." She pointed at the sword on her neck. "I'm kind of leashed to the city at the moment, remember?"

Julius opened his mouth to remind her that didn't mean Amelia couldn't do something *inside* the city, but Marci cut him off. "I'm doing this."

The way she said that made it clear there'd be no changing her mind, and Julius sighed. "Fine," he said. "Just...just promise me you'll be careful. I don't want you to get hurt."

Marci smiled like that was the best thing he could have said. "That's amazingly sweet of you, Julius, but it's perfectly okay. I'm not going to get hurt, and I'm not going to do something dumb. Have a little faith."

"I do," he said earnestly. "But…"

She arched an eyebrow. "But?"

But you're a human, he wanted to say. And she's an ancient dragon who sees mortals as playthings and pawns. That match never ended well, but as much as he wanted to grab Marci and run away so Amelia couldn't take her, doing so would make him just as bad—another dragon ordering a human around like he owned her. Julius could never do that, which put him in a conundrum. One he'd been in for a while, actually, which stung, because it meant his brother had been right.

He had to pick. Was Marci his friend or his human? His equal or his servant? Because he couldn't have it both ways. He didn't want a human, though. He wanted his clever partner and ally. He wanted *her*, and so he stepped back with a shaky breath. "I trust you," he said quietly. "Do whatever you think is right."

She beamed and squeezed his hand before turning back to Amelia. "I'm ready."

"Thank goodness," the dragoness said. "That was getting too sappy to stomach." She knocked back the rest of her giant mimosa and vanished the bucket-sized glass with a flick of her hand. "So what's your pleasure? Waffles? Pancakes? The heads of your enemies on sticks?"

"Whatever you like is fine with me," Marci said, scooping up Ghost and placing him carefully in her shoulder bag, along with several notebooks. "I just want to get there quick. I have so many questions to ask—"

The slam of a door cut her off, and everyone jumped. Well, everyone except Amelia. She merely turned at a leisurely pace to face the doorway where Justin was now standing shirtless with Julius's sword in his hands.

Julius didn't even know how his brother had found Tyrfing's hiding spot in the ceiling, but he had it now, and he was pointing the needle-sharp tip straight at Amelia's face. "How did you get in here?"

"Justin, stop," Julius said. "Can't you see she's our sister?"

"Impossible," his brother growled, looking Amelia up and down. "She doesn't have the eyes."

"And you, clearly, don't have the brains," Amelia said, glancing back at Julius. "Which one is this? I can't keep all you babies straight."

"This is Justin," Julius said quickly. "The Fifth Blade of Bethesda. Justin, this is our sister Amelia."

Justin's scowl faded. "Amelia?"

Julius nodded.

"*A*-melia?"

Amelia rolled her eyes to the ceiling. "Yes," she said loudly. "*AAAAAAAA*-melia. Seriously, do you kids do that to everyone? Because if so, we're going to have a long talk about manners."

She flashed them both a condescending smile, to which Justin responded by baring his teeth. "How do I know you're who you say?"

"Hmm," Amelia said, tapping her finger against her chin. "I could turn you into dragon hamburger. Would that suffice? But then, how do *I* know *you're* who you say?" She looked pointedly at Tyrfing's narrow blade. "You seem to be short the necessary equipment for a Fifth Blade."

Julius winced. Of all the things she could have chosen to pick on, she had to pick that.

"You'll be missing something soon!" Justin snarled, taking a menacing step forward. "If you really are Amelia, then I don't need my Fang to teach you a lesson. Everyone knows you're a coward who ran to hide on the outer planes rather than doing her duty to the clan."

"Is that what they're saying about me now?" Amelia said, clutching her chest dramatically. "I'm wounded. But then again—" her hurt look fell away "—even after being branded for cowardice, my position is *still* better than yours. How many Fifth Blades have there been now? Ten? Eleven?" She shrugged. "They die so fast, I can't keep track. But I guess that's how it is when your job is to be Bethesda's attack dog." She gave Justin a cruel smile. "Maybe I should be congratulating you for slipping your leash? Who's a good boy?"

By this point, Justin's growl was rattling the floorboards, and Julius decided it was time to intervene before structural damage occurred. "Let's just stop," he said, putting his hands up. "We're all on the same team here."

"She's on no team of mine," Justin snapped, looking down his sword, which was still pointed at Amelia's head. "She's a traitor, Julius. A Heartstriker in name only. She's been living on the outer planes for years, refusing all of Mother's summons. I don't know why she's back now, but it's not to help us."

Amelia lifted her chin. "Maybe it's different for you, whelp, but *dragons* don't come when called. I'm here because it suits me. No more, no less. Now."

She flicked her finger, and magic roared into the room. It slid through the air like a heated knife, overpowering even the scent of Marci's spellwork before turning to focus on Justin. He jerked a second later, his whole body shooting bolt upright on his tip-toes like he'd been grabbed and lifted by a giant, invisible hand. He was wiggling there in vain when Amelia walked over to pat him on the head.

"That's better," she cooed, plucking Tyrfing from his frozen hands and tossing it to Julius, who caught it only by reflex. "Angry children shouldn't play with knives."

Justin's eyes widened, but with her magic holding him, he couldn't even open his mouth. Amelia knew it, too, and she grinned like a fiend as she reached up to pinch his cheeks. "Poor little baby. You might be big for your age, but we both know you're just an overgrown whelp pretending he can keep up with the big kids." She tilted her head back toward Julius. "You clearly think your brother is less than you, but at least he has the good sense to know when he's outclassed. You, on the other hand, are like a mad bull in a bullfight, and unless you wise up real quick, with about the same life expectancy. That's why I'm going to do you a favor."

She touched him on the shoulder, and Julius felt the magic holding Justin double. "There," she said, smiling. "Now you *can't* be stupid. See what a loving sister I am?"

By this point, smoke was pouring out of Justin's mouth. Amelia ignored it completely, turning instead to beckon Marci over.

"You stay here with your adorable brother and think about your poor life choices," she said as the mage hurried to her side. "Meanwhile, Marci and I are going to go discuss my price for dispatching Vann Jeger in private. We should be back with your salvation in an hour or so." She lifted her arm and smiled at Marci. "Shall we?"

If Marci had beamed at Amelia before, she was now looking at the dragon like Amelia was her own personal hero. She grabbed her offered arm, hefting the bag containing the still sleeping Ghost onto her shoulder as she waved goodbye to Julius and, more pointedly, to Justin. That only made the trapped dragon puff smoke harder, but it was all for nothing. Amelia and Marci were out the door, their footsteps hurrying down the stairs. But then, when they reached the first floor, the footfalls vanished. Marci's scent vanished as well, leaving the house unmistakably empty. A few seconds later, the magic holding Justin vanished as well, dropping the dragon on the floor in a furious heap.

"Where is she?"

"I think they're gone," Julius said, already worried. He had no idea how a dragon and a mage could vanish instantly like that, but it couldn't be good. But as much as he wanted to run down and check, he had to deal with his brother first, because Justin looked ready to burn the house to the ground. "Would you calm down?"

"Calm down?" Justin yelled. "*Calm down?* What is wrong with you?"

"What's wrong with *you?*" Julius cried. "Barging in here and threatening our sister when she's just trying to—"

"If you say 'help,' I'm going to throw you out that window," his brother snarled. "Amelia doesn't help anyone but herself."

"How is that different from every dragon?" Julius asked, shaking his head. "What's your grudge against her, anyway? She's been off this plane since before we were born."

Justin drew himself to his full height. "Unlike you, I'm not ignored by everyone important. I've heard plenty about the Planeswalker. She's a high-functioning alcoholic who'd sell out her own mother for an inch up the magical ladder."

"Again," Julius said. "How is that different from every dragon? Mother tried to sell me out just last month, in case you forgot."

"Would you stop being bitter and listen?" Justin snapped. "Amelia isn't like the rest of us. Even before she started spending all her time on the outer planes, she was weird. Plenty of dragons like having humans around, but Amelia's a crazy cat lady, except replace 'cats' with 'humans.' Conrad told me once that she had a whole village of the bastards back in the old days, and now you're trusting her with yours?"

"That's just gossip," Julius said, trying not to sound alarmed. "And anyway, this is Marci's decision. She's not an idiot, and her life's the one on the line here. I trust her to take care of herself and make her own decisions."

"Are you stupid?" Justin shouted, getting in his face. "She's *your* human! If she's making any decisions, it should be how best to serve *you!*"

Julius stepped back. "What the—*You're* the one who told me I had to choose if she was my human or my friend!"

"I didn't think you'd pick *friend!*" Justin roared. "Seriously, who does that?" He looked away with a growl. "I swear, Julius, if I hadn't hatched next to you, I wouldn't believe we were the same species."

Julius looked away as well. He was so tired of constantly coming up short in his brother's estimation, especially when Justin was being such a stubborn, pig-headed *idiot.* "Well, it doesn't matter now, anyway," he said. "Marci will bring Amelia around because she's brilliant like that, and then this'll all be over."

"Not happening," Justin said. "Vann Jeger is *my* kill!"

"You mean your death," Julius snapped, turning to face him head on. "I know you think you can beat everything, but it's time to face the truth, Justin, and the truth is that if you go up against Vann Jeger, you will *die*. Marci and I will probably die, too, and Algonquin will get a nice new set of dragon heads for her collection. Amelia might well be everything you say, but she's also the only one of us who has a real chance against that monster. I understand you're desperate to prove you're hot stuff and get your sword back, but you're going to have to find somewhere else to show off. I'm not letting you gamble all our lives for your stupid pride!"

He was yelling by the time he finished, and Justin's eyes narrowed. "Big words from a whelp who can't even swing a sword properly," he growled. "But I don't take orders from the Failure of the Heartstrikers. I *will* have my fight, and there's nothing you can do to stop me."

He stalked closer with every word, his eyes gleaming a menacing green. Normally, that kind of pressure would have sent Julius scrambling back, but not today. There was too much at stake to back down now, and Julius was so, so *sick* of being pushed around.

"I don't have to stop you," he said, glaring up at the towering dragon. "Because you don't know where it is."

His brother arched a skeptical eyebrow, and Julius reached up to tap the side of his neck. "The fight location is marked on Marci's tattoo, and since she's not here, that means you have no idea where to go. I'm not telling you, either, because I don't want you to die."

Justin bared his teeth. "You can't be—"

"I am," Julius snarled. "I am deadly serious. You are *not* going to the fight tonight, and if you try to crash it, the Planeswalker will just lock you down again. Either way, your life's going to be saved whether you want it to be or not, so you might as well accept it."

Justin's answer to that was to blow a long, hot plume of smoke through his teeth, and for several terrified heartbeats, Julius was sure this was it. He'd finally pushed his brother too far, and now he was going to be burned to death. But just as he was preparing for the end, Justin turned away.

"You always were the master of hiding behind bigger dragons," he said, resting Tyrfing on his bare shoulder. "But one day, Julius, you're going to wake up and realize that there's more to life than merely staying alive. I just hope, for your sake, that there's something left worth conquering."

"Not all of us want to conquer everything in our path," Julius reminded him, but his brother was already stomping down the stairs. Seconds later, Julius's bedroom door slammed so hard, several of Marci's empty chalk boxes fell off the shelves. Julius picked them up again with a sigh, fighting the urge to go down and apologize. So what if Justin was mad? He had nothing to say sorry for. His brother would just have to deal with not committing suicide by Vann Jeger tonight.

But even as he told himself that he was right and Justin was being a stubborn idiot, the knotted feeling in his chest only got tighter. He wrote it off as being exhausted, starved, and magically drained. He just needed rest and food and maybe a do-over button for this whole horrible twenty-four hours. Since that last one was out of the question, he settled for going downstairs to raid the fridge, emptying the contents of every takeout box onto a single plate. He didn't even bother warming it up, just shoveled the whole thing into his mouth as fast as possible before collapsing on the living room couch. Upstairs, he could hear his brother stomping around in his room, but Julius couldn't deal with Justin anymore right now. He couldn't deal with anything, so he turned over, shutting his eyes against the world as he willed himself into instant, exhausted, dreamless sleep.

CHAPTER NINE

When she followed Amelia downstairs from the workshop, Marci expected her to take them outside to a car, maybe even a limo like the one Bethesda had arrived in. Instead, the dragon led her into the kitchen, where a door-sized hole in reality was hanging in the air in front of their refrigerator.

Marci stopped cold, eyes wide. "Is-is that—"

"A portal?" Amelia finished, ducking through. "Naturally. Now come along so I can let the idiot go before he wastes all my magic."

Marci could only suppose Amelia was talking about Justin. Another time, the implications of that comment would've been interesting to explore, if only to shed some light on how dragons actually cast spells. At the moment, though, Marci was too distracted by the *floating gateway* to properly follow up. "Is that really a portal to another dimension?!"

"Nope, this one goes uptown. Portals to the planes are way more dramatic. Now come on."

She stuck her arm back through the hole and snapped her fingers impatiently. Eyes wide as they could go, Marci obeyed, carefully stepping through the door-shaped gap. The moment she reached the other side, the hole vanished, leaving her standing alone with Amelia in a small, cement room with a single metal door.

The similarities to the bleak prison cell where Vann Jeger interrogated her were enough to make Marci instantly nervous, but there was no drain in the floor this time, and the "door" was nothing but a flimsy, corrugated metal sheet that slid up on a track. Once she got over her initial shock, the little room actually reminded Marci more of a storage unit than anything else.

"That's because it *is* a storage unit," Amelia answered proudly when she asked. "Best security you can get for the price! Plus, no one bothers you."

"You *sleep* in a self-storage unit?" Marci said, horrified. The closet-sized room was barely big enough for the two of them to stand in.

"Of course not," Amelia scoffed. "I just needed somewhere safe to hide *this*."

She reached out as she spoke, rapping her knuckles against the unit's rear wall. A split second later, the painted cement bricks vanished to reveal the most beautiful beach Marci had ever seen.

Turquoise water lapped in small, gentle waves in a crescent bay under a pink and blue sky just on the cusp of sunset. The white sand beach was speckled with black, volcanic boulders and bordered by an explosion of tropical vegetation so dense, it looked like a wall of green. Directly in front of them, in the dry sand above the surf, someone had set up a wooden table shielded from the sun by a large beach umbrella with heaps of beautiful, ripe, tropical fruits and a metal bucket loaded with ice and what appeared to be bottles of high-proof rum.

The whole setup was so absurdly picture-perfect, Marci would have sworn it was an illusion, but even the best illusions covered only two to three senses at the most. Here, though, not only could she see the beautiful landscape stretching out in front of her, she could smell the warm sea air coming in like a caress. The setting sunlight that streamed through the gap was hot and balmy on her skin, and when Amelia kicked off her shoes and stepped through, her bare feet slid into the sand with a silken *kush*.

After that, Marci had no choice but to accept that there really was a hole in the wall in front of her that led to paradise. But when she reached down to plunge her own fingers into the warm, white sand, pain shot through her neck like a knife, making her jump back with a strangled gasp.

"Interesting," Amelia said, glancing back at Marci's pained sound before resuming her stroll to the fruit-laden table. "Looks like your curse is pretty literal. You really can't set so much as a finger outside the DFZ."

"So it would seem," Marci said, rubbing her throbbing neck. "So is *that* another plane?"

"Wrong again," the dragon replied, grabbing the heaping bowl of fruit off the table. "Keeping a portal to the outer planes open for more than a few minutes is beyond even my abilities. This is a little island of no consequence in what you now call the Philippines. I've been using it as my base of operations in this world for centuries. The tropical climate agrees with my plumage." She walked back to the portal and stuck the bowl through, placing the fragrant fruit just below Marci's nose. "Mango?"

Marci took the offered yellow fruit without looking. She'd never been to the Philippines personally, but the island's beauty certainly matched any tropical postcard. Also, being on the other side of the planet would explain why the sun looked to be on the verge of setting behind Amelia despite the fact that it was early morning in Detroit. But what she still didn't get was, "How?"

Amelia arched an eyebrow. "How what?"

"How can you do *this*?" Marci said, flailing her arms at the gently cresting waves. "Dimensional magic is one of the most competitive fields in modern sorcery. All the top universities are working on it, but the biggest portal I've ever heard of was MIT's last year, and that was barely the size of a dime. You've got a whole wall! And you opened it *inside* the same dimension. I didn't even know that was *possible*."

"Hey, they don't call me the Planeswalker for nothing," Amelia said smugly, grabbing a mango for herself before dropping the bowl back onto the table. "Don't worry about it too much. Proper portal creation takes longer than a single human lifetime to master. You see those seams?" She pointed at the edge where the beach met the storage unit like a razor slice. "It takes centuries to get to that level

181

of precision. But I had a lot of time to practice, and portals to my own private island are much more convenient than actually trying to live in Algonquin's playpen. But enough about me." She plopped down into the folding beach chair beside the table, leaning back to face Marci with a wide grin. "Let's talk about your spirit."

Her voice was still casual and friendly, but the abrupt subject change was enough to remind Marci that this wasn't actually a beach trip. "Why are you so interested?" she asked, clutching her bag where Ghost was still snoozing, blissfully unaware.

"He's a unique specimen," Amelia replied, reaching into the ice-filled bucket beside her to grab a frosted bottle of rum. "So are you, for that matter. New sights are a rarity at my age, so when I find one, I don't waste time." She popped the cork with her teeth and took a long swig of the cold, amber liquor. "Assuage my curiosity," she ordered when she finished. "Tell me how you ended up bound to him."

Marci frowned. She hadn't needed Julius to warn her that telling dragons anything before you knew their end goal was a bad idea. That said, Amelia *had* answered all of her questions so far. It seemed wrong not to return the favor. Besides, the entire reason she'd agreed to go with Amelia had been to get a chance to pick an ancient dragon's brain. Maybe if she told the truth, Amelia would be able to shed some light on what had happened in the alleyway?

"I kind of got him by accident," Marci confessed. "My very first job in the DFZ was a haunting job. Most so-called hauntings are actually caused by spirits, so I came prepared for a banishing, but when I reached my client, Ghost was sitting on her chest draining her magic. I'd never seen a spirit do anything like that before, but I didn't exactly have a lot of time to investigate since my client was nearly dead by the time I got there. So, since banishing Ghost would have meant I'd never get to answer my questions, I decided to bind him instead. That was a little over a month ago. We've been together ever since."

"Hold up," Amelia said, leaning forward in her beach chair. "You found an unknown spirit sucking the life out of another human, and you decided to bind him to your own soul for the rest of your life just so you'd get a chance to poke at him later?"

Marci's cheeks began to burn. "It's not as bad as it sounds," she said quickly. "I'm no expert at spirits—my training is in Thaumaturgical spellwork theory—but even I could tell that Ghost was too small to be a threat. The only reason he was able to over-power my client in the first place was because she was already old and sick. I was perfectly safe, and I couldn't send him away without at least trying to figure out what he was."

That came out more defensive than she'd intended, but Amelia was grinning ear to ear. "You mistake me," she said. "I wasn't being critical. I appreciate your audacity. Were you successful, then? Do you know what he is?"

Marci had no choice but to shake her head. "My first hypothesis was that he was a death spirit. I'd never heard of a non-human one, but the house where I found him was overrun with cats, and there was more than enough death for a manifestation."

"A death spirit of cats," the dragon said, pausing for a long, thoughtful draw off her rum bottle. "That's a new one. And do you still think that's the case?"

"No," Marci said. "At the time, I was hoping I'd discovered a new classification, but Ghost has never acted like a death spirit, so now I'm not sure what he is. I was actually about to start experimenting when this Vann Jeger nonsense blew up." She smiled at the dragon, crossing her fingers in secret where she held her bag. "Do you know what he is?"

She'd just meant to fish for clues, but to her amazement, Amelia actually seemed to be giving her question serious consideration. "There's a lot of answers to that," she said at last. "You claimed you weren't an expert on spirits. What does that mean?"

"Well," Marci said. "I mean, obviously I know the basics. Every licensed mage in the U.S. has to learn how to bind and banish and so forth for their own protection. But the study of spirits is part of the Shamanic branch of magic, and I'm a Thaumaturge. We deal with the more rigorous, scientific aspects of magical theory."

"I've been gone for fifty years, so I have no idea what you're talking about," Amelia said with a shrug. "But I'm guessing all of that was a fancy way of saying spirits aren't your area?"

Marci sighed. "More or less."

"Don't worry," Amelia said. "If spirit studies are like the rest of modern magical theory, they're all wrong anyway. It's actually easier if you don't know anything, because that means I can start with the basics. Here."

She took another quick drink off her rum bottle and set it back in the ice bucket. With her hands free, she turned her chair around and started digging a hole in the wet sand behind her.

"Think of magic in this plane like this water," she said, moving her hands to show Marci the seawater that was seeping up through the bottom of the sandy hole she'd dug. "It wells up constantly from the Earth at a more or less even rate. Like water, magic's not picky. It'll fill anything that'll hold it." She expanded the simple hole into a cross shape as she said this, and sure enough, the water followed, filling the canals with foamy salt water.

"On the beach, of course, we're uphill, so the water only goes part way. But if this beach were perfectly flat, the water would fill each of these depressions to overflowing before moving to the next one. Magic is the same."

She turned her chair back around to face Marci again, grabbing her rum for another swig before continuing. "It's like water welling up in a flat field. If there are any depressions—ditches, holes, low areas, etc.—it will fill those first before flowing on. Once filled, these puddles of magic take on the characteristics of the land that contains them. This is why magic feels different in different places. It's literally taking on a different shape depending on what it's filling. *But*, if the vessel in question is large and deep enough, eventually the enormous amount of magic filling it will reach critical mass. When this happens, the magic itself can develop sentience and become what we know as a spirit."

She paused there, shooting Marci an *Are you following all this?* look, but Marci could only stare back in awe. She'd never heard anything like this. Everyone knew that magic rose from the ground, but no one yet understood why that was, or why certain locations had different magic than others. There were dozens of competing theories as to why some places—like the Great Lakes—had spirits while others did not, but nothing had ever been proven. This, though, this made *sense*.

"Spirits are sentient magic," she said, her voice shaking. "I always thought a domain was just the specific place a spirit had control over, like Algonquin and her lakes, but it's the other way around! The domain is what contains the magic that becomes the spirit, because spirits *are* magic!"

Amelia smiled. "Like that, huh?"

"*Like* it?" Marci plunged her hands into her bag, pulling out her notebook so fast, she tugged them right through Ghost. "I have to write this down!"

The more she thought about Amelia's explanation, the more things clicked together. Her whole life, all of her teachers had talked about spirits like they were just a different, more powerful type of magical animal, but that had never really made sense. A tank badger had magic, sure, but it was nothing like a spirit. It couldn't vanish and reappear like Ghost could, and no magical animal had ever talked to her in her head. But if she accepted the idea that spirits weren't physical at all, but *sentient magic* that thought and acted for itself, that explained so much! That was why she'd been able to bind Ghost in the first place, because he was just more magic, the same stuff she touched and moved around all the time.

And the drought! She'd always thought the name for the thousand-year span when there'd been no magic was just poetic, but what if it was *literal*? What if the magic really had dried up like a river in a drought? That would explain why the spirits had all been forced into sleep, and why they'd all come roaring back the moment the meteor got the magical flow going again. Unlike magical animals—including human mages—who'd merely been altered by the sudden influx of magic, spirits had been practically reborn on the spot, because they *were* magic. Unified, self-aware, sentient *magic*.

Grinning like a maniac, Marci paused scribbling her notes and jumped back to the top of the page, writing the words *SENTIENT MAGIC THEORY* across the head of her notebook in bold stokes. Forget earning her doctorate, *this* was the sort of magical break-through that got your name in the history books! All she needed now was proof—some kind of experiment that would show defini-tively that spirits weren't a separate class of magical animal or gods or whatever the current popular theories claimed, but thinking, moving blobs of self-aware magic—and she'd be famous *forever* as the mage who finally cracked spirit theory. They'd awarded the Nobel Prize in Magic for less. And here she'd thought her academic career was over!

That thought snapped her back to the present, and Marci looked up to see Amelia watching her with a bored expression and a nearly empty bottle of booze. That wouldn't do at all. She'd finally found an immortal willing to talk to her about magic, and the results had already gone beyond her wildest expectations. She couldn't let Amelia get bored with her now. Who knew what other secrets she had to offer?

"Sorry," Marci said, scanning her page one last time to be sure she had all the key points down before closing her notebook. "Got carried away." She paused, suddenly worried. "You don't mind if I tell other people about this, do you?"

"Knock yourself out," Amelia said, downing the last inch of rum and tossing the empty bottle into the sand at her feet before dig-ging into the ice bucket for a fresh one. "Believe it or not, this stuff used to be common knowledge. If I'd known human magic was this far behind on the fundamentals, I'd have come back decades ago just to save myself the pain of watching you all make the same mis-takes all over again."

"That's not our fault," Marci said hotly. "There was no one teach us! All the old books and resources on magic were either destroyed by time or burned by the ignorant as heretical. By the time magic actually came back, most people believed it had never existed in the first place. That's not even starting at zero. The first mages had to work their way up from negative knowledge, and the whole time, the spirits and dragons were just watching and not telling us anything!"

"Why should they?" Amelia said, popping the cork on her new bottle. "Human mages used to be at the top of the food chain, killing dragons and banishing spirits. The only thing that kept you in check was the fact that most of you died of preventable causes before you could become really dangerous. With the modern explosion in the human population, though, there are more mages alive right now than have ever existed in all the previous history of mankind combined. Your astounding ignorance is the only thing that keeps you from ruling the world on all levels. Frankly, I wouldn't be surprised if there were hidden dragons embedded in academic magic circles purely for the purpose of feeding you false information to keep it that way."

Considering how long a few incredibly stupid theories had stuck around in otherwise respectable circles of magical thought, Marci didn't actually find that idea too far-fetched. "So why are *you* telling me now?"

"Because I don't have to stick around for the aftermath," Amelia said with a wink. "I can leave this plane anytime I want. Also, I'd love to see certain individuals taken down a peg or two. Watching a new generation of dragon slayers rise up to take down the old guard would be *very* satisfying." She paused for an evil grin before taking another slug off her bottle. "Shall we continue? I still haven't actually answered your question, and I'd like to get this over with before the sun goes down and the mosquitoes come out."

"Of course," Marci said, flipping her notebook open again. "Please go on."

"You asked me when we started if I knew what kind of spirit your kitten there was," Amelia said, settling back into her chair. "The short answer to that is yes, but the long answer is a bit more complicated, and has to do with you."

Marci blinked. "Me?"

Amelia nodded. "As you might have guessed from what I said earlier, spirit classification is a tricky business. Traditionally, spirits

187

are organized into four types according to their vessels. The most common type of spirit are those whose power gathers in physical landmasses, like, say, the Great Lakes. We call these spirits Spirits of the Land, and they tend to be the heavy hitters of the spirit world since they're the magical embodiment of freaking giant mountains and whatever. Really, though, anywhere magic pools for long enough can become a spirit. Animals, for example. If enough animals get together in a population, their collective magic pools to form an Animal Spirit."

"I've seen plenty of those," Marci said, thinking of the tank badger spirit she'd banished yesterday evening. "They don't seem to be as powerful, though."

"They're not," Amelia said, nodding. "But that's a volume issue. Even if a critter is super magical, it takes a *lot* of them all living together to create a magical depression as big as the Great Lakes. Most animal populations simply never reach that size, and so Animal Spirits tend to be weaker, smaller, and stupider than their geological counterparts."

Marci nodded, writing all this down as fast as her pen would go.

"Animals and land are the obvious ones, though," the dragon went on. "Stuff gets really crazy when you get into death spirits. Strictly speaking, death spirits aren't even really a formal category. It's more of a catch-all term for the phenomenon that occurs when so many individuals die all at once, the combined release of their magic creates a temporary glut big enough to become a spirit. This is why death spirits come in so many different forms, and why they almost never stick around for very long. Because they're formed by a temporary magical surge instead of filling a vessel, there's nothing permanent holding them together. Once the natural ebb and flow of magic disperses the glut that created them, death spirits fade right back into oblivion, never to be seen again."

Marci jotted that down, looking up again when Amelia didn't continue to find the dragon sitting back in her chair, drinking her rum in long, thoughtful sips.

"Um, that's only three," she said nervously. "You said there were four classifications of spirit."

Amelia nodded. "I did."

"So what's the last one?"

The dragon's smile turned cryptic. "You tell me," she said with a tip of her bottle. "It goes against my nature to give away too much for free, and Julius spoke *so* highly of you."

Marci began to sweat. "You want me to guess?"

"It's not hard," Amelia said with a shrug. "Spirits occur anywhere the naturally welling magic flows into a definite shape: a lake, a wolf population, a slaughtered city. But there's another force at work that moves and shapes magic all the time which we haven't mentioned yet. What is it?"

Marci bit her lip. Being put on the spot always made her nervous, but she didn't think Amelia was the sort who'd ask her a question she couldn't answer. She just had to look at what she already knew and follow the clues. What force hadn't they mentioned yet? What power could push and hold enough magic together to reach the critical mass necessary to gain sentience and—

"Humans," she blurted out. "We move magic. That's the final kind of spirit."

Amelia's face split into a wide grin. "I knew you were a clever monkey," she said. "You're right. The final classification of spirits are what used to be called Mortal Spirits, the magic that gathers in the dips and scars left in magical landscape by mankind."

"Is that what Ghost is?" Marci asked, too excited to even write this down. "But how? He doesn't look human."

"It's more complicated than that," Amelia said. "Haven't you ever wondered why there's a spirit of wolves, but not a spirit of humans?"

Marci nodded. "People have been looking for our Animal Spirit pretty much since we knew they were a thing, but we've never found one. The articles I read on the subject theorized that humanity was simply too divided to have a single spirit that represented us as a whole."

"That's actually not too far off," Amelia said, looking impressed despite herself. "The factor you're missing, though, is that the human animal is unique. There are thousands of magical species that burst back into the ecosystem in the years after the meteor hit, but of all those plants and animals and insects and fish and whatnot, humans are the only ones who have the ability to actually *manipulate* magic. All of you, even non-mages, are capable of leaving eddies in the magical landscape, and when you get enough of those eddies all working together, you create ruts for magic to fill."

Marci added that to her notes. "What kind of ruts?"

Amelia shrugged. "Whatever you believe in. The more importance humans collectively give to something, the deeper a mark it leaves in your collective magical landscape. Take death, for instance. All mortals fear dying to the point where they will do nearly anything to avoid its inevitable grasp. That sort of universal preoccupation has *weight*, it leaves a very deep chasm indeed."

"Hold up," Marci said, eyes going wide. "You're saying Mortal Spirits are *concepts*?"

"That's exactly what I'm saying," Amelia said. "There are over nine billion humans on the planet right now. Every one of those nine billion, mage or not, has the ability to alter the magical landscape around them. Individually, of course, those changes are minute, but the more humans as a whole care about something—a belief, a fear, an ideology, whatever you want to call it—the bigger a space they carve out for it in their lives. Each one of these hollows creates a place for magic to pool, and where magic pools, spirits are born." The dragon smiled. "As you might imagine, the combined weight of humanity's concerns made for some very large spirits indeed. Many Mortal Spirits were worshiped as gods before the magic vanished, just to give you an idea of the scale we're talking about."

"And you think Ghost is one of these?" Marci said, looking down at her cat, who was still sound asleep at the bottom of her bag. "I'm sorry, but I'm having trouble buying this. If Mortal Spirits are as big as you say, why haven't we seen any? Why isn't the Grim Reaper riding through war zones taking heads right now?"

"Because there hasn't been enough time, yet," Amelia said. "Magic's only been pouring back into the world for six decades. That's enough to fill the shallow vessels—the lakes and mountains and animals—but Mortal Spirits are as large as human ideas. The impressions you gouge into the Earth's magical landscape have gone from the weight of millions to the weight of billions since the last time magic was here to fill them. Add in the advent of world-wide media and mass communication, and the ruts of humanity's shared beliefs and values have become so deep and so vast, modern magic simply hasn't had time yet to fill them. The water is running, but the bucket is just too big. Make sense?"

It did, but Marci still didn't understand what this had to do with Ghost. "But," she said, feeling slightly foolish. "If that's true, how is Ghost here?"

"Well, that's the question, isn't it?" Amelia said, sitting up with a grin. "Mortal Spirits have always been a particular fascination of mine. I wasn't actually planning on returning to this plane for at least another fifty years since that was the earliest my calculations suggested a Mortal Spirit could appear. Imagine my surprise, then, when I come back to do a favor for my brother and find not just a Mortal Spirit, but one that's already stably bound to a mage. Do you even know how amazing that is?"

"I'm starting to get an idea," Marci said, clutching her bag where Ghost was sleeping even tighter. "So, is he premature or something? Is that why he's so small?"

"That's a good theory," Amelia said. "Honestly, though, I have no idea. He's a mystery!" She beamed with excitement. "Now do you see why I wanted to talk to you so badly?"

Marci did, but the more she thought about all of this, the more what Ghost had said in the alley bothered her. "You said Mortal Spirits are created by collective human ideas, like death. That means they're not all good?"

"Good is relative," Amelia said dismissively. "But being doomed to die makes humans a fairly pessimistic species, so I suppose most Mortal Spirits could be classified as unpleasant, yes."

Considering her cat seemed to feed off death and was cold as the grave, Marci wasn't feeling optimistic about her chances. "Is there a way to identify them, then?" she asked. "I asked Ghost what he was straight-out yesterday, but he claimed he didn't know his name. He said he couldn't remember unless I fed him power."

"He probably can't," the dragon said, squinting at Marci's bag. "Poor little thing's barely more than a flicker. If he wasn't anchored to you, I doubt he could even hold himself together. It's no wonder he doesn't know his name."

"So he *was* telling the truth," Marci said, relieved. "I was a little worried he was just playing me for more power."

"He was probably doing both," Amelia said. "Like I said, all spirits are self-aware magic, but *how* self-aware depends on how much power they have access to. Given how low yours is running, it's completely possible he doesn't even know what he's a spirit of."

"So what happens if I do feed him magic, then?"

The dragon frowned thoughtfully. "Difficult to say. Without knowing what type of Mortal Spirit we're talking about, it's impossible to predict how he'll react once he gets above the threshold for true self-awareness. But that's a question for later. All you need to understand right now is that your spirit could potentially be a Very Big Deal. Equally important, though, is the fact that he allowed *you* to bind him."

Marci nodded. "You said something like that before. Why is the binding part so important?"

"It's the choice that's important, not the binding," Amelia said. "Mortal Spirits are the magical creations of humanity's fears and beliefs and so on. As such, they tend to be *really into* whatever aspect of your kind they represent. Depending on what they're a spirit of, this obsessive focus can make them critically unstable. So, to prevent a collapse, most Mortal Spirits are drawn to mages whose strengths help to balance them out." She frowned. "Or, at least, that's how it used to work before the magic vanished. Since we don't know what kind of spirit we're dealing with yet, I don't know if that's why Ghost picked you specifically, but however it came to be, binding him was a pro move on your part."

"How so?" Marci asked.

"Because by tying your magic to his, you've now effectively plugged into the domain of Mortal Spirits, which is basically all human magic," Amelia explained, her eyes flashing. "That's *big*, Marci. Way too big to risk losing to an obsessed idiot like Vann Jeger, or a fool like Julius."

Marci jerked back. "What?"

"Oh, come on," Amelia said, rolling her eyes. "He's a sweet kid, but you have to know by now that your baby dragon isn't exactly a power player. You're a mage with a Mortal Spirit, possibly the *very first* Mortal Spirit to re-emerge. I don't know how or why Ghost happened, but your connection to him puts you decades ahead of the curve." The dragon flashed her a knowing smile. "You are a very valuable commodity, Marci Novalli, and you deserve better than some random kid at the bottom of Heartstriker. You *need* better. You need me."

It took Marci a few seconds to be sure she'd heard that right. "Are you trying to *recruit* me?"

"Don't sound so surprised," she said. "Did you not understand what I just told you? You are a prime asset. I'm just happy I decided to drop by Julius's and found you before Vann Jeger ruined everything."

She said this casually, like she was just pointing out the obvious, but Marci could already see the writing on the wall. "That's the deal, isn't it?" she said, staring the dragon down. "That's why you wanted to get me alone. You'll save us from Vann Jeger, but only if I join you."

"You make it sound like a bad thing," Amelia said, pouting. "Surely you've grasped by now just how much a real alliance with a proper dragon would benefit you? Or did you think I spent the last thirty minutes telling you the secrets of magic out of the goodness of my heart?"

Marci had. Or, rather, she'd been too excited about what she was hearing to worry about the cost, and from the smug look on her face, Amelia knew it.

"The first hit is free," she cooed. "But there's *so* much more. I was born only a century after Bethesda herself. That makes me a contemporary of many of the mages you now think of as legends." She pointed up the coast toward the main body of the island. "You can't see it through the trees, but I have a tower on the northern coast with a library full of their writings. Books, scrolls, letters explaining the highest workings of magic, I have it all. That's *my* treasure. While other dragons hoarded gold and weapons and the various other material trappings of power, I hoarded *knowledge*, which we both know is far more valuable. It's all still there, too. Even while I was away on the outer planes, my protections kept it safe all this time. You think what I just told you was amazing? That's nothing. Child's play. My collection of magical texts was the envy of the world even before the new generations of mortal idiots became terrified by the idea of magic and started burning the treasures of their past. Now, it can be yours as well. Yours *specifically*, Marci Novalli, and all you have to do is promise your life to me."

By the time she finished, Marci's heart was hammering. "What do you mean, 'promise my life'?"

"It means you would be my human," Amelia explained. "I understand if you have some confusion with the concept given the ridiculous way Julius treats you, but I promise you'd enjoy it. Unlike some dragons, I treat my mortals like treasures. You'd live here with me in this paradise, and I'd give you the best of everything. One month in my library would be enough to make you the greatest mage alive. The knowledge you'll emerge with will make the last sixty-years of magical theory look like the dark ages, and that's only the beginning. Once we get your Mortal Spirit up to speed, the full potential of human magic will be within our reach once again."

"*Our* reach?" Marci said, confused. "But you're a dragon. What do you care about human magic?"

"I care because this is *your* world," Amelia said, rising to her feet. "Dragons are just interlopers on this plane, but you were born to master it. There are places here that only you can go, things you can do that no spirit or dragon can touch. I want to see that. Like you, I want to *know*, but, being a dragon, I can't do it on my own. You and your spirit are the chance I've been waiting on for ten centuries. Ally with me, and I'll give you everything you could ever want: power, knowledge, safety, comfort, fame, wealth. Also, and I only bring this up because apparently it needs to be repeated, you won't die tonight. Unlike some, *I* can keep *my* humans safe from dragon hunters."

"But not Julius's," Marci finished for her.

Amelia lifted her shoulders in an elegant shrug. "Now you see the benefit of having a proper master. Really, though, I don't understand why you're hesitating. I'm offering you everything a woman in your position could possibly want. But maybe I read you wrong? Maybe you're not someone who cares about reclaiming your race's lost knowledge?"

Marci swallowed. That wasn't true at all. Amelia couldn't have baited her hook better if she'd tried. Even now, the urge to run into the jungle to find that library and start digging through it was making her twitchy. The dragon's words had rekindled childhood dreams. With Amelia's help, Marci could become an archmage in the classic sense. Someone who wielded the true power of magic, not just an academician who wrote theoretical papers for peer review. She could reclaim the glory of the old mages for *herself*. No more scrabbling in the dirt or being looked down on by more powerful creatures, because she would be one of them, an equal at last. But amazing as all of that was, the way Amelia offered it bothered her.

"It's very tempting," she admitted. "But…you make it sound like I'd be your slave."

"Treasure," Amelia corrected. "You'd be my *treasure*. Big difference."

"But still a possession."

"Well, what else could you be?" the dragon said, scowling. "I take care of you. That makes you mine. But I'm not a harsh master. Cruelty is a waste of time and resources. I want you happy, eager, and productive. I would, of course, require you to breed once in a while to help me rebuild my population, but I'd only pick the strongest, most handsome specimens for you to partner with, so it's not like it'd be a hardship. Plus, you'd be my first, which means you and your children would have rank over all the other mages I'll be bringing in. You'd pretty much be a queen, answerable only to me. Tell me that's not a great deal."

She finished with a show-stopping smile, but Marci could only stare. Even now, part of her still wanted to take it, to seize the power Amelia offered. And that was the problem, because it wouldn't be power at all. She'd be a possession, and hungry as Marci was for the knowledge Amelia dangled in front of her, she didn't know if she could live like that. Then again, if she *didn't* take Amelia's offer, she probably wouldn't live past tonight, period. At best, she'd be under Vann Jeger and Algonquin's thumb for the rest of her life, the human they'd "rescued" from the dragon. Next to that, being queen of Amelia's slaves actually sounded like a pretty good deal, but there was one issue they hadn't touched on yet.

"*If* I agreed," Marci said cautiously. "Could I still see Julius?"

"I don't think you'd have the time," Amelia said. "And weak as he is, he's still a dragon, which is a problem." Her smile turned pointed. "We don't share."

Marci sighed. "Then I can't do it."

Amelia's smile faded. "I'm sorry," she said. "I couldn't have heard that right. There is no way a smart woman like yourself would possibly turn down infinite power for a *boy*."

"That's because I'm not turning it down for a boy," Marci said, glaring. "I'm turning it down for a friend. You claim you're offering me power, but not being allowed to stand by a friend when he needs you sounds a lot like being powerless to me, and I don't do that."

As she spoke, Amelia's friendly expression fell away until, by the end, she looked every bit as haughty and dreadful as her mother.

"Aren't you forgetting something, mortal?" she growled. "I am your *only* hope. If I don't defeat Vann Jeger, you and your *friend* will die. Is that how you show your loyalty to your dragon? Condemning him to death?"

"Julius isn't my dragon," Marci said, pulling herself straight. "He's my partner, and he would never want me to be become a slave for his sake."

"I keep telling you," Amelia snapped. "You're not a slave. You're a treasure."

"Same difference," Marci said proudly. "But I'm not any of those things. I'm a person. Just because mortal lives are short doesn't mean they're cheap, or that they aren't our own. If you can't see that, then you're no better than Bethesda."

That insult must have hit harder than she'd intended, because Amelia recoiled like she'd been struck. "I am *nothing* like her!"

"Then prove it," Marci said, seizing the opportunity with both hands. "Kill Vann Jeger and save us anyway. Once I'm free, I'll come work for you of my own accord. I'll gladly share everything I learn, anything you want, but I will *not* be a possession, treasured or otherwise, and I will *not* turn my back on the one dragon who actually treats me like an equal."

"Arrogant mortal," Amelia snarled. "Normally, I like that, but you go too far. You claim friendship with a dragon, but when you go back to your precious Julius empty-handed, you'll see he's no different than the rest of us. He can't save you. He can't even save himself. I am holding every card. You have nothing to bargain with."

"And I respect you for that," Marci said, lifting her chin high. "I'm a firm believer that when you do the work to get someone over a barrel, it's your right to shake them as hard as possible, but that's not what's happening here. In a negotiation, the person who can walk away is the one with the power, and that's me."

"You mean walk to your death," Amelia scoffed. "You know as well as I do that it's impossible for you and that whelp to defeat Algonquin's Hunter on your own."

"I'm a mage," Marci said haughtily, clinging to her pride like a shipwrecked sailor would cling to a rock in a stormy sea. "Doing the impossible is my vocation. But you're the one who messed up, Amelia."

"Really?" the dragon drawled, her brown eyes narrowing to slits. "And how do you figure that?"

Marci breathed deep. Here went nothing. "Because you let me know how badly you want Ghost. That means *I'm* holding the cards, and if you don't want the human attached to the world's first Mortal Spirit to end up as a notch on Vann Jeger's spear, you'd better come up with a new offer."

Amelia's jaw dropped. "Damn," she whispered, shaking her head. "That was *good.* You turned my own threats back on me. I'm… actually very impressed."

"I've had a bit of experience with dragons," Marci said smugly. "So if you're looking for a pushover slave, I suggest you find another human."

"You are utterly *wasted* on Julius," Amelia said, breaking into a grin. "Fine, you win. I can't let a chance like you die. I'll kill Vann Jeger, and then we'll renegotiate, because I am *not* giving—"

She froze mid-word, her whole body going still. If she'd been a cat, her ears would have been swiveling. Marci was about to ask what was wrong when Amelia suddenly leapt at her, tackling her to the ground just in time as a spear of ice blasted through the storage unit's flimsy door.

CHAPTER TEN

Marci didn't even get a chance to scream. She was too busy protecting her face, hiding behind the shelter of Amelia's arms as the hail of metal scraps and broken ice landed around them. As soon as she was sure she wasn't going to lose anything vital, she wiggled out of the dragon's grasp and scrambled to her feet, sucking magic out of the air and into her bracelets as she turned to help Amelia face...whatever it was that had just happened. When she saw what was waiting, though, Marci's hopes of being useful vanished like frost in the sun.

Two tall, blond women were standing in the blasted-out shell of what had once been the storage unit's metal door. Marci recognized the one on the left immediately, but the one on the right was new, though she didn't doubt for a second that they were both dragons. Nothing human could be that beautiful, or that scary. Unfortunately, Svena didn't seem to recognize her at all. Her pale blue eyes were locked on Amelia, who'd already rolled back up to her feet. But even though the blast of ice had clearly been Svena's doing, she didn't attack again. Instead, she moved back, clearing the path for the unknown dragoness, the one with hair like snow and a smile like a razor, to step forward.

"Estella."

Marci flinched. In hindsight, she supposed it should have been obvious. But scary as it was to be within reach of the seer whose plans she, Julius, and Justin had ruined just last month, Amelia's reaction was what really petrified her. Even when Justin had been roaring and breathing fire, Marci had never heard anything as predatory or draconic as that growled name.

"Let me guess," Amelia said, moving to stand between the new dragons and Marci. "You foresaw your own death today, so you came here to make sure it was quick. That's the only logical reason I can think of for why you'd approach me."

"I did, in fact, foresee a death today," Estella replied with a coy smile. "But it wasn't mine." She tilted her head toward Svena behind her. "It seems you and my sister have unfinished business, Planeswalker."

"Really?" Amelia drawled. "That's funny, because I thought our business was *quite* finished. As I recall, the last time we met, the White Witch ended up swimming for her life because I burned off both her wings."

She glared at Svena as she said this, clearly daring her to reply, but the dragoness said nothing. She just stood there, staring at Amelia with oddly detached hatred, like her face had been frozen that way. If her silence was supposed to be a scare tactic, though, it was working. Even Amelia looked taken aback before she turned away with a huff.

"I don't have time for this," she grumbled, stepping back through her portal to the beach. "If you want a beating so badly, follow me and let's get it over with. I have bigger fish to fry today."

Still silent, Svena stalked after her. Marci, however, could not believe what she was seeing. "You're going to fight them *now?*" she cried, running as close as she dared to the portal's edge. "But—"

"Better to finish this here than have her hounding us," Amelia said, marching past her beach chair to the edge of the surf. "And it's not like you can run."

With those words, Marci became perilously aware of her position. Thanks to the curse, she couldn't follow Amelia through the portal, and Estella was blocking her only way out.

"I see you finally comprehend your position."

The whisper washed over her like ice water, and Marci whirled around to see Estella standing right beside her.

"Hands off, Snow Queen!" Amelia yelled from the beach. "That one is mine!"

"I would never stoop to using mortals as hostages," Estella replied, looking down on Marci like she was a bumbling puppy. "Unlike your clan, *we* still have our honor."

Amelia's snort eloquently expressed what she thought of *that.* "Honor must be all you have, then, because if you still had your foresight, you'd know better than to bring your sister to her death."

Estella laughed. "I see the Heartstriker's arrogance bred true, at least."

"It's not arrogance to speak the truth," Amelia said, glaring at Svena, who had yet to say a word as she stepped through the portal to take up position opposite the Heartstriker heir on the beach. "But if you need another lesson in the dangers of challenging those greater than yourself, I'll be happy to be your teacher."

"And *I* will be happy to finally see that smug mouth silenced," Estella said, turning to her sister. "When you're ready."

At this point, Marci was torn as to what to do. On the one hand, Svena and Amelia seemed to be getting ready for a straight up brawl. But while seeing a battle between two ancient dragon mages was definitely an item on her bucket list, this was a little closer to the action than she was comfortable being. Also, she might not know Svena personally, but they didn't have to be best friends for Marci to notice that the dragon was acting *really* weird. Put those two together, and a call for outside assistance was *definitely* in order. She was scrambling to think how she could manage that with no phone and Ghost still dead asleep when a cold, hard hand grabbed her hair.

"You," Estella said, ignoring Marci's gasp of pain as she yanked her off her feet, lifting her up into the air until she was at eye level with the much taller dragon. "You're one of Brohomir's little pawns, aren't you?"

Before Marci could recover enough to answer, Estella set her back down again, but she didn't release her grip. "Watch," she ordered, yanking Marci's head back around to the beach where

Svena and Amelia were faced off like gunmen at high noon. "Be his eyes so that he can see when my White Witch tears his beloved sister apart."

"Not going to happen," Marci choked out, blinking back tears from the painful pressure on her scalp. "Amelia is the oldest Heartstriker. She'll make dragon sushi out of both of you."

There was a pause, and then Estella burst into laughter. Not maniacal villain cackling either, but honest *I-can't-believe-you-just-said-that* giggling. If Marci hadn't been sure Estella was laughing at *her*, it would almost have been endearing.

"You really believe that?" the seer gasped, wiping her eyes. "Foolish mortal. Svena was a legend before the Heartstriker was *born*. Her daughter is nothing, just another of Bethesda's prodigies. But then, that's why the Broodmare breeds so much. She's playing the odds. Lay enough eggs and a few are guaranteed to hatch into winners. In the end, though, poor breeding will always show. The Planeswalker might be good for a Heartstriker, but Svena is the daughter of *gods*."

She knotted her fingers tighter in Marci's short hair, locking her head in place. "Watch," she ordered again. "We wouldn't want the Great Seer of the Heartstrikers to miss a moment of this, would we?"

Marci didn't bother to answer. One, reasoning with the dragon was clearly impossible, and two, she was too busy staring.

The whole time Estella was talking to her, Amelia and Svena had been standing on opposite sides of the beach, sizing each other up. Then, like the first shot in a fight, Svena changed.

Marci had seen a dragon change twice before: once when Justin had reached the end of his patience and literally exploded into a giant, fire-breathing dragon, and again this morning when Katya had changed back into her human shape. Svena's transformation was different from either. One second, she was standing on the beach at sunset in her white gown like she was modeling for a perfume ad. The next, she was engulfed in a pillar of blue-white fire so bright it whited out every other light, and so cold Marci could feel it from here. The flare lasted only a second, though it took several more before Marci could blink the glare out of her eyes. When she could see again, Svena was gone, and in her place was a white dragon.

It was heartbreakingly beautiful, a white dragon with scales like new snow and wings as delicate as frost-covered glass. She was also *enormous*, easily three times as big as Justin had been, and that wasn't even counting the trailing, feather-like tendrils of frost decorating the end of her long tail. Her curved talons were large enough to easily encircle a car, and her white fangs were as long as Marci was tall. Of course, given how old Svena supposedly was, that made sense. From the hints she'd picked up from Julius, Marci didn't think dragons ever stopped growing, and since they made their own magic, this meant they only got larger and more powerful with age.

This was bad news for Amelia, who was still standing in her human form at the edge of the surf with her neck craned back to look up at the enormous white dragon towering over her. But when Svena spread her glittering wings to block out the light of the setting sun and throw the beach into shadow, the Planeswalker smirked.

"This is all you've managed?" she called, looking Svena up and down. "You've barely grown a foot since the last time we fought. I have little brothers bigger than—"

A blast of blue-white fire cut her off. Svena opened her mouth to bathe the beach in freezing flames that turned the surf behind Amelia to ice mid-wave. But the unnatural fire only blazed for a moment before another flame, this one orange and bright as a summer sunset, burst through, melting everything again as Amelia emerged from the attack with smoke pouring from her human mouth.

"That's how you want it, eh?" she yelled, eyes flashing in fury. "No finesse, no challenge, just a brawl?" She spat on the ground, causing the sand at her feet to start smoking. "*Fine.*" Her eyes flicked to Estella, still standing with Marci on the other side of the portal. "You wanted to see the difference between us, Northern Star? Study closely, because it will be the last thing either of you ever see."

The air around her shimmered as she spoke, and then the beach exploded in fire. Orange flames washed over the sand, turning the surf to vapor and blackening the green foliage at the forest's edge. Even Svena was forced into the air to avoid the blast, flapping up a dozen feet on her frosted wings. By the time she set down again, the entire beach was smoking, the sand hardened into a burned glass landing zone for the biggest dragon Marci had ever seen.

Oddly enough, Marci's very first thought was how much she looked like a Heartstriker. This dragon had the same feathered wings, serpentine body, scaly clawed feet, and crested triangular head as Justin. But where Justin's plumage had been a tropical mix of greens and blues, Amelia's feathers were pure, uninterrupted crimson. Likewise, her brown eyes were now the color of molten gold. Her scales, where they were visible, were black as volcanic glass, and her claws were even darker, like they'd been tempered in fire. But the most telling difference of all was her size.

It was actually difficult for Marci to comprehend how large Amelia was. She was so big, she made the island trees look like models, so huge that Marci couldn't actually see all of her through the portal. Even Svena, who'd looked enormous up to this point, suddenly looked like a kitten. The white dragon knew it, too, and for the first time since she'd appeared, her eyes widened in fear.

Above her, the red dragon chuckled. "Now you see," she said in a deep, terrible voice that Marci only recognized as Amelia's because she'd seen her change. "*Now* you understand the difference between us." She laughed again, landing on the beach with enough force to topple the nearby trees. "Foolish, Svena. While you wasted your time in this magicless plane, bowing and scraping for sisters too hide-bound to abandon their lands even as they became worthless, I knew better. I alone was brave enough to go to planes where magic still lived, and as you see—" she lifted her massive head, throwing the entire beach into shadow, "—I've reaped the rewards."

She stopped there, waiting for Svena to reply. As always, though, the white dragon remained silent, and Amelia bared her teeth in disgust. "Look at you," she snarled "Look what you've let yourself become. But while you and your sisters were content to merely be the daughters of gods, *I* have hunted and eaten them. Now look at you. You're nothing but shadows, arrogance without ambition." Her amber eyes narrowed to glowing slits. "You do not deserve to be called dragons."

When she started, she'd been looking at Svena, but by the time Amelia finished, she was staring through the portal straight at Estella. The seer's grip tightened on Marci's hair in response, and Marci closed her eyes, hoping against hope that the dragons would remember they had reasons to not let her die. But to her amazement, no fire came. Instead, Estella released her entirely, lifting her hands to raise a glowing barrier around herself and Marci as she ordered, "Bring her down."

The words were scarcely out of her mouth before Svena obeyed. The white dragon launched into the air, leaving a blast of frost on the sand that melted immediately in Amelia's heat. As soon as she was off the ground, Svena swung out over the sea, using the cool water to form massive spears of ice that shot from the waves as she passed. Each one moved faster than the speed of sound, creating little sonic booms as they rocketed toward Amelia's sky darkening wings. But as the spears closed in, they began to shrink. Even at top speed, the heat was too intense, and by the time they actually reached Amelia's feathers, the shots were little more than cold water.

"Is that the best you can do?" Amelia teased, brushing her damp feathers. "You were better than this the first time we fought."

Svena's answer to that was to launch another volley of ice, this time at Amelia's head. Again, though, the shots melted before they reached her, the seawater falling harmlessly down onto the melted sand below. Amelia shook her head with a final, disgusted look and opened her massive mouth. Marci got a brief glimpse of a wall of teeth the size of support pillars before the dragon breathed a river of fire that made Justin's green flames look like a sparkler.

If Svena hadn't been over the water, that would have been the end. Amelia's fire consumed the entire bay. Orange flames stretched to the horizon, covering the water from one end of the beach to the other, leaving nowhere to run. But even that much fire couldn't boil away the sea, and that was where Svena escaped, diving below the waves seconds ahead of the fire. Seeing her retreat, Amelia stopped her flames as quickly as they'd started, her glowing eyes watching Svena's white shadow as she darted through the water as fast as a swordfish before exploding back to the surface with her own blast of icy fire.

At first, it looked like a pretty good shot, but the exit from the water must have spoiled her aim, because Svena's attack missed Amelia entirely, blasting into the sand below her instead. Even though she was rooting for Team Heartstriker, Marci couldn't help feeling bad about that. Whatever magic Svena had put into that attack, it was killer, creating a spire of ice that didn't melt even though the sand around it had long since turned to sticky, black glass. If Svena was upset about the loss, though, she didn't let it show. She just turned around and breathed on herself next, coating her scales in a protective shell of that same, unmelting ice, much to Amelia's amusement.

"Are you sure you want to waste that much cold?" she said, her voice booming over the waves as she swooped down to tap her claw against the pillar of frozen water below her. "That ice comes from your own life's fire, White Witch. We both know you can only make so much, and the fight's barely started."

Svena's answer to that was to attack again, breathing a plume of white fire at Amelia's claws. Again, though, she missed by miles. Amelia didn't even have to dodge as the ice flew under her to crash harmlessly into the smoldering trees at the beach's edge. But while this attack was just as ineffectual as the others, Amelia was no longer amused.

"What are you doing?"

When Svena didn't answer, Amelia flapped her sky spanning wings, sending out a wave of super-heated air that hit Svena like a wall, throwing her down into the surf. Amelia was on top of her the second she hit, pinning the smaller dragon into crashing waves with her claws.

"What are you doing?" Amelia snarled, sparks flying from her mouth as she bent low over her pinned enemy. "You're better than this, I know you are. The White Witch doesn't waste her life's magic on missed shots. What has she done to you?"

Her eyes flicked to Estella as she said this, but the seer wasn't the one who answered. Instead, Svena hauled back and breathed fire straight into Amelia's face.

This time, the attack actually got through. Amelia jerked back, shaking her head as ice coated her red feathers. She raked her claws down Svena's body at the same time, and the white dragon screamed, the first sound she'd made since she'd arrived. But though the wounds looked horrible, Svena was already pushing back on her feet, ignoring the blood that ran down her scales as she advanced on Amelia again.

"Stop this," Amelia hissed, melting the ice from her face with a smoky huff as she retreated up the beach. "*Stop*, Svena. You're killing yourself."

But the bloody dragon didn't stop. She just kept pushing forward, and Amelia, clearly unwilling to injure her any further, had no choice but to keep moving back. "Have you gone as insane as your sister?" she growled. "You're not in your right mind. You always were a good enemy, Svena. That's almost the same as being friends. Don't make me do this. I refuse to slaughter you when you can't fight back."

Again, though, the dragon didn't stop, and Amelia's glare turned murderous. "Last warning," she said, planting her enormous clawed feet in the blackened sand. "Back *down*."

With every word she spoke, the air grew hotter. Even through the portal, it burned Marci's skin. She had no idea how Svena could stand being in front of that, but just as she was bracing for what was clearly going to be the end, Estella said, "Now."

The word rang like a bell across the battlefield, and Svena's body jerked. That was the only warning they got before Amelia's rising heat was buried under an avalanche of cold.

Marci had felt dragon magic plenty of times before, but this was another level entirely. Just standing near it made her feel like claws of ice were stabbing into her stomach. But though it felt horrible, Marci still didn't understand what it was supposed to do. There was no blast of white fire, no attack. Amelia didn't even seem to be in pain. But then, when Marci was wondering if Svena had just lost control for good, it happened.

All over the beach, all the chunks of unmelting ice Svena had thrown around during the fight began to hum. The eerie sound was enough to make even Amelia look alarmed, but it wasn't until the enormous dragon actually turned around that Marci finally figured out what was going on. All of those times where Svena's attacks had missed hadn't been misses at all. The failed shots had fallen around the bay in a wide circle, and Amelia was now standing directly at its center.

Amelia must have noticed this just a hair faster than Marci, because she was already launching into the air, but still not fast enough. Her claws had barely left the sand before the humming ice exploded in a massive cloud of frozen crystals that caught her mid-flight. Amelia turned and breathed fire at once, but this time, even that wasn't enough. Though the beach outside the circle was still smoldering, the inside was so cold, the air itself didn't move. Only the ice kept spreading, and by the time Svena pushed herself back to her feet again, Amelia was frozen from her claws to her wings.

"You can't keep this up forever!" she roared, breathing another wave of scorching fire over her icy prison. "You idiot, this is your life's magic! You're going to kill yourself trying to hold me down, and for what? You can't even hurt me in the time it'll take me to break free." As she said this, the ice holding one of her wings shattered, and Amelia bared her teeth in triumph. "You feel that? I'll be out in less than a minute!"

"But a minute is all we need."

Marci jumped. She'd been so transfixed on the epic battle going down on the other side of the portal, she'd forgotten that Estella was still standing right beside her. Now, though, the seer stepped forward, raising her hand to point at the sky overhead.

Marci looked before she could think better of it, squinting into the glare of the setting sun. She was starting to wonder if the seer was bluffing them when she spotted it.

It was a plane. Not a passenger jet or an island jumper, either, but one of those massive, long haul cargo planes, and it was going down. Had been for a while if the smoke pouring from its four engines was any sign, but between all the fire and magic, no one had noticed. No one, that was, except Estella.

"Right on time."

"You've got to be *kidding* me," Amelia roared, slamming the full weight of her body against the icy prison, but it was no use. Fast as her heat was melting it, it wasn't fast enough. Marci was still watching her struggle in horror when Estella turned and pressed something flat and papery-feeling into her hands.

"For Brohomir," the seer said sweetly. "A parting gift."

"Wha—" Marci began, but the dragon was already walking away, dispersing her shimmering barrier with a careless flick of her hand as she stepped through the portal and onto the blackened beach. Like she was just taking a stroll on the beach, Estella walked to her sister's side, throwing up another, much thicker barrier just as Amelia cracked the ice holding her second wing. But though the huge dragon was now more than halfway free, it was far too late. The crashing cargo plane was nearly on top of her. She barely had time to put her newly-freed wings up as a shield before the jet slammed into her, crushing the dragon under six hundred thousand pounds of flaming steel.

"*Amelia!*" Marci screamed, or she started to. Before she could actually make a sound, though, the blast wave from the plane's impact shot through the portal, slamming her off her feet and into the cement wall behind her.

• • •

When the rumbling finally stopped, Estella lowered her frozen barrier to reveal a smoking wasteland. Amelia's famous beach was now a smoldering crater. Inland, a forest fire was beginning to rage, though whether it had been sparked by the jet fuel or Amelia's own attacks, Estella didn't know. Nor did she care. She had more important business to take care of, but just as she was about to set off into the smoke, something cold and sharp wrapped around her ankle.

She looked down, eyes narrowing as she saw Svena's claw, the tip of which was hooked around her leg. "What?"

Her sister responded with a rattling gasp, her pain-dilated blue eyes pleading through the haze of smoke. Below her, the sand was now red with her blood. Her white scales were stained as well, and Estella sighed.

"It won't be much longer," she promised, reaching out to touch her sister's scorched nose. "But we can't rest yet. There is no room for weakness."

The dragon's blue eyes narrowed, but Estella was having none of it. "Start working on the spell to take us home," she ordered, snatching her hand away. "This will only take a moment."

A growl rumbled through the sand, and for a heartbeat, Estella thought her sister was going to balk. But she'd already made sure there was no more disobedience in Svena's future, and in the end, the bloody white dragon bowed her head. Still, Estella waited until she actually felt the freezing wind of her sister's teleportation spell before she turned back to the task at hand, unraveling the next to last black chain from her hand as she began picking her way through the plane's smoking wreckage in search of the red dragon lying beneath it.

• • •

Marci woke to the feeling of a deathly cold paw gently patting her face.

Alive?

She groaned and turned her head, wincing when the motion jostled the newly formed lump on the back of her head.

The paw tapped again.

"I'm up," she grumbled, opening her eyes to see Ghost standing on her chest. "What happened?"

The spirit flicked his ears. *Not sure, was asleep.* He looked over his shoulder. *Explosion, then nothing.*

Marci frowned, confused for a moment, and then it all came back. She sat up with a curse, ignoring the pain as she looked for Amelia, but the room was empty. Other than the door Estella and Svena had ruined, there was no sign the storage unit had ever housed a portal to paradise. Or a dragon. And that was a big problem.

What are you doing? Ghost asked as Marci shoved herself to her feet.

"Don't know yet," she said, grabbing the wall for support as a wave of nausea swept over her. "Something."

Tell someone, she added to herself, and fast. She didn't want to believe a dragon as old and powerful as Amelia could be killed by a rogue aircraft, but she wasn't willing to rule out anything when a seer was involved, especially since the whole thing had obviously been a trap. She wasn't sure why Estella would go through all that trouble and *not* kill Amelia, but assuming the dragon mage was dead didn't help anyone. There was no way Marci could do anything on her own in any case, which meant her first priority had to be getting word of the attack to someone important as soon as possible. Normally, that would be as simple as calling Julius and letting him relay it up the chain, but even that was complicated since Marci had crushed her phone last night to prevent traces, a scorched earth policy she was beginning to regret.

Well, it was too late to cry over crushed phones now. Fortunately, she still had Ghost, and he was actually awake. Convincing him to play messenger cat again would take some doing, but this was an emergency. When Marci glanced down to ask, though, her eyes were drawn instead to a paper envelope lying on the floor where she'd fallen.

What's that? Ghost asked, nosing curiously at her hand when she bent over to pick it up.

"I think it's the thing Estella gave me for Bob," she replied, turning the envelope over in her hands. Given the disasters going on at the time, she hadn't actually looked at the thing when Estella had handed it to her, but the envelope felt right. But while there was clearly something inside it other than paper, it didn't feel magical or dangerous. She was about to open it up and see for herself when she felt Ghost tense in her mind.

"What?"

Someone's coming, he said, ears swiveling. *Quickly.*

Probably security, Marci thought grimly, glancing at the storage unit's busted door. They'd certainly made enough noise to attract even the laziest rent-a-cop. But as she was leaning through the broken door to peer down the hallway for a glimpse of what was coming, her spirit tensed again. That was all the warning Marci got before a leather-gloved hand closed over her mouth.

"You have five seconds to tell me where Amelia is."

She couldn't help it. She screamed, jumping off the ground. Or, she would have if the person behind her hadn't instantly wrenched her back down.

"Try that again and you'll lose an arm," the deadly voice growled. "And you now have four seconds left."

Marci froze, eyes wide. Beside her, Ghost was hissing silently, his glowing fur standing up on his back. He wasn't attacking, though, and since Ghost was more than capable of taking out a human, that told Marci that whatever was behind her was *not.* Not that that was a surprise considering the question about Amelia, but the realization was enough to make her stop panicking and start thinking.

She went limp immediately, lowering her head in obvious surrender. Even so, the hand over her mouth stayed firm for another few heartbeats before letting her go.

"*Thank* you," Marci said, rubbing her bruised lips in exasperation as she turned around. "There was no need for—"

She stopped, eyes wide. The female standing directly behind her was only a little bit taller than Julius, but a thousand times more terrifying. Her black hair was cut military short, and her wiry body was clothed from neck to boots in the same sleek, urban combat armor SWAT teams wore when they were going on a night raid. A sword that looked like a smaller version of Justin's was belted onto her hip, and her eyes, though clearly Heartstriker green, looked more like gemstones than anything soft enough to be alive. Likewise, her face—which, like all dragons, should have been inhumanly beautiful—was the cold, efficient mask of a career killer. It was probably the most intimidating sight Marci had ever seen, and she was still trying to get up the courage to speak when the dragon growled, "Three seconds."

"Who are you?" Marci said, trying not to let her voice shake. Interrogating angry magical predators was usually the sort of suicidally stupid antic Marci tried her best to avoid, but as she'd just told Amelia, she had some experience with dragons now, and withholding useful information was a pretty good tactic if you wanted to stay alive. Besides, even though it was obvious that the dragon in front of her was a Heartstriker, she didn't know *which* Heartstriker, and she wasn't about to give up information on Amelia to just anyone.

The dragon had clearly picked up on this as well, because she released her death grip on Marci's shoulder. "You're Julius's human."

It wasn't a question, but Marci nodded anyway. "And you are?"

Rather than answer, the dragon began to inspect the storage unit's destroyed door. "Svena's work?"

"That depends," Marci said, crossing her arms over her chest. "Name?"

The dragon gave her a cutting look, but she answered. "Chelsie."

Marci's eyebrows shot up. Chelsie was the dragon Justin was always going on about, the one who'd taken his sword. That immediately put her up several notches in Marci's estimation. Anyone who saw Justin as a menace rather than a champion was clearly a sensible creature.

"Svena and Estella attacked us," she reported now that she was satisfied Chelsie could be trusted. "Amelia had a portal open to her island. We were talking through it when they came, and then she and Svena fought. Amelia was winning until Estella hit her with a plane. I got knocked out after that."

Chelsie looked like she wasn't sure if she wanted to believe that or not. "A plane?"

"A cargo jet," Marci explained. "It was seer work. Svena played like she was losing for the first part of the fight, and then she trapped Amelia in the exact right spot where the plane would crash. By the time Amelia noticed, it was way too late."

"You know a lot about seers for a mortal," Chelsie said, arching an eyebrow. "But that's useful at the moment." She lowered her gloved hand to the hilt of her sword. "Do you think she's still on her island?"

Marci nodded. "That's where they all were when the portal closed. I suppose she could have left after the crash, but—"

"No," Chelsie said firmly. "Even Amelia can't make portals when she's seriously injured, and if she was trapped by Estella, injured is the best we can hope for." She drew her sword with a ringing sound. "Looks like we're going to the Philippines."

"W-*we*?" Marci sputtered, backing away from the long, naked blade that was much too close to her. "Why me?"

"Because you're my only witness," the dragon explained. "I can't leave you here, but I can't leave my sister either, so we're going to do both at once." She raised her sword. "You might want to stand back."

Marci jumped back to the wall. "But I can't leave the DFZ! And Amelia's on the other side of the *world*. How are you—"

Before she could finish that question, Chelsie answered it. The dragon swung her sword down in a beautiful arc. Where the blade passed, the air split open like paper, opening a rift into what looked like a warzone. Smoke and wreckage were everywhere. If the shape of the island itself hadn't been identical, Marci wouldn't have believed it was the same beach. More importantly, though, she didn't see Amelia anywhere.

For a horrifying second, Marci was convinced the giant dragon had been blasted to pieces. Then Chelsie jumped through the portal, skidding down the edge of the massive crater of wet sand to what looked like a heap of dirty, water-logged trash at the bottom. It wasn't until the dragon fell to her knees beside it, though, that Marci realized the pile wasn't trash at all. It was Amelia. A human, naked, very bloody Amelia lying face down in the water at the bottom.

"Is she—"

"She's breathing," Chelsie said, hauling her bloody sister into her arms. "Barely. Do you know any healing magic?"

Amelia looked way beyond any of the spells Marci knew. Considering the trail of blood she was leaving in the sand as Chelsie sprinted back up the crater, Marci wasn't sure how the dragon was still alive. "I can do basic first aid," she said. "But I can't move from this spot. I told you, I'm trapped—"

"Trapped in the DFZ, I heard," Chelsie snapped, giving her a hard look.

Marci bit her lip, terrified she'd just identified herself as more trouble than she was worth. But to her enormous shock, Chelsie didn't say a word more about it. She just ducked back through the hole she'd cut in the air, cradling Amelia in her arms as she moved back to Marci's side. "Guess we're doing this the hard way, then," she said, offering Marci her shoulder. "Grab on."

Marci blinked. "Grab on to what?"

"Me," Chelsie growled, shifting Amelia's body to one side to free her sword arm. "And hold on tight. This is going to be a rough ride."

Her tone didn't allow any backtalk, and Marci really didn't want to stay here alone, so she shoved her bag back onto her shoulder and latched on, wrapping her arms around the dragon's armored waist as tight as she could. "Where are we going?"

"Don't know," the dragon said grimly, lifting her sword again. "I just hope my brother does."

Before Marci could remind her again that she really, *really* had to stay in the DFZ, Chelsie brought her sword down. Like before, the air split beneath them, peeling away from the blade's razor edge to drop them into the unknown.

CHAPTER ELEVEN

Julius woke to someone pounding on his door.

He sat up groggily, blinking the sleep out of his eyes as he checked his phone. What he saw made him wince. According to the clock, he'd barely been asleep an hour. He needed another seven at least, but whoever it was at the door wasn't going away. By this point, the knocking was starting to rattle the windows, so Julius hauled himself up. He'd already grabbed the doorknob before it occurred to him he probably should have checked the peephole first. When he yanked the door open, though, it wasn't one of Algonquin's anti-dragon units or even a pizza delivery guy. It was Bob, and he did *not* look happy.

"What's wrong?" Julius asked, instantly awake.

"You'll see in a second," Bob said, pushing past him into the house. His pigeon fluttered in after him, landing on the back of the living room couch. "Lock the door, and get some towels."

"Towels?" Julius asked, clicking the deadbolt back in place. "What do you need—"

Before he could finish his question, a slice appeared in the air in front of him, literally cutting him off. For a heartbeat, a line hung in the air like a silver seam, and then it burst open, dropping Marci, Chelsie, Amelia, and several buckets worth of what smelled like beach sand drenched in burning jet fuel into the middle of his living room.

"What was *that?*" he cried, rushing to help his sisters as the hole closed behind them. "How did you…where did…*what just happened?*"

"It's her sword," Bob said, pushing past him to grab Amelia, whom Julius had only just now realized was naked, bleeding, and apparently unconscious. "Chelsie's Fang has the ability to cut to any Heartstriker, no matter where they are."

"*DON'T TELL HIM THAT!*" Chelsie roared.

"It's a bit late to try and hide it now," the seer said, ignoring her as he turned to gently lay Amelia down on the couch. "Julius? Towels?"

The question snapped Julius out of his shock, sending him racing up the stairs. So *that* was how she did it, he thought as he grabbed their entire stack of clean towels. *That* was how Chelsie was always behind you. Her sword let her teleport.

He'd never actually heard of the Fangs having powers like that. Then again, given whose Fang it was, he wouldn't have. If the truth of Chelsie's blade got out, her reputation as the all-knowing, ever-present Heartstriker boogeyman would be ruined. She certainly looked pissed when he made it back to the living room. Fortunately, her attention, like everyone else's, was on Amelia.

His oldest sister looked like she'd been hit by a fleet of trucks. The amount of blood that had already seeped into their couch made Julius's stack of towels feel inadequate as he handed them to Bob. "What happened?"

The question was meant for no one in particularly, but Marci jumped to answer. "We were talking through her portal on her island in the Philippines when Estella and Svena attacked," she said, racing through the explanation like she'd done this before. "Amelia fought Svena, but it was all a set-up to let Estella hit her with a plane. I got knocked out in the blast. I'd just woken up when Chelsie appeared. She cut her way to the island and found Amelia, but as you can see, she's pretty messed up, so we decided to bring her here." She looked at Chelsie. "Why did we do that again?"

"Ask him," Chelsie said, nodding at Bob. "He's the one who called and told me to get to Amelia, but couldn't tell me where she was."

Everyone turned to stare at the seer, who was kneeling beside his sister with an uncharacteristically serious look on his face. "I was worried something like this might happen," he said softly, reaching up to pat the blood off Amelia's face with a towel. "But I didn't think it would actually work."

"Why not?" Julius asked. "Didn't Estella attack Conrad just last night?"

Chelsie's hand was on his throat before he realized she'd moved. "*How do you know about that?*"

"Katya told me," he choked out, putting his hands up in instant surrender. "She ran from her sisters while it was happening and came here."

For the first time in his life, Chelsie looked surprised. "She came to *you?*"

He nodded, and she let him go. "Why?"

Julius was too busy recovering from the near choking to answer immediately, so Bob did it for him. "Because Julius is nice," he said. "But we knew that. I'm far more concerned about the parts of this we don't understand. Namely, why Amelia, like Conrad, is still alive."

"She almost wasn't," Marci pointed out, but Chelsie was shaking her head.

"A plane crash, even a big one like this, isn't enough to kill a dragon like Amelia. Estella would know that. This was clearly an attack to wound, not kill." She glared at Julius. "Not that I should be telling you this, but since you already know, Conrad was the same. So far as we can tell, Estella and Svena attacked him in his room early this morning. Likewise, I smelled both Estella and Svena at the beach on top of the scent of burning fuel. That means they were both there *after* the plane crashed, so why did they leave? Svena's been trying to kill Amelia for years. I don't believe for a second she'd stand over her unconscious body and not finish the job."

"I don't know about that," Marci said. "Svena was acting *really* weird."

"Katya said the same thing," Julius agreed. "What's going on?"

Once again, everyone looked at Bob. This time, though, the seer just sighed. "I don't know."

A cold chill went up Julius's spine. "You don't know? How do *you* not know?"

"I already explained this to you last night," Bob said, annoyed. "Ever since Estella returned, the future has been a mess. Threads of possibility are vanishing all over the place. First Svena, then Conrad, and now—"

"Amelia," Chelsie finished with a growl.

"But how is that possible?" Julius asked. "You specifically told me last month that our family was safe. 'My brothers, my pawns,' that's what you said. Svena I can understand, but how could she get Conrad and Amelia?"

"If I knew *that*, we wouldn't be having this conversation," Bob grumbled, sitting down on the floor. "A seer's work is dominated by probability. We look at all the things that might happen, and then we do whatever it takes to ensure that *might* becomes *will*. But even with the power of foresight, there are still some events that are *so* unlikely, they're functionally impossible. For sanity's sake, seers learn to ignore these extremes, but over the last twenty-four hours, those seemingly impossible futures are exactly what has been happening." Bob bared his teeth. "It's like Estella's just yanking the future into whatever shape she pleases. I could accept that as just really good seer work if it wasn't for the fact that she's also yanking *my* pieces away with no setup whatsoever."

The seer was growling by the time he finished, and the sound was enough to make Julius want to run for the hills. He'd never seen Bob actually angry before, and he never wanted to again. Even Marci looked spooked, stepping back toward the wall. Chelsie was the only one who looked unaffected. "So how is Estella able to do it?" she asked.

"There's only one explanation," Bob growled. "She's cheating."

Marci frowned. "How do you cheat at the future?"

"I don't know," the seer said, glaring down at Amelia. "But I intend to find out."

Chelsie sighed. "Be that as it may, we still have two siblings down. Conrad—"

She stopped, looking pointedly at Julius and Marci, but Bob just rolled his eyes. "They're in neck deep already," he reminded her. "Might as well put everything out there and get more minds working on the problem."

"Fine," Chelsie growled. "It's not like they can make things worse." She turned to Julius, folding her arms over her chest. "Unlike Amelia, Conrad suffered no injuries at all from his attack. The only reason we know something happened at all was because I found him unconscious in his room with Estella's scent on his clothes. When he woke up, he had no memory of what had occurred. Now, Amelia's situation is obviously different, but given that she still hasn't woken up, I wouldn't be surprised if her memories were altered as well. Since they both came out of Estella's clutches alive and in our custody, however, we have no choice but to assume they've been compromised."

"Compromised?" Marci squeaked. "You mean like bugged or mind controlled or—"

"I don't know," Chelsie said sharply. "But there's no way Estella would take out two of the most powerful Heartstrikers only to turn right around and give them back to us without a hitch. Even Mother's accepted that and ordered Conrad be restrained until we know exactly what's going on. Unfortunately, Amelia's situation is a little more complicated."

"More complicated how?" Julius asked, staring at his sister, who was starting to look deathly pale. "Shouldn't we be getting her back home as well? She needs a doctor if nothing else, and Heartstriker Mountain's the only place—"

"*No.*"

They all jumped. On the couch, Amelia's eyes shot open. "No," she gasped again. "Not the mountain. Never. *Never*—"

Magic began to surge. It rose from Amelia's body in a desperate strike, digging into Julius's chest before he could defend himself. But then, just when he was sure the power would rip him open,

Chelsie grabbed Amelia's head and slammed down with magic of her own. It happened so fast, Julius couldn't even tell what Chelsie had done. Whatever it was, though, it worked. Amelia collapsed back onto the couch, her whole body going limp as her magic vanished as quickly as it had risen. Chelsie kept her hands tight on her sister's head until the last of it was gone, and then she unclenched her fingers with a grimace. "That was close."

"Too close," Marci said, shaking. "She nearly sliced and diced us."

"What did you expect?" Bob asked, glaring at Julius. "He threatened to take her to Mother."

"I said she needed a *doctor!*" Julius cried. "I know Bethesda isn't exactly Mother of the Year, but unlike my house, she has physicians on hand who actually know how to treat a dragon. And how was I supposed to know she'd freak out like that? Amelia was at the mountain just last night." He looked back down at his sister, who looked terrifyingly pale. "I still think taking her back is the best option. I don't know what Mother's beef with Amelia is, but there's no way she'd risk starting trouble inside the family while we're under attack from another clan."

That logic made perfect sense to Julius, but by the time he finished, Chelsie and Bob were both staring at him like he'd lost his mind.

"Please tell me he's kidding."

"I don't think he is."

Julius's cheeks began to heat. "What did I say?"

"Julius," Chelsie said, exasperated. "Amelia is Bethesda's *heir.* Do you have any idea what would happen if she arrived at the mountain injured and vulnerable? It wouldn't matter if there was an army at our gate, Mother would never overlook a chance like that."

"You can't be serious," Julius said, horrified. "I know Bethesda's ruthless, but she's not stupid. Using whelps as pawns is one thing, but a dragon like Amelia is an irreplaceable asset. There's no way she'd throw away a dragon that valuable. I mean, Conrad's there chained up right now, and you're not worried about him."

"That's because Conrad's male," Chelsie growled. "Not to mention he's two clutches down. Plus, he has the eyes."

Julius grew very still. "What do you mean, the eyes?"

"Heartstriker Green isn't exactly a *natural* development," Bob said grimly, blinking his own neon green eyes. "But that's not what's important right now. The real issue here is that Amelia is *female* and only a hundred years younger than Bethesda herself. That makes her a threat of the highest order, or have you forgotten how Bethesda became the Heartstriker?"

Julius hadn't. The story of how their mother betrayed their grandfather and took his clan was the legend of their family. He'd been taught from birth to revere Bethesda's ruthlessness and cunning, using the confusion caused by the sudden disappearance of magic and her status as her father's favorite daughter to take down an ancient dragon ten times more powerful than herself. What he'd never considered, though, was how that kind of treachery would color Bethesda's own view of her children. Even so.

"I can believe she'd be suspicious of Amelia's intentions," he said. "She certainly didn't look happy to see her at the party, but we're under siege here. You said yourself that Amelia's the only one who can stand toe-to-toe with Svena." He shook his head. "I just can't believe that Bethesda would risk losing an asset that powerful just because she's paranoid about her heir, especially since Amelia doesn't even seem to like being on this plane."

"Oh, Julius," Bob sighed. "Sweet, naive Julius. Never change."

"What?" he said, defensive. "How is that wrong?"

"You're giving our mother too much credit," Chelsie said dryly, glaring at him. "Or do you really think all the A's died of natural causes?"

He hadn't actually thought about that. "I—"

"Mother killed them," she said, cutting him off. "She used them until they were old enough to be a threat, and then she killed them one by one, a preemptive strike against the one clutch strong enough to do to her what she did to her own father. The only reason Amelia's still alive is because she was smart enough to stay away. That's why she's been out on the planes so long. It's the one place Mother can't get to her. She only came to the party last night because she knew she could get away if she had to, and because she never could resist a chance to rub her new power in Bethesda's face. Now that she's injured, though, it's a different game, and that's why your argument won't work. It doesn't matter if we're under attack. Estella could have a sword to Bethesda's throat, and our mother would lean right into it if that meant getting a chance to finally take Amelia down. It's all about target priority. The Daughters of the Three Sisters are a major threat, but at the end of the day, all they can do is kill Bethesda. Amelia, on the other hand, is one of us. If she challenged our mother and won, she could take her power and become the Heartstriker in her place, and it is *that*, not death, that Bethesda fears most."

By the time she finished, Julius was chilled to the bone. He'd never heard Chelsie sound so bitter, but he didn't doubt her words for a second. If there was one thing he was learning not to underestimate, it was his mother's ruthlessness when it came to preserving her own position. "Okay," he said with a deep breath. "No mountain. But should she really be on my couch?"

"No," said Chelsie.

"Yes," said Bob at the same time.

Chelsie shot him a dangerous glare, but Bob stood firm. "You're busy," he reminded her.

"You really want to entrust our sister's safety to *Julius*?"

"Yes," Bob said. "Honestly, I can't think of anyone better."

Chelsie bared her teeth. "Have you finally gone insane?"

"No more than usual," the seer said, clapping a hand on Julius's shoulder. "But if you can name another dragon who could be trusted to look after the unconscious heir to the Heartstrikers *without* betraying her to Mother the moment we're gone, I'm all ears."

Chelsie's face fell into a stubborn scowl. "Fair point," she grumbled, turning her glare back to Julius. "Don't let me down, whelp."

Julius swallowed. On the one hand, this was quite possibly the highest compliment he'd ever received. Two of his most powerful siblings were entrusting him with a job that could change the course of their whole clan, and they were doing it because he was who he was, not who he wasn't. He'd earned their trust by being *loyal*, not ruthless. But as much as he wanted to swear up and down that he'd guard Amelia with his life, there was still a fjord-sized problem in his way.

"I want to help," he said. "Really, I do. But Amelia *can't* stay here."

"Why not?" Chelsie demanded.

He began to sweat. This was not how he'd intended to break the news to his family, but there was no hiding it now. "Because," he said, voice shaking. "I'm being hunted by Vann Jeger."

"*What?*"

Chelsie's shriek made him jump. Or, rather, start to jump. He hadn't actually made it off the ground before she grabbed him by his collar and slammed him into the wall. "And you were planning on reporting this *when?*"

"It only happened last night," he said, trying not to panic as she lifted him off the ground. "After the party. I wasn't trying to hide anything, I swear! It just went down so fast."

"At least this explains why your human has a killing curse on her neck," Chelsie said, glancing at Marci. "That's how they trapped you, wasn't it?"

She made it sound like a personal failing, but Julius didn't care. "Yes," he said. "And unless I go with her to face Vann Jeger tonight, that sword is going to cut off her head."

"And you were just going to *go?*" she cried. "What were you going to do when you got there? Nice him to death?"

"We *had* a plan," Julius said. "Amelia was going to—"

"Amelia isn't doing anything now," Chelsie growled, dropping him as she turned her wrath on Bob. "Did you know about this?"

"I might have seen something," the seer said. "But it didn't seem immediately important."

"*Not immediately important?*" Chelsie yelled. "Being targeted by the most powerful dragon hunter in the world didn't strike you as *immediately important?*"

"It's not exactly easy to read a future that's in constant flux," Bob said defensively. "There was a lot going on."

Chelsie closed her eyes with a long sigh. "Done is done," she growled, turning back to Julius. "Pack your things. We're leaving."

"Leaving?" Julius choked out. "But what about Amelia?"

"I'll find somewhere else for her," his sister snapped. "But *you* are going back to the mountain. Right now."

"What?" he cried. "*No!* I can't go home. Weren't you listening? If I don't show up, Marci will *die.*"

"All mortals die," Chelsie said. "It's time you accepted that."

Behind them, Julius was aware of Marci going very still. She didn't make a sound, but it didn't matter. He could smell her fear like acid in the air, and it sent his fists clenching as he said, "No."

Chelsie froze. "Excuse me?"

"No," he said again, forcing himself to stand straight and meet her glare. "It's my fault Vann Jeger put that mark on her neck, and I'm not leaving her to deal with it alone. I'm not leaving her to die."

"You say that like you have a choice," Chelsie sneered. "But you have *nothing*. No chance, no hope. What do you think is going to happen when you face Vann Jeger?"

It took Julius several seconds to realize that question wasn't rhetorical. "I know the odds aren't good, but—"

"Aren't good? Vann Jeger is the Death of Dragons. Hunting and slaughtering our kind is his crusade. A monster like him would be a tough fight even for Amelia. You don't have a prayer."

"But we don't *have* to beat him," Julius explained. "The curse just requires her to show up with a dragon."

Chelsie rolled her eyes. "And what? You think you'll just waltz in, punch your ticket, and go?"

Julius fought the urge to growl. In the end, though, Chelsie didn't even give him a chance.

"If you get within striking distance of Vann Jeger, you will die," she said sternly. "Both of you. But while you seem to be content to let your mortal do whatever she likes, *your* life belongs to Heartstriker.

As clan enforcer, that makes it my responsibility, and I'm not about to let you throw it away on doomed, childish heroics."

He grit his teeth in frustration. "It's not like that. I—"

Chelsie drew her sword faster than he could blink. One moment, the Fang was sheathed on her hip, the next, the bone-colored blade was pressing against the soft skin of his throat. "Pack," she ordered. "Now."

And just like that, something in Julius snapped. He hadn't even known he was so close to the edge until the whisper of a blade at his neck pushed him right over. "Or what?" he growled.

"I think that's pretty obvious," Chelsie growled back, nudging the blade a little closer.

"Then do it," Julius said, lifting his chin to give her a better opening. "Cut my head off."

Chelsie's eyes narrowed. "You can't bluff me, so don't even try. This is not open to debate. You're going back to the mountain. The only choice you have left is whether you do it intact or in pieces."

"Are you even listening to yourself?" Julius cried. "You're threatening to *kill me* if I don't let you save my life. Do you have any idea how ridiculous that is?"

"Maybe," Chelsie snarled. "But I wouldn't *have* to do it if you weren't determined to be such a suicidal *idiot*."

He'd said almost the exact same thing to Justin not an hour ago. Now though, Julius was finally beginning to understand his brother a little. There was no question that Chelsie was right. He *was* utterly outclassed, and he was being suicidally stupid to keep resisting her attempts to save his life. Even now, every survival instinct he had was screaming at him to stop being a moron and just do what she said, but Julius didn't move. He couldn't, because after a lifetime spent running from the terrifying monsters he called family, Julius had finally found something bigger than fear. He was still terrified, probably always would be, but it didn't matter anymore. Even death paled in comparison to the thought of an immortality spent knowing that he was the reason Marci had died, and that he'd left her to do it alone.

"I'm not going," he said again, fisting his hands at his sides to keep them from trembling. "I know you're strong enough to make me, but I'll fight you every step of the way. That's my choice, but you still have yours. You can take me back to the mountain in pieces, or let me stay here and guard Amelia for you as long as I can."

His whole body was pounding in time with his heart by the time he finished, but Chelsie didn't even blink. She just stood there with her weapon pressed against his neck, and the longer she waited, the more Julius was convinced that this was it. He'd called Chelsie out, and now she was going to kill him. But just as he was making his final peace with death, Chelsie lowered her sword with a curse.

"Of all the times for you to grow a spine," she grumbled, shoving the blade back into its sheath. "Fine. I'm only doing this because I care more about Amelia than I do about you. Stay here and die if that's what you want, but from this point on, everything that happens is on your head. No more last second saves. Understood?"

Julius nodded.

She nodded back. "Now, where's your idiot brother?"

He blinked. "Sorry?"

"Where's Justin?" she growled. "I let you go after him at the party because I thought you were the sensible one, but apparently suicidal tendencies are a trait of J clutch. You've already gotten away with it, but I'm not about to let Justin run around loose in Algonquin's city with all of this going on. I'm taking him home immediately, so where is he?"

Julius opened his mouth only to close it again. When he'd gone to sleep, Justin had been upstairs. He hadn't even thought about him in the confusion, but now that Chelsie was asking, Julius couldn't believe his brother would stay quietly in his room through all this chaos. They'd been making tons of noise for at least fifteen minutes now, but the house above them was quiet. Too quiet, almost as though it was…empty.

Chelsie's eyes narrowed to slits. "You don't know where he is, do you?"

"He was here just a few minutes ago," Julius said, following her as she turned and charged up the stairs. "I only lay down for a moment!"

"A moment's all he needs," she said, throwing open the door of Julius's obviously empty bedroom. The far window had been left open, as was the hidden panel where he'd kept Tyrfing.

"He's gone," Julius said, shoulders slumping. "And he has my sword."

Chelsie turned without saying a word, taking the stairs two at a time.

"I'm sorry," Julius said, running after her. "I didn't—"

"Save it," she snapped, drawing her sword. "I'll be back to deal with you later. *Do not move* from this house until I return."

She swung her blade as she spoke, cutting a hole in the air. Where to, though, Julius never got to see. By the time he caught up, she was already gone, vanished through her portal without a trace.

● ● ●

He was still staring at where she'd been when Bob's hand landed on his shoulder.

"Standing up to Bethesda's Shade," the seer said. "Who are you, and what have you done with Julius?"

"Quit it, Bob," Julius whispered, shrugging out of his grip. "This is serious." He could hardly imagine a worse situation than Justin running off alone and angry into the DFZ. "Will she reach him in time?"

"Hard to say," Bob replied. "But Chelsie's the best at what she does. If Justin can be saved, she'll do it. She might kill him herself when it's over, but she won't let him die to outsiders."

Julius was having a hard time finding that comforting. "This is all my fault."

"I guess it could be if you wanted to take it that way," Bob said. "But guilt is such a waste of time. I'd have thought you'd be more interested in working on keeping yourself and your human alive."

His head shot up. "Is that possible?"

"Possible, yes," Bob said. "Probable?" He shrugged.

Julius grit his teeth. Normally, Bob's jovial nature just rolled off him. Now, though, it was hard not to be offended. Lives were at stake, and Bob was still acting like this was all a big joke. "This isn't a game, you know."

"Of course it's a game," the seer said, walking back over to the couch where Marci was standing over Amelia. "Everything's a game, Julius. It has to be. Life is whimsical, random, and cruel, but a game is something you can *win*."

"Not if your opponent is cheating," Marci said. "I saw Estella. She certainly didn't look like she was playing fair. It was like she knew everything that was going to happen. She even gave me this to give to you."

She pulled an envelope out of her bag, and the smile slipped off Bob's face.

"I don't know if it's a bomb or a threat or what," she said, holding it out for him. "I was going to show it to Chelsie, but she was kind of preoccupied. Still, I thought if Estella's cocky enough to send you messages, maybe she messed up and left a clue?"

Bob took the envelope without a word. He ripped the top off and turned it over, sliding something white and small into his open palm. It didn't smell magical to Julius, but his brother was staring at it like he'd seen a ghost.

"What is it?"

The seer cleared his throat. "It's a comb," he said, holding it up so they could see the four delicately carved bone tines.

"Why would she send you a comb?" Marci asked.

"Because it's mine," Bob said. "I gave it to her a long time ago as a courtship gift."

"Wait," Julius said, because he'd obviously heard that wrong. "You gave Estella a *courtship* gift?" When his brother nodded, he cried, "*Why?*"

The moment the question was out, Julius regretted it. For the first time he could remember, Bob looked…sad.

"Because I was courting her," he said, dropping the comb back into its envelope. "Estella wasn't always like she is now. There was a time, centuries ago, before she dedicated her life to my downfall, that the Northern Star and I were very close. She was the only one who actually understood what it was like to live as a seer. Add in her legendary beauty and I was quite the smitten young dragon."

Julius couldn't believe what he was hearing. "What happened?"

Bob sighed. "The inevitable. Estella's greatest weakness has always been her tragically narrow vision. For all her brilliance, she could only ever conceive of two types of relationships: pawns and enemies. Once she discovered I'd never be the former, I became the latter." He smiled sadly. "I saw it coming, of course, but that's the dirty secret of seers. We're forever trying to change our own fate, even when we know better."

"Is that why she hates you so much?" Marci asked softly. "Because you wouldn't be her pawn?"

"Of course not," Bob scoffed. "What do you think this is, a soap opera? Estella dumped me the moment she realized I wasn't going to be her fawning lackey. She only cared enough to start hating me when I started *winning*."

He turned around, tossing the comb and the envelope into the trash can at the foot of the couch. "I'm not sentimental enough to believe she treasured this as a keepsake," he said matter-of-factly. "She's a dragon; hoarding beautiful objects is her nature. The only reason she sent it back now is because she saw an opportunity. She's trying to get under my feathers, to distract me from her real goal."

"Which is?"

"The absolute destruction of our clan."

Julius winced. "That seems a little extreme."

Bob cocked an eyebrow. "What about Estella made you think she was anything less?"

He couldn't argue with that.

"Of course, I'm still unraveling the particulars," Bob went on. "Genius that I am, it pains me to admit that Estella has the upper hand this time, but not for long." His lips peeled away from his teeth in a snarl. "She's not the only one who can cheat."

The anger in his voice at the end made Julius shudder, but Bob's happy mask had already snapped back in place when he looked up again.

"I have to go away for a while," the seer said casually as he leaned down to press a quick kiss against Amelia's cheek. "I realize you've got a lot going on this evening what with your imminent demise, but if you could look after my sister for as long as you can, I'd be very grateful. Amelia and I have been together for a very long time now. She is…precious to me."

That was the most sincere thing Julius had ever heard his brother say, and he nearly tripped over his own tongue in his rush to return the favor. "Of course I'll protect her," he promised. "She's my sister, too. I'll do whatever I can."

Bob gave him a dramatic look of shock. "Not even trying to take advantage of my obvious emotional distress?" He shook his head with a *tsk*. "You really are the worst dragon, Julius Heartstriker."

"Thank you," Julius said. "But if you wanted to give me some inside information, I wouldn't say no." Because if ever he needed a heads up on his future, it was now.

"I *did* have one important piece of advice I meant to give you," Bob said solemnly. "Listen closely, because this might just save your life."

Julius nodded, holding his breath, eyes locked on his oldest brother as Bob leaned in to whisper in his ear.

"Be yourself."

Julius yanked away. "That's it?" he cried. "*That's* your important advice? Justin is missing, we have two siblings down, Marci's got a killing curse on her neck, I'm being hunted by Algonquin's personal dragon slayer, and all you can say is *be yourself?*"

Bob looked hurt. "It's very good advice."

"It's *meaningless* advice!" Julius yelled. "I know you said the clan is always in danger, but this is *different.* You know it's different, that's why you're leaving. But I'm the one who has to stay and deal with all of this, so for once in your life, can you drop the mysterious seer act and just tell me something useful? Unless a miracle happens, I'm going to have to face Van Jeger in less than twelve hours. How is being myself going to stop that? I can't keep Amelia safe if I'm dead!" He grabbed the seer's hand. "*Please*, Bob, I'm begging you here. Give me something I can work with. Anything will do."

He knew he was being pathetic, but he was too desperate to care. The last twenty-four hours had been one disaster after another, and now that Amelia was down as well, Julius was officially out of tricks. If the Great Seer of the Heartstrikers couldn't help him, he had nothing. But Bob didn't give him an answer. He just smiled, reaching out to rest his hand on Julius's shoulder. "Do you know why I picked you?"

Julius sighed. "Of course not. But I don't see how this is—"

"It's because you're a failure."

"We've established this," Julius grumbled. "But—"

"Truly terrible," Bob went on. "Absolutely the worst. I've seen all of Bethesda's clutches—past, present, and future—and I've never seen anything like you. You would not *believe* what a Herculean task it was to keep Mother from getting fed up and eating you when you were still a whelp, but against all odds, I succeeded, and as a result, you've grown into something unique. The things you value, the decisions you make, they're inscrutable to the rest of dragonkind, including me."

He said this like it was vitally important, but Julius didn't understand. "How is that useful?"

"Because you are an enigma, Julius Heartstriker," Bob said solemnly. "And that is your strength. Anyone who challenges you expecting a dragon will get something else entirely, something they are completely unprepared to fight. Something they do not, and most likely *cannot*, understand. So when I say, 'be yourself,' I'm telling you to use the advantage no other dragon in the world possesses." He stepped back, looking Julius up and down. "You."

Julius swallowed. "That doesn't sound like much of an advantage."

"It's our only advantage," Bob said grimly. "As much as I hate to admit it, Estella's been steadily backing us into a corner. From the moment Svena vanished from my sight yesterday morning, carefully orchestrated plans years in the making have been dropping like flies. Given everything I've learned over centuries of being a seer, that should be impossible. But even if Estella has somehow managed to get access to a higher level of control over the future than I can reach, she still has to understand what she's looking at to use it. That's the one factor she can't cheat her way around, and so long as you are you, I'm gambling that even the Northern Star won't be able to make heads or tails of what you're doing until it's too late." He grinned. "Or, at least, that's the plan. Even I can't say for sure what will happen with so much in the air, but I know you'll find a way. You have to, or we're all toast!"

"That's hardly a motivational speech," Julius said, feeling a little shell-shocked. "And why do you seem so happy about it?"

"Personal eccentricity," Bob said, grinning even wider. "It's not often a seer doesn't know the ending ahead of time. Can you blame me for enjoying the forbidden thrill of the unknown?"

That did *not* make Julius feel better. "Are you sure you can't tell me something more useful?"

"But I *have*," Bob said. "You didn't think I said all that just to boost your ego, did you? This is why I picked you. *This* is your purpose. Because when I saw these disasters coming, I knew I'd have to play my most unexpected card. The only thing Estella—who knows me better than anyone—wouldn't see coming. *You.*" He grabbed Julius's hands, clutching them together. "Help us, Juli-wan Kenobi, you're our only hope."

For a moment, that almost, *almost* made Julius feel like a hero. And then he remembered. "Doesn't Obi-Wan die in that movie?"

Bob dropped his hands with a cryptic smile and started for the door. "I must be off," he said as his pigeon flapped after him. "Make sure you have food and booze on hand for when Amelia wakes up. She's not exactly a morning dragon."

"Wait!" Julius cried, running after him. "*Bob!*"

But the seer was already gone, jogging down the stairs toward his antique of a car. Julius would have run after him, but there didn't seem to be much of a point. Bob had clearly already said all he was going to say, so Julius just shut the door and put his back against it with a pained sigh. When he opened his eyes again, Marci was standing in front of him.

"Thanks for what you said earlier."

His ears began to burn. "It was the truth."

"I know," she said, smiling. "That's why I'm saying thank you."

"Don't thank me yet," he said, looking pointedly at Amelia. "I guess we'd better get some food."

"I'll go," Marci volunteered. "You should stay here in case Justin comes back so he doesn't freak when he sees Amelia."

Julius didn't think Justin was coming back, but he wasn't exactly keen to disobey his sister by leaving the house, and besides, he was tired. He'd been tired when this whole thing started. Now he felt like his legs were going to give out if he didn't sit down.

"Just be careful," he said, moving off the door so she could leave. "Fate has it out for us today."

"Always am," Marci said, leaning in to kiss him on the cheek.

He barely had time to register the touch of her lips before she was off, running down the stairs to her stolen wreck of a truck. He would have chased after her, but Amelia was already stirring on the couch, blowing out long lines of angry smoke as she struggled toward consciousness. So, with a final, longing look at Marci, Julius closed the door and went to his sister, standing over her protectively as he pulled out his phone and hit Justin's number. He was calling more out of thoroughness than any real hope Justin would answer, but that couldn't keep his heart out of his throat as the call rang… and rang…and rang.

CHAPTER TWELVE

On the opposite side of the city, Justin Heartstriker stepped out of his cab and into the middle of nowhere.

He paid his fare and sent the cheap little coffin of an automated car away, keeping Julius's pathetic excuse for a sword loose in his grip as he walked down what was left of the crumbling sidewalk. Down the street, the collapsing church he'd used as his stakeout slumped dejectedly in the morning sunlight, its broken steeple bobbing slightly in the cool breeze. But though it was oddly comforting to see something familiar in this horrible city, the broken-down church was not his destination today. *That* stood in front of him.

He stopped at the sidewalk's edge, looking up at the two-story tall chain link fence that cut across the landscape like a line on a map, bisecting the flood-ruined ranch homes that stood in its way. Hanging high on the links, well above what few slumping roofs remained, rusted metal signs the size of small billboards proclaimed what everyone already knew in huge, block capitals.

WARNING!
ALGONQUIN CORPORATION RECLAMATION
PROJECT IN EFFECT BEYOND THIS POINT
AUTHORIZED PERSONNEL ONLY

The notice was repeated every ten feet in multiple languages. There were no threats to back it up, no listed fines or penalties, not even cameras. But then, none were needed. All the land in this part of the

DFZ was saturated with the magic of wild places humans could not tame. It scared away even the most drugged out, desperate humans, which was why, despite the fact that parts of the fence stood within sight of the skyways, no one lived in the ruined houses that lined the cracked streets. Of course, this also meant there was no one to see Justin as he marched into the closest overgrown lot, trampling the tall grass under his boots as he made his way to the fence. But though his mind should have been on his surroundings, all Justin could think about was how his brother had betrayed him.

He'd thought they understood each other. He'd thought—or he'd thought that Julius thought—they were *friends*. So how could he have done this? How could Julius have just handed Justin's fight, the one *he knew* meant earning his Fang back, to another dragon? And not even a proper dragon like Conrad, but *Amelia*.

It was insulting. It was *shameful*. But if Julius thought he could control the Fifth Blade of Bethesda by holding back something as stupid as a duel location, he was even more of a fool than everyone took him for. That, or he'd forgotten that this was the DFZ, and Justin was a dragon who'd spent the last three days planning his incursion into Reclamation Land. It wasn't like getting Vann Jeger's attention would be hard.

With that, he lifted his sword and cut a Justin-sized hole in the fence, stepping through the sundered chain link into the place were no other dragon had set foot for over sixty years. But when he stopped to survey Algonquin's secret base, all he felt was a sharp sense of disappointment.

The forbidden side of the fence looked exactly like the rest of this part of the DFZ. Every direction he looked, it was just more of the same cracked asphalt streets, sagging, abandoned houses, and overgrown lots like you'd see anywhere else in this part of the city. Of course, Justin had known *that* just from looking through the fence, but after all the build-up, he'd expected something more dramatic. A giant illusion covering a portal to another dimension maybe, or a hidden army of spirits. So far, though, Algonquin's Reclamation Land just looked like…land. Justin couldn't even tell what she was supposedly reclaiming. He could, however, feel the heavy magic coiling around him like an angry snake, followed by the unmistakable sense of being watched.

Good, he thought, pulling himself taller as he resumed his march through the tall grass toward the nearest street. Let them watch. Let them *fear*. Dragons had been too cautious for too long, and Algonquin's hold on this place had solidified as a result, but he was different. Julius and the others could cower all they liked, but Justin was going to make history. When he brought home Vann Jeger's dripping head for his mother to hang in her collection, all the world would learn what it meant to challenge the Heartstrikers, and he would finally earn his rightful place at the top of the clan.

As always, that thought brought a smile to his face. He was so busy going over what he'd say to Julius and Chelsie when it happened, he didn't notice the fog rolling in until he was neck deep in it.

Justin froze with a curse, readying his sword. Fog wasn't normally a problem for a dragon with his nose, but this was no ordinary water vapor. It was magic. Wild, cold magic that drenched everything with the scent of rain and rotting leaves. He couldn't even smell the crumbling asphalt under his feet, but it wasn't until Justin looked down that he realized this wasn't because of the fog, but because the street he'd been following into Reclamation Land wasn't there anymore.

Ten steps ago, he'd been walking through the same dilapidated neighborhoods that surrounded all of Restoration Land. Now, he was standing on what could only be described as loam. Dense, soft leaf litter, the sort you only found in deep forests, covered the ground at his feet. Likewise, the shadows in the thick fog were no longer the shapes of rotting houses and abandoned cars, but trees. Massive, gnarled, ancient trees as thick as Justin was tall. One trunk was actually right next to him, its heavy bark saturated with water from the fog as though it had always been here, and Justin was the one who'd moved.

With that realization, a cold sensation that might have been fear began to creep up his neck before Justin banished it. There was no point in getting spooked. He'd come in expecting something like this, and given the amount of magic in the air, a suddenly appearing forest was actually pretty mild. He wasn't sure what kind of trees he was looking at, but given their size, they were obviously older than the sixty years since Algonquin took this land, which meant either the forest was magically created, or he really had stepped through a portal and hadn't noticed. Either way, he was in too deep for caution now. But just as Justin was about to say screw it and change so he could fly up and get a view of this place from the sky, his ears picked up an unusual sound.

It was rhythmic, regular, and deep. Almost like a drum, but not, because it was also getting rapidly closer, each beat vibrating the ground under his feet. It sounded like something he should know, but Justin was so unfamiliar with horses, he didn't actually recognize the sound of charging hoof beats until the rider burst through the fog directly in front of him.

Justin jumped back with a growl, sword ready. But even before he knew what he was looking at, he knew it wasn't human.

The rider in front of him was eight feet tall, seated on a horse made of what appeared to be nothing but water. His shape was that of a large, menacing man, but his skin was the color of deep water and his beard was the glossy green of sea kelp. He wore his long seaweed hair braided back from his face like a Nordic warrior, and his huge body was covered in thick-shelled muscles, which he wore like armor. But while the long dragon spear in his hand was as good as an engraved announcement, what really gave him away was the scent. Even through the heavy fog, the warrior in front of him smelled of salt water and dragon's blood, and Justin lifted his sword with a triumphant grin.

"Vann Jeger."

The spirit looked down on him with utter disdain. "You know my name, and still you trespass here." He tipped his huge wooden spear forward, pointing the dark stained tip at Justin's chest. "You must want to die very badly, wyrm."

Justin ignored the weapon in his face. "I could say the same of you for daring to speak to me," he said proudly, pulling himself to his full height. "I am Justin Heartstriker, the dragon who attacked the Pit, and we have unfinished business."

Vann Jeger's black eyes went wide. "You?" He threw back his head in laughter, showing a mouthful of flat, yellow teeth. "*You?*" he cried. "Impossible! I saw the green fire in the distance with my own eyes. The dragon who attacked the Pit was clearly a powerful scion of the Quetzalcoatl himself, one of Bethesda's best. You are a *baby*."

"I am the Fifth Blade of Bethesda," Justin snarled. "A Knight of the Mountain!"

The spirit's laughter cut off as quickly as it had begun. "Do you think me a fool?" he said angrily, his black eyes dropping to the sword in Justin's hands. "That is Tyrfing. A fine blade and a legend, but not a Fang of the Heartstriker." He sat back on his horse. "If you're going to lie, serpent, at least make it believable."

Justin's jaw twitched. "I don't need my Fang to defeat an old has-been like you," he growled, stepping into position. "Fight me, and we'll see who's lying!"

"Me? Fight you?" Vann Jeger's lips curled in disgust. "Do you know who I am? I am the Death of Dragons, the one who has dedicated his immortality to ending your kind. You're a braggart who can't even manage to show up with a suitable weapon."

Justin bared his teeth in fury, but the spirit was already turning away. "I challenged the dragon from the Pit because I wished to fight against a Fang of the Heartstriker," he said as his horse began walking back into the fog. "You have no such weapon, therefore, you are beneath my notice."

"What the—You're not going to fight me?"

"Of course not," the spirit said without looking back. "My weapons are treasures, the lost masterworks of their age. To use them on a baby like you would be an insult to the brave heroes to whom they once belonged. But fear not. Just because I do not wish to waste my time or blades on insignificant insects doesn't mean you'll leave this place alive. I shall send my human team to grant your suicide wish."

"Then you'll be sending them to their deaths!" Justin roared. "I came here to kill *you*!"

Vann Jeger looked back over his shoulder with an expression of absolute disgust. "Kill me? A pathetic creature like *you*?" He turned back away again with a snort. "Impossible. You couldn't even kill my boredom."

That was the last straw. After a month of being looked down on by everyone in his family, being condescended to by his prey was the absolute end of Justin's patience. He didn't care that he was facing Vann Jeger's back, he didn't even care that the spirit had not yet accepted his challenge. He simply attacked with a roar, swinging Tyrfing as hard as he could.

The tiny sword wasn't meant for dragon magic. It bucked in his hands, actively rejecting the power Justin forced into it. But Justin had practiced this strike until it was a part of him, and he pushed it through anyway, sending a slice of magic sharp as his fangs and hot as his fire flying straight at Vann Jeger's back.

The attack cut through the tree trunks like wire through butter, setting the chunks of wet wood ablaze as they fell. It cut through the fog, incinerating the choking, wild magic until the forest was clear. And when the strike reached the spirit, it sliced him, too, going through Vann Jeger like a scythe through grass. It sliced his horse and spear, too, dividing each into neat halves.

Justin froze, staring at his enemy, whom he'd apparently just cut in two. Surely it couldn't be that—

Before he could finish his thought, the sundered spirit and his horse collapsed, pouring to the forest floor in a cascade of water only to instantly reform—horse and rider, both whole and uninjured—directly in front of him. That was all he had time to see before the spirit grabbed him around the neck and lifted him bodily off the ground.

"You will pay for that," Vann Jeger rumbled, his huge hand squeezing the dragon he was dangling like a caught fish in front of him.

"Sounds like someone's a poor loser," Justin gasped, dropping Tyrfing so he could use both hands to pry the spirit's hold from his neck. "What's the matter, water drop? Did I break your stick?"

He glanced pointedly over Vann Jeger's shoulder at the giant wooden dragon spear, which, unlike the miraculously re-forming spirit and his horse, was still lying in two pieces on the ground, and the Hunter began to growl. "Do you know what you have done?" he snarled. "You've disgraced a treasure!"

"How great can it be if it breaks in one hit?" Justin snarled back, kicking his dangling legs at Vann Jeger's stomach.

The spirit smacked his attack away. "You have no respect! I am the soul of the deep fjord! From the very beginning, the humans who lived on my shores have burned their heroes on my waters. They believed that their souls would be lifted to Valhalla, but their weapons became mine, as do all things that fall into my depths. For thousands of years I have kept their treasures, the work of their hands, and now you treat them as mere tools?"

He tossed Justin down, slamming him into the ground. "I have changed my mind," Vann Jeger said, hopping off his horse to land with a crash next to the prone dragon. "I was going to grant you an honorable death against a well-matched, if human, foe. But I have no mercy for a wyrm too stupid to recognize a priceless artifact when he sees one."

"So you're going to fight me now?" Justin said, grabbing his sword again before shoving himself back to his feet. "And here I thought you were scared."

Vann Jeger scowled. "Still delusional, but it matters not. If you wish so badly to be crushed, I will oblige, if only because it will give me a chance to teach you the value of true treasures before I take your head."

He reached out his hand as he said this, and the broken spear vanished, fading into the mist that still crawled across the ground.

In the same instant, a new weapon appeared in Vann Jeger's grasp. A long sword this time, its four-foot-long, rune-marked blade condensing from the mist like a water droplet. Just like the wooden spear he'd just broken, it was obviously magical. Justin was staring at it, wondering just how many weapons the spirit had at his fingertips, when Vann Jeger attacked.

For a slower dragon, that would have been the end. The spirit moved like water, his giant body warping and shifting unnaturally as he drove his sword straight at Justin's heart. But Fang or no, Justin was a Knight of the Heartstrikers. He dodged with time to spare, using Tyrfing's small size to his advantage as he slipped the little blade up under Vann Jeger's defense to stab the spirit in the ribs.

The short sword slid through the spirit's armor, sinking into his flesh like a stone into a pond as Justin watched in triumph. But when he tried to yank it out again for another stab, the blade refused to budge. Confused, Justin yanked again, but the short sword was stuck fast. He was still pulling with all his might when the spirit chopped down at his arm from above.

Cursing, Justin released Tyrfing, snatching his hand out of the way a split second before the spirit took it off. But as he was leaping back to avoid Vann Jeger's sword, his own weapon sunk into the spirit's armored chest, vanishing into Vann Jeger's body like a coin dropped into a deep pool.

"What did you do to my sword?"

Vann Jeger's black eyes gleamed. "Delusional *and* stupid, I see." He ceased his attack and straightened up with a cruel grin, patting the spot on his massive chest where Tyrfing had vanished. "Did I not just tell you, little whelp? *Everything* that falls into my waters belongs to me."

Justin couldn't believe his ears. "You *ate* my sword?"

"Think of it as a requisition," the spirit said haughtily. "An idiot like you was unworthy of a work of art like Tyrfing. And as you see…" He shifted his long sword to one hand and flexed the other. The moment his fingers closed, Tyrfing appeared in his off-hand grip, gleaming in the silver, misty sunlight as the spirit turned both blades on Justin. "It's in much better hands now."

"Then I'll just have to take it back," Justin growled, smoke curling from his mouth. He didn't care about Tyrfing, but like hell was he going to lose anything to this freak. It was also time to try a new tactic. From the way he'd instantly put himself back together after Justin's first attack, it was clear Vann Jeger was a water spirit in the most literal sense of the word. But while being made of water apparently meant you didn't care if you got stabbed or chopped in half, a sword was only part of Justin's arsenal, and losing one now wasn't going to set him back.

With that, Justin retreated, ceding ground to the spirit. Vann Jeger eyed the distance cautiously, but eventually he stepped in just like Justin knew he would. Opponents who thought themselves superior always fell for that trick because they thought they had nothing to fear. What Vann Jeger didn't know, though, was that Justin had been looked down on by every serious opponent he'd ever fought. He was always the challenger, the one fighting up, and he knew how to draw his enemies in, leaving his chest temptingly open to attack while he kept his eyes on Vann Jeger, daring him to try.

It was an invitation no fighter could resist, and wise as he claimed to be, Algonquin's Hunter was no exception. He charged after only a few seconds of taunting, stampeding across the soft, wet ground with his two swords—the long blade and the stolen Tyrfing—positioned to stab Justin through the lungs and heart. Even so, Justin waited, watching the spirit's swords until they were mere inches from his chest. Only then, when his enemy had committed to the attack and could not turn back, did Justin let go, dropping his human mask in an explosion of fire.

Under normal circumstances, the explosion would have been green, the undying emerald fire of his grandfather. Without his Fang, though, Justin's blast was the rich, molten orange of his own fire, but it was still more than enough. Everything his flames touched—the loamy ground, the tall trees, his clothes, Vann Jeger's surprised face—turned instantly to ash. Justin alone was immune, because the fire *was* him, the burning magic that made him what he was. And when the glare died down a heartbeat later, he was looking down on the now burning forest from his true height.

"Who's a whelp now?" the dragon roared, breathing another blast of flame at the trees, spreading the forest fire until even the ever-present fog was overwhelmed by smoke. "Still want to leave me to your humans?"

His taunt was still echoing when he smelled the spirit's bloody, seawater scent behind him. Justin swiveled his head, turning just in time to see Vann Jeger condense from what was left of the mist at the top of one of the smoldering trees with another weapon, a metal spear this time, glinting in his hands. He hadn't even finished forming before he threw it, launching the weapon straight at the soft spot below Justin's jaw. But fast as the spirit was, Justin was faster.

Without even the conceit of a human shape to weigh him down, the dragon moved like lightning, ducking under the spear before lashing out with his tail to knock the spirit's tree completely out of the ground. The blow caught the spirit off guard. He stumbled, bracing against the falling tree. He was beginning to dissolve back into the mist when Justin lashed out with his claws, pinning the water spirit to the still falling tree before he could get away.

There was nothing held back this time, nothing saved for later. From the moment Justin had realized what it would take to win, every move had led up to this. In just a few seconds, Vann Jeger would turn back into water and slip away. Right now, though, the spirit was pinned beneath his talons, and like any true dragon, Justin came down on him with everything he had.

He opened his mouth with a roar, engulfing Vann Jeger in a blast of fire so hot, it changed the consistency of the air itself. Brilliant, orange-white flames snaked around the spirit's blue body like chains, and everywhere they touched, Vann Jeger vanished, his water instantly turning to vapor.

But even after he'd boiled the spirit away completely, Justin didn't stop. He couldn't. Fire like this could only be summoned once. Already, Justin's throat was cracking under the heat. It'd be days before he recovered enough to pull off an attack like this again. If he didn't end things now, he wouldn't get another shot, so Justin decided to make sure he wouldn't need one.

From the moment he'd realized Vann Jeger could reform himself from the mist, he'd known the only way to actually defeat him was to keep burning until there was no water left at all. With that in mind, he pulled back, bathing the entire forest in a wash of orange fire. He pushed his fire hotter with every breath, pumping the bellows of his magic until the soil beneath him began to vaporize and the trees at the far edge of his vision spontaneously burst into flame. He pushed until his own feathers began to smoke and the rapidly expanding air created a shockwave that blasted the ancient trees flat in all directions. He pushed until every molecule of oxygen was consumed, smothering his own flames and leaving nothing for him to breathe. Even then, he pushed a little further, pouring his heat into the landscape until even the rocks were burning. Only then, when everything that could be destroyed had been, did Justin finally let his fire die.

It was like standing on another planet. The misty forest was gone, as was the soil below it. Even the omnipresent, oppressive magic of the Reclamation Land had been burned away, leaving him standing alone in a bone-dry crater of fine, powdery ash. But satisfying as it was to witness the absolute thoroughness of his victory, even Justin couldn't remain in the heavy carbon dioxide bubble his intense heat had created. His lungs were already empty from creating the massive fire, and so Justin had no choice but to use the last of his strength to spread his wings and fly up, forcing his body through the unnaturally heavy air until he finally broke through the ceiling of smoke and exploded into the clear sky above.

He sucked the cold, clear air into his ravaged lungs with a gasp, knocking the ash out of his feathers with a powerful beat of his wings. When he was no longer in danger of suffocating, he took a different kind of breath, scenting the air for any lingering trace of his enemy, and found nothing. Even up here where there was still water, his sensitive nose didn't pick up so much as a trace of Vann Jeger's briny scent, which could only mean one thing.

He'd *won.*

Satisfaction struck him like a physical blow. He'd done it. He'd gambled everything on a single attack, and it had *worked.* He'd known it would, of course, but to actually be on the other side, to *feel* his victory…there was nothing better in the world. He alone had dared to enter Algonquin's land and face her champion, and like all who dared greatly, he'd been rewarded. He, Justin Heartstriker, had defeated the Death of Dragons!

Now all he needed was proof.

Sucking in a lungful of clean air, Justin dove back down into the smoke. He'd been hoping to bring home a head, but that was impossible since he'd evaporated Vann Jeger, so he'd have to settle for some other trophy. One of the spirit's prized weapons would have been perfect, but unfortunately his own power had made trophy hunting nearly impossible. The ash bowl he'd created was as fine as silt, a quarter mile in diameter, and swallowed everything that fell into it. Even using his wings to blow the ash back, hunting for a weapon in that pit was like searching for a needle in the desert. Already, his search had taken longer than he was wise to spend, and so, with a growl of frustration, Justin decided to go back to his original plan: ripping open the secrets of Reclamation Land.

He changed course instantly, shooting out of the cloud of smoke that marked his victory and into the clear air beyond to take his first real look at Algonquin's hidden land. But while his plan was to do a military assessment—noting landmarks, weak points, obvious weapons, and so forth—what was waiting below him blew all such practical thoughts out of his head.

When Justin had first found himself standing in the old-growth forest, the obvious explanation was that it was some kind of illusion, a trick of the mist. Looking down from the sky, though, Justin saw the truth was the other way around. The run down houses and overgrown lots were the illusion. Even the primeval forest where he'd faced Vann Jeger was nothing but a border, a narrow band of green wrapped protectively around a landscape like nothing he'd ever seen.

It was like looking into a child's illustration of fairy land. Inside the forest's protective circle, giant mushrooms stood in rings around flowering trees the size of skyscrapers. Wolves as big as buses lounged by perfectly circular pools of cobalt blue water while deer with golden coats and silver antlers grazed in the rolling meadows beside them. Even the grass was different, growing thick as a carpet and too green to possibly be real all the way to where the lake shimmered in the distance.

It was all so strange and beautiful and overwhelming that even Justin, who could never be accused of romanticism, took several heartbeats to realize that he was staring at *spirits*. Thousands of them in every type he could imagine. But while a spirit refuge actually made a great deal of sense for Algonquin's Reclamation Land, nothing explained the *magic*.

Even before he'd actually stepped inside, the power of Algonquin's Reclamation Land had been overwhelming. Now, flying high over what he could only assume was its heart, the wild magic clung to him like tar, and that set off warning bells. Justin normally prided himself on being willfully ignorant of anything beneath the notice of a proper warrior dragon, but even he could tell that this was more magic than should ever be in one place without actually being part of a spell, and he was hundreds of feet in the air. How strong must the magic be down on the ground, where it originated?

He couldn't imagine, but one thing was absolutely clear: this much magic in one place could not happen naturally. Whatever the spirits were doing down there, the end result was a massive buildup of magic that, if this section of Reclamation Land was representative of the rest, went on for *miles*.

He couldn't begin to guess how much power that added up to in total, or what Algonquin could possibly be planning to do with it all, but he didn't have to. Magic this big in the hands of their enemy could not be tolerated. But while he couldn't do anything to stop a magical buildup of this magnitude, just knowing about it before Algonquin played her hand would give whoever had the information a huge advantage.

Justin broke into a sharp-toothed grin. Forget killing the dragon hunter, this was the true prize. Information this valuable would put him at the top of Heartstriker for sure. Even if they didn't fight the Lady of the Lakes themselves, even if she didn't use it for a century, just knowing about the magic Algonquin was stockpiling in Reclamation Land would give Bethesda leverage over the other dragon clans for years to come, and she'd have Justin to thank for it.

With that happy thought, he pivoted in the air and started flying as fast as he could for the border. He was gleefully imagining how his mother would react to his news when a shadow passed over his head.

His first thought was that it was a cloud, but then he remembered that he was above the clouds. Confused, Justin swiveled his head up, squinting into the glare of the bright morning sun. Sure enough, something was in the sky above him. It wasn't a cloud, more like a haze of water vapor shimmering in the sunlight. Shimmers that condensed into a hail of spears right before his eyes.

Justin barely had time to comprehend what he was seeing before the falling spears crashed into him like a wall. The bladed shafts stabbed into him from tail to crest, shredding his wings like paper and punching him out of the sky. For ten terrifying seconds, he tumbled in freefall, and then he crashed into the meadow where he'd seen the golden deer grazing only seconds before, the long spears pinning him to the too-green grass like a bug on a board. He was struggling to rip himself free when the shadow passed over him again, and he looked up to see Vann Jeger standing over him, sitting relaxed on his horse like he'd been here the whole time just waiting for the dragon to fall.

For a second, Justin could only stare in shock, and then rage like he'd never known consumed him whole. "*How?*" he bellowed, tearing himself against the weapons that held him down. "I destroyed you! *I burned you to ash!*"

"So you did," Vann Jeger said, dismounting with a smile that stabbed as deep as his blades. "I admit, you caught me off guard. But while your fire was unexpectedly impressive, you're a thousand years too young to understand that fire will never be enough."

He held out his hand as he spoke, and an executioner's ax formed in his palm, its half-moon blade glinting in the sunlight. "You dragons think of yourselves as conquerors," he said solemnly, positioning the blade over Justin's neck. "But no matter how fast you breed or how big you grow, you will never win, because we are the will of the land itself. We are undefeatable as the sea, indestructible as the wind. We are the life of this world, and when my Lady's work here is done, we shall be its sole rulers once more."

"Never," Justin snarled, baring his fangs. "You are nothing but prey!"

The spirit chuckled. "Arrogant to the end. How typical." He planted his boot on Justin's head, stomping him down into the bloody grass. "It really is a pity. You had promise. In another few centuries, you might even have been a challenge. Now, though," he lifted the blade, "all you are is dead."

Justin narrowed his eyes, watching the ax rise over him. If he'd had fire left, he would have melted it to slag before Vann Jeger could swing, but he had nothing. He'd already exhausted his magic on what he'd thought would be his final attack, and with the spears bleeding him dry, he didn't have the strength left to even snap at the spirit's boots. He was about to try anyway, if only so he could die with his teeth in his enemy as a dragon should, when the ground beneath him rumbled.

Considering all the other weirdness going on inside Reclamation Land, Justin didn't think much of it. Vann Jeger, however, looked up like someone had shouted his name. "No," he growled, lips peeling back in a snarl. "This is *my* hunt."

With Vann Jeger's boot on his forehead, Justin couldn't turn to see who the spirit was talking to. He didn't smell another presence, but with magic this thick, he didn't trust his nose like he usually did. He was about to ignore whatever it was and just focus on biting off whatever part of Vann Jeger he could reach when the ground rumbled again. This time, though, the vibrations had a tonality to them. It was almost like whale song, but miles deeper, the notes so low they were more feeling than sound. But though Justin still couldn't make heads or tails of what that meant, he knew a command when he heard one.

"*No!*" Vann Jeger shouted again, removing his boot from Justin's head so he could turn and face whatever it was properly. "So long as I guard the city, I am free to hunt when and what I choose. *That* was our oath, or is Algonquin going back on her word?"

Now that the spirit's weight was off his head, Justin could move. He'd intended to use this unexpected freedom to bite off Vann Jeger's leg, but he'd always had an excellent sense for danger, and at this point, his instincts were certain that the fjord spirit was no longer the greatest threat. So, though it went against years of training, Justin turned away from his enemy and looked up.

And up.

And up.

Well, at least there was nothing wrong with his instincts.

Like everyone on the planet who'd paid any attention to the news in the last decade, Justin knew what Algonquin's leviathan looked like. He didn't know where it came from or what it was, no one did, but he could recognize it when he saw it. But even though his brain technically had a name for what his eyes were seeing, comprehension did not follow. There simply weren't words big enough for the shadow towering over the meadow like a small mountain.

Funny enough, his first thought was that the whale song comparison had been unexpectedly accurate. The giant shape *did* look kind of like a bizarre, deep-water fish. Its skin was mottled brown and black, like an eel's, and it crawled on tentacles like an octopus. If it had a mouth or eyes, Justin couldn't find them, but though it looked like it belonged in some deep, dark place, it didn't seem to mind the sunlight or the dry land. It actually seemed to be floating over the grass with a grace that belied its bulk, its tentacles waving in a mesmerizing dance, like a cobra shifting before it struck its prey. Even Justin, who should have known better, was transfixed, staring up at the leviathan in horrified wonder when the strange, alien song came rumbling through the ground again, and Vann Jeger threw down his ax with a snarl.

"It seems you have received a temporary stay of execution," he said, reaching out to yank the myriad spears out of Justin's body with a violent jerk. "It will not be a long one, I promise."

"I don't know about that," Justin said, grinning through the pain at his enemy's discomfort. "Looks like you've just been put in your place, water spirit."

Vann Jeger's only answer to that was a sneer as he pulled the last of the spears out of Justin's body. Before the dragon could even try to slip away, though, Vann Jeger scooped up his discarded ax and swung it like a golf club, slamming the blunt side of the shaft down on Justin's skull. Magic followed the strike like a lungful of cold seawater, and Justin's mind went blank.

And a mile away, on the edge of Reclamation Land, as close as she could get to the fence without alerting their enemy, Chelsie drew her sword with a vile curse, cutting a hole through the world back to Heartstriker Mountain to deliver the bad news to her mother.

CHAPTER THIRTEEN

Justin woke to cold water splashing over his head.

He came to with a start, opening his mouth to bite whoever would dare only to find that he couldn't. He was back in his human shape, dressed in what looked like spare medical scrubs and bound on his knees to a damp stone floor with chains large enough to hold an ocean liner. He couldn't even turn his head thanks to the metal cage that had been fitted over his skull, its lower half and sides sharpened so that if he opened his mouth more than it took to speak softly, he'd slice his jaw open.

Another time, the overkill security would have struck him as a sign of respect. Now, though, the unwelcome obstacle was nothing but an annoyance. Every muscle in his body hurt, and his burned throat was spasming in pain. All he wanted to do was go back to sleep, but that was impossible thanks to the magic.

Strange, cold power covered him like tar inside and out. Even if he hadn't used up all his fire on Vann Jeger, he couldn't have gotten enough out to light a candle under these conditions. As it was, he could barely lift his head, but considering he'd been one ax blow away from losing it, Justin supposed he should count this as a step forward. Quitting was for pathetic dragons who'd lost their ambition, anyway, and so, summoning up all his pride, Justin forced his throbbing head up to take stock of his situation.

He was in what appeared to be an underwater cavern. An obviously fake one since Justin was fairly certain natural caverns didn't have tasteful recessed lighting, but it was still impressive if only for its size. The cave was as large as an aircraft hangar, though aside from the little stone island in the center where he'd been chained, it seemed to be mostly water. Lake water from the smell, which only made him more wary. So far as he could tell, though, the giant room seemed to be empty. There was no scent of Vann Jeger, and he was pretty sure he couldn't miss the leviathan. He was wondering if this place was meant to be a prison when a voice whispered.

"Welcome."

He froze, eyes darting. The voice had come from everywhere and nowhere, but while that was unnerving, Justin was having a hard time being alarmed by something so beautiful. Just the way the sound of it had flowed over the words reminded him of floating weightlessly in placid waters. He was about to ask it speak again when it ordered. "Lean forward."

Justin set his jaw stubbornly. Beautiful voice or not, he didn't obey anyone but his mother. But just as he resolved to never move again, magic crashed into him like an iron rod to the back of the head.

He resisted on principle, but after his fight with Vann Jeger, he couldn't even slow himself down as the magic forced him to lean over until he was staring straight down at his own reflection in the dark water. He froze after that, bracing for the attack he was sure was about to leap at him out of the water, but there was nothing. Just his own reflection staring back at him in the cave's tasteful light, its lips curled in a cold, cruel smirk.

A smirk which Justin was dead certain was not on his own face.

He jumped back with a curse, or he tried to. Once again, the magic held him fast, forcing him to watch as the reflection's cruel smile grew wider

"You're slow for a dragon."

Justin jerked again. The words had come from his lips in the water, but the voice was the smooth, beautiful sound from before. He was still wrapping his brain around that when the reflected Justin bent over, reaching through the water to grab the ledge at his—*their*—feet.

Now he *did* manage to jump, shoving against the magic with all his might as he jerked away from his reflection as it pulled itself out of the dark water to stand beside him on the little stone island. Water pooled around it, leaving a cold, slimy trail on the rock, but the reflection itself looked every bit as dry as the original as it undid the cuffs and muzzle that mirrored Justin's own with a quick flex of its hands.

"You are bigger than I thought," it said when it was free, tossing the reflected chains back into the water, where they vanished with a splash. "But smaller than I'd hoped."

It smiled at Justin as it finished, clearly waiting for him to speak, but his mouth didn't seem to work. When the silence had gone on too long, his reflection shook its head.

"Surely the dragon who could surprise my Hunter long enough to get a look at my secret garden is smarter than this?" it cooed, reaching down to pat Justin's cheek with his own deathly cold hand. "You know my name, cockroach. Say it."

Justin didn't want to. He didn't want to do anything that would make the creepy thing wearing his face happy, but the hated word was already on the tip of his tongue.

"Algonquin."

The reflection smiled his own cocky grin back at him. It was a tiny detail in the larger scheme of creepy nonsense Justin had dealt with today, but the sight of his own mocking smile on something else's face gave him the final kick he needed to snap out of his shock.

"Why am I here?" he demanded, pulling himself as straight as he could with the chains. "Why did you stop Vann Jeger from killing me? You hate dragons."

"You give yourself too much credit," Algonquin said, looking down on him with his own green eyes. "Hate implies investment, but your kind are merely pests to me, a troublesome nuisance I wish to exterminate. It's nothing personal."

Justin didn't believe that for a second. "If that's so, then why stop the ax? Why not kill me and be done with it?"

Algonquin smiled wider. "Again, you overestimate your own importance. I could kill you right now without lifting a finger. This cavern is normally underwater. All I'd have to do is let my lake back in and watch you drown."

"So why don't you?" Justin growled, lifting his chin. "I'm not afraid."

"Because there's no point," the spirit said with a sigh. "Dragons are like roaches. For every one you kill, ten more scurry in the shadows. Vann Jeger enjoys the hunt, but I have a city to run."

His reflection turned away, walking across the wet stone island with Justin's own no-nonsense gait. "Normally, I would have been content to let my Hunter have you," Algonquin went on. "Vann Jeger needs to kill things on a regular basis or he grows surly. Unfortunately for him, your presence today is part of a larger plan that, unlike your miserable life, is actually worth my time."

"Plan?" Justin scoffed. "Impossible. I didn't even decide to enter Reclamation Land until an hour ago."

Algonquin chuckled. "Deluded creature. You are directly related to a seer, and yet you still believe your decisions are your own?"

She shook her head, waving the reflection of Justin's hand over the water, which immediately parted to reveal a very expensive looking, and apparently waterproof, augmented reality projector. It was an industrial model, the kind Five Sense Theaters used to project three-dimensional images into the crowd, but just as Justin was wondering why Algonquin would have a projector in her prison, the spirit reached down to turn it on.

The machine came on with a hum, projecting a crystal clear, 3D image of an empty room into the air in front of them, almost like they were looking through a window. The whole thing happened so suddenly and unexpectedly, Justin didn't even realize what he was looking at until a tall, beautiful, terrifying figure stepped into view, flanked by her shorter, but equally terrifying, shadow.

"Lady of the Lakes," Bethesda said, motioning for Chelsie to stand beside her as she took in the sight of Justin, bound on the floor, and his doppelganger, smiling beside him like a cat who'd gotten into the canary coop. "I was wondering when you'd call."

"Good," Algonquin replied coolly. "If you were expecting my call, then we can get right to the point." She reached down to grab the cage surrounding Justin's face. "I have something that belongs to you," she said, turning his head from side to side like he was an animal up for auction. "Would you like it back?"

"That depends," the Heartstriker said, crossing her arms. "How much is it going to cost me? Justin's value isn't what it was."

Justin knew she had to say that, this *was* a negotiation, but his mother's words still hurt. Algonquin, however, seemed delighted by her apparent disinterest. "How nice it must be to have so many children that you can afford to be spendthrift with their lives!" she cackled, giving Bethesda a wide grin. "But don't worry, the price on this one is rock bottom."

"Then get on with it," Bethesda snapped. "Some of us are busy."

"Very well," Algonquin said, releasing Justin's head. "If you want your son back in one piece, all you have to do is say please."

Justin jerked in alarm. That couldn't be right. It *couldn't* be that easy. His mother was clearly thinking the same thing, because her scowl deepened. "That's it?"

"That's it," Algonquin echoed, smiling wider than ever. "One little word is all you have to say, and your whelp can scurry home only slightly worse for wear."

She paused to let Bethesda answer. When she didn't, the spirit shook her head. "I don't think I need to mention that this generous offer will not be repeated," she warned. "My Hunter gets very put out when I take his prey, even a little minnow such as this. He's still all worked up over missing the Heartstriker who was breathing green fire all over my Pit last month. This one claims to be his target, but there's no way a little whelp like him could possibly wield a Fang of the Heartstrikers."

Justin held his breath, but his mother didn't correct Algonquin. "Your Hunter is no concern of mine," she said casually, looking down at her nails. "I only accepted this call to hear your deal. If you can't give me a serious offer, then we have nothing more to discuss."

"So you don't care if Vann Jeger kills one of your knights tonight?" Algonquin said, arching an eyebrow. "He's already got their human trapped in a curse."

"Any knight of mine who'd risk his neck for a human deserves what he gets," Bethesda snapped. "Are you going to bargain or not?"

"Not," Algonquin said. "My offer is what it is. Personally, I don't care about your baby's life one way or the other. This is just an experiment to see if I can't get the great Heartstriker to *ask* for something instead of demanding it."

"Then you're in for a long wait," Bethesda growled, her face growing serious at last. "I do not beg, spirit. Not for you, not for him," she nodded at Justin, "not for anyone."

Her words landed like blows on Justin's shoulders, hammering him into the stone. He couldn't actually believe what he was hearing until Algonquin broke it down for him.

"You're just going to throw him away?" the spirit said, eyebrows shooting up. "That's a little wasteful, don't you think?"

"I don't care what you think," the Heartstriker said haughtily. "Justin is mine to use as I see fit." Her voice grew condescending. "I know you can't understand this, Algonquin, seeing how your kind can't breed, but children exist to be useful to their parents. I learned ages ago that lowering myself to save one defeats the entire purpose of having them in the first place."

"Is that so?" the spirit said, looking back at Justin. "Then you don't mind if I use your son as fish food?"

"It's none of my concern how you waste your time," Bethesda said flippantly. "Now, unless you have something of actual value you want to discuss, this conversation is over. I have work to do."

Algonquin shrugged and turned to Justin. "Would you like to say goodbye?"

He opened his mouth. To say what, he wasn't sure. In the end, though, it didn't matter. Bethesda had already hung up, cutting off the video feed with a click.

"I can't claim that was unexpected," Algonquin said, smiling down at him with a cold, cruel curve of his own lips. "Like all dragons, your mother has always been a selfish, wasteful creature. But I have to admit, I didn't think she'd throw you over quite *that* easily."

Justin wanted to yell that she was wrong. That this was all a ruse and his mother would never abandon him like that. But badly as he wanted to believe that, the empty air where his mother's image had stood taunted him with the truth. It'd finally happened, a voice that sounded very much like Julius's whispered. She'd finally thrown him away.

"Don't look so down," Algonquin said, reaching over to pat him on the head. "I'm not actually going to feed you to my fish. They deserve far better."

"Then what are you going to do?" he croaked, doing his best to sound like he didn't care.

"I've already done it," the spirit replied. "I told you at the beginning, you're just a cog. A small, insignificant detail in a much larger machine. I knew your mother would throw you away before I called, though I have to say I'm delighted she played her part so well. You see, you're already sold, and it would be very awkward if Bethesda turned out to actually care."

Justin bared his teeth. "What do you mean sold?"

Algonquin's face—which is to say, his own face—turned mocking. Instead of answering, though, she waved his hand over the water yet again, pushing it back this time to reveal a stone walkway that ran from the island to a hidden door on the far side of the cave Justin hadn't noticed in the gloom. He was wondering if she was going to march him down it when his nose caught the unmistakable smell of sea ice. He'd only smelled it once before, but like all threats to his family, he'd memorized it instantly. But with the evidence literally in his lungs, Justin still couldn't believe what his nose was telling him until he saw the dragoness emerge from the gloom.

"*You*," he snarled, baring his teeth.

"Who else?" Estella said, smiling a predator's triumphant smirk as she strolled down the narrow stone walkway. "How are you even surprised? Have I not been the one pulling all the strings so far?"

Justin dismissed that with a sneer. "I don't care if you hate our family, but how can you work for *her*?" He jerked his head toward Algonquin, who was watching the exchange with an amused expression. "You're a seer, can't you see she's just playing us against each other? You're betraying our whole race!"

"Don't be so dramatic," Estella said, stepping onto the island. "The Lady of the Lakes here would have my head on a pike in an instant if she could manage it. At the moment, though, we share a mutual enemy, which is as close to allies as our kind gets."

"Don't lump me in with you," Algonquin said with a disdainful sniff. "But the white wyrm is correct on one issue at least. Eliminating Bethesda the Heartstriker is something I've desired for many years now. The Quetzalcoatl was at least wise enough to stay on his continent, but the broodmare's brats are forever squeezing into my domain. That is an annoyance I would give much to end, including delaying my own gratification that would come from killing one of the three dragon seers for as long as it takes to hand you over."

Estella nodded like the implied death threat was a great compliment. Justin, however, had had about enough of this. "You'll never win," he growled. "Heartstriker is better than you in every way. We will crush your plans to dust."

"But there is no *we* anymore, is there?" Estella said sweetly. "Or did my ears deceive me when I heard Bethesda throw you away."

Justin clamped his jaw shut, and Estella knelt beside him. "There, there," she whispered, brushing the water from his bruised face. "I saw this would happen. I knew she would betray you. That's why I came."

He opened his mouth to tell her where she could shove the compassionate act, but Estella put a finger on his lips, casting Algonquin a pointed look before leaning in until her lips brushed his ear. "I know we've been enemies since before you were born," she whispered, each word leaving little puffs of frost on his skin. "But you're not in a position to be judgmental. The Lady wants to give you back to Vann Jeger. His anger is an inconvenience for her.

The only reason she's not dragging you back to him right now is because she knows I want you."

"Why?" Justin growled. "Are you looking to die?"

That was supposed to be a threat, but Estella smiled like he'd told her a joke. "Do you know what I am?" she whispered. "You might be a whelp now, but I've looked into the future. I've seen what you become: a prodigy, a *legend*. Your mother was a fool to throw you away. I am not. I know what you are worth, Justin, and I want it for myself."

He jerked away, eyes wide in confusion. "What are you talking about?"

"I want you to join us," Estella said, looking him up and down. "Times are changing, and the Daughters of the Three Sisters are no exception. We can no longer afford to ignore strength when it appears, and unlike your mother, we're smart enough to know that." Her fingers trailed down his shoulder to trace lightly over his bicep. "*We* would not throw you away. The fact that I'm willing to bargain for your life with the Lady of the Lakes proves how much we need you. I will set you free of this tomb where your foolish mother left you to be food for Algonquin's fish, and all I ask in return is your sword at my side."

Justin opened his mouth, the *No* already on his lips, but it never got out. Ideas were forming in his head. Dangerous ideas that quickly became dangerous plots. Just considering it was a huge risk, but Justin already knew he was going to take it. At the end of the day, there were ways dragons were supposed to die, and being chopped up and fed to fish was not one of them.

"*If* I came with you," he said. "Would I get a sword?"

"The very best we have," Estella promised.

Justin thought a moment longer, and then he nodded. "You have a deal."

Estella smirked one last time and shot to her feet. "Svena!"

Justin looked up in surprise. He hadn't even realized there was another dragon in the room until Estella yelled for her. When she stepped forward, though, he saw why. Svena looked terrible. Her scent was next to nothing, and she limped down the stone bridge like she'd been on the losing end of multiple fights. She hardly looked like the great and powerful White Witch everyone was always going on about, but Estella didn't seem to notice her sister's terrible condition. She just nodded at Justin. "Take our newest treasure home and let him have his pick of our mothers' arsenal. Nothing is too good."

Svena nodded silently and grabbed Justin's shoulder. A cold wind rose at the same time, filling the cave with the scent of snow and the bite of dragon magic. Both grew stronger by the second, filling Algonquin's grotto with arctic ice, which the spirit didn't seem to like at all. Justin had just enough time to appreciate that before Svena's magic bit down hard on his chest, yanking him to the other side of the world.

• • •

"Your sister looks very ill."

Estella turned away from the falling snow to look again at Algonquin. As usual, the ever changing Lady of the Lakes had shifted while her attention was distracted. Now, instead of the idiot Heartstriker whelp's face, the spirit wore Estella's own, smiling coyly at her from the water's edge. It was unnerving as always, but Estella had seen Algonquin's tricks before, and she didn't let them get to her now.

"My sister is my concern, not yours."

Her reflection laughed. "You don't seem very concerned," she pointed out. "That's unlike you, Northern Star. When we first met, your clan was your life."

"My clan is still my life," Estella snapped. "Nothing has changed."

Algonquin's eyebrows lifted in Estella's own skeptical look, and the dragon turned away with a glower. A spirit could never understand the sacrifices required of a seer. Of course it hurt her to make Svena suffer, but it was the only way to destroy Heartstriker for good. Besides, her sister would recover eventually, which was more than Estella could say for Brohomir. Or herself, for that matter.

As always, that thought darkened her mood, and Estella hurried on to other things. "I believe our business here is complete," she said stiffly. "I will take my leave."

"Not quite yet."

Algonquin's words were still echoing when the water around them began to surge. That was probably meant to be frightening, but it was hard to scare a seer who already knew her own end, which was why Estella didn't even flinch when the Leviathan's black tentacles emerged from the water at Algonquin's feet, rising up to encircle the little stone island in a wall of slick, black flesh.

"I'm always happy to help dragons tear each other apart," Algonquin said, strolling over to the wall of tentacles to sit on the lowest slimy appendage like it was a throne. "But before I can let you go, there's still the matter of my payment."

Estella's eyes went wide. "Payment?" she cried. "What payment do I owe you? I was the one who set this up! I handed you the Heartstriker's children on a platter. You'd still be hunting for the dragon from the Pit if I hadn't tipped you off about his human mage, and that was only the beginning." Estella pressed her hand against her chest. "Thanks to *my* efforts, the world's largest dragon clan is about devour itself from within. Is the fall of the Heartstriker and her clan not payment enough for your very small part in this?"

"The death of the Heartstriker would be a prize indeed," Algonquin admitted. "*If* you can pull it off."

Estella scoffed. "You doubt me?"

"I doubt everything," the spirit said, shooting Estella's disdainful look right back at her. "You forget, white snake, I am old. Older than you, older than your vaunted mothers, older than any of your kind. I have seen the impossible happen more times than you've drawn breath, and I do not trust anything blindly, especially not little dragon seers who think themselves clever."

"She *will* die," Estella growled, holding up her arm to show the spirit the last remaining black chain on her wrist. "The future is bound in chains, Algonquin. I could not save the Heartstriker now even if I wished to."

The spirit's smile widened even as the circle of tentacles surrounding the island began to close in. "And what if you don't live to see it?"

Before Estella could reply, the already heavy magic in the cavern doubled, sending her to her knees. She caught herself at the last second, but not fast enough to hide her weakness from Algonquin, who laughed in delight.

"Foolish little serpent," she cackled, her watery voice rippling with anticipation. "You came willingly into my domain. Even your sister's spell cannot pierce this place again without my permission. So tell me, Northern Star, how does your future look as a head on my wall?"

By the time she finished, The Lady of the Lakes' dark, heavy magic was like an anvil on Estella's shoulders, but it could not push her down. Algonquin was powerful, even for a spirit, but when push came to shove, she was still just a lake. Estella, on the other hand, was the daughter of gods, and she bowed to no one but her mothers.

"Save your threats for someone who can't see through them," she said haughtily, calling her own magic to freeze the leviathan's writhing tentacles. "The first vision any seer has is their own death. I've known mine all my life, and it has nothing to do with you or this filthy cave. But even if I couldn't see what was coming, I wouldn't be afraid, because I know you can't kill me."

"Really?" Algonquin asked, leaning forward as ice encasing the leviathan's tentacles began to crack. "And how do you figure that?"

"Because you know as well as I do that if I die, another seer will be born to take my place, and the Heartstriker will continue to be a thorn in your side," Estella said calmly, crossing her arms. "Only an idiot would throw away long-term benefits for short-term gratification, and for all your faults, you've never been an idiot. Or has that changed since you woke, Algonquin?"

The spirit sighed. "It seems my bluff's been called," she said, waving her hands to send the tentacles back down into the lake below. "You have no idea how badly I want to plunge your smug face under the water until you drown. Alas, the deal you offer is simply too good to pass up. If you succeed, the Heartstriker dies. If you fail, you'll die. Either way, I win." She sighed. "It's still a pity, though. I always wanted a seer's head for my collection."

"Then go after Brohomir's," Estella said, tossing her white hair. "He would look lovely mounted on a pike."

"He *is* prettier than you are," Algonquin said thoughtfully. "But, sadly, his head is not yet yours to offer."

"Let me go and I'll change that," Estella snapped, crossing her arms over her chest. "Haven't you wasted enough of our time with this?"

"Not yet," Algonquin said, hopping down off her perch on the leviathan's tentacles. "There's still the matter of my fee. So long as you are in my domain, you are at my mercy, and you of all creatures should know there's no getting out of that without a price."

"Then stop prattling on and name it," Estella snapped. "I have more important things to do than stand around humoring a senile old spirit in a cave that stinks of fish."

"No need to be rude," Algonquin said. "It's a simple request. Just a boon, really."

"What?" Estella growled.

The Lady's smile turned coy. "Give me your hair."

Estella had little experience with being surprised, and she did a very poor job now of keeping the shock off her face. She couldn't see Algonquin's future, but she'd known from her own that the spirit would want something, though she never would have guessed *hair*. The more she thought about it, though, the more the request made sense.

Despite being a spirit, Algonquin relied primarily on human mages to do most of her dirty work, and hair was a powerful magical link. With it, Algonquin would be able forge a magical connection to Estella from anywhere in the world, even through the protections of her mothers' hidden fortress below the ice. It could be used to trace her movements, or even kill her from afar, and then there was the part where Estella *liked* her hair.

But while her first instinct was to turn the spirit down, Estella had an advantage that even an ancient force of nature like the Lady of the Lakes couldn't match, and that was absolute knowledge of the future. She could see the rest of her life like pictures in a book, and after this meeting, Algonquin played no part in it. The mere fact that she hadn't foreseen the spirit's demand proved that giving Algonquin her hair would make no difference in the end. Whatever Algonquin was planning, she wouldn't pull it off before Estella brought the Heartstriker to her knees, and after that, well, nothing much mattered.

With that in mind, the choice became simple, and Estella reached back to gather her hair, savoring the feel of the smooth strands one last time. "You want it?" she said, turning her head to show Algonquin the long white ponytail. "It's yours. But only after you let me go."

The spirit spread her arms, and all the leviathan's tentacles slid back into the water, once again revealing the path out. "Be my guest."

Never taking her eyes off the spirit, Estella strode down the still wet stone walkway across the dark water to the door in the cave's outer edge. When she was physically standing in the exit, she called her magic, honing it to a fine edge. Then, before she could regret it, she yanked the power up, slicing clean through her gathered hair.

"There," she spat, dropping the severed ponytail into the water at her feet. "The payment is made."

"And accepted," the spirit said as Estella's hair vanished into the depths. "You are free to go, Northern Star."

Ignoring the creeping feeling that she'd made a terrible mistake, Estella turned on her heel and marched out of the cavern, climbing up the damp stairs toward the surface where her hired boat was waiting to take her away from Algonquin's Tower in the lake and back to the mainland of the DFZ.

• • •

The last twenty minutes had been the longest of Julius's life.

Marci was still out, there was no word from Justin, and though Amelia was stirring, she had yet to actually wake up. That last one was particularly worrying. Generally speaking, it took a lot to keep a dragon down. He wasn't sure what Chelsie had done to knock her out earlier, but he was certain it should have worn off by now. But even though she hadn't opened her eyes yet, Amelia did look much better. Julius was trying to feel hopeful about that when his phone buzzed.

He'd barely registered the motion before he had the thing in his hands. When the name flashed on the screen, though, his heart stuttered, because it wasn't Justin or Marci or anyone he actually wanted to talk to.

It was his mother.

For a few seconds, Julius actually considered not answering. But two decades of enforced obedience were difficult to ignore, and there was always the chance Bethesda would have information about Justin. It was that more than anything that made his decision. Not wanting to disturb Amelia, Julius stepped out of the living room into the hall that led to the kitchen, raising the phone to his ear as he grimly accepted the call. "Hello, Mother."

"*Julius!*"

He jumped, eyes going wide. Maybe he was hearing things, but he would have sworn it sounded like Bethesda was *crying*. "What's wrong?"

"It's your brother. He's been captured by Algonquin."

Julius took a ragged breath. Capture wasn't the worst scenario he'd imagined, but it was close. "What happened?"

"He went into Reclamation Land alone and challenged Vann Jeger," she sobbed. "Now my brave baby boy is in the hands of that lake monster!"

"Mother," Julius said, shocked. He'd never heard her sound so upset. "It's all right," he reassured her. "We'll save him. I'm sure there's a way—"

"There isn't," she sniffled. "Algonquin already made it clear she won't bargain. Our only option is a direct assault on her tower to take him back. An attack like that would take the very best of Heartstriker working together, and that's not even counting Algonquin's army of mages. The entire tower is layered with wards." Her voice began to break. "I couldn't even begin to think how to get around them without Amelia's help, but she never answers my summons. She thinks I want to hurt her." Bethesda paused there with a sniffle. Then, almost like an afterthought, she added, "You were talking to her at the party. Do you know where she is?"

A cold shiver went down Julius's spine. His mother's voice was more hopeful and sincere than he'd ever heard it, and why not? It was no secret that Justin was Bethesda's favorite. If she was going to get emotional over anyone, it would be him. But even so, even when he was trying to think the best of her, the question about Amelia set off alarm bells in Julius's head. Chelsie had *just* warned him that their mother would try anything to kill Amelia, and while he wanted to believe that Bethesda was genuinely concerned enough about Justin to put aside her paranoia, he knew his mother better than that. Bethesda the Heartstriker was a true dragon. She put aside nothing when it came to her own well-being.

"Julius!" Bethesda snapped when he didn't answer immediately. "This is very important! We need to move fast if we're going to save Justin. Now, tell me where your sister is."

Part of him, the better part, wanted to believe her. He *wanted* so badly to believe she was telling the truth, that she wouldn't use her son like this. But the rest of Julius, the dragon who'd grown up in the Heartstriker's shadow, couldn't take that risk, and when he replied at last, the lie slid easily from his lips.

"I don't know."

There was a long pause, and then his mother sighed. "You always were a terrible liar."

Julius tensed. There were no more tears in her voice, no more distress. The whole thing had been an *act.*

"I'm not a fool, Julius," Bethesda continued in a calm, business-like voice. "I know Amelia latched onto you last night, and I will not tolerate you keeping secrets. Now, tell me, where is Amelia?"

"I don't know," Julius said again, clutching the phone. "Where's my brother?"

"Oh, that part was all true," his mother said. "And I really am very upset about all this. But *really*, what did Justin think was going to happen when he walked into Reclamation Land?"

"So you're just going to let Algonquin have him?" Julius cried. "You're going to let him *die?*"

"Don't say that like this is my fault," she snapped. "Justin brought this on himself and you know it. That said, it doesn't mean we can't come to an arrangement."

Julius blinked, confused. "What arrangement?"

"Come now, darling," Bethesda chuckled. "I know Justin's your favorite brother. He's been saving your life since you were both the size of my claw, which explains why you're so desperate to help him now. Speaking as the clan head who has to consider the good of all Heartstrikers, I, of course, have already been forced to write off saving Justin as more trouble than it's worth. However, I *could* be convinced to change my mind, provided you made it worth my while."

She paused expectantly, but Julius was so angry he could barely speak. "Let me be sure I have this right," he ground out at last. "You want me to pay for saving my brother, your *son*, by betraying my *sister?*"

"Don't be stupid, dear," Bethesda said. "You can't betray Amelia because you owe her no allegiance. That belongs to me."

"But you're going to kill her?"

"I have no choice," his mother replied. "Amelia is a drunken, grasping whelp who's been after my throne since she was born. Not that I don't admire her ambition, but she'd be a terrible leader for our clan, and I have to think of the family. Her death would be for the good of everyone, something you'd understand if you paid any attention whatsoever to clan politics. But I don't understand why you're so worked up about this. You'd never even met Amelia until last night, but Justin's been there for you your whole life. Really, I fail to see how this is a hard decision."

"*I shouldn't have to decide!*" Julius roared. "They're both my family! I shouldn't have to choose between my brother and my sister, and you *definitely* shouldn't be making me!"

The moment he said it, Julius knew he was dead. For once, though, he didn't care. With Amelia down, he was probably dead tonight anyway, so he might as well speak his mind. "You're always going on about how you're our mother and you know best, but what kind of mother bargains one child's life for another?"

"An effective one," Bethesda snarled. "Did I accidentally seal your brain when I sealed your magic, or do you truly believe a clan like ours can be ruled with *kindness*?"

"I do," Julius snapped. "Because kindness and weakness are *not the same thing*. You treat us all like pawns, throwing us away whenever it benefits you, and you can't even stop to see what a waste it is! Can't you understand how much more powerful Heartstriker could be if you actually acted like we're your children instead of potential enemies?"

"That's the stupidest thing I've ever heard," the Heartstriker sneered. "The only thing dragons respect is strength. If I took your advice, if I acted like *you*, Heartstriker would tear itself apart. I would know, too, because it happened to my father." Her voice turned bitter. "If the Quetzalcoatl had loved his children less and suspected more, he might still be alive. But he was a fool, and now *I* am the Heartstriker, and I will not make the same mistake."

"But that's not how it has to be," Julius said. "We're not all like *you*."

"No," Bethesda growled. "You're not, and that's why you'll always be a failure."

Julius bared his teeth into the phone. "I am *not* a failure."

"Yes, you are," she said. "And unless you grow some claws, that's all you'll ever be. The road to the top is one you have to claw your way up, Julius. The moment you flinch, the moment you show weakness, your enemies will eat you alive unless you eat them first. That's

269

what it means to have power, Julius. That's what it means to be a *dragon*."

She stopped there, waiting for him to try again, but Julius had nothing to say. If that was what his mother thought a dragon was, then he didn't want anything to do with it.

"I'm not here to argue philosophy with a child," Bethesda continued when it was clear he was staying silent. "This is your last chance, and I do mean your *very* last chance, Julius. I know all about your troubles with Vann Jeger. Algonquin even mentioned it, which means there's no hope for a last minute save from Justin trying to claim your spot. The Hunter is coming for you in just a few hours, and if you don't want to be the shortest lived of your clutch, you'd better tell me where Amelia is. She never even has to know you were the one who told me. Just give me a location, something I can work with, and I'll not only give the order to save you, I'll save Justin as well. You can save everyone: yourself, your brother, even your pathetic little human, and all you have to do is stop being a traitor to your clan and tell me where my daughter is."

"You have to believe in something to betray it," Julius said quietly. "But if selling out my sister is what it takes to make the Heartstriker clan head rescue the son she should already be scrambling to save, I think I'm better off taking my chances with Vann Jeger."

"Then you are already dead," Bethesda said with a sigh. "No loss, really. You always were my greatest failure. I'm only surprised it took this long."

Julius closed his eyes. This had been his decision, and he was sure it was the right one, but Bethesda was still his mother, and her words still hurt. He knew that made him a fool, chasing after the approval of someone who'd never loved him, never even liked him, but he couldn't stop his voice from cracking as he whispered, "Goodbye, Mother."

He waited, holding his breath, but there was nothing to hear. Bethesda had already hung up. He was still listening in vain to the silence when a voice said, "Do you mean it?"

Julius jumped, almost dropping the phone as he spun around to see Amelia sitting up on the couch. "How long have you been awake?"

"Long enough," she said. "The last thing I remember was being attacked by Svena on my island." She glanced down at the bloody towels covering her body. "I'm guessing it didn't end so well?"

Julius shook his head. "They did something to you. We're not sure what, but you were unconscious when Marci and Chelsie brought you here. Bob was here, too. He told me to take care of you."

"He would," she said, reaching up to rub her forehead with a wince. "Though that does explain why I had Chelsie's hammer of a knockout spell on me. She never could learn finesse when it came to magic."

"It was for our protection," Julius said. "You started freaking out when I mentioned taking you to the mountain."

Amelia's face fell. "Did they tell you why?"

He nodded, and she sighed. "I don't know why I bother," she grumbled. "I should probably just kill her and take the stupid clan at this point. It's certainly what she's always expected of me, but…"

"But you can't," Julius finished.

Amelia shook her head. "Don't get me wrong. Bethesda deserves whatever I can give her, but if I do it, I'd have to be the Heartstriker, and eff that."

"Why?" Julius asked, genuinely curious.

"Uh, because running a dragon clan is like trying to ride herd on hundreds of fire-breathing, sociopathic cats who all want to murder me?" Amelia said, like this should be the most obvious thing ever. "I've told Mother as much a thousand times, but she can't see past her own paranoia." She snorted. "Not that I'm any better."

"What do you mean?" Julius asked.

"I mean that the cynical part of me wants to believe that whole conversation with Mother just now was all for my benefit," she said, looking him straight in the face. "It's a good setup. I'd hear you defending me, finally learn to trust, and then *bam*," she clapped her hands together, "down comes the hammer."

"B-but it wasn't!" Julius stuttered, horrified. "I *didn't*! I…"

He faded off, feeling like a fool. He had no idea what he could say that would convince someone who'd been rightfully paranoid her whole life that he was being sincere. But while Julius was thrashing his brain to come up with something that would prove he wasn't in league with their mother, Amelia just lay back with a smile.

"Like I said, that's what the cynical part of me thinks, but I'm sick of being cynical. I'm tired of assuming everyone wants to do me in. Basically, I'm tired of acting like Bethesda, so I'm not going to." She put up her hands. "I quit. You're not that good a liar, anyway, and Mother didn't sound like she was faking those death threats."

"So you believe me?" he asked hopefully.

Amelia shrugged. "That depends. You never did answer me when I asked if you meant what you said about not selling me out?"

Julius nodded, and her face grew grim. "Why?'

"Because selling out one family member to your *mother* so you can save another is awful!" he cried, exasperated. "Maybe I watched too much human television growing up, but I've always assumed that *not* killing your own family was kind of a given."

"Depends on who's doing the giving," Amelia said with a wry smile. "Okay, okay, easy tiger. I believe you."

Julius blinked. "Really?"

She nodded. "I guess this means I owe you an apology."

"No, no, it's all right," he said quickly. "Most people don't believe me the first time." Katya certainly hadn't, but Amelia was shaking her head.

"Not about that," she said. "I'm not sorry I didn't believe you right off, that's just common sense. But I am sorry for how I treated you." She looked away. "I thought you were a fool and a coward. At the party, I was having fun stringing you along because you were a cute kid, but when you went to try and help Katya, I just thought you were stupid. Why would anyone try so hard to save a clan that treated them like dirt? I thought you were too naive for words, and that meant you didn't deserve nice things, especially not a human mage of Marci's caliber." She glanced back at him. "I tried to steal her from you, you know."

He couldn't have heard that right. "You did?"

"'Try' is the operative word there," Amelia said, laughing. "I made her an offer she couldn't refuse. You two didn't have a prayer of defeating Vann Jeger without me, and Marci was smart enough to know it, so I told her I'd save you both if she came to work for me."

Julius had to fist his hands to keep them from shaking. "And did she agree?"

"No," Amelia said, almost making him collapse in relief. "Though it wasn't from lack of trying on my part. I sweetened the deal like you wouldn't believe, but she still turned me down flat. At first, I thought it was because she was being an idiot, too, falling for a dragon's charms, but now I get it. Marci isn't stupid or weak, and neither are you. You're nice. *Actually* nice, even when people don't deserve it, even when you probably shouldn't be, and I'm just contrary enough to find that inspiring."

Now Julius *knew* she was messing with him. "Really?"

Amelia's look grew grim. "You're not the only dragon who hates the way things are," she said. "I don't regret my years on the planes. I got stronger out there than I ever could have here, but…"

She stopped with a long sigh, running her hands through her bloody hair. "Can you imagine what it's like to be exiled from your own home? To never be able to even drop by for a visit without being terrified that your mother will make one of the few siblings you actually care about try to kill you? And it's not like I'm a special case. *Every* Heartstriker has suffered under Bethesda. But unlike the rest of the clan, who're willing to put up with anything to keep their seat on the Heartstriker ride to the top, I'm sick of being afraid. I'm *done* putting up with this, Julius, and from the sound of things just now, so are you. If that doesn't put us on the same side, I don't know what does."

Julius was so shocked by his sister's words, he didn't notice she was moving her hand until she'd stuck it right out in front of her, magic sparking from her fingertips. "What's that?"

Amelia arched an eyebrow. "What does it look like? I'm offering you a life debt."

"What?" he cried. "*Why?*"

"Gee, I don't know," she said, rolling her eyes. "Maybe because you saved my life? That's generally how these things work. You could have sold me out to Mother half a dozen times just now, but you didn't. I'm pretty sure that counts."

Julius hadn't thought about it that way, but now that Amelia said it, the thought of her listening while he yelled at their mother made him blush from his chest to his ears. "I'm honored," he said. "Really, thank you very much, but I can't accept."

Amelia looked at him like he was insane. "Why not?"

"Because I don't like being in debt, and I try not to do things to other people that I don't enjoy myself."

That sounded kind of corny even to him, but the Planeswalker just shook her head. "You really are something, aren't you? I thought Bob was playing a joke on us when he chose you, but now I get it. You're the anti-dragon."

Julius winced. "Thank you?"

"It was meant as a compliment," she assured him, shaking the sparkling magic off her fingers. "But if you won't accept my debt, I don't know what to do. It's not like I can leave this hanging. I might not be a particularly honorable dragon, but I do have *some* standards." She frowned, thinking. "Maybe we could enter a pact of service for the next year?"

That sounded even worse than a life debt. "What if we just agreed to be friends?"

From the look on Amelia's face, you'd have thought he'd suggested they swallow frogs. "Why would we do *that?*"

"Because friends help each other without obligation," Julius explained ruefully. "And, all debts aside, I could really use some help right now."

"You need a lot more than help," Amelia said with a snort, but her expression was thoughtful. "So even after hearing about the whole planning to kill you and steal your mortal thing, you *still* want to be my friend?"

This was the first Julius had heard of killing, but he nodded anyway. "I've gotten over worse, and Marci's not my mortal, anyway. Though I would appreciate it if you wouldn't try that again."

"Nah," Amelia said. "If she wouldn't dump you for a library, I've got nothing. Though, as your friend, I *would* get to stick around her." That must have been the deciding factor, because Amelia's face brightened immediately. "Okay, you've got a deal." She stuck out her hand again, without magic this time. "Let's be friends."

"Deal," Julius said happily, shaking on it. "See? That wasn't so hard."

"Speak for yourself," Amelia grumbled. "I just gave up any chance of ever getting your mage. Not that I'm an expert on this stuff, but I'm given to understand that friends don't steal friends' girls."

Something about the way she said that struck Julius as odd, and since they were friends now, he went ahead and asked. "What's so special about Marci?"

Amelia looked at him in appalled horror, and Julius scrambled to backtrack. "Don't get me wrong! I think she's amazing!" Understatement of the year. "But I don't understand why you're so determined to have her as your human."

"What's to understand?" Amelia said with a shrug. "I like humans. I particularly like the females, and Marci's pretty freaking cute. She's also talented, ambitious, smart, has a lead on a Kosmolabe, *and* she has the guts to turn my own ultimatums around on me. How could I not want her all to myself?"

That wasn't what Julius had expected her to say, but he couldn't argue with his sister's logic. "So what about Ghost? You seemed really excited about him this morning."

"He's the icing on the cake," Amelia said, folding her arms behind her head with an unsettling grin. "Suffice it to say we're on the cusp of great things. Assuming we don't all die tonight, your human might just be the world's first Merlin."

Julius frowned. "The world's first what?"

Amelia opened her mouth to explain, but before she could begin, her eyes went wide. A few seconds later, Julius understood why. A wonderful scent was drifting on the air, followed by the even better sound of Marci unlocking the front door. When she came into the room a moment later, she was carrying four of the most delicious smelling bags on the planet and a pair of condensation-soaked plastic milk jugs filled with bright green frozen slush.

"Oh good," she said, beaming at the two of them. "You're up."

Amelia nodded, but her eyes were locked on the milk jugs. "Are those...?"

Marci held them up with a grin. "Margaritas."

And that was when Julius learned frozen drinks really could raise people from the dead.

CHAPTER FOURTEEN

Amelia finished the first jug of margaritas in under a minute, chugging the entire gallon container without even pausing for breath. Marci had the second jug ready by the time she finished, along with a bag of tacos, earning herself a look of pure, unabashed love from the Planeswalker.

"You are the Best. Human. *Ever.*"

"I try," Marci said with a smirk, handing a bag to Julius, who also dug in. "But shouldn't you take it easy? Your stomach might still have extra holes in it."

"I'll be fine," Amelia said, shoving a taco into her mouth and washing it down with another glug of alcoholic frozen slush. "Have you seen a dragon eat?"

"Fair point," Marci said, walking down the hall to the kitchen to grab a chair. "So what did I miss?"

Julius started to answer, but his sister beat him to it. "Bethesda tried to blackmail Julius into selling me out, so he rage quit the clan."

Marci ran back into the room. "*Really?*"

Julius made a face. "It didn't go quite like—"

"It was awesome," Amelia interrupted. "He pretty much told her to take her clan and shove it. I've never been so proud!" She stuck another taco into her mouth, eating it in one bite. "I tried to give him a life debt for it, but he apparently hates getting the best debt on the planet, so now we're just BFFFLs."

"BFFFLs?" Marci repeated, bewildered.

Amelia shrugged. "I don't know the modern slang, but basically it means I'm joining Team Nice Dragon. Looks like we'll be working together after all!"

Marci crossed her arms over her chest. "I thought you said you didn't share?"

"I don't," Amelia said, nodding at her brother. "But, apparently, he does. But that's all water under the bridge now, right?"

Marci looked at Julius, who smiled. "I can only speak for myself, but I bear no grudge against Amelia, and I'm always happy to have a friend."

"Spoken like a true Julius," Marci said with a sigh. "Fine, I'm in too, but I still want access to your library *and* I want you to tell me everything you know about Mortal Spirits." She smiled sweetly. "No secrets between friends, right?"

Amelia laughed. "Eyes on the prize as always. I *knew* I liked you." She emptied the last of the tacos into her mouth and crumpled the bag, tossing it into the trashcan across the room for a perfect three-point-shot before offering her hand to Marci. "You've got a deal, but it'll have to wait. It's almost noon already, which means we've only got seven hours and change before sunset."

Marci's expression turned grim as she shook the dragon's hand. "So what do we do now? We've already determined that breaking my curse is impossible, and you're too injured to fight. What options do we have left?"

"The obvious one," Julius said solemnly. "We go and face him."

They both whirled around to stare at him. "But," Marci said at last. "Isn't that exactly what you've been saying we *shouldn't* do?"

"It is," he said, nodding. "But the situation's changed. Vann Jeger has another hostage now: Justin."

Marci's eyebrows shot up in alarm. "How did *that* happen?"

Julius looked back down at his food. Marci's opinion of Justin was bad enough without hearing about how his brother had charged into Reclamation Land rather than let Amelia hog the glory of defeating Vann Jeger. Her question deserved an answer, though, so he stuck to the best possible interpretation of events. "He tried to get the jump on Vann Jeger and got caught."

"And your family isn't up in arms to save him?" she asked, confused. "I thought he was a big deal in Heartstriker?"

"No one's a big enough deal for Bethesda to inconvenience herself," Amelia said bitterly.

"Mother doesn't think he's worth the risk of running an assault on Algonquin," Julius explained. "She *did* offer to save him, but only if I told her where Amelia was, which I wasn't willing to do."

"Wow," Marci said. "No wonder you told her to go jump in a lake. Good job, Julius."

Julius stared at her in wonder. After so many years of being told everything he valued was wrong and weak, it was hard to wrap his head around how much it meant to him that Marci thought he'd made the right decision. He wanted to stop there and just enjoy the feeling, but time was ticking down, so he forced himself to move on.

"Strategically, the rescue angle makes things more complicated," he said quickly, clearing his throat against the sudden tightness. "Mother said he's still alive, but I can't imagine Algonquin will let him stay that way once she realizes Bethesda isn't going to bargain. If we're going to have a chance at saving him, it has to be tonight."

"But how?" Marci asked. "He's Algonquin's prisoner, right? It's not like Vann Jeger's going to show up to the fight with a captured dragon in tow. How will fighting him change Justin's situation?"

"Because that's how we get leverage," Julius replied. "Algonquin's only keeping Justin alive to wring concessions out of Bethesda. Concessions we already know she's not going to give. The second Algonquin realizes this, Justin's toast, so if we want to keep him alive past that point, we have to figure out a way to give his life value beyond his status as a Heartstriker. The easiest way to do that is to have something to trade for him. Something Algonquin wants more than killing a dragon."

"And it just so happens that her most prized hunter is headed right for us," Amelia finished with a bloodthirsty smile. "Not bad, Baby-J. Not bad."

"Hold up," Marci said. "Maybe I'm not following, but it sounds an awful lot like your plan is to defeat Vann Jeger and ransom him back to Algonquin in exchange for Justin?"

Julius nodded. "That's exactly my plan. Vann Jeger's a spirit, which means he can't technically be killed, but he *can* be defeated. It's like Justin said earlier: Vann Jeger might be strong, but he's also a long way from home. Whatever he's using for power here, it's not his actual domain, which means there has to be a limit. If we can make him use up his local reserve, he'll have no choice but to flee back to his fjord in Norway." He glanced at his sister. "How long do you think it would take Vann Jeger to recover if we forced him to retreat?"

"For a spirit his size?" Amelia pursed her lips, doing the math in her head. "Five years, minimum. Realistically, probably more like ten to get back up to full power after a total defeat."

That was even better than Julius had hoped. "There's no way Algonquin wants to be without her dragon hunter for ten years," he said excitedly. "That *has* to be more valuable than Justin! If we can just find a way of making Vann Jeger use up all his local magic, but stop just short of actually forcing him to retreat, we can barter his continued usefulness in the DFZ for my brother's life *and* get the curse off Marci's neck in the process. It's a win-win!"

"That's a pretty big *if*," Amelia said. "Not to rain on your parade, but how are you planning on making Vann Jeger fight that hard? You're not exactly a combat powerhouse, and he's clearly not lacking for magic here in the city. What are you going to do to him that'll make him go so ballistic, he'll have to run home for a refill?"

"I haven't actually worked that part out yet," Julius admitted sheepishly. "How were *you* going to defeat him?"

Now it was Amelia's turn to look sheepish. "I wasn't, actually."

Marci and Julius gasped in unison. "*What?*"

"I didn't get to this age by being stupid!" Amelia said defensively. "It's called fighting smarter, not harder. My plan was to show up, stall until I was sure the Sword of Damocles was off Marci's neck, and then bail through a portal. I would have solved everyone's problems and kept all my promises without risking a hair on my head."

Julius scowled. It wasn't that Amelia's strategy was bad, but he didn't appreciate how easy his sister had made defeating Vann Jeger sound, especially since she hadn't actually been planning to *try*.

"Don't look at me like that," Amelia grumbled. "Vann Jeger's called the Death of Dragons for a reason. He's not the sort of fight I can just waltz through, and I've found my long term survival strategy works best if I avoid direct confrontations with dudes who can kill me."

"What about the portal thing?" Marci asked. "Could you still do that? Like, could we open a portal under Vann Jeger's feet and drop him into a lake of lava or a black hole or something?"

"I've done both of those, actually," Amelia said with a smile. "But there's something else I haven't told you. Watch."

She stuck her hand out in front of her, and Julius flinched instinctively, bracing for the sharp bite of dragon magic. A bite that did not come.

"Um, was something supposed to happen?"

"Yes," Amelia said glumly, dropping her hand. "And that's exactly my point. That *should* have opened a portal large enough to drive a truck through, but I haven't been able to open so much as a pigeonhole since I woke up."

Julius stared at her. "You tried to open a portal from my couch?"

She nodded. "While you were on the phone. But as you see, it didn't work."

"Why not?" Marci asked.

"I think it's the injuries," Amelia said, patting the bloody towels covering her chest. "Rapid healing and cutting through the fabric of time and space both require a lot of magical oomph, and apparently I don't have enough to do both at the moment." She reached into the bag on her lap for another taco. "That's why I'm eating so much. I'm hoping food will help get me back up to speed. Well, that and tacos are freaking delicious."

"Could it be something else?" Julius asked, remembering Chelsie's theory that Amelia might be compromised. "We know Estella did something to you, and ruining your ability to portal would definitely count as effective sabotage."

"It would," Amelia said with her mouth full. "But I don't think that's what's going on here. Messing with a dragon's magic means messing with the core of what makes us what we are. That's not something you can do without the victim noticing. I mean, even if Mother had knocked you out for the process, could you overlook your seal?"

Never. "Then I guess we're just going to have to wait and hope your power comes back," Julius said, defeated. "Because, barring a miracle, I have no idea how we're going to beat Vann Jeger without you."

"I don't know about that," Marci said, tapping her lip in the way she did when she was thinking of something big. "Vann Jeger's a tried and true monster, but at the end of the day, he's still a spirit. What if we tried banishing him?"

Julius frowned. "Does that even work on spirits his size?"

"Why not?" she asked. "Spirits vary wildly in size, intelligence, and ability, but—as your sister explained to me earlier today— they're all just basically sacks of sentient magic. If that's true, then, mechanically speaking, Vann Jeger should be no different than the tank badger spirit we pulled off that dude yesterday."

That didn't sound right to Julius. "I don't know—"

"It's very simple," Marci said, digging a piece of casting chalk out of her pocket as she sank to her knees and began sketching a circle on the scuffed hardwood floor. "One of the core tenets of Thaumaturgical Theory is that all magic can be reliably manipulated regardless of the source. That's why, unlike Shamans who just grab whatever magic is available and throw it around, Thaumaturges always take the time to write out our spells, because no matter how crazy the magic might feel when you're pulling it in, it all acts the same once you put it through your spellwork. It's just like electricity. It doesn't matter what generated it or even what form it arrives in. Once you run that current through a voltage regulator, it's all just power."

"We're still talking about a *lot* of power," Julius reminded her.

"Doesn't matter," Marci said. "If Vann Jeger is made of magic like every other spirit, there's no reason the normal banishing spellwork shouldn't work on him. It's just a matter of scaling it up."

"How are you even going to get him into the spellwork?" Julius asked, looking down at the hula-hoop sized circle Marci had just finished drawing at his feet. "The badger was happy to sit on our client, but I don't think Vann Jeger's going to stand politely in one place."

Marci smirked. "He will if we draw a big enough circle."

"She's right," Amelia said excitedly. "This whole thing started because Vann Jeger wanted to fight a dragon. If we give him what he wants, he's not going to leave the battlefield, so if we draw a circle around *that*, he might not even notice he's in a trap until it's too late."

"How is he not going to notice?" Julius asked. "We've done a lot of banishing jobs, and the spirits never look happy about it."

"That's because I generally trap them in a ward first so they can't get away," Marci explained. "They're struggling because they're stuck, not because of the rest. At the simplest level, banishing a spirit is just a transfer of power from one place to another. Once you've got your target trapped in your circle, you suck out its magic to shrink it down to a size you can manage, and then you use the magic you just took to power a spell that will banish the spirit back to its domain or bind it or do whatever it is you want to do."

"And again, how is that not noticeable?" Julius said, exasperated. "You've sucked magic out of me, remember? It's not exactly a subtle operation."

"That's different," Amelia cut in. "You're a dragon. We make our own magic. If a mage takes some, then we're left with a gap until we do something to regenerate what we lost, like eat or sleep.

This makes us very attuned to even minor changes in our power, but spirits are different. They're more like empty pots that magic gets poured into. This doesn't mean they won't notice when they're getting empty, but if they're busy with other things—like, say, a long-awaited epic fight with a dragon—they might not notice someone siphoning off the top until it's too late."

That was encouraging, but, "How would we even get an 'epic fight with a dragon'? You're down for the count, remember?"

"*I* am," Amelia said with a smirk. "But you're not."

Julius's eyes went so wide they hurt. "You're joking."

"Do I look like I'm joking?"

She didn't, which was insane. "You just said Vann Jeger would be a tough fight even for *you*," he reminded her. "You're an A! I'm a J, and not even one of the good J's. I'm also *sealed*. I couldn't give Vann Jeger an epic *anything*, except maybe a laugh."

"All true," Amelia said sadly. "But you're forgetting something very important, which is that you are in the company of two incredibly talented mages." She looked at Marci. "Once he's in your circle, how long do you think it would take you to whittle Vann Jeger down to a manageable size?"

"Impossible to say without knowing how big he actually is," Marci replied thoughtfully. "Maybe half an hour?"

Julius gaped at her. "Seriously?"

"I drained that tank badger in less than two minutes," she reminded him with a proud look. "The time sink part of banishing a spirit is getting the spellwork set up. Once I actually start pulling, they go down quick."

"So you really think you can drain enough to banish Vann Jeger in half an hour?"

"I wouldn't have said so if I didn't," Marci replied with a huff, folding her arms over her chest. "Pulling in magic is only slow if you're dealing with power that's spread out. Give me a proper, concentrated source, like a dragon, and I can drain that puppy in minutes."

Her example made him wince, but if there was anything Julius had learned to trust about Marci, it was her knowledge of magic. If she said she could do something, then she could. "Okay," he said, running his hands through his hair. "I believe you, but that still means I'm going to have to keep Vann Jeger in the circle and distracted for thirty minutes, and I just don't see how that's going to work."

"That part's easy," Amelia said. "We'll just make you look like something else."

At this point, Julius would have sworn nothing could surprise him anymore. And he would've been wrong. "What?"

His sister's smile grew smug. "You might be at the bottom of the magical food chain, but injured or not, *I'm* a total boss. Just because I don't have enough juice to open a portal right now doesn't mean I can't smother you in enough raw dragon power to make you look like the Quetzalcoatl himself. Vann Jeger will eat it up."

"Okay, so I'll look scary," Julius said slowly. "How does that help me not die when he hits me?"

Amelia shrugged. "It won't, so I suggest making sure that doesn't happen."

Julius could feel himself going pale, and his sister sighed. "It won't be that bad," she assured him. "Like most geologically ancient spirits, Vann Jeger's old-fashioned. He prefers banter and drama over modern efficiency. Also, remember that you'll look like the sort of super powerful dragon he'll want to savor, not rush through. Between all that, keeping him talking for thirty minutes should be child's play, especially for someone who talks as much as you do."

"Thanks," Julius grumbled. But though he still didn't like Amelia's plan in the least, he was starting to see how it could work. From what Marci had told him in the closet, Vann Jeger *did* seem like the type who could grandstand forever given a proper audience, and between his sister's magic and Marci's skill with illusions, he would definitely look the part. He still wasn't optimistic about his own ability to keep an ancient spirit talking for thirty minutes straight, but it was definitely more viable than any scenario that required him to fight, which made this the best plan they had.

"Okay," he said with a sigh. "I'm in. What do I have to do?"

Amelia's face grew slightly terrifying. "Just hold still."

That was the only warning Julius got before he was engulfed in fire.

• • •

It took almost five hours to get everything perfect. Or, at least, it took five hours to reach Marci's definition of perfect. Julius had his own opinion of the situation.

"I feel ridiculous," he growled, scuffing his feet on the workroom floor as he waited for Marci to finish packing her bag.

"But you look amazing," Marci reminded him, looking him over for what had to be the hundredth time.

Even sulking like he was now, Julius looked absolutely incredible. As well he should, too, because the illusion Marci had done for him was quite possibly her best ever.

She'd covered him from head to toe, replacing his worn sneakers, t-shirt, and comfy jeans with pointed Italian leather shoes and a super expensive-looking dark gray power suit before topping the whole thing off with one of those perfectly styled messy haircuts you only saw on male models. But while that would have normally been enough, this was *not* a normal situation, and so Marci had gone over him again, adding lighting and shadow effects to bring out the angles of his face and body, ensuring that every side was now his good side. Finally, she'd spent an hour sharpening and refining his features, transforming the normally boyishly handsome Julius into an intimidatingly handsome, extremely draconic version of himself. But as much as Marci wanted to claim all the credit, what really took Julius to the next level was his magic, and *that* was all Amelia.

As promised, she'd shellacked Julius with her fire until he was positively radioactive with power. Even his seal was gone, buried under the layers of intense dragon magic that glittered like banked coals just waiting for a chance to burst back into flame. The smoldering burn of magic followed his every glance, and even standing perfectly still, energy radiated from his body like he was barely holding his fantastic powers in check.

Even knowing it was all fake, Marci still got a chill every time she looked his way. Between the magic and her illusion, Julius really did look every inch the ancient, terrifying dragon he was pretending to be. Now, if she could just get him to stop looking so miserable about it, everything would be perfect.

"Cheer up," she said, tucking several cans of spell-ready spray paint into her bag. "You really do look fantastic."

He stared down at himself in disgust. "I look like a *jerk*."

"That's kind of the point," she reminded him. "Last I heard, ancient dragons aren't known for their kind and friendly demeanor."

She turned in a circle, checking her lab one last time. When she was certain she hadn't forgotten anything, she zipped up her bag and loaded it onto her shoulder, stopping just long enough to let Ghost, who'd been anxiously waiting on her desk, jump inside. "Okay," she said when the spirit had vanished into her bulging sack of supplies. "I'm all set. Let's go do a final check with Amelia, and then we can head out."

"I'm still not comfortable leaving her here alone," Julius said as they started down the stairs.

Marci shrugged. "It's safer than bringing her with us. And anyway, she's an ancient dragon. It's not like she needs a babysitter. You should be more worried about her eating us out of house and home."

When the tacos had run out, they'd ordered pizza. An hour later, that was gone, too. So was Marci's entire fifth of emergency vodka, which was *highly* annoying. Amelia might be easier to get along with, but when it came to being a houseguest, she was even worse than Justin. At least he didn't drink.

"She's healing," Julius said by way of an explanation. "And she did promise to buy you another bottle. An expensive one."

Marci laughed, trying to imagine what an ancient, wealthy dragon like Amelia would consider "expensive" vodka. "I just hope I'm alive to enjoy it."

She'd meant that as a joke, but Julius looked more dour than ever, which wouldn't do at all. Their plan depended on him playing his role as the terrible and fearsome dragon, which was tough to pull off when you looked like a kicked puppy. Before she could think of something properly motivating to cheer him up, though, she spotted Amelia at the bottom of the stairs, wrapped in a bloody towel and holding herself up by the railing.

"Should you be up?" Julius asked, hurrying past Marci to help her.

"I'm not made of paper," Amelia said, smacking his hands away. "I was just coming to ask if I could bum some new clothes. Not that blood-stained isn't my style, but I usually prefer it to be someone *else's* blood."

"Sure," Marci said. "I'm basically running a dragon clothing service at this point, anyway." She handed her bag to Julius. "Would you mind putting this in the truck for me?"

"Do you even have keys for that hunk of junk?" he asked, tilting sideways as he slid her criminally heavy bag, complete with cat spirit poking his head through the zipper, onto his shoulder.

"Nope, but there's a screwdriver in the ignition."

Julius's eyebrows shot up. Thankfully, though, he didn't say anything more about her dalliances in car theft. He just waved and headed for the front door. Amelia watched him the whole way, her brows knitted.

"What?" Marci asked.

"Nothing," Amelia replied. "We just did a bang up job. I never would have expected it, given the material we had to work with, but ruthless is a surprisingly good look on Julius. Mother would have a heart attack if she saw him like that."

Marci started back up the stairs. "And I suppose that's part of the appeal for you?"

"How well you understand dragons," Amelia said with a grin, using the wooden banister to pull herself along as she followed

Marci up to her room. "Also, I have to say you're doing a fantastic job at controlling your fear. You don't smell afraid at all to me."

"I've been too busy to be afraid," she said, digging into her dresser in search of something that might fit yet another crazy tall dragoness. "I'm sure it'll all catch up with me later."

"I wonder," Amelia said, sitting carefully on the footboard of Marci's bed so as not to get blood on the comforter. "Ghost was in the bag you handed Julius. I assume that means you're taking him with you?"

"I can't leave him," Marci said. "He's my cat." She glanced over her shoulder. "Why? Do you think I shouldn't?"

Amelia pursed her lips. "I'm not sure, to be honest. He seems very loyal, which isn't something I'd have expected, and I can't imagine he'd make things worse."

"But?" Marci prompted.

The dragon sighed. "Remember what I told you on my island? Mortal Spirits draw their magic from mortal concepts. That's what makes them so incredibly powerful, but it's also their greatest flaw, because most global concepts humans share aren't the sort of things you want to be bound to. Until Ghost remembers his name, there's no way of knowing what his domain actually is, but just going off what I've observed of him so far, I don't think it'll be something warm and cuddly."

After what had happened in the alley, Marci didn't either, but she *did* believe that whatever Ghost turned out to be, he would still be himself, and he would still care about her. "Don't worry," she said, flashing the dragon a confident smile. "I can handle it."

"I'm not saying you can't," Amelia replied. "Normally. But you're going into a situation where your life will be at risk *and* you'll be drawing enormous amounts of magic off of one of the biggest spirits in the world. That's a lot of temptation for a newborn Mortal Spirit on the edge of guessing his name. I don't want to lose you both just because someone got desperate."

Marci hadn't considered that angle. Again, though, Ghost had seen her at her worst and her best. He was surly and grumpy, and more than a little disobedient, but he was hers. When the chips were down, he'd come through for her every time, and Marci always repaid loyalty.

"I promise I'll be careful," she said, digging out her maxi-dress, the only item of clothing she had left that might fit Amelia. "But I can't go up against Vann Jeger with anything less than my best, and Ghost is part of that. It'll be what it'll be."

"I suppose that's the most I can ask for," Amelia said, holding out her hand to accept the dress Marci offered. "You've already made it clear I can't order you around. But would you take some advice from an old dragon?"

"Always," Marci said. "What?"

Amelia smiled, but the expression didn't reach her eyes. "Don't let him see you weak."

"Why now?" she asked, instantly suspicious.

"Because the thing you think of as your loyal cat is actually a spirit with more potential than any other in the world right now," Amelia replied, smoothing the borrowed dress in her hands. "That kind of power doesn't stay subservient willingly. I'm not saying it's guaranteed, but if you don't want to end up being his pet instead, I suggest you make sure that, whatever happens, you *always* have the upper hand."

By the time she finished, Marci was cold inside. She didn't want to believe what the dragon was saying, but at the same time, it made a lot of sense, especially since she could still hear Ghost's purring voice in her head.

We can be very powerful together.

The memory made her shiver, and Marci turned away, walking to the door in long, purposeful strides. "Thanks for the advice. I'll keep it in mind."

"See that you do," Amelia replied, standing up. "I'm going to use your shower. Good luck tonight."

"You too," Marci said, hurrying into the hall without looking back.

She went down the stairs just as fast, rubbing her arms to get rid of the creepy feeling that still clung to her like glue. She didn't have time for this right now. It wasn't that she was not grateful for Amelia's advice, but Marci had talked a big game to Julius earlier about banishing Vann Jeger. To actually pull that off, she was going to need her wits about her, not off worrying about Ghost.

With that in mind, Marci pulled herself together, plastered a smile on her face, and raced out the front door. "Sorry that took so long!" she cried as she bounded down the steps. "Amelia had some last minute advice for…"

Her voice trailed off. As she'd asked, Julius was waiting for her beside the running truck, but he was no longer alone.

• • •

When his sister had gone upstairs with Marci, Julius had quietly fled outside to focus on calming down.

He knew he was being a wuss, freaking out about wearing a disguise when everyone else was doing their part, but he hadn't expected to feel so…different. It wasn't that he had any complaints about the illusion. If anything, Marci and Amelia had done their job *too* well. They'd transformed him into a picture perfect specimen of an ancient, ruthless, tyrannical dragon, which meant he now looked like the thing he hated most in the world.

This was even more horrible than he'd imagine. He'd gone into this with low expectations, but now that the illusion was finished, he couldn't even look at himself without feeling like he'd done something he should apologize for, and the magic itself was even worse. Where Marci's magic had always felt like a comforting blanket, Amelia's felt like being caught in a dragon-sized bear trap, changing him from the inside out. He felt different, he walked different, he even *smelled* different. And while that was probably a good thing if Vann Jeger had anything resembling a dragon's sense of smell, having your nose constantly filled with the scent of ancient, terrifying predator was stressful to the max. Even knowing it was fake, Julius couldn't stop his subconscious from constantly freaking out about the giant dragon it was convinced was standing right behind him, which was a real liability when your plan for survival depended on you looking confident.

But awful as all this was, it was way too late to change the plan now. Like it or not, the illusion was here to stay, and so, after carefully placing Marci's bag inside the truck like she'd asked, Julius closed his eyes to focus on not making a fool of himself. He was still working on it when his nose caught a new scent that made his own constructed menace feel like nothing. A scent that, in hindsight, he really should have expected an hour ago.

Under more normal circumstances, that would have been enough to send him over the edge, but apparently there were only so many shocks a dragon could take. He mostly just felt a sense of resignation as he turned to face the terrifying dragon who was *actually* standing behind him.

"Hello, Chelsie."

The Heartstriker enforcer stepped out of the shadows beside the front porch, her green eyes glowing. "Not surprised to see me?" she said, resting her hand on the hilt of the Fang at her waist. "You're getting better, Julius."

"Never too late to improve," he replied, trying for a smile only to fail utterly. "I guess you're here to kill me, then?"

"If I was, we wouldn't be having this conversation."

Julius's eyes widened. "So, Mother didn't order you here to… you know…"

"Oh no," Chelsie said. "Bethesda's orders were very specific. I'm to kill Amelia first, then you, and then your human, just for good measure. After that, I'm supposed to sneak into Algonquin's Tower and kill Justin so he can't be used against us. You know, just make a nice, clean sweep of things."

She swept her hand through the air as she finished, and Julius swallowed. "So why aren't you?"

That was a suicidal thing to say, but Julius was genuinely curious, and it wasn't like he could stop his sister from doing whatever she wanted anyway. Also, despite the cold, casual way she was talking about killing them all, Chelsie didn't look half as deadly as she usually did. She looked more tired than anything. Tired and sad, her face haggard in the porch light's dim glow.

"It's been a long day," she said at last, walking over to lean on the rusted truck beside him. "And surprising as you might find it, I don't relish the idea of killing the one sister I've ever been close to and my baby brother in the same swoop. Especially not when said baby brother has finally grown the fangs to say something to Bethesda that wasn't 'yes' or 'I'm sorry.'"

Julius winced. "You heard that?"

"I was in the room when she called," Chelsie said, her lips quirking in what might have been the ghost of a smile. "Ironic, isn't it? The one time you actually act like a dragon, Mother decides to kill you for it."

"But not you?" he said hopefully.

Chelsie frowned up into the dark. "I don't believe in punishing whelps for learning what we teach them," she said slowly. "And I don't think you were wrong."

"You *don't?*"

He hadn't meant for that to come out sounding so skeptical, but his sister just nodded. "Mothers shouldn't ransom one family member against another," she said quietly. "I told her as much a long time ago, and I'm still paying for it."

There was a lifetime of anger simmering under that last sentence. It made Julius curious, but he knew better than to poke at old wounds, especially now. "So what are you going to do?" he asked instead. "If you're not here to kill me, why *are* you here?"

"Because I can't disobey," she growled, turning to glare at him in the dark. "I don't do this job because I enjoy it, Julius. I'm bound by oaths I can never break to obey the Heartstriker until she dies or I do. Fortunately, when Mother ordered me to go to the DFZ and kill you all, she neglected to set a time limit. By coming here tonight, I've obeyed her order to the letter, if not the spirit, but that's still enough to free me from my obligations for the time being. So now the question becomes, what are *you* going to do?"

Julius blinked. "Me?"

"You're all dolled up for something," Chelsie said, looking him up and down. "Unless you've taken up cosplaying as an actual dragon, I can only assume this get-up is part of a plan to take down Vann Jeger, and I want in."

He couldn't have heard that right. "*You* want to help us fight Vann Jeger?"

Chelsie nodded.

"*Why?*"

"Weren't you listening?" she snapped. "I. Don't. Want. You. To. Die. I told you that last month. I told you that this *morning*. I've been bending over backwards to keep you alive ever since Mother booted you out of the mountain. I'm not about to throw all that work away just because you're overly attached to your human and your brother's a pig-headed moron."

Julius stared at her in wonder. The way she said it made it sound like he was being chewed out, but that didn't change the fact that Chelsie's rant was still the nicest thing anyone in his family had ever said about him. "Thank you."

"Don't start," she growled, looking away. "I'm doing this for me, not you. Mother loves a winner. I don't know what crazy plan you've concocted tonight, but if I help you defeat Algonquin's champion, there's a chance Bethesda will be so impressed, she'll rescind her order, and then *I* won't have to kill you."

Julius nodded rapidly. "And we can save Justin!"

Chelsie gave him a sideways look. "Say what?"

He quickly explained the plan to leverage banishing Vann Jeger against Algonquin to ransom Justin. Going through the steps again, it actually sounded a lot more solid than Julius remembered. By the time he finished, though, Chelsie was looking more skeptical than ever. "Do you really believe your human can banish an ancient spirit like Vann Jeger in thirty minutes?"

"She's never been wrong about this sort of thing before," Julius said. "I'm way more worried about my ability to keep Vann Jeger from crushing me before she finishes."

"That makes two of us," Chelsie said with a scowl. "But it's too late to shift gears now. We'll start with your plan, and when things go south, I'll come and bail you out. If Vann Jeger doesn't know I'm there, I should be able to land at least one good shot on him."

"Thank you," Julius said, sincerely touched. "I can't tell you how much I appreciate—"

"Then don't."

He winced at her harsh tone, and Chelsie sighed. "Save your gratitude until after I've actually done something," she said, a little more gently this time. "Vann Jeger came by his reputation honestly, and I'm specialized to kill dragons, not spirits. If your plan to keep him distracted can buy us ten minutes, I can probably hold him off for the last twenty. After that, all bets are off." She glanced up at the brightly lit house. "I just hope your mage isn't a lot of hot air, or this is going to be a very short fight."

"If she says she can do it, she can do it," Julius said firmly. "I trust her."

"That must be nice."

Given who was speaking, Julius would've expected that to be sarcastic, but there was no venom in Chelsie's voice. She actually sounded sincere, which, in turn, made him feel ridiculously grateful all over again. "I'm *really* glad you're here," he said, reaching out to squeeze her shoulder with a smile. "Thank you, Chelsie."

His sister's eyes widened and she jerked away, but not before Julius saw the flush that spread over her cheeks. "Yeah, well, you can consider it payback for you keeping your lips shut about how my Fang works," she growled. "Which you *are* going to do, or I will take your lips *off*."

"Of course," he assured her, "I wasn't going to say anything, anyway."

Chelsie's look told him she didn't buy that for a second, but before she could say as much, Marci burst through the front door.

"Sorry that took so long!" she cried, running down the steps. "Amelia had some last minute advice for…"

She trailed off, her eyes jumping from Chelsie to Julius and back again, and then the air filled with the scent of her magic right before her bracelets lit up.

"Marci!" he cried, jumping between his battle-ready mage and his sister. "It's okay! She's here to help."

"Is she?" Marci said coldly, not dropping her magic an inch. "Because the last time I saw her, she was trying to make you leave me to *die*."

"That *would* have been easier," Chelsie said, crossing her arms. "But Julius has convinced me you're a vital part of the plan, so you may live for now."

"And what about Amelia?" Marci demanded. "I'm no Heartstriker, but I know you're Bethesda's Shade. How do we know you won't betray her to your mother while we're gone?"

Chelsie shrugged. "Amelia is the Planeswalker. *If* she was injured, she would never be stupid enough to remain on this plane, so I see no reason to waste my extremely limited time looking for her until after the current crisis is resolved."

That was some excellent logic if your goal was to avoid Bethesda's orders. Terrible for everything else, of course, but Julius had the sneaking suspicion that his sister did this kind of mental side-stepping a lot. Not that he had a problem with that.

"Sounds great to me," he said, yanking open the pick-up's rusty door. "Shall we go? We've got a lot to do and not a lot of time to do it in."

Chelsie was in the car before he finished, settling into the passenger seat with her legs crossed and her sword resting on the dash like she was being chauffeured. Still scowling, Marci got in next, grabbing her bag from the back where Julius had set it and moving it to her lap. Ghost hopped out a second later, jumping up to sit under the windshield like he couldn't wait to go on a trip. If

Chelsie was surprised to see the spirit, though, she hid it perfectly, watching with her unnerving, all-seeing gaze as Julius climbed into the driver's seat and turned the screwdriver, starting the engine for what would hopefully *not* be their final journey.

CHAPTER FIFTEEN

They arrived at 8 Mile Road an hour before sunset.

As the official northern border of the DFZ, 8 Mile was the farthest you could get from the skyways and still be inside Algonquin's
domain. But where the other DFZ borders came with a buildup of
businesses servicing state-side customers looking to jump the border just long enough to take advantage of the DFZ's anything-goes
vice laws, up here, there was nothing. Just grass, the rotting founda-
tions of strip malls, and the perfectly straight skeleton of a road that
hadn't been used in decades.

"It's kind of surreal," Marci said, turning around to look back at
the skyways rising like a double-layered reef behind them. "All this
empty space not ten miles from downtown."

"With good reason," Julius said, covering his nose with his hand
as he opened the door. "This magic's even thicker than the stuff at
your old place."

That was a drastic understatement. Marci's apartment at the
hoarded cat house had been bad, but the magic here was like nothing Julius had ever experienced. Normally he had to focus to pick
up on ambient magic, and even then it was only by smell. Now, he
could actually *feel* the magic like a physical pressure on his skin.
The only thing that even came close was the Pit where they'd faced
Bixby last month. But while 8 Mile magic didn't reek of death like
the Pit had, it still made him nervous, prickling the back of his neck
like he was being hunted.

"That's because we are," Chelsie said when he mentioned it, glaring at the landscape like it had insulted her. "The magic here is too thick for what you'd normally find this far from the Reclamation Land border. It could just be backlash from Justin kicking the ant-hill, but I wouldn't bet on it." She climbed out of the truck, stepping into the tall grass silently as a cat. "I'm going to have a look around. Keep your nose sharp."

Julius nodded, but his sister was already walking away at a speed that would have been a run for a human. A few seconds later, she vanished into the long shadow of an abandoned car. There was no flash, no portal, not even a blip in the pea-soup magic. The moment she stepped into the shadow, she was simply gone, leaving only the empty grass swaying in the evening breeze.

"Wow," Marci said. "What is she, Heartstriker Batman?"

"Close enough," Julius said, looking down the road at the line of abandoned gas stations, strip malls, and fast food joints. Or, at least, those were his best guesses. After sixty years of neglect, it was getting hard to tell what any of the crumbling buildings had been, especially since nature seemed to be working overtime to take the ruins back.

Everywhere his eyes fell, plants were growing. Huge tufts of grass had cracked the old parking lots and sidewalks into a lattice-work, while trees and bushes grew out windows and doors, explod-ing out of the old buildings wherever the sunlight touched. If it wasn't for the creepy magic hanging over everything like an anvil in a cartoon, the view would have been peaceful in a return-to-nature, post-apocalyptic sort of way. With the magic, the lovely, overgrown ruins only served as a reminder of whose land this was, and how unwelcome they were in it.

Julius turned away with a shudder, holding out his hand to help Marci out of the middle seat. "Come on. Let's get set up."

"Way ahead of you," she said, placing a brand new can of spell-ready spray paint into his offered hand.

He looked at it in confusion. "What's this for?"

"We're drawing a circle big enough to trap a fjord," Marci explained, pulling two more cans out of her bag. "We're going to need a lot of coverage. You take that can and paint a line on the ground going left until it runs out. I'll go right and do the same. Once both cans are empty, we'll come back, get two more, and do it again going north and south to form a cross. Once we've got our guide lines, we'll just connect the four ends in a roughly circular fashion. Just make sure you arc out so we don't end up with a diamond."

"That doesn't sound very accurate."

Marci shrugged. "We're talking about free-handing a casting circle big enough to hold the yearly magical output of the entire DFZ. A few bumps are unavoidable. Just do your best to get it round-ish and I'll adjust at the end."

Julius still wasn't sure, but this was Marci's area of expertise, so he took his can and got going, laying down a line of glittering silver paint over the tall grass behind him.

• • •

Marci's circle ended up being nearly a quarter mile in diameter. It took them almost the entire hour just to draw the thing, which left Marci barely fifteen minutes to frantically write out the spellwork as the sun sank toward the horizon.

Julius tried his best to give her space, but as the minutes ticked down to the wire, he found himself edging closer until he was standing almost on top of her, nervously watching as she set down what he hoped were the last lines of the spell on the edge of the giant circle where it crossed one of the few remaining unbroken sections of sidewalk.

"Almost there," she said, sticking her tongue out of the side of her mouth in concentration as she dragged the chalk across the dirty cement so fast, the dust flew up like a cloud. "Just need to add in a protection so everything stays in place and…done!" She sat up with a grin. "What do you think?"

300

"It's definitely big enough," Julius said, looking down the silver spray-painted line that ran glittering off into the distance. "But isn't it a little noticeable?"

"Only because I haven't activated it yet," she said. "Observe."

Marci leaned over and placed her hands on the spray-painted line. The moment her skin touched the paint, the scent of her magic cut through the syrup-thick power in the air, and then the whole circle lit up. For a heartbeat, it flared like burning phosphorus, and then the silver spray-painted line vanished without a trace.

"How did you do that?" Julius said, leaning down to poke at the now completely normal looking grass that had been covered in paint only seconds before.

Marci stood up with a cocky smile. "Illusion master, remember? I'm not going to go through the trouble of making a circle this big without taking out some insurance. I also added in a few lines to make it all waterproof because, you know, obvious reasons."

She grinned, clearly expecting him to laugh, but Julius was too nervous to find anything funny. Now that the spell was done, it was starting to hit him that this was it. The sun was now as low as it could go in the sky. Vann Jeger would be here any second, and even though they were as prepared as they could possibly be, it was hard to be calm. He didn't doubt Marci for a second, but a spray-painted circle, however big, suddenly felt like very poor protection against the world's most infamous dragon hunter.

"Maybe we should just try to break the curse and run?"

Marci's head snapped up. "What?"

Since it wouldn't matter to the illusion, Julius ran a shaking hand through his hair. "I know I was the one who said we should fight Vann Jeger to save Justin, but now that we're here, I worry we're trying to do too much. If we had more time, it'd be different, but this just feels so rushed. Don't want to reach too far and end up losing everything, you know?"

"But that's how it works," Marci said, her face growing serious. "Risk and reward are intrinsically linked. We don't get anything if we take the safe route every time."

"I know," Julius said, looking down at her. "But…"

But I don't want to risk you.

That was what he wanted to say, but admitting it out loud where she could hear terrified him way more than Vann Jeger. Thankfully, Marci interpreted his speechlessness as fear of a different sort.

"We *can* do this, Julius," she said with that supreme, unquestionable confidence that had drawn him to her in the first place. "Everything's been planned, everything's in place. All you have to do is get Vann Jeger in the circle and keep him there, which shouldn't be hard at all. I mean, look at you!" She threw out her hands. "You look like the most terrifying dragon I've ever seen! Vann Jeger will eat you up."

"That's what I'm afraid of."

Marci winced. "Okay, bad choice of words, but I'm telling you it's going to be *fine*. How many banishments have we done over the last month?"

"Thirty-two," he said.

"You see?" she said, spreading her arms wide. "We've got this thing down to a science. I don't care what nonsense Vann Jeger shows up with, his butt is getting *kicked*. For good, too, because I'm sick of being the weak human. I'm going to show that stupid spirit what it means to mess with a mage."

Her eyes were flashing when she finished, almost like she was daring him to argue, but Julius had nothing to say except, "Thank you."

Marci blinked. "For what?"

"For not letting me back down," he said with a nervous smile. "For everything, really. You're the best thing that's ever happened to me, so I wanted to tell you thank you. Just in case the worst happens."

"Well, it's not going to happen," Marci said firmly, stepping closer until he couldn't have looked away from her if he'd tried. "Listen to me, Julius. I know your family likes to put you down, but I've met my share of dragons at this point, and I can say without a doubt that you are every bit as sneaky and slippery and cunning as the rest. Just because you don't use your powers to be a colossal jerk doesn't mean they're not there, so you can kick your worst case scenarios to the curb, because if anyone can pull off this insanity, it's you."

That was such an odd, Marci-esque mix of insult and praise, he couldn't help but grin. There was nothing romantic about standing in a trash-littered field at sunset waiting for a spirit who was coming to murder you, but in this moment, Julius couldn't imagine anywhere he'd rather be. After so many years of being a failure, the shame of the Heartstrikers, the idea that someone as undeniably capable as Marci trusted him—*believed* in him—was more than he could ever hope to ask for.

But then, she always had been.

The truth of that sudden realization made his breath catch. From the very first time they'd met, Marci had been more than he had any right to expect. She was his ally, his teammate, his clever, brave, beautiful *friend* who'd stood by him with a loyalty other dragons paid kingdoms for. Three days ago, he'd thought he'd be happy forever if he could just hold on to that, but now, after everything that had happened, merely holding on was no longer enough.

Maybe it was the looming threat of death, or maybe there really was a risk-taking dragon inside him somewhere, because suddenly, Julius couldn't wait another second. So he didn't. He did something better, something he'd been wanting to do almost from the moment he first saw Marci marching toward him across that crowded restaurant.

He kissed her.

• • •

In hindsight, his timing left much to be desired. Kissing someone out of the blue when you both were waiting to be attacked was not very considerate. He should have given her some warning at least, because Marci nearly jumped out of her boots when their lips met. If he hadn't been a dragon with superhuman speed, she would have head-butted him, which would have been awkward all around. But ill-advised as he knew this was, Julius didn't regret it for a second. Vann Jeger could have landed on his head right now and he wouldn't have cared so long as he didn't have to stop kissing Marci.

He just wished she'd kiss him back.

Julius froze, eyes shooting open. Why wasn't she kissing him back? He'd thought she'd wanted to in the closet. Had she changed her mind? Maybe he'd read things all wrong. Maybe she didn't want this at all.

With that splinter of doubt, the reality of what he'd just done hit Julius like a punch. He'd *kissed* Marci. Without asking. Right before a fight. No, forget the fight. Going up against the world's best dragon hunter was nothing compared to a reckless kiss that might have just cost him the most important friendship of his life.

Feeling like the absolute worst, Julius jerked away, his brain scrambling to think of how in the world he was going to fix this. But as he opened his mouth to start apologizing, Marci grabbed his shoulders and yanked him back down.

"Don't stop," she commanded against his lips, wrapping her arms so tight around his neck he nearly choked. "Don't you dare stop."

Julius slumped into her, happily pressing his body into hers. He was so relieved he could have laughed, but doing so would have meant stopping his kiss with Marci, and now that he knew she was okay with it, he wasn't doing that again for anything. Just like the night in the hotel, she was warm and soft in his arms, only now it was even better, because she wasn't kissing him out of obligation or gratitude. She was kissing him because she wanted to. Because she wanted *him*.

Just thinking about that made him feel like he was flying. The fear, the heavy magic, the constant sense of impending doom, it was all gone. It was like he'd closed a door on everything that wasn't Marci in his arms right now, which was why he didn't notice his sister standing directly beside them until she cleared her throat.

It was a sign of just how giddy he was that Julius actually considered ignoring her. Fortunately for everyone, Marci's survival instincts were still functioning. It only took her a handful of seconds before she untangled herself, her face flushed but completely unrepentant as she turned to look at Chelsie, who was watching the two of them with a thoroughly unamused expression.

"*If* you're finished," she said, looking pointedly at the setting sun. "It's time."

Julius was not finished. He didn't think he'd *ever* be finished, but Chelsie was right. The edge of the sun was now undeniably touching the horizon, which meant Vann Jeger was due to arrive any second. But even with the Death of Dragons incoming, Julius couldn't let Marci go before he explained himself.

"Listen," he said, turning his back to Chelsie so he could pretend he wasn't saying this in front of his sister. "I—"

The word was barely out of his mouth when something icy touched his foot. He looked down in surprise, expecting Ghost, but it wasn't the spirit. Or, at least, it wasn't Marci's spirit.

Water was rising from the grass at their feet. It seeped up through the dirt like a welling spring, rapidly turning the hard, dry ground to sludge. Unlike a natural spring, though, this water reeked of salt and dragon blood, pushing back even the oppressive, wild stench of the Reclamation Land magic as it rushed over the empty roads and fields of the DFZ side of the border.

"Crap," Marci whispered, her face turning serious as she splashed back to her thankfully—and, in hindsight, *brilliantly*—waterproofed spellwork. "Battle stations."

"No, wait," Julius said, running after her. "I might not get another chance to—"

"You will," she said, whirling back around to face him. "Because we're going to win this. After that, we'll pick up where we left off, but right now you have to stop being sweet and go be a terrible and ruthless dragon or the whole gig is up."

She was right. He *knew* she was right, but—

"Listen to me, Julius," Marci said fiercely, cutting him off before he could say another word. "Do you have any idea how long I've wanted you to kiss me? There is no way on Earth I am dying after that, so go do your part." She broke into a giddy grin. "The sooner we get this done, the sooner we can get back to what we were doing."

That was the best motivation for survival Julius could imagine, but he couldn't stop himself from darting in to press a quick, final kiss against Marci's cheek. He held on for as long as he could, savoring the smooth, soft feel of her skin until the very last second before turning away and striding out to the center of the circle where the rising water was deepest.

By the time he reached the assigned meeting place, the freezing water was up to his knees. As promised, Chelsie had already vanished, and with Marci hanging back to keep a hold on her hidden circle, that meant Julius was taking his stand alone. He was trying not to be intimidated at the prospect when his ears caught the distant thunder of horse hooves.

Julius had never been a particularly good student during his strategic combat lessons—partially because he didn't like violence, but mostly he'd been too busy defending himself from his siblings to worry about outside threats—but even he knew what that sound meant. But knowing what was coming didn't make it any less scary when a giant warhorse made of crashing waves burst through the center of the mini-ocean Vann Jeger's magic had created in the fields surrounding 8 Mile Road.

It exploded up like a torpedo, rocketing out of the water only to come crashing down again seconds later, its dinner-plate-sized hooves splashing water all over Julius's front as it landed in front of him, bringing its massive rider face to face at last with the dragon he'd come to fight.

Oddly enough, Julius's first thought was that pictures he'd seen didn't do Vann Jeger justice. The spirit in the old news footage they'd studied at the mountain merely looked like a large, oddly-colored human with an impressive weapons collection. In reality, standing in front of Vann Jeger felt like standing in front of a hurricane. Flat pictures, even video, simply could not capture the force-of-nature menace that poured off him like water down a hill. A sensation that only got worse when the spirit set his enormous wooden spear on his shoulder and scanned the ruined landscape with his black eyes before finally resting them on his enemy.

"Well, well," Vann Jeger said, the words crunching like cracking sea ice as he looked Julius over. "That's more like it. I'd hoped for a Fang, of course, but you are not as great a disappointment as the whelp I faced earlier."

The mention of Justin made Julius flinch. A detail that did not escape Vann Jeger.

"Concerned about your brother?" The spirit taunted with a grin. "Don't worry. Algonquin saved his head for herself, but yours is another matter." He leaned forward on his horse, eyes gleaming. "What do they call you, wyrm?"

Julius clamped his jaw tight as he let the illusion Marci and Amelia had put together do the work of maintaining proper draconic disdain. Good thing, too, because inside, he was nearing full panic. The others had tried to warn him, but knowing that Vann Jeger was a big spirit and experiencing it firsthand were two very different things. Nothing could have prepared him for the reality of the murderous intent that emanated from the spirit like cold from an iceberg. And he was supposed to stall *this* for half an hour?

Oddly enough, that thought was his salvation. Though his body was screaming at him to escape as fast as he could, there was nowhere to go. Vann Jeger was here—huge and implacable and right in front of him—and the only chance Julius had of surviving was to follow the plan as closely and calmly as possible. Any panic, even the normal, healthy kind, would only guarantee defeat, which was intolerable. He'd only just gotten up the guts to kiss Marci. He couldn't fail now. Forward was the only option, so Julius embraced it, shoving his fear aside as he threw himself into the role he'd agreed to play.

This was actually a lot easier than he'd expected. He'd never considered himself any sort of actor, but in this case, the sheer quantity of examples he had to pull from made up for his lack of natural talent. He didn't even have to think about it too hard. All he had to do was think of Ian and Svena and Bethesda and Chelsie and pretty much every dragon who'd ever looked down on him, and the words just came rolling out.

"My name is not for the likes of you."

If things had been less dire, Julius would have cheered. That cold, haughty voice didn't sound anything like him. Vann Jeger, however, looked more dreadful than ever.

"Then you are unique among your kind," the spirit sneered. "Most dragons are all too eager to recite their ridiculous titles. But I suppose it matters not." His sneer turned back into a smirk. "I don't need your name to kill you."

"And I didn't come here to listen to uninspired threats," Julius said, looking at Vann Jeger with the bored, I-have-nothing-better-to-do-so-I'm-deigning-to-interact-with-you expression that Ian used in all their conversations. "You said Algonquin saved my brother's head for herself. Does that mean he's already mounted on her wall?"

Please say no. Please say no.

"He lives for now," the spirit said with a shrug, almost making Julius sigh in relief. "But why do you care? Your mother didn't seem to."

Julius wasn't sure how to answer that one. *Channel Ian.* "The Heartstriker knows better than to let spirits know her real intentions," he said haughtily, lifting his chin so high he got a crick in his neck. "And beyond idle curiosity, I *don't* care. I'm only here because you inconvenienced my human."

The spirit laughed, making the ground tremble. "Your human? A pathetic baby mage who let herself get caught."

"A brilliant mage who is very precious to me," Julius said, not even needing the illusion to make him sound cold this time. "Normally, I would make you pay for what you did to her, but that's what you want, isn't it?"

That question was his best chance for a stall. Even when it was obvious what they wanted, no dragon would ever just admit their true goal. He'd hoped to trick Vann Jeger into going around in coy circles for at least another few minutes. But, sadly, this was where Julius's vast experience failed him, because Vann Jeger *wasn't* a dragon, and he didn't take the bait.

"It is," the spirit thundered, his face splitting into a terrifying grin. "I'd thought she'd led me false when she claimed you were powerful, but it seems your human was telling the truth after all. I do not know what son of the Heartstriker you are, serpent, but you are clearly worth my time, and that pleases me greatly." He waved his hand sharply through the air. "The Sword of Damocles is lifted," he announced. "Your human may live."

The words were barely out of the spirit's mouth when Julius heard Marci's delighted gasp. Before he could even feel happy about it, though, the spirit added, "You, on the other hand, will have to fight for your head."

Julius jumped back. All around them, the ankle-deep, freezing water covering the ground was now flowing away. It was like watching the tide go out, only instead of racing out to sea, Vann Jeger's water began to churn around them in a circle, spinning up until they were surrounded by a whirlpool of water as tall as a five-story building.

Until this point, Julius hadn't even realized there *was* that much water on the ground, and for a horrible moment, he was sure the whole thing was about to crash down and drown him. Bad as that would be, though, the truth was actually worse, because the wave didn't crash down at all. It went *up*, shooting into the evening sky before curving over on itself to create a domed cage of surging, spinning, obviously magical water cutting them off from the rest of the world.

By the time he realized he was trapped, Julius's panic was almost enough to break the illusion. He couldn't even see Marci through Vann Jeger's wall of water. For all he knew, he was cut off from Chelsie as well, which meant he was alone, trapped in a watery arena with the Death of Dragons. About the only thing that had gone right was that they were still inside Marci's giant circle, not that that was much comfort when Vann Jeger planted his spear on the ground and used it like a pole vault, leaping off his horse to land in front of Julius with a crash.

"Since the challenge was mine, I shall allow you the first move," the spirit said, banishing the horse back to water with a wave of his spear. "You may attack when ready."

That offer struck Julius as oddly fair. It also gave him an idea. The wall of water had been a surprise, but otherwise, Vann Jeger was behaving exactly like the archaic warrior Amelia had described him as earlier. With that in mind, Julius switched gears completely, keeping his hands at his sides as he asked, "Why?"

Vann Jeger scowled. "Why what?"

"Why do we have to fight?" Julius clarified. "You've gone out of your way to provoke me, harassing my human and forcing me into the open, yet I've done nothing to harm you or Algonquin or this city. There are plenty of arrogant, destructive dragons in the DFZ for you to fight. Why waste your time hunting those of us who just want to be left alone?"

A dragon would have seen through that question before it got out of Julius's mouth, but as he'd just seen, Vann Jeger *wasn't* a dragon. He was a spirit, a proud soul who clearly got his values from a very different time. And, as Julius had learned as a teenager trying to argue on the internet, if you wanted to get a proud person talking, all you had to do was ask them to explain why they thought they were right. It didn't hurt that he was also legitimately curious, which made his attention all the more believable when Vann Jeger snapped up the bait.

"I hunt you because you are what you are," the spirit thundered. "You say you've done us no harm, but that is impossible when your very existence harms those around you. Consumption and destruction are a dragon's nature. It's why you came to our world in the first place, because you'd already destroyed your own with your never-ending greed." He bared his teeth. "You are all parasites feeding off a world that does not belong to you, and it is my pleasure as well as my duty as a soul of this land to make you bleed."

That was much more of an answer than Julius had been expecting, and one that sadly made a lot of sense. But even so, "We're not all like that," he said earnestly, forgetting his role as a ruthless, terrible dragon for a moment. "Some dragons are what you describe, but there are plenty who just want to live in peace. Surely this world is big enough for both of us?"

"No world is big enough for your greed," the spirit said bitterly. "Enough of this. I didn't come here to explain what you should already know."

"But I still don't understand," Julius said quickly. "Dragons didn't destroy the world in the thousand years you were sleeping, why would we do it now? We just want to live here, too."

"But none of us want to live with *you*," Vann Jeger snarled, stabbing his spear through the air at Julius. "Understand *that*, wyrm. This is our world, not yours, and we will not share it with the likes of you. Now." He bared his yellow teeth. "Change and fight, or I will go back on my offer and strike you down like the mortal you pretend to be."

Julius took a step back. He'd been doing surprisingly well up until now, but apparently he'd trodden on sacred ground with that last question. He was scrambling to think of a way to sidetrack the spirit onto another topic when Vann Jeger charged straight at him.

It happened so quickly, even Julius's speed wasn't enough. Despite his bulk, Vann Jeger moved faster than Julius's eyes could track. One second he was standing several feet away, the next, all ten feet of homicidal, dragon-hating spirit was right in front of him with his giant spear already crashing into Julius's chest.

If not for Marci, that would have been the end. Forget dodging, Julius hadn't even *seen* the attack until it was way too late. But in addition to her fantastic illusion work, Marci had also given him some insurance in the form of a ward against blades similar to the one she'd used on herself to stop bullets when she'd confronted Bixby. But while the magical barrier did indeed stop the point of the spear from actually stabbing through his chest, it couldn't do anything to stop the force, which was still enough to send Julius flying across the soggy field and into the spinning wall of water.

He bounced off it like a rubber ball, thrown face first back into the field by the magic current. But this, too, was a stroke of luck, because the muddy dirt actually absorbed most of the impact. It still hurt like crazy, but at least he didn't break anything. Unless, of course, you counted Vann Jeger's willingness to believe that Julius was actually an ancient and powerful dragon.

"*That's it?*" the spirit roared, stomping over to grab Julius out of the dirt. "Where is your fire? Where is your *strength?*"

He shook Julius violently with each word, making it impossible to answer, not that Julius could have given him one. His power was entirely on the surface, and by the time Vann Jeger let him go, it was obvious the spirit knew it.

"Is this what Heartstriker has come to?" he growled, throwing Julius back into the mud. "I came here because I was promised a true fight, but you're even weaker than the whelp this afternoon! At least he had fire."

Julius tried to come up with something disdainful and witty to say to that, but between the shaking and his second impact with the ground, he could barely form words. Everything in his head was ringing and shaking. He was still working on pushing back up to his knees when he saw the spirit raise his spear.

"Pathetic," Vann Jeger growled, lining up his spear to skewer Julius's heart. But as he pulled back his arm for the killing blow, a whistling noise sliced through the air, followed by Vann Jeger's roar of pain.

Julius gasped in surprise, yanking his still-ringing head up just in time to see Vann Jeger drop his spear and reach around with both hands to grab at something on his back. The spirit was so large though, Julius couldn't actually see what he was trying to catch hold of until Chelsie jumped down, her sword glinting wetly in the light of the setting sun.

Not counting the few seconds after she'd first fallen into his living room, Julius had never actually seen Chelsie's Fang out of its sheath. Not surprisingly, the bone-colored, curving blade looked very much like Justin's. But where his brother's sword was clearly designed for power, Chelsie's was narrow and sharp as a surgeon's scalpel. It was also dripping with a black liquid Julius could only assume was Vann Jeger's blood. *Literally* dripping, as in Julius couldn't understand how she'd gotten that much blood out of a single attack. When Vann Jeger whirled around to face her, though, he understood.

Chelsie hadn't just stabbed the spirit in the back, she'd *gutted* him, slicing him open from the base of his neck to the small of his back. If he'd been human, he'd have been cut him in two. But Vann Jeger was no more human than he was dragon, and the dripping wound closed before Julius's eyes, the dusky blue flesh sealing over in seconds until it was impossible to tell the spirit had even been injured.

If Chelsie was upset her surprise attack hadn't worked, she didn't let it show. Vann Jeger, on the other hand, looked like he'd just stumbled over a hidden treasure. "I was expecting a trap," he rumbled, his blue face splitting into an inhumanly wide grin. "But Bethesda's Shade herself?" He laughed again, a joyous, delighted sound. "You are known to me, black snake! And to think I fell for that pretender when you were within my grasp all along, but no matter. It shall be my great pleasure to take your hide." His black eyes dropped hungrily to the sword in her hands. "And your Fang."

"Try it," Chelsie snarled, lifting her blade. "And we'll see who ends up getting skinned."

Her taunt only made Vann Jeger happier. "Change, then!" he cried, spinning his spear with a flourish. "I've waited centuries to face a Fang of the Heartstriker. Return to your true self, Shade of Bethesda, and give me a battle worthy of your name!"

Chelsie's lip curled in pure disgust, and she spat on the ground. "Make me."

Vann Jeger's eyes widened. So did Julius's. He didn't know the details of Chelsie's Fang, but if it was anything like Justin's, turning into a dragon would give her a massive boost in destructive power, which seemed like a pretty good idea right now. But Chelsie must have known something he didn't, because she stayed stubbornly human, her green eyes narrowed to slits like she was daring the hunter to attack. A dare Vann Jeger was more than ready to take.

"So be it," he said, letting go of his spear.

Julius's breath caught, his eyes locked on the spear as it tumbled to the ground, but didn't hit. The moment the spirit released his weapon, the long wooden spear turned to water, then vapor, and then nothing at all. It was as though it had simply dissolved into thin air, and by the time it was gone, Vann Jeger was holding two new weapons, twin iron swords that looked even deadlier than the spear.

The whole exchange couldn't have taken more than a heartbeat. Julius wasn't even sure where the new swords had come from, but they definitely looked real. Real and highly magical, their edges glowing green with a power that smelled both human and very, very old.

"I've always wanted a Fang of the Heartstriker," Vann Jeger said casually, crossing the two giant swords in front of him. "When I first heard reports of green fire in the Pit, I knew I'd found my chance at last. But if you will not give me a proper demonstration of your weapon's power, then I have no choice but to force one out of you." He chuckled. "I don't think it will be hard."

His deep voice was mocking by the end, but Chelsie refused to be riled. She just stepped into a defensive stance, raising her sword in front of her like a wall. When it was clear she wasn't going to join in the banter, Vann Jeger's face turned sour. "Haughty to the end, I see. How like a *dragon*."

On the word *dragon*, he vanished. He didn't charge or jump, he was just *gone*. Then, before Julius's eyes could even move from the place where the spirit had been, he heard the clash of weapons. By the time his head whipped around, Vann Jeger was bearing down on Chelsie with both swords.

She looked as surprised as Julius had been by the seeming teleportation, but apparently getting the drop on Chelsie was as impossible for spirits as it was for Heartstrikers. Even though her enemy had literally appeared from thin air in front of her, Chelsie met him like she'd had ages to prepare, blocking his attack with both hands on her sword: one on the hilt, and one grabbing the upper half of the blade as she pushed back with all her strength.

With a bloodthirsty grin, Vann Jeger started swinging, pounding his swords down on her defense over and over like hammers on an anvil. Every blow pushed her boots deeper into the ground, but though her guard didn't break, she was still trapped. Vann Jeger was completely on the offensive, his swords slamming into hers so fast and furious, she couldn't drop her guard long enough to even try for a strike. Worse still, his constant blows were pushing Chelsie backwards toward the wall of surging water. If she hit it, she'd be thrown just like Julius had been, and then everything would be over.

She must have known it, too, because when they got within five feet of the water, Chelsie dropped her defense and lashed out at last, swinging for the spirit's left arm to force him to dodge and give her a way out of the trap. But even when it was obvious her sword was coming right at him, Vann Jeger didn't try to get out of the way. He just kept swinging, letting her cut deep into his forearm below the elbow and then through his arm altogether, slicing off his hand and wrist in a quick, clean strike.

The moment the path was clear, Chelsie darted away, rolling across the field before the spirit's sliced off hand could even hit the ground. Trouble was, it never did.

Like the spear, Vann Jeger's severed hand—and the sword that was still clutched in it—turned to water before it hit the ground. Likewise, the black-bleeding stump of his wound was only visible for a second before a new hand formed on top of it with a bow clutched in its fingers. Julius was still trying make sense of that when the sword in the hand Chelsie hadn't cut off dissolved as well, reshaping itself into a jagged, iron-headed arrow in the blink of an eye. That was all the warning they got before Vann Jeger began shooting arrows at Chelsie like a machine gun.

Giving credit to her reputation, Chelsie dodged every one, sliding between the onslaught like a bird in the wind. But though her defense was flawless, she still wasn't attacking, and Vann Jeger didn't seem to be tiring. He actually seemed to be enjoying himself, his face split in an enormous smile. "You're very good at running away," he taunted, shooting even faster. "Shall we see how fast you can go?"

The question was still rumbling when Julius saw the wall of water behind his sister ripple. "*Chelsie! Behind you!*"

He barely got the words out before a wall of glinting spears shot out of the water like knives through a curtain. But Chelsie was the Heartstriker all others feared for a reason. She'd jumped the moment Julius shouted her name, launching herself straight up almost to the peak of the domed prison to let the spears fly by beneath her.

Even Vann Jeger looked impressed, letting his bow fall back into water. "Marvelous!" he cried as Chelsie landed neatly in front of him. "You are everything your reputation promised, so how about we make things more interesting?"

He waved his hand, and the entirety of the watery cage—the dome, the walls, even the puddles that still lay on the ground at Chelsie's feet—began to ripple. Chelsie raised her sword in answer, but Julius already knew it was hopeless. The fight so far had proven that his sister was even better than he'd realized, but there was no way she could dodge simultaneous attacks from so many angles. It was too late for her to get out, though. The points of Vann Jeger's summoned weapons were already breaking through the water on all sides. So, with no other options to save his sister, Julius did the only thing he could think of.

He shot to his feet, yelling at the top of his lungs. "*Cut to me!*"

The attack launched at the same time. It came from all sides: spears, arrows, daggers, swords, and other sharp weapons Julius couldn't even name came shooting out of the water in a volley at his sister. There were so many blades in the air, he couldn't even see Chelsie anymore. He could, however, smell her blood. But then, just when he was sure he'd yelled too late, the air in front of him split open, and his sister tumbled out.

"Chelsie!"

He dropped to her side, but she pushed him away just as fast, reaching up to yank the arrow—which he hadn't even seen hit her—out of her shoulder. The moment it was out, she rolled back to her feet and turned to face Vann Jeger, who'd already dissolved the arsenal he'd thrown at her.

"So your Fang can cut through space?" he said, chuckling as he turned to face the Heartstrikers. "Now I *must* have it."

"Try and take it," Chelsie taunted, stepping into position. Julius, however, had had about enough.

"Are you crazy?" he hissed. "Don't keep fighting him! He's clearly doing all of this through water. If you turn into a dragon, you can vaporize him!"

"That's exactly what he wants," Chelsie whispered back, never taking her eyes off Vann Jeger. "Turning into a dragon is the worst thing you can do when facing a dragon hunter." She nodded at the water on the ground, all that was left of the volley of weapons Vann Jeger had just launched. "All of his attacks are tuned for big, flying targets. By staying human, I'm harder to hit. That gives me the advantage."

Julius didn't see how the word "advantage" could be applied to anything that had happened over the last few minutes. "So you're just going to keep dodging until he wears you down?"

"Stalling is the entire point of this," his sister snapped. "Or did you forget your own plan?"

"Keeping him busy is different from losing," Julius said frantically, pointing at her bloody shoulder. "How are we going to hold out if you're the only one taking hits?"

"I won't be for much longer," Chelsie growled, looking down her sword toward the far side of the circle formed by Vann Jeger's wall of water. "When I attack, go stand over there."

Julius couldn't see why. That stretch of muddy, torn up grass looked just as bad as everywhere else. Before he could ask what she was planning, though, Chelsie was gone, stalking toward Vann Jeger with her sword held low.

"Tired of running?" the spirit taunted, reaching out with both hands to catch an enormous sword—the sort ancient infantry used to cut down horses—as it condensed from the air.

"Tired of you," Chelsie snarled, planting her feet in the mud. "When you're ready."

Vann Jeger attacked before she'd even finished, charging her with his massive sword clutched in both hands like a bat. Chelsie let him get almost all the way before she jumped, landing on the edge of his raised blade like a bird. She lashed out with her much smaller sword at the same time, cutting down to take Vann Jeger's head.

This started an exchange of blocks and counters that went too fast for Julius to track, so he didn't even try. Instead, he focused on doing what Chelsie had said, quietly sneaking around the side of the water prison until he was standing where she'd pointed. When he got to the right spot, he looked back up to see how things were going, and immediately regretted it.

Despite attacking all out, Chelsie was still getting pushed back. Not because she was slower or less skilled—she and Vann Jeger's swordwork actually seemed to be pretty evenly matched—but because the spirit didn't seem to care about getting hit. She was drawing blood with almost every attack, but while that would have been enough to whittle down any other opponent, Vann Jeger's blue skin just closed right back up. She might as well have been trying to slice up the sea for all the good she was doing, but while Vann Jeger was grinning like he could do this forever, Chelsie was looking significantly worse for wear.

Other than the arrow wound from earlier, nothing looked major, but she was bleeding from multiple small cuts across her arms, legs, and torso. It had to hurt like crazy, but the pain wasn't slowing her down at all. If anything, she actually seemed to be moving faster, but it didn't matter. A fight where one opponent could be injured while the other couldn't had only one outcome, and Julius was starting to think they'd made a fatal mistake when Vann Jeger's sword finally landed a solid hit, flinging Chelsie backwards into the wall of water.

Julius gasped, eyes wide. But though that looked like the beginning of the end, Chelsie was smiling as she flew through the air. Then, just before she should have smacked into the geyser of water and been thrown right back at Vann Jeger, she vanished.

The spirit jerked, looking around. Even Julius was confused. He was starting to think Chelsie had given up and cut her way back home to the mountain when a boot landed on his shoulder.

He stumbled, fighting to keep his balance as Chelsie dropped out of the cut in the air she'd made over his head, almost taking him to the ground. It wasn't until she pushed off him again, though, that he understood. The place she'd told him to be was directly behind Vann Jeger. The spirit hadn't landed a hit, she'd *let* him launch her so she could cut to Julius, putting herself in the perfect position for an attack from behind. An attack she clearly meant to be final.

Julius had never seen Chelsie attack for real before. He'd thought he'd seen it earlier, but now he knew he was wrong. She'd been playing defense this whole fight, doing only what was necessary to stay ahead of Vann Jeger's one spirit army. Now, though, she attacked in earnest, her magic roaring through the air like dragon fire as she shot toward Vann Jeger. Fast as he was, the spirit didn't even have time to turn around before Chelsie plunged her sword into his back, burying her Fang's bone-white blade between his shoulder blades so deep, the point emerged from his chest.

As soon as he was impaled, Chelsie planted her feet on the ground and yanked the blade up, clearly intending to slice straight up through his neck and into his head. But while Julius could see her muscles straining, Chelsie's sword didn't budge.

For the first time in his life, Julius saw real surprise on his sister's face. He was sure his looked the same. He'd seen Fangs of the Heartstriker slice through solid stone without even trying. A water spirit should have been nothing. But no matter how hard Chelsie pushed, her sword didn't move. She was still trying when Vann Jeger's body flickered like the water had earlier.

Chelsie let go with a curse, leaping out of the way just in time as the wooden dragon spear Vann Jeger had been carrying when he'd first arrived shot out of the spirit's body at her face. She landed back by Julius, her heavy boots sinking deep into the sodden ground. Meanwhile, on the other side of the water prison, Vann Jeger reached over his shoulder and calmly yanked Chelsie's Fang out of his back.

Julius had seen his sister angry plenty of times. It was always a terrifying sight, but nothing, *nothing* compared to the fury rolling off her now as she threw out her hand. Magic shot out at the same time, snapping at the sword in Vann Jeger's hands like jaws. But though the Fang clearly wanted to fly to her, it couldn't seem to escape Vann Jeger's grasp, and every time it failed, Chelsie's fury grew even hotter.

"How?" she demanded, caution completely forgotten as she stomped toward him. "How are you holding it? That sword belongs to Heartstriker magic! It will never be yours!"

"But everything that falls in my water belongs to me," Vann Jeger replied, turning his hand to show Chelsie her Fang as it began to dissolve, turning into water, then to vapor, and then vanishing entirely, just like all his other weapons.

Standing behind his sister, Julius couldn't see her face, but it must have been horrible, because Vann Jeger smiled wider than ever. "There it is," he cackled. "There's the *hate*. Poor little snake. You thought you were clever with your bait and switch, but I've been jumping around battle fields since the mountains were young. I allowed you to hit me because I wanted your sword, and now that I have it, I'm afraid my interest in this fight is at an end."

"Does that mean you'll let us go?" Julius asked hopefully.

Vann Jeger looked at him like he was very, very stupid. "It means that if you want to keep living beyond this moment, you'd better figure out a new way to be entertaining." He flicked his hand, and a new bow—this one longer and heavier than the one he'd used before—appeared in his hands. "Let's start with something simple, like seeing how fast you can run."

"Julius," Chelsie growled as Vann Jeger summoned an arrow and slowly began to notch it. "Split left. I'll go right. Focus on weaving."

Julius stared at her in horror. Surely she wasn't actually suggesting they try to stay ahead of the monster who could teleport, summon infinite weapons from any direction, and who'd just *eaten* one of the Fangs of the Heartstriker before their eyes? But Chelsie just smacked him on the shoulder.

"Remember the plan," she growled, darting her eyes pointedly toward the place where Marci was hidden behind the wall of water. "We're not dead yet. Now," she shoved him. "Go!"

Julius stumbled backwards just in time to miss the arrow that sank into the mud where his feet had been. Chelsie was already sprinting away in the other direction. Vann Jeger's shots seemed to be following her, and Julius took his chance to run the other way. He still thought it was insane, that there was no way they could get out of this mess, but then, they didn't have to. All they had to do was survive long enough for Marci to drain Vann Jeger's magic down to a level where they could beat him, which, by his reckoning, should only be about another ten minutes. Of course, considering what they were up against, ten minutes might well be nine minutes too long.

Please Marci, he thought, running faster than he'd ever run before. *Please hurry up!*

That was all the conscious thought he had time for before instinct took over, pushing him faster still as Vann Jeger's arrows began whistling over his head.

CHAPTER SIXTEEN

*W*e *are so screwed.*

This was the refrain that ran through Marci's head as she crouched in her circle just beyond the edge of Vann Jeger's water cage…bell jar…whatever, ignoring the horrible sounds coming from inside as she stared at her spellwork, trying to figure out how her simple plan had gone so wrong.

It hadn't started out that way. The beginning was perfect. Vann Jeger had removed her curse and stepped into her trap without a twinge. He'd then proceeded to lock himself inside an even *smaller* circle right in the middle. She couldn't have invented a better setup for a banishing, and she'd gotten right to work, stealing his magic in whisper-light touches that rapidly became greedy tugs once she realized the spirit wasn't reacting. She wasn't sure if this was because Vann Jeger was simply too caught up in the dragons to notice her, or if he knew what she was doing and was too convinced of his superiority to care, but until he came out of his water palace to stop her, Marci was going pedal to the metal. And, ironically, that was her problem.

Marci bit her lip, shaking her head to fling off the sweat that was dripping down her brow. She'd been sucking down magic at top speed without stop for the last twenty minutes. The giant circle she and Julius had drawn was already nearly full, which meant she'd moved more magic tonight than in the entire rest of her life combined. She could do nothing but sit around casting her biggest spells over and over for a year and *still* not use all the power she'd pulled out of Vann Jeger, and yet, inexplicably, the spirit was no smaller he'd been when she'd started

"Screwed," she muttered, glaring at the faintly glowing circle under her fingers. "So screwed."

She wouldn't have been so upset if the problem had made *sense*. Like any mage worth the name, she'd built contingencies into the spellwork, but all of her fallbacks had been designed assuming Vann Jeger would be fighting her for his magic. Never in a million years would she have dreamed the spirit just wouldn't care, or that he'd have more than she could fit in a freaking quarter mile circle, or that it wouldn't be doing any *good*. Despite losing the equivalent of a municipal power grid's worth of magic, Vann Jeger was as strong as ever, which should have been completely impossible. No spirit was infinite, especially not one so far from his domain. There *had* to be a bottom to Vann Jeger's power somewhere, but damned if Marci could find it, and she was almost out of time.

With that grim thought, Marci stopped pulling. The holding circle was almost full anyway, and just sitting around sucking more magic out of Vann Jeger clearly wasn't going to solve the problem any time soon. If she didn't want to be the reason this whole thing failed, she was going to have to come up with a new strategy that *would* work, and fast. So, with that, Marci forced herself to quit worrying about how screwed they were and started digging into Vann Jeger's magic.

Since there was no way he didn't know she was here at this point, Marci didn't bother with subtlety. She just dug in, peeling open the magic she'd just been sucking down to try and find the reason *why*. Why was it endless? Where was it all coming from?

But while she'd hoped to find something obvious, Vann Jeger's magic just looked like chaos. Even Ghost hadn't been that disorganized when she'd found him. Not being a spirit expert, Marci had no idea if the disarray was normal for spirits this size or if Vann Jeger was in a class by himself. Either way, it was time for a second opinion.

"Ghost!"

The spirit had been at her side the whole time, watching the water dome that hid Vann Jeger, Julius, and Chelsie like it was the most interesting thing in the world. She'd specifically kept him out of her spell at the beginning due to Amelia's warnings, but Marci had passed caring about such things ten minutes ago, and she didn't hesitate now to shove Vann Jeger's magic in his face. "What do you make of this?"

The cat wrinkled his nose. *Mess.*

"That's what I thought," she said, scowling. "Is that the way magic normally looks for a spirit this size?"

Normal is relative, Ghost said, flicking his ears. *But that's not his magic.*

"Don't joke," she scolded. "If that's not his magic, then what have I been siphoning for the last twenty minutes?"

Ghost yawned. *His weapons.*

"His weapons," Marci repeated slowly. "You mean like the knife he formed out of water and put against my throat?"

It wasn't formed out of water, Ghost said, looking at her like this was all too obvious for words. *Water isn't metal. Vann Jeger is a fjord. The knife was dropped into him long ago. All he did was pull it out again.* The cat turned to stare again at Vann Jeger's wall of water. *He has hundreds, all different.* His transparent tail began to lash back and forth. *They have voices.*

Marci had no idea what that last part meant, but her mind was racing too fast to care. "Are we talking magical weapons?" she asked quickly. "Like Tyrfing?"

The cat blinked his glowing eyes. *Do you know anything else that can hurt a dragon?*

Marci could have hugged him. Despite legends that described them as being forged by gods, magical weapons—like magical anythings—were usually the product of human mages. Like the Kosmolabe and so much else, the knowledge of how to make them had been lost during the thousand-year drought, but Vann Jeger was much older than that, *and* his domain was a fjord that ran through land that had been settled by humans since Neolithic times. She'd never actually heard of a spirit using human weapons, but if that's where Vann Jeger was getting his arsenal, then it would also explain why his power seemed limitless, because it wasn't his at all! The endless magic she'd been pulling on wasn't just the reservoir of an ancient and powerful spirit, it was also *all the powerful magical artifacts that had fallen into him.*

But while that hypothesis, if true, would totally explain everything that had been going on tonight, it actually made Marci's current problem worse. Unlike spirits, who were loose embodiments of magic, magical weapons were basically super dense spells. The few times Julius had let her poke at Tyrfing, she hadn't even been able to get past its surface thanks to the enormously complex and powerful enchantments that surrounded it like vacuum-sealed packaging. Even assuming Tyrfing was super high grade and therefore far more powerful than average, it wouldn't take that many enchanted objects of any caliber to make a pool deeper than Marci could ever hope of draining, not to mention Vann Jeger was stupidly old and seemed to be a collector. Who knew how many magical swords and spears and whatevers he had stashed away?

Too many seemed to be the answer. Now that Marci knew what she was looking for, she could actually feel the different threads of spells that wove through Vann Jeger's magic. The chaos she'd seen when she first dove in wasn't actually chaos at all. It was a weave, a complex braid of power made up of far more than just Vann Jeger's personal magic, and all her efforts tonight had barely been picking at the edges.

No wonder Vann Jeger hadn't cared that she was pulling on his magic. She could drain him for a year and barely make a dent, because Vann Jeger wasn't a simple spirit living off the power of his domain. He was an amalgam, a living arsenal of integrated, supermagical weapons, and she had no idea how to stop him.

That realization was crushing. She didn't know how to beat him. She didn't know how to win. From the sounds coming from inside the dome of water, Julius and Chelsie were clearly fighting him right now. Even if Marci could figure out a way to extract Vann Jeger's weapons, there was no way she could do it before the two dragons went down. That must have been why Vann Jeger had told her in advance where the fight would be, and why he hadn't spared her a glance when he arrived. Why be afraid of a trap when you knew you were too big to catch?

The more she figured out, the lower her hopes sank. Forget being screwed, she'd screwed them all. She'd told them she could handle this, told them to trust her, and she'd failed. She wasn't sure how much time had gone by at this point, but she had to be over her thirty-minute deadline, and from the sound of Vann Jeger's taunting laughter from behind the curtain of water, Chelsie and Julius were rapidly nearing the limit of what they could do. Even if they did manage to hold out five or ten more minutes, it wouldn't matter. She couldn't possibly do anything to stop Vann Jeger in so little time, which meant they were dead. *All* of them were dead, and it was all her—

No.

Marci shook her head violently, curling her hands into fists above her glowing circle. This was not how great mages behaved. There'd be time for self-recrimination after she was dead. Right now, though, she was alive. They all were. So long as that was true, the fight wasn't over, and Marci was going to do everything in her power to keep it that way.

First, though, she had to *get* power.

Ghost must have known it, because when Marci looked over, he was already waiting, standing beside her with his head up and his tail swishing back and forth.

Ready?

The fact that he knew what she was going to ask before she asked it was a giant warning flag, but Marci didn't care. It was amazing how unimportant personal safety became when you had your back to the wall. Besides, at this point, she couldn't imagine how Ghost could possibly make things worse.

"Ready," she replied, staring straight into his glowing eyes. "I want power."

His satisfaction was like a warm caress on her mind. *No conditions?*

"That depends on if you can give me what I need to beat Vann Jeger," Marci said firmly. "This is a huge risk for me. I have to know if it's worth it."

You help me, I help you, that was always the offer, Ghost said, pawing at her mental hold on the massive circle stuffed full of the magic she'd stolen from Vann Jeger. *Give it to me,* he whispered, his glowing eyes narrowing to slits. *And I will bring him to his knees.*

Marci took a deep breath. She'd come into this prepared to do whatever it took, but even for someone with her back against the wall, that was a lot. She wasn't even sure if she *could* channel that much power back through herself and into Ghost without permanently damaging her ability to move magic in the first place. And then there was the part where, if she lost control at any point during the transfer, she'd set off the magical equivalent of a nuke. But while both of these possibilities were terrifying, what really worried Marci was the fact that, if she fed Ghost all that magic, she wouldn't have anything left to rein him back in if he decided to go rogue.

Considering Amelia's warning, that felt like way more fire than Marci would be wise to play with. As much as she wanted to save Julius and his sister, she didn't think either of them would thank her for setting off a possible magical apocalypse in the process. Then again, though, there was no guarantee that Ghost was a bad, power hungry sort of spirit, right?

Marci grimaced. She couldn't even think that last bit with a straight face. Like she'd said to Julius earlier, though, it all came down to risk and reward. Was beating Vann Jeger really worth possibly setting whatever Ghost actually was free on the world?

She wasn't sure. Couldn't be, really, without knowing the truth in advance. One thing, however, *was* clear: whatever disaster Ghost brought would have to be pretty freaking bad to outweigh losing to Vann Jeger. Also, Marci already had the first inklings of a backup plan, assuming things did go to pot. She could feel Ghost prowling around in her head, though, so she turned her thoughts carefully away, looking the spirit in the eye as she gave her answer.

"Let's do this."

The words were barely out of her mouth when she felt Ghost's claws dig in. It was just like in the alley when he'd yanked the magic through their connection, only this time, everything was multiplied by a thousand. The magic didn't just burn as it came back in, it was blistering, the most intense pain Marci had ever felt. Likewise, the cold Ghost left behind wasn't just cold, it was a physical presence, an anchor of ice that dragged her down until she didn't even feel human anymore. She was just a wire, a conduit feeding Vann Jeger's magic into something else. Something huge and cold and terrifying that she barely knew anymore.

Marci never knew how long the transfer went on. It felt like forever, but it couldn't have been more than a few minutes, because when she became aware of the outside world again, the evening sky wasn't yet full dark, and Vann Jeger's cage of water was still up. Everything was just as it had been before, only now the giant circle stuffed full of power she'd had a death grip on was empty, and Ghost was nowhere to be seen.

I'm here.

Her breath caught. The spirit's whisper was no longer a whisper, but a voice in her head just as loud and clear as her own. That probably should have been her first concern, but Marci was more pissed that she'd gone through all that only to wake up and find Vann Jeger was still attacking Julius.

It's not finished.

"How can it not be finished?" she demanded, forcing herself to sit up. "I gave you everything."

A whisper of amusement floated through her head. *You don't have to talk out loud, you know,* the voice chided. *You did indeed give me everything I asked, but I can't help you yet.*

Marci rolled her eyes impatiently. Why not?

Because doing so would kill you, too, the presence that had once been Ghost replied. *You did it, Marci. You bought my name. But the bond between us is no longer strong enough for what I am now. If we are to continue together, a new pact must be made.*

She grimaced. The spell she'd used before was the only binding she knew.

Not a spell, he said, his voice smooth and deep in a way Ghost's had never been. *If I'm to continue as your spirit, I have to be part of you. For that, I need something of yours. A sacrifice.*

That word conjured up bloody images of hearts on trays, and the spirit laughed.

I'm not that kind of cat.

"You're not a cat at all," Marci reminded him. Out loud, too, because speaking helped maintain the semblance of equal ground. "But if you don't want blood,"—which was a huge relief—"what *do* you want?"

There was a long silence, and then, *A memory.*

"That's it?" Marci laughed. "You're already inside my brain. Just take your pick."

What followed was the strange sensation of someone shaking their head while still inside hers. *It doesn't work like that. The memory is an offering, a sacrifice to forge the bond. I cannot pick what you offer. You must choose what you sacrifice, and you must surrender it willingly.*

Fair enough, she supposed. "Any particular kind of memory?"

Someone who has died.

The answer came instantly, which struck her as odd. Just what kind of spirit was he?

You'll see, he promised. *Choose.*

"Bixby," she said at once.

Revulsion flooded her mind. *You would offer me something you hate? What kind of a sacrifice is that?*

Marci sighed. So much for the easy out. Then again, she supposed it made sense. Deals with the devil never worked when you tried to foist off something you didn't care about.

I'm not the devil, the voice said grumpily, sounding much more like Ghost than he had before. *I chose you because I thought you knew that. You accepted me as I was.*

"Sorry," Marci said, and she was. For all his creepiness, Ghost had always done right by her. That said, though, if he wouldn't take Bixby, that left only one person.

Marci's hands went unbidden to the rectangular shape at the bottom of her shoulder bag. With so much going on, she hadn't had a chance to move her dad's ashes somewhere safer, or maybe she just hadn't wanted to let them go. Either way, surrendering his memory to a spirit, even Ghost, felt unspeakably wrong. She was his last living family, the only one who still remembered the big-hearted, overly-generous man that was Aldo Novalli. If she gave that up, he'd be forgotten forever.

The dead are always forgotten.

"Not helping," she muttered, looking up again at Vann Jeger's prison. She still couldn't see through the wall of water, but she could hear the battle inside, which she hoped meant both dragons were still holding out. That was a miracle in and of itself, and Marci wasn't foolish enough to think it would continue much longer. Unlike her father, Julius and Chelsie were still alive and depending on her. Her dad would understand. If he were here now, he might even volunteer. Aldo Novalli never had been able to resist playing the hero.

The thought brought a smile to her lips, and Marci lowered her head. Slowly, reverently, she pulled the box of ashes out of her bag and placed it in her lap, stroking the name printed on the cardboard with loving fingers. "Okay," she whispered, blinking back the tears the blurred her vision as she tried her best to remember her father as she'd loved him best: the mage who'd taught her magic, the trickster who'd made her laugh, the one person who'd always believe in her no matter what. She gathered those memories and held them tight as she could, like she was hugging him one last time. And then, all at once, she let go.

"Goodbye, daddy."

The moment the words left her mouth, the world went dark. Not night dark or closet dark or even the dark of the Underground, but absolute pitch. But while that should have been terrifying, Marci wasn't afraid, because she wasn't alone. There was a weight on her shoulder, a large, ice-cold hand squeezing gently.

The price is paid, the voice said loud and clear behind her. *The bond is forged. What will you do with it?*

The image of Vann Jeger's smug blue face flashed through her mind, and Marci bared her teeth. "Take him down."

It was impossible to see in the dark, but Marci would have sworn the spirit smiled.

As you wish.

His voice was still hanging in the air when the hand on her shoulder vanished, and then a wind began to rise, blowing away the darkness as Marci got to her feet to see what she had brought into the world.

• • •

"Chelsie!"

Julius rolled in the dirt, dodging the giant hammer seconds before it landed on his head. On the other side of the circle, his sister jumped at Vann Jeger, slamming her boot into the spirit's arm and throwing his next attack crooked just long enough for Julius to scramble away. Ten minutes ago, the daring escape would have been cause for celebration. Now, with his lungs burning and every muscle in his body on the edge of giving out, Julius couldn't even spare it a thought.

"Come on," his sister growled, snatching him onto his feet again as she raced by. "Keep moving."

Julius nodded and tried to move faster, though he wasn't sure if the effort made an actual difference in his pace, or the fight's seemingly inevitable outcome. "He's just toying with us," he panted, looking back over his shoulder at Vann Jeger, who was making a great show of selecting his next weapon.

"That's why we're still alive," Chelsie said, her face grim. "Beggars can't be choosers."

That was true enough, but Julius was no longer sure he preferred death-from-exhaustion over death by whatever crazy tool
Vann Jeger pulled out next. He'd lost all track of time after Vann
Jeger had eaten his sister's sword, but they had to be well past Marci's
deadline, and there was still no end in sight. Just more running, the
two of them avoiding Vann Jeger's attacks by smaller and smaller
margins while the spirit stood in the center, blatantly enjoying the
sight of dragons scurrying like mice.

Even for Julius, who was used to running, it was a humiliating
experience. Or, he would have been humiliated if he hadn't also
been so terrified. Even Bethesda had never brought him as close to
death as he'd come to tonight, or half as many times. Chelsie was
the only reason he hadn't gone over. She'd stuck by him like glue,
constantly pulling him out of danger and keeping him moving even
when he was sure he couldn't take another step. But grateful as
Julius was for his sister's help, it had taken everything both of them
had to survive this long, and he didn't have any illusions about their
chances going forward.

"Come on, Marci," he whispered, risking a glance at the wall of
water where he thought she was, though he'd been around so many
times now, he couldn't be sure anymore. "Come *on*."

"Forget her," Chelsie snapped, reaching back to yank him forward. "The plan's failed. I don't know what she's been doing, but
Vann Jeger's no weaker now than he was when we came in."

Julius didn't want to believe that, but it was getting harder and
harder to keep up hope. Still. "Marci will think of something," he
said firmly. "She always does."

"Keep telling yourself that."

"What else is there?" he cried. "We can't run forever!"

"If you've got a better idea, I'm all ears," Chelsie replied, and
then she shoved him hard. "On your left."

He stumbled to the ground just in time to miss the ax flying
through the air where his head had been. As always, the weapon
turned to water vapor before it could hit the ground, but the little
glimpse he caught of the wickedly curved blade before it vanished

confirmed it was different from the others, just as they'd all been. "How many of those has he got?!"

"From what I've seen? Infinite." Chelsie pointed across the circle. "Go north. We'll pincer."

Julius didn't see the point in attacking. In the short time since she'd lost her sword, he'd seen Chelsie rip off Vann Jeger's arm, both legs, *and* split his head to the teeth with just her bare hands. Every time, though, the spirit had reformed good as new in seconds.

The obvious difference in power was unfair enough to make even Julius feel murderous. If it wasn't for the seal, he'd have changed and blasted Vann Jeger ages ago, whatever his sister said. But then, just as he was imagining how good it would feel to burn Vann Jeger until he evaporated, a wind rose in the dark.

If they'd still been in the open field, that wouldn't have been remarkable, but here inside Vann Jeger's watery prison, the only wind Julius had felt was the gust of a weapon as it narrowly missed him. That alone made the breeze remarkable, but what really caught his attention was the cold.

Given that it was mid-September, the nights were starting to get chilly, but no amount of seasonal change could explain this kind of dry, creeping, bone-chilling cold. It was like someone had let in a draft from the abyss. Even Chelsie stopped when she felt it, a move that nearly cost her her head when Vann Jeger whipped a long sword in her direction.

The attack must have been habit by this point, because Vann Jeger wasn't even looking at them when it happened. He was standing still at the center of the circle, his black eyes darting from side to side like he was searching for something. But while the spirit's distraction gave them a chance to catch their breath, Julius didn't think it was a good development. An opinion that only grew stronger when the freezing wind picked up, blowing the dirt into dust devils that stung his eyes and smelled of old graves.

"Get back."

Julius jumped and turned to see Chelsie standing right beside him. "What's going on?"

"I don't know," she said, covering her nose with her hand. "But something's here. Can't you smell it?"

Julius wished he couldn't. In the few moments they'd been talking, the graveyard smell had become overpowering. The temperature had dropped as well, plummeting from normal evening chill to meat locker levels, and as it got colder, the wind grew stronger.

It came from everywhere and nowhere, ripping the loose soil from the torn-up battlefield and spinning it into shapes that looked almost like people in the dark. A few seconds later, there was no "almost" about it. The dust figures *were* people—shuffling, faceless human forms of every age, sex, and race. Some looked like they'd walked straight out of ancient paintings, while others looked like dust copies of normal people you'd see on the streets of the DFZ. All of them were silent, their bodies blown in and out of existence by the freezing wind that had no beginning and no end as they circled around Vann Jeger, the apparent center of the strange, spontaneous storm.

"Enough!" the spirit roared, forming a large, wicked-looking ax in his hands. "Who are you?"

The one who remembers.

Julius nearly jumped out of his skin. That deep voice had been *inside* his head, the words blowing though his mind just like the freezing wind blew over his skin. It wasn't just him, either. Chelsie jumped, too, her head snapping around as she looked for the voice's source. Vann Jeger was doing the same, turning in a tight circle with his teeth bared and his ax ready. "You are not known to me," the spirit thundered. "And you are not welcome. This is my fight. Show yourself or be gone!"

But I have always been here.

Despite the bitter cold, Julius began to sweat. Maybe it was his imagination, but he'd have sworn the voice had sounded *familiar* that time. He was desperately trying to remember where he could have possibly heard something that terrifying before when Vann Jeger froze in his tracks. Chelsie grabbed Julius's shoulder a split second later, yanking him around until he was facing the prison's

far edge. But while both his sister and Vann Jeger were clearly looking at something, Julius had no idea what. So far as he could tell,
that side of the circle was filled with the same ghostly, shuffling dust
figures as everywhere else. A second later, though, he realized that
wasn't quite right. One figure in the crowd, a shadow of a soldier
in the tattered armor of the Roman Legion, was standing still, and
his eyes—two angry slits that glowed like blue fireflies in the empty
dark of his helmet—were looking straight at Vann Jeger.

Had Julius been in Vann Jeger's shoes, this was the point where
he would have started running. But being functionally unkillable
must have been a crazy confidence booster, because the spirit just
looked pissed. "I'm in no mood for games," he growled, swinging
his ax through the swirling ghostly figures. "What are these shades?
Answer truthfully, or die."

For some reason, the soldier seemed to find this hilarious. *Die?*
he cackled, his voice growing stronger. *But they already have. They are
the forgotten dead, memories lost to all but me.*

"And who are you?" Vann Jeger demanded.

The soldier raised his head, and when he spoke again, the
words were no longer in Julius's head, but actual sound—a man's
deep voice, warped by the blowing wind into something much more
terrifying. "I am the Empty Wind, Spirit of the Forgotten Dead, and
I have come for what is mine."

By the time he finished, Julius was petrified. He'd never heard
of a spirit of the forgotten dead, but it didn't sound friendly. The
only positive thing he could say about their situation was that at
least none of the terrifying, ghostly dust figures were looking at him
or Chelsie. Their attention was fixated on Vann Jeger, who looked
pretty terrifying in his own right.

"Spirit of the Forgotten Dead?" he roared, his blue face turning
navy with anger. "*Impossible!* You are an illusion, a trick!"

The soldier tilted his head. "Does this feel like a trick?"

The wind picked up as he spoke, nearly blowing Julius over.
Even Vann Jeger was starting to look spooked as ice crystals began
forming in his kelp beard, but that didn't keep him from yelling.

"There are no more Mortal Spirits!" He swung his ax through the dust figures, who didn't seem to care. "This is Algonquin's land, the domain of millions of years of water! We have no place for fears made flesh."

"You speak as if you have power," the Empty Wind said calmly. "But you're nothing but a misplaced drop of water riding on stolen magic and hiding in Algonquin's shadow. Even the Lady of the Lakes is nothing but a pond who's overflowed her bounds." He held out a ghostly hand, pointing down at the ground. "This land is more my domain than it ever was hers. All that you call the DFZ was built on the forgotten, the unknown thousands who drowned beneath Algonquin's wave and now lie lost without even a monument to their name."

The wind rose higher as he spoke, bringing more figures out of the dirt. But while the ghosts were still little more than faceless shapes in the swirling dust, Julius could feel their anger like a weight as they pressed in around Vann Jeger.

"They called to me," the Empty Wind continued, his deep voice shaking with fury. "Their pleas woke me from my slumber, and I will give them satisfaction." He stepped forward, his eerie blue eyes glowing brighter than ever. "They *will* be remembered, Spirit of the Geirangerfjord! And you who put on airs and claim power not your own, you will be forgotten."

The moment he finished, the ghosts charged in, plunging their transparent hands into Vann Jeger's body. The spirit roared in reply, swinging his ax in great, sweeping circles as water surged up from the ground to fill the arena. By the time Julius realized what was going on, the icy saltwater was already up to his chest. But though the dust that gave the ghosts their shape was now crushed under several feet of water, it was too little, too late. The dead were already here, and even without the dirt that had defined their edges, they kept swarming, plunging their glowing hands into Vann Jeger, and when they pulled them out again, his weapons were clutched in their transparent fingers.

"*No!*" Vann Jeger roared, grabbing at the ghosts, but his hands passed right through them. When it was clear he couldn't stop them, the spirit turned to the only figure that *was* solid. "You shall not have them!" he thundered, lobbing his massive ax straight at the soldier's head. "They are *my* offerings! My treasures!"

The Empty Wind caught the tossed ax with one hand, and Julius gasped, waiting for the weapon to turn to water vapor like all the others. But this time was different. This time, the ax stayed, its blade cracking where the Empty Wind's gloved hand pressed down.

"Nothing is yours," the soldier said, dropping the broken ax into the pile of ancient weapons the ghosts were building at his feet. "These are human weapons forged for human hands. You are merely the low they sank to when the funeral boats stopped burning. But human treasures do not belong to the land. Those warriors whose names are dust and whose songs are long forgotten, *they* remember what was once theirs, and I will not rest until I have seen them reclaim what you have stolen."

With every word the Empty Wind spoke, more ghosts appeared. Ancient ones this time, men and women in furs and armor who ran through the rapidly rising water without leaving a ripple to plunge their hands into Vann Jeger. Each one yanked out a single weapon and vanished, but there was always another to take their place. And as the ghosts came and came and came, Vann Jeger began to look truly afraid.

"*NO!*" he screamed, his voice breaking like the waves around him as he whipped the water into a storm. "*I'll drown you all before you take what is mine!*"

There was more, countless curses and threats, but nothing Vann Jeger said or did could touch the dead. They just kept coming, passing effortlessly through the surging water to plunge their hands into the fjord spirit one after another, taking their weapons back under the Empty Wind's glowing gaze. But while Julius could have happily watched Vann Jeger get cut down to size forever, they had bigger problems.

RACHEL AARON

The waves Vann Jeger had summoned in his effort to crush the swarming ghosts were now tall enough to wash over Julius's head. The water was still rising, too, the new waves picking up momentum from rushing currents that formed the prison's walls until the whole circle resembled a giant whirlpool. Already exhausted, Julius didn't even try to fight the current. He was just focusing on keeping his head above water when Chelsie swam to his side.

"We have to get out of here," she yelled over the waves. "This place is filling up."

"Get out how?" he yelled back, jerking his head at the swirling wall of water. "We're still trapped in here!" He swam closer to her, grabbing her shoulders to keep them together in the maelstrom. "Let's just hold on a moment. I think Marci's plan is working!"

Chelsie shoved her sopping black hair out of her face. "Why in the world would you think that?"

He pointed down at the glimmering ghosts under the surface. "Because that's her spirit."

Chelsie's eyes went so wide Julius could see the green of her iris all the way around, but he didn't have time to explain. He still wasn't sure of the details himself, but as he'd been fighting to keep his head above water, he'd finally remembered where he'd heard the Empty Wind's voice before.

"Boost me up," he said, climbing onto his sister's shoulders. "I need to check something."

Chelsie grabbed his legs so hard they nearly snapped. "Check *what?*"

It was simpler to show her than answer, so Julius just stood up, trusting his sister to keep them above the waves as he scanned the surging water for the one human who wasn't transparent.

"There!" he shouted. "Look!"

Vann Jeger's walls must not have been as good at keeping things out as they were at keeping them in, because Marci was now swimming toward them across the current. After all his running earlier, Julius was too tired to meet her half-way, but he put his arms out

338

when she got near, yanking her into the relative safety of the lee he and Chelsie had created. "What's happening?"

"No time to explain," she yelled back. "Just stick to the plan!"

"*Plan?*" Julius thrust his hand into the water where hordes of ghosts were swarming over Vann Jeger like ants. "Summoning armies of the undead was *not* the plan! We need to get out of here!"

"Do you want to save Justin or not?" she said, pulling a marker out her hair, where she'd stuck it to keep it dry. "You have to trust me on this. I just need a little more time and a dry surface to write on."

"Good luck finding that," Chelsie said. "I'm with Julius. We should go."

"No!" Marci cried, her voice pleading. "We're about to win this whole thing. Look."

She pointed down through the icy water, and both dragons turned to see a very different scene than the one they'd witnessed barely a minute ago.

Beneath the surging whirlpool, the once unconquerable Vann Jeger was on his knees. His massive body, now half its former size, was ringed with more ghostly figures than ever. Likewise, the pile of reclaimed treasures at the Empty Wind's feet was now higher than the waves, and with every weapon Vann Jeger lost, the swirling water got lower.

"See?" Marci said as she turned and started swimming for the emerging island of weapons. "What did I tell you? We've got this in the bag."

"You're right," Julius said, though he wasn't sure how he felt about that. The horror movie scene below was very different from the victory he'd envisioned. But victory was victory, he supposed, and if Marci said she had things under control, then he believed her. It was certainly better than the alternative.

"What can we do to help?" he asked, swimming after her.

"I need your disguise," she said, hauling herself up onto the shifting pile of swords, axes, and other things the ghosts had pulled out of Vann Jeger. "You're not using it anymore, and I'm going to need all the power I can get."

"Gladly," he said, climbing up beside her. "But why? Vann Jeger's almost done for."

"It's not Vann Jeger I'm worried about," Marci said grimly as she dropped to her knees, digging through the pile of priceless magical artifacts until she found a large leather Viking shield that her casting marker would write on. "I'd pull magic out of these, but I still haven't figured out how to get magic out of enchanted weapons, and I don't think it would be a popular move right now."

Julius didn't need her pointed glance at the ghosts to understand that last part. Even if the ghosts had no intention of using them again, sucking magic out of the weapons they'd just reclaimed from Vann Jeger would most definitely *not* go over well. "Here," he said, offering her his hand. "All yours."

She grabbed his fingers tight, and Julius sighed in relief as the heavy coating of magic Amelia had painted over him drained away. But while he was feeling immeasurably better, Marci looked grimmer than ever.

"It's not enough," she said, scowling down at the spellwork she was writing on the shield. "I need more."

He shoved his hand at her again. "Then take more."

"No way!" she cried, smacking it away. "I just pulled off you this morning."

"I'm not giving up when we're this close," Julius said, sticking his hand out again. "Just—"

He cut off with a yelp as Chelsie grabbed his wrist. "You've given too much already," she growled as she forced his arm back. "You don't even have that much to give." She turned to Marci, putting out her own hand where Julius's had been. "Use me."

Marci looked uncomfortable. "Uh, are you sure? Not that I'm complaining, but—"

Chelsie cut her off with a stern look. "I don't know what dark pact you struck with whatever-it-is down there to pull this off, but you've made more progress against Vann Jeger in the last five

340

minutes than we've made all night. That's proof enough for me." She grabbed Marci's hand. "Just do it."

Marci shot Julius a terrified look, but he just shrugged. If Chelsie wanted to help, who was he to stop her?

"Okay," she said, turning to face his sister. "This might feel a little strange."

Having been Marci's battery before, Julius could feel the moment she started pulling. Chelsie, being Chelsie, didn't even wince. She knelt there still as a statue as the mage took and took and took. By the time Marci finally let go, she was glowing even brighter than the time she'd nearly sucked Julius dry, and her expression was one of wonder.

"Wow," she whispered, eyes round. "That was *amazing*. And here I thought Julius was high grade, but *that*—"

"Is it enough?" Chelsie interrupted, her face pale and strained.

Marci jumped and looked down again, reprimanded back into seriousness. "It'll have to be," she said, writing the final lines of spellwork onto the shield. "We're almost out of water."

She was right. In the time it had taken her to drain Chelsie, the water—both the rising tide and the walls that had penned them in—had drained away almost completely, and so had Vann Jeger. The once giant spirit was now little taller than Julius. He collapsed as they watched, falling to his knees as the last of the ghosts finally retreated, leaving only the Empty Wind.

Blue eyes gleaming, the ghostly soldier stepped forward to face his defeated foe. He bent down as he walked, picking up the ax he'd caught earlier out of the pile. He was raising the cracked blade to take Vann Jeger's head when Marci ordered, "Stop."

The word was full of magic, and the Empty Wind froze.

"I told you to bring him to his knees," Marci said, clutching the round shield she'd covered with her spellwork. "He's there. Mission accomplished."

The Empty Wind looked over his shoulder, and Julius flinched as the glowing blue eyes floating in the empty helmet slid over them. "He has stolen from us," the spirit growled. "He must pay."

"And he will," Marci said, standing up. "But I think being at the mercy of dragons is the worst punishment Vann Jeger could receive."

The soldier's glowing eyes narrowed. "Then you do not know mine."

"And I'm not going to," she said stubbornly, holding out her hand. "Your part in this is done, Ghost. You're still my spirit, and I say it's time to come home."

Julius cringed down into the wet weapons. He'd guessed the truth already, but hearing Marci say the spirit's name somehow made it all real. But though she'd clearly given her order, the Empty Wind just tilted his head.

"And what if I say you're my human?"

Marci's scowl turned dangerous, but the Empty Wind didn't seem to care. "Do you know how many dead this city has forgotten?" he asked, looking across the once again open field toward the glowing wall of the skyways on the horizon. "They call to me, begging for justice. What would you have me tell them? That my *master* was too busy working for dragons to hear their voices? That she would rather stay a servant than embrace what we could become?"

He turned back to Marci and held out his gloved hand, which was no longer transparent, but real as Julius's. "We are bonded, you and I," he said. "I am more like you than those cold blooded snakes could ever be. Leave them to their fate and come with me, and we shall do great things together."

Fear began to curl in Julius's stomach, but when he saw Marci's stubborn expression, he didn't know why he worried. "We *will* do great things," she said, lifting her chin haughtily. "But you above all others should know by now that I am *no one's* servant."

She reached down as she finished, slamming her hand against the spellwork she'd scribbled along the circular shield's edge, and the magic crashed down on them like a hammer. It shut down the freezing wind, dispersing the last of the ghosts and knocking what was left of Vann Jeger into the dirt. Even the Empty Wind, who'd been pretty much untouchable this entire time, stumbled under its weight, and when he got his head up again, his blue eyes were blazing with anger. "What are you doing?"

"What I did before," Marci said, her voice humming with power. "I'm binding you." She turned the shield to show him the markings she'd drawn on its surface. "Did you know that spellwork written anywhere inside a larger circle applies to the whole? Once you said your name, it was a simple trick to change the ritual's target from Vann Jeger to you."

The Empty Wind's blue eyes went wide in the empty dark of his helmet. "*Why?*"

"Because I was warned it would come to this," she said sadly. "I knew that you would try to take control the moment you had the upper hand. For the record, I don't fault you for that. You've got your dreams just like I've got mine. But just because I understand doesn't mean I'm going to let you do it."

Julius couldn't believe she was just *telling* him that. But though he fully expected the Empty Wind to go ballistic over Marci's confession, the spirit did nothing of the sort. Just the opposite, he actually sounded impressed. "You planned this from the beginning, didn't you?"

"Of course." Marci said, lifting her head high. "Who do you think I am? A good mage always has a backup, and speaking of." She flexed her fingers, and the magic pushing down on the field doubled, sending the Empty Wind to his knees.

"Now that I've got your attention," she said. "Here are my terms." She tapped the shield in her hands. "I haven't completed my spellwork yet, but I've got enough grade-A dragon magic here to do pretty much whatever I want. With one line, I can finish the spell that will rebind you as my servant. With another, I can banish you so hard you won't reform for another sixty years. Your choice."

"You would banish me?" Ghost cried, incredulous. "Give up all this power?"

"Power someone else gives you isn't power at all," Marci replied stubbornly. "And you should know I'm not bluffing."

"I never doubted it," the spirit said, scowling. "But what would you gain by binding me again? We're already linked as deeply as can be."

"We are," Marci agreed. "But this is for me, not you. I had no idea what I was doing the first time I bound you. This time, I know exactly what's at stake, and I've made a lot of improvements." She pointed at the spellwork on the shield. "You'd still be my spirit and subject to my orders, but you'll keep your name and free will, and I've also added in a clause that binds *me* to help you with your work as much as I can, no more questions asked."

Julius had no idea what that meant, but the Empty Wind looked extremely touched. "You'll help?"

"Of *course* I'll help," Marci said, exasperated. "Just because I'm taking precautions so I don't end up your slave doesn't mean I don't respect your mission. Your work is important—even the dead need a champion—but I am *not* going to be your pet mage. I've done my best to be fair to both of us here. If that's agreeable to you, then stop wasting time and come back, but if you want to keep being a menace, I won't hesitate to do what I have to do."

The spirit stared at Marci for a long time after that. Then, at last, he lowered his head. "I knew it," he said as the last of the icy wind died down. "Even when I knew nothing, I *knew* I chose right in you."

Marci grinned. "So you'll take the binding?"

The Empty Wind nodded. "There is no shame in being bound to a worthy master, and Mortal Spirits, like mortals themselves, were never meant to be alone."

"Then come home," she said, adding one final stroke to the spellwork on the shield before holding out her hand. The circle on the shield in her hand flared at the same time, and the enormous weight of magic vanished, melting away like snow in the sun. When it was gone, the soldier with the glowing eyes was gone, too, and Ghost was sitting in the crook of Marci's arm, his fluffy white body curled contentedly against her chest.

"Really?" she said, arching an eyebrow. "All that and you couldn't even keep the badass haunted Roman Legion look?"

The cat gave her a nonchalant look, opening his mouth in a silent meow that made Marci roll her eyes.

"What did he say?" Julius asked.

Marci tossed the spellwork-covered shield back on the pile. "He claims it's less work to be a cat. He's also complaining that he's tired. Oh, and we're not to touch any of the weapons."

"Pity," Chelsie said, her voice strained. "They'd make fine trophies."

Julius glanced at his sister, suddenly worried. He'd never heard her sound so exhausted, but there was no weakness in Chelsie's movements as she hopped to the ground. "Julius?"

He slid down the massive pile of weaponry to stand beside her. "Yes?"

She turned to Vann Jeger. "It's time to finish what you started."

Julius's stomach sank. Even now that Marci's magic was gone, Vann Jeger was still doubled over, his head pressed down into the once again dry field. It was a truly pathetic sight, and it filled Julius with unexpected hesitation, especially since he'd been daydreaming about burning Vann Jeger to a crisp not ten minutes ago. But his sudden attack of sympathy dried up as fast as it had started when the hunter lifted his head to shoot them a look of pure hate.

"Get on with it," he whispered, his breaking ice voice now little more than a crack. "Send me home, it makes no difference. I will always rise again, and when I do, I will hunt you all to the ends of the Earth for what you've done tonight."

"What *we've* done?" Julius cried, stomping over. "*We* were minding our own business. This whole thing was your fault!"

"You know nothing," Vann Jeger growled, his black eyes moving to Marci, who was still making her way down the weapon pile. "Your human brought death himself back into this world. Do you have any idea how many will suffer because of this? But you snakes don't care about preserving. You only know how to destroy. But the last laugh shall be ours." His pinched face split into a grin. "The Lady has already repaired the damage from your idiot brother's rampage. The Reclamation Project marches on. With or without me, it's just a matter of time."

Chelsie's expression darkened. Julius didn't like the sound of this "Reclamation Project" either, but he knew better than to ask. The only reason a beaten enemy dropped hints like that was when he was laying bait. For all they knew, Algonquin was already on her way.

"Enough," Julius growled, crouching down in front of the defeated spirit. "Where's my brother? You said he was alive?"

"Very," Vann Jeger said with a toxic grin. "It barely took a scratch before he sold you out."

Julius opened his mouth, but Chelsie beat him to it. "Impossible. Justin's a thick-headed idiot, but he'd die before he betrayed the clan."

"Think that all you like," the spirit said. "But my Lady set up the deal herself. Your whelp of a brother sold you out to the Northern Star for a sword and a chance at revenge. Not that it's surprising. Your kind *was* born to betray."

"Shut *up*," Chelsie growled, reaching down to dig her nails into the spirit's neck until he gasped in pain. "How is Estella involved in this?"

"How should I know?" Vann Jeger choked out. "You snakes are the ones who're always meddling with the future. Algonquin merely played you against each other, and your brother was more than happy to play along."

Chelsie let his neck go with a muttered curse, sliding down to press her palm against his chest. A moment later, Julius felt the bite of her magic, and Vann Jeger went stiff with a cry, his head jerking back in pain as Chelsie's stolen Fang ripped its way out of his chest and returned to her hand.

She clutched her blade with a smile, shaking off the black blood as Vann Jeger fell gasping to the ground. When she'd cleaned the blade to her satisfaction, Chelsie turned to position it over the prone spirit.

"What are you doing?" Julius asked as she took aim.

"Finishing this," Chelsie said, swinging down.

"Wait!" he cried, but it was too late. Chelsie's Fang was already slicing through Vann Jeger's neck. Still weakened from having his final stolen sword ripped out, the spirit didn't even try to dodge. He just lay there, grinning at them as his head rolled off his shrunken body, and then the corpse collapsed back into water.

"*Why did you do that?*" Julius cried, staring in horror as the puddle that had once been Algonquin's greatest dragon hunter seeped back into the ground. "What happened to ransoming him to Algonquin for Justin?"

"You heard what he said," Chelsie said, cleaning her Fang once more before returning it to its sheath. "Estella's involved."

Julius couldn't believe this. "And you took him at his word?"

She nodded. "On that, yes."

"What about Justin?"

Chelsie's eyes narrowed. "The situation's changed. I don't want to believe Justin would sell us out, but seer plots are never straight-forward, and we're neck deep in one designed to bring us all down. If Algonquin's working with Estella, then keeping Vann Jeger alive only complicates matters. Better to remove him from the situation entirely than risk having him come back and bite us later."

"And what if she's *not* working with Estella?" Julius said. "I've never heard of Algonquin working with a dragon."

"Then we've just proven we're a force to be reckoned with and given the Lady of the Lakes even more reason to keep him alive for bargaining," Chelsie said, glaring at him. "Use your head, Julius. What makes more sense? That Vann Jeger would lie for Estella, or that he'd try and rub it in our faces? Considering every disaster over the last two days has led straight back to the Northern Star *and* the fact that she's been specifically targeting high-ranking Heartstrikers, we'd be stupid not to suspect her now."

He shook his head. "But—"

"The last thing we need on top of a seer is a vengeful, dragon-hunting spirit with a chip on his shoulder coming back to screw things up," his sister snapped. "Especially if Algonquin really did give Justin to Estella and thus *can't* trade him back to us."

Julius didn't want to believe it, but his sister's argument made a cynical sort of sense. "So this was all for nothing, then?"

Chelsie scoffed. "You call saving your human and bringing about the death of one of our greatest enemies nothing?" She nudged the mud where Vann Jeger had dissolved with her boot. "This was a great victory, and since your human was the one who actually took him down, I won't even be lying when I tell Mother you were at the heart of it. It doesn't matter what you said before, Bethesda would never kill the dragon who slew Algonquin's dragon slayer. She'll have no choice but to welcome you back to the clan, which means *I* won't have to come home with your head." She shrugged. "It might not be what we planned, but I'm prepared to call that a win."

It didn't feel like a win to Julius. "And what if I don't want to go back?"

Chelsie's head whipped around. "What?"

Julius pulled himself straight. "It's not that I don't appreciate your efforts to save me, but I meant what I said on the phone. I *don't* want to be a part of a family that makes you sell out your sister to save your brother, and I *don't* want to get back into mother's favor. I don't want any part of this."

"Too bad," Chelsie growled. "You *are* part of it. There is no out, Julius. You were born a Heartstriker, and you'll die a Heartstriker. There's no escaping that, but you've got a second chance right now to make something for yourself in this clan. Don't waste it."

He shook his head. "But I don't want—"

"Then act like a real dragon and change the situation!" she yelled. "Do whatever you have to do. Take over the clan and rebuild it from scratch if that's what it takes. Just find *some way* you can live with being a Heartstriker, because so long as Bethesda rules this family, the only way out is at the tip of this sword." She reached down to clutch the Fang at her side. "Don't make me kill you just when I've started to like you."

Julius's shoulders slumped. The last thing he wanted to do was fight the sister who'd just saved his life, but now that he'd finally stood up to his mother and told her how he felt, just going back to the clan, even as a hero, felt more like failure than lying down and dying to Vann Jeger. It must have shown on his face, too, because Chelsie sighed.

"Don't think about it now," she said, reaching out to rest her hand awkwardly on his shoulder for a moment before snatching it back. "Just focus on getting yourself and your human back to your house. You need to go check on Amelia, anyway."

"What about you?" Julius said. "Why don't you come with us? You could cut us all there right now."

His sister rolled her eyes. "First, I'm not a taxi, and second, you're an idiot if you think Algonquin doesn't know what just happened and isn't arranging a counter attack as we speak. You're still sealed, which should put you beneath her notice, but I've been standing out here being an obvious dragon for almost an hour now. When they come, I'll be the natural target, so I'm going to try and lead them as far away as possible while you are going to go home and keep your promise to guard our sister. Is that understood?"

Julius didn't like the idea of Chelsie using herself as bait, but if there was anyone who was a master at keeping ahead of the hammer, it was Bethesda's Shade. "Understood," he said. "Just be careful."

For a second, he thought he saw her smile at that. It must have been his imagination, though, because Chelsie's face was as grim as ever when she drew her sword. "You, too."

By the time the words were out, she was gone, vanishing into the dark like the shadow she was named for.

CHAPTER SEVENTEEN

Chelsie reappeared seconds later less than a block away, collapsing against the trunk of a tree growing out of what was left of a convenience store as she fought to catch her breath.

It was her own fault. She hadn't realized Julius's mage could take so much. Just cutting her way this far had taken what little reserve she had left. It probably would have been wiser to just stay with Julius, but being weak in front of her baby brother was more shame than Chelsie could stand, and she hadn't been lying to him about Algonquin's counterattack. She was actually surprised the anti-dragon SWAT teams weren't here already. Apparently, today was their lucky day. But no luck held out forever, which meant it was time to get moving.

Gritting her teeth, Chelsie shoved herself upright and pulled out her phone, dialing up the car she kept in long-term storage for just such an emergency. It would have been safer to just cut back home and report, but she was supposed to be laying a false trail, and it wasn't like she had enough power to get back to Heartstriker Mountain anyway. At this point, just standing unassisted was a challenge, so getaway vehicle it was. But as she was sending her GPS coordinates to the car's autodrive for the pickup, a breeze brushed the back of her neck.

It was a tiny thing, just the briefest sensation of cool air wafting over her flushed skin, but Chelsie hadn't survived as long as she had by ignoring the little signs. She dropped her phone and drew her sword in a single motion, spinning around with her blade up just in time to see the dragon step out of the shadows behind her.

"Gotcha," Estella whispered, her arm shooting out to throw something long, black, and snaking around Chelsie's neck.

She jerked back with a gasp, dropping her sword as she reached up to rip away whatever it was the seer had thrown at her throat, but there was nothing. No weapon, no talisman, nothing but her own skin and horrible feeling of a noose tightening, cutting off her air.

"You should be proud," Estella said as Chelsie fell choking to her knees. "Of all Bethesda's spawn, you were by far the hardest to corner."

Chelsie ignored her, fumbling across the ground for her dropped sword only to have it knocked from her fingers when the seer kicked it away.

"I might not have been able to pull it off at all had you not shown me your weakness last month," Estella continued, crouching down beside her. "I can't tell you how hard I laughed when I discovered that the Heartstriker Enforcer has a weakness for whelps, but I must say it worked like a charm. All I had to do was drop a hint to Algonquin's hunter so he'd put pressure on the babies, and *pop*." She snapped her fingers. "You appear like a rabbit out of a hat."

She smiled as she finished, but all Chelsie saw was red. "It was you," she whispered. "Vann Jeger, the trap, it was all *you*."

"Oh, child," Estella said, her eyes gleaming like ice in the dark. "Haven't you learned by now? It's *always* me. Now go to sleep. We have much to do."

The suffocating feeling grew heavier with every word Estella spoke, but Chelsie would have none of it. She would *not* go down like this. Not with so much left unfinished. Not to Estella. She had to escape. Had to get away.

The thought had barely cleared her mind when fire washed over her body, igniting the grass at her feet as her human disguise burned away. At this point, changing wasn't even a conscious decision. It was instinct, the overwhelming need to run taking physical shape. But as she spread her still-forming wings to take off, Estella's noose cinched tighter.

Maybe if she hadn't been so weakened to start with she could have made it, or maybe she'd been doomed from the beginning. Either way, Chelsie barely made it ten feet into the air before she came crashing right back down, collapsing into the still smoldering grass at Estella's feet. The last thing she saw with her darkening vision was the seer's smug face hovering over her as sirens began to wail in the distance.

• • •

"Marci," Julius said, nervously looking over his shoulder in the direction of the approaching sirens. "Time to go."

"Just a sec," she called from her crouch on top of the mountain of priceless, ancient, magical weapons that now stood like a monument in the middle of the field where they'd defeated Vann Jeger. "I'm almost done."

Julius sighed. If he had a dollar for every time she'd said that… "I thought we were supposed to leave the weapons alone?"

"The ones that don't belong to us, yes," she said, grunting as she moved a battle ax that was almost as tall as she was. "But Ghost says Tyrfing's in here. Vann Jeger must have taken it when Justin lost."

"Not that I don't appreciate the effort, but I can get another sword, and the cops will be here any second."

"But I've almost—ah ha!" She yanked her arm up, tugging a short, familiar, mirror-bright blade out of the pile. "Ta da!"

Happy as he was to see his sword again, Julius was far more relieved that she was finished. "Thank you," he said quickly, running over to take it from her. "Now can we *please*—"

A flash of light cut him off. Somewhere on his left, something was flaring emerald green in the night. By the time Julius whipped his head around, though, it was gone. He was wondering if he'd imagined it when Marci yelled, "What was *that?*"

Julius wasn't sure. It'd *looked* like dragon fire, but there was only one dragon currently in the DFZ who could produce green fire, and she certainly wouldn't do so now. But even as he told himself it was probably just a really desperate hobo throwing weird stuff into his campfire, the wind shifted, bringing him the scent of ash and blood. *Very* familiar blood.

"Come on," he said, stomach clenching as he ran back to the truck. "Let's go look."

Marci ran after him. "But didn't you just say we had to get out of here?"

He nodded, tossing his recovered sword into the back of the truck cab before jumping in himself. "We're just going to take a look," he assured her as she got in. *And make sure I'm wrong,* he added to himself.

Any hope of that vanished as soon as they started driving. Even with the windows up, the smell of dragon smoke rapidly became overpowering as they drove less than a block to the place where they'd seen the light. Julius tried to hold on to a silver of optimism by telling himself that the smoke was probably just left over from the dragon's escape, but even that hope went out the window when they rolled to a stop in front of a ruined convenience store that had been completely taken over by a tree.

"Holy—" Marci cried, leaning out the open window. "What is *that?*"

Julius swallowed against the knot in his throat as he stared wide eyed at the dragon curled in a ball at the base of the tree. "That's my sister."

Until this moment, Julius had never actually seen Chelsie in her true shape. Even when she'd snatched Justin out of the sky in front of him last month, he hadn't caught more than a glimpse of a long, snaking shadow in the dark. He'd always just assumed she had some kind of magic that let her be so sneaky, like a camouflage spell or something. Now, though, he saw that the truth was much, much simpler. He'd never seen Chelsie flying because the feathered serpent lying on the grass was black. Not shiny black, either, but matte black, the kind of color even dragon eyes passed right over.

"Are you *sure* that's your sister?" Marci whispered, pulling herself back inside the window. "I thought you guys were, you know, tropical colored?"

"We are," Julius whispered back. "I think she dyes them, but that's *definitely* Chelsie." No other dragon in the world had that scent.

Marci grimaced. "What happened to her? Wasn't she supposed to be leading the cops away?"

Julius had no idea, but with the sirens getting closer by the second, he knew what they had to do. "Come on," he said, throwing open his door.

Marci scrambled out after him, and together they crept across what was left of the overgrown parking lot toward the sleeping dragon. The closer they got, the more worried Julius became. Given who they were approaching, he'd expected to be knocked on his back with a claw in his throat by now, but his sister hadn't even cracked her eyes.

"Chelsie!" he called softly, reaching down to brush his fingers over her black feathers. "It's me. Wake up."

The dragon didn't move. Worse, she didn't even twitch, which made Julius's blood run cold. Dragons were paranoid creatures by nature, but Chelsie was in a class by herself. If she wasn't even demonstrating an involuntary threat response to another dragon touching her, something was seriously, seriously wrong. "Is she under a spell?"

"Nothing I can see," Marci said, staring at the sleeping dragon in wonder. "You guys are seriously pretty in this form, though."

Julius wasn't sure if she meant magically or literally. Knowing Marci, probably both. Then again, weird as it felt to admit about his own sister, there was no denying that Chelsie—with her lithe snaking body, delicate eye-ridges, and elegantly tapered feathers—was a ridiculously beautiful dragoness. She was also a soon-to-be dead one if they didn't get a move on.

"Chelsie!" he yelled, louder this time. "*Chelsie!*" Again, no response, and Julius stepped back with a curse, peering around the bushes at the flashing lights he could now see in the distance. "We have to get her out of here."

"How?" Marci said, standing up from where she'd been cautiously petting Chelsie's long feathers. "Look at her. Even curled into a ball, she's the size of a tractor trailer. It's not like we can just roll her into the back of the truck." She bit her lip. "Isn't there someone you can call for help with stuff like this? Like a Heartstriker hotline or something?"

"She *is* the Heartstriker hotline," Julius said, pulling out his phone, though to call whom, he had no idea. Amelia was down, Bob was who knew where, and he didn't trust any of his other siblings not to seize the opportunity to take Chelsie out while she was defenseless. He supposed he could call Bethesda, but given how she'd treated Amelia, Julius didn't know if that was a good idea or not. Also, he *really* didn't want to call his Mother for help after their last conversation.

He had to do something, though. Already, the first wave of police cars were pulling into the field where they'd killed Vann Jeger. No one was looking their way yet, but it was only a matter of time before they started searching the area. He was about to say screw it and call Bethesda anyway when his ears caught the soft but unmistakable sound of a phone vibrating.

Since his phone was currently in his hand, Julius knew it wasn't him, and Marci didn't even have a phone right now. But while his ears had never been half as good as his nose, they were still sharper than a human's. Sure enough, after with a little hunting, he found Chelsie's vibrating phone lying under a half-burned clump of grass next to her left forefoot with the words UNKNOWN CALLER shining bright on the screen.

The answering wave of relief almost made Julius drop the phone. He caught it at once, accepting the call and jamming the speaker to his ear. "*Bob!*"

"What happened?"

It was on the tip of Julius's tongue to say Bob was the one who should know, but he couldn't say a word. He'd heard Bob sound uncharacteristically serious several times over the last two days. Now, though, the seer sounded *terrifying*. Julius had never heard anything like the quiet, killing rage in his brother's question, and he decided then and there to stick purely to the facts.

"I don't know," he said honestly. "We just found Chelsie unconscious." Images of Amelia's bloody body flashed through his head, and he clutched the phone tighter. "Do you think Estella got her?"

"Given that her future just vanished, I'd say that's a safe assumption," Bob growled. "How badly is she hurt?"

"She isn't, actually," Julius said, looking his sister over. "Or at least no more than she was after our fight with Vann Jeger. But she's in dragon form and unconscious, and Algonquin's task force is almost here."

There was a moment of silence, and then Bob said. "Oh."

"*Oh?*" Julius cried. "That's it?"

"Of course not," his brother said, sounding much more like himself. "I'm just relieved. That's not half as bad as I expected."

Julius didn't want to know what Bob had expected if their current situation was a relief. "Well, she's too big to move and she's not responding to anything we say. If Algonquin's security goons catch her like this, they'll kill her before she can open her eyes."

"Calm down," Bob said. "Believe it or not, this actually is one of the better outcomes. Now listen carefully, because I'm going to tell you a fool-proof way of waking Chelsie up. Normally, I'd make you swear never to tell a soul before divulging this information, but your future's one of the few remaining that hasn't been scrambled into chaos yet, so I already know you'll keep your lips zipped."

"Of course," Julius said, glancing over his shoulder at Marci, who was making frantic *hurry up* gestures. "What do I do?"

"It's easy," Bob assured him. "Just stand back and shout, 'I know what happened in China.'"

"That doesn't even make sense," Julius snapped. "This is *serious*, Bob!"

"When it comes to Chelsie, China is as serious as it gets," the seer replied. "Trust me, it works every time."

"Every time?" Julius repeated skeptically. "How many times have you done this?"

"Well, not me *personally*," Bob said. "I'm not suicidal enough to mention China around Chelsie myself. I was referring to all the times I've seen it work in the future, which, counting you, is one. Coincidentally, you'll probably want to get behind something fireproof."

That wasn't a comforting thought. "So what happened in China?"

"You'll have to direct that question to Chelsie," Bob said. "Right after you pick out your funeral clothes. Now are you going to do this or not? I thought you were in a hurry."

Julius was, and he didn't have any more time to waste with Bob's Bob-ness. "I'll give it a try."

"Let me know how it goes," Bob said. "I have to hang up. I'm just leaving the airport now. I'll call you again when you get home."

There was a lot to unpack in that sentence, like which airport? And how would he know when they got home? But Julius had been around seers long enough now not to sweat the details, and he didn't bother asking questions. He just hung up, shoving Chelsie's phone into his pocket as he took cover behind the truck, motioning for Marci to do the same.

"What are we doing?" she whispered, crouching drown beside him.

"Your guess is as good as mine," he whispered back, glancing over the hood at his sister as he took a deep breath. Here went nothing.

"*I know what happened in China!*"

He yelled it as loud as he dared and then ducked down, covering his head and Marci's, but there was no giant fireball. Nothing happened at all, actually.

"Um," Marci said. "Was that it?"

"It was supposed to be," Julius said, alternating between angry with his brother for leading him wrong and terrified at the implications. If Bob no longer knew what was happening, they were beyond screwed. "Maybe I should try again?"

"I don't think that'll be necessary," Marci said, peeking up over the truck's hood. "Look."

Julius raised his head, and his breath caught. The black dragon still hadn't moved, but she was no longer asleep. Narrow green eyes were glowing like embers in the shadows of her black feathers. That was all he was able to make out before the dragon attacked.

Later, Julius was never actually able to accurately describe what happened next. One second he was crouching behind the truck, the next he was on his back in the grass with a giant dragon coiled on top of him, her flames lighting up the back of her throat as she demanded, *"What do you know?"*

"Nothing!" Julius said frantically. "I swear, I don't know anything! I was just repeating what Bob told me to say to wake you up!"

The dragon blinked her green eyes in confusion, looking around the overgrown convenience store parking lot like she was only just now realizing where she was, or whom she was pinning to the ground. "Julius?"

"Yes," he said, panting in relief. "It's me, and you need to change back right now. Algonquin's people are barely a block away."

The first cars that had pulled into the field where they'd fought Vann Jeger had now been joined by several more, plus a SWAT truck. Fortunately, the officers were all too busy gawking at the mountain of ancient weaponry to notice the giant black dragon crouched in a parking lot just down the street. That luck wouldn't last for long, though. Already, Julius could hear the *wump wump* of helicopter blades, and he turned back to his sister with his hands clasped together. "Please," he begged. "*Please*, Chelsie, change back."

The dragon stared at him a moment longer, her eyes glowing like green lanterns, and then, fast as she'd attacked, she collapsed, her enormous body crumpling until there was nothing to see but black feathers. Seconds later, even those were gone, leaving only Chelsie standing in front of them, human and—other than the empty sheath on her hip—completely naked.

Julius dropped his eyes at once, cheeks flaming. "Here," he said, pulling off his still damp t-shirt and handing it to her.

Chelsie didn't seem to care one way or the other about her nudity, but she accepted the clothing without comment. "Never mention this again," she said stiffly as she pulled the shirt over her head. "Either of you. Is that understood?"

"Yes," Julius said, elbowing Marci until she nodded too. "Now can we go?"

Rather than answer, Chelsie leaned down and scooped her Fang off the ground, sheathing the sword in a smooth motion before climbing into the truck. Julius closed the door behind her, cursing under his breath when he saw more security vehicles coming toward them down the road. "Marci?"

"Already on it," she said, jumping into the driver's side and reaching up to tap the circle of spellwork she'd written on the underside of the truck's roof the last time she'd had to sneak away from Algonquin. "Gird your loins."

The illusion washed over the truck before she finished, leaving Julius standing beside what looked like empty space. Fortunately, it still felt like a truck when he climbed inside, becoming invisible himself as well the moment he passed through the door.

"Now remember, we can only do this when we're out in the boonies," Marci's disembodied voice whispered beside him. "I hope I don't have to explain the dangers of driving an invisible car in actual traffic."

Julius nodded before he remembered she couldn't see him. He still kept his mouth shut, piloting their invisible truck out of the parking lot and between the incoming lines of Algonquin's anti-dragon task force trucks. Only when they'd made it through the flashing lights back to the semi-inhabited University Heights neighborhood where Marci had lived when he'd first met her did Julius finally release the breath he'd been holding. "I think we're clear."

Marci must have agreed, because the invisibility illusion vanished seconds later to reveal her grinning face. "Quality spellwork," she said proudly. "Take the time to do it right, and it works the first time, every time."

"Very high quality," Julius agreed, flashing her a thankful look before turning to check on his sister. "Are you okay?"

"No," Chelsie said quietly. She was sitting as far from the two of them as possible, leaning against the passenger door with her sword in her lap and her eyes locked on the dark road ahead. "I can't remember anything after the fight with Vann Jeger."

"That's probably because of Estella," Julius said quickly. "But it's okay. We made it, and now we're going to get you somewhere safe."

He finished with a smile that was meant to be comforting, but Chelsie's eyes were as cold and hard as green stones when they met his. "Do you have my phone?"

That seemed like a weird question, but Julius didn't comment as he pulled it out of his pocket and handed the device over. "Bob called you," he explained quickly. "That's how I knew how to say the…um…thing I'm not supposed to mention."

Chelsie nodded, though she didn't actually seem to be listening. She was just staring at her phone with an odd expression.

"What's wrong?" he asked nervously.

"We'll find out when we get back to your house," she said, closing her eyes. "I need to recover. Wake me up when we get there."

Julius shifted nervously. But before he could think of a polite way to ask how she could possibly sleep at a time like this, Chelsie was out, curled in the corner with her head resting on the passenger window.

The sight filled him with decidedly mixed feelings. Happy as he was that his sister trusted him enough to sleep in his presence, he was also afraid that the sleep wasn't by choice. Whatever had just happened to Chelsie, it clearly wasn't over yet. But there wasn't anything he could do for her in the car, so Julius forced himself to turn back to the road, manually adjusting the pickup's ancient controls to avoid as many potholes as possible as they raced down the ruler-straight streets back to the glittering, double-layered city rising like a cliff face in front of them.

• • •

Amelia was waiting when they got home, sitting on the porch steps in the ill-fitting dress Marci had given her with a half-empty bottle of whiskey dangling from her fingers. She set it down as soon as they pulled in, pushing herself to her feet with a pained grin. "You lived!" she cried happily. "I guess that means we… *What happened to you?*"

This was directed at Chelsie, who half-stumbled, half-fell out of the passenger door the second the truck stopped moving. "I'm fine," she muttered, regaining her balance. "Get inside."

"Fine?" Amelia cried. "You're missing half your magic!" Her eyes turned murderous. "Did one of Algonquin's mages do this?"

"No," Marci said sheepishly, scooting out of the truck behind Chelsie. "It was me."

"Because I told her to," Chelsie snapped.

"And why would you do something stupid like that?" Amelia snapped back. "Was your life not complicated enough already?"

Chelsie's reply to that was a silent glare, leaving Amelia steaming. "What bit her?" she grumbled, crossing her arms with a hurt look as Chelsie marched up the steps into the house. "And why is she naked? Did she fight Vann Jeger as a dragon?" Her face turned spooked. "Do we need to start digging an air raid shelter?"

"No," Julius said, shutting down the car. "We beat Vann Jeger. Well, really Marci did, but—"

"It was a team effort," Marci interrupted, though she still beamed when Amelia gave her two thumbs up.

"—we've got another problem," Julius continued. "Chelsie was attacked by Estella."

For the first time since they'd arrived, Amelia was speechless, and Julius took advantage of the lull to get her back into the house.

Inside, they found Chelsie lying in what had been Amelia's spot on the bloody couch with her head back and her eyes shut. Amelia, who probably shouldn't have been standing either, sat down on the couch's arm with an uncharacteristically grim expression. "Are you cold?"

"Freezing," Chelsie said.

Julius, who remembered all too well how awful he'd felt after Marci had taken all of his magic, ran upstairs to get her a blanket that wasn't covered in blood. When he came back down, Chelsie was eating an entire bag of frozen chicken wings.

"It's all we had left," Marci said before Julius could even ask. "I offered to order food, or at least put the wings in the oven, but—"

"No time," Chelsie said, eating the raw, frozen wings bones and all. "We have to move fast."

Amelia crossed her arms stubbornly over her chest. "Not before someone tells me what happened."

"We distracted Vann Jeger," Chelsie said in a clipped voice. "Marci's spirit defeated him, after which I helped her bind him again, and then I took Vann Jeger's head."

Amelia's eyes were huge by the time she finished. "You used your Mortal Spirit?" she cried, turning to Marci. "That's amazing! What's his name? How did he do it? TELL ME EVERYTHING!"

"Later," Chelsie growled, baring her teeth when Amelia shot her a furious look. "There's more to life than your curiosity. Estella attacked me just like she did you. The last thing I remember is chopping off Vann Jeger's head. After that, there's nothing until I woke up as a dragon with Julius in my face and Algonquin's task force on my tail."

Amelia's look turned smug. "Nice Dragon saves the day again, huh?" She turned to Julius. "Is bailing us out of disasters your new hobby or something?"

Julius's ears began to burn at that. But while it was nice to finally get some appreciation, he couldn't claim credit for this one. "It was Bob," he said quickly. "I just did what I was told. But while we managed to get Chelsie out safely, none of us saw the attack, so we still have no idea what Estella did. We can't even go back and investigate since the whole place is overrun with dragon hunters."

"We don't need to go back," Chelsie said, holding up her phone.

Julius frowned in confusion, and his sister sighed. "Estella hasn't been targeting Heartstrikers at random," she explained. "First Conrad, then Amelia, and, assuming Vann Jeger was telling the truth, Justin. I'm not sure if she's specifically attacking Fangs and just went after Amelia because she could, or if she's been systematically taking out any Heartstriker who could pose a threat, but either way, I was next. That's why, after what happened to Amelia, I went ahead and rigged my phone's camera and mic to record at all times."

"You bugged yourself?" Julius said, impressed. "That's clever."

"Clever is Chelsie's middle name," Amelia said proudly, ruffling her younger sister's short hair before Chelsie could smack her hand away. "So what are you waiting for? Play it!"

Chelsie glared and tapped her phone, turning it around so they could all see the video on the screen since her obviously disposable phone was too cheap to have public AR. Fortunately, the video quality was reasonably good even with the dark, though oddly, the first thing they saw was the phone falling out onto the ground as Chelsie collapsed against a tree.

"Never mind that," Chelsie muttered, skipping ahead several seconds. "Here."

After all that buildup, Julius was braced for something epic, but the exchange was actually astonishingly short. The whole thing couldn't have lasted more than five seconds before Chelsie's fire whited out the camera.

"What happened to Estella's hair?" Amelia asked. "Cancer patient is not a good look for her. Was it like that when she attacked me?"

"Who cares about her hair?" Marci cried. "Is she freaking serious? Did she s*eriously* set up all that Vann Jeger nonsense—me getting interrogated and having a curse put on my neck and all that stuff with Ghost—just so she could get the drop on *Chelsie*?"

"Actually, I thought that part was pretty clever," Amelia said. "How else could you bait Bethesda's Shade out into the open? Chelsie's always had a soft spot for the babies."

"Excuse me for not condoning child murder," Chelsie growled, skipping the video back to replay the attack. "But I still don't see how she knocked me out. She barely even touched me."

Marci leaned over the phone. "I think she put something on you," she said, backing the video up again and pausing it on the second when Estella's hand shot out toward Chelsie's neck. "See? Right there. She has something in her hands."

Julius squinted at the barely visible black line. "What is that? A rope?"

"I think it's some kind of chain," Marci said, tilting her head sideways.

Amelia's whole body jerked. "Say that again," she demanded.

"What?" Marci asked, frowning. "Chain?"

The dragon mage's face collapsed into a scowl Julius didn't like one bit. "Is that bad?" he asked.

"Potentially apocalyptic," Amelia replied, her voice deadly serious. "We need to call Bob."

"I'm surprised he hasn't called us," Julius said, suddenly worried. "He said he'd call when we got home."

"Maybe he's busy?" Marci said.

"Or maybe he can't see now that two of our futures are gone," Amelia said grimly.

That was enough to make everyone look dour, and then Chelsie closed the video to bring up her phone's number pad. She dialed a long string of numbers and waited, fingers poised over the numbers to dial again when the call suddenly picked up.

"You answered," Chelsie said, obviously shocked.

"I told you I always pick up when it's important," Bob replied. "Put me on speaker. This is a group discussion."

Chelsie did as he asked, turning the phone so everyone could hear. "I take it you know why we're calling, then?"

"Yes, but only through Julius," Bob said. "Can you show him the video again? I want to double check something."

"How about I just send it to you and you can watch it yourself?" Chelsie said, hitting a button.

"Or that," Bob replied, falling silent as he watched the short clip. "Please tell me that's not what I think it is."

"No can do," Amelia said, taking the phone from her sister. "That's a chain all right, which explains our memory loss nicely. Though I still don't understand how Estella got one, let alone multiples."

"Never underestimate what Estella is willing to put herself through for victory," Bob said darkly. "Why else do you think she almost killed her sister trying to get a Kosmolabe last month?"

Amelia gasped like this was the vital piece of new information that solved the puzzle, and Marci rolled her eyes. "Okay stop," she said, putting up her hands. "Can we please get some context for those of us who *don't* know what's going on?"

"I can try," Amelia said. "You know that dragons didn't originate on this plane, right?"

Marci nodded. "Vann Jeger said something about that. He also said dragons originally came here because they destroyed their own home, but he's not exactly a reliable source."

"Unfortunately for us, he was telling the truth," Amelia said grimly. "We're what Algonquin would call a 'non-native invasive species.' The first dragons came to this world as refugees roughly ten thousand years ago. No one knows anymore if we picked this place for a reason, or if it was just the first one we found, but either way, we've never gone back."

"Wait," Julius said. "I thought we came as conquerors? That's how I always heard it."

"That's just the spin," Bob said. "Surely you don't expect any proper dragon to admit we were forced to flee to this world after cataclysmically failing to manage our own?"

That explanation rang too true to be a lie. "So what happened?"

"Exactly what you'd expect from a place where dragons were the dominant species," Amelia said bitterly. "We fought amongst ourselves until there was nothing left to fight over, and then we jumped ship."

Again, that made a horrible sort of sense, but Chelsie looked fed up. "I've never heard any of this," she growled. "How is it that you two know it all?"

"Because we knew grandfather," Amelia said sadly. "He was one of the last living dragons who actually came through the original portal."

"Wait," Julius said, breathless. "You've *met* the Quetzalcoatl?"

"Of course," Amelia said. "*A*-melia, remember? The Quetzalcoatl used to dote on his grandchildren, especially Bob."

"I'm innately lovable," Bob said. "But this story has a point other than horrifically dating ourselves. With the exception of trusting Bethesda, our grandfather was a very wise dragon. He was young when he was forced to flee to this world, but he never forgot what happened to his home, and he was determined that his clan would not make the same mistakes as our ancestors. But while Amelia's version of the story makes for a nice moral tale, the situation that destroyed our original home plane wasn't entirely due to the natural draconic urge to conquer. What really ruined things for everyone were the seers."

"Seers?" Julius said. "As in more than the usual three?"

"Exponentially," his brother replied. "Dragon seers used to be as common as human mages. They were literally everywhere, meddling atrociously, tangling the future into knots." He shuddered. "I don't even want to think about it."

Julius didn't, either. Two seers fighting was bad enough, but thousands? "I can see why our ancestors had problems."

"I still haven't gotten to the bad part," Bob said. "With so many seers fighting each other for control of the future, some started pursuing new, more inventive strategies to get a leg up on their enemies. This kicked off an arms race which eventually culminated in the creation of a new weapon unique to seer magic. A tool that, when applied to your enemies, would enforce your single vision of the future over all others, no matter how unlikely."

Julius's eyes went wide, but Marci beat him to it. "The chains!"

"Bingo," Bob said. "Give the girl a prize."

"Let me get this straight," Julius said slowly. "You're saying Estella went to the old home of the dragons and brought back a weapon that will make her version of the future come true over yours?"

"Over everyone's," Bob said grimly. "No matter what. She's *literally* bound the future in chains, and now we're in a pickle."

They were in a lot worse than a pickle. Julius was still trying to wrap his head around how bad this could be when Marci asked, "So where does my Kosmolabe come in? Don't dragons know how to get back to their own plane?"

"Not any more," Amelia said sadly. "You gotta understand, we didn't just trash our home plane. We *obliterated* it. Our ancestors flew out of there one step ahead of total collapse. Things got so bad there at the end, the sphere of our reality actually disconnected completely from the other planes. Now, the only way to get back is by tunneling through the void between worlds, and the only way to do *that* is if you have something pointing you in the right direction."

"Like a Kosmolabe," Marci said.

"Exactly," Amelia said, nodding. "Why do you think I've been trying for so long to get my hands on one? I've been working on opening a portal back to the remnants of our home plane for centuries. Can you imagine how much lost history might still be buried there?"

"History, of course," Bob said drolly. "And the rumored mountains of treasure abandoned by the fleeing dragon kings has *nothing* to do with your interest."

Amelia shrugged. "Can't I be interested in both?"

"Be that as it may," Chelsie said. "Let's get back to the point. You're saying Estella used the Kosmolabe she stole last month to go back to our ancient home plane and acquire a seer weapon that forces a specific future onto us?"

"If you want to squeeze it all into one sentence."

"Then why hasn't the chain kicked in yet?" she asked, ignoring his sarcasm. "If Amelia and I are already on Estella's rails, how are we even able to have this conversation?"

"I don't know," Bob said, sounding uncharacteristically frustrated. "I told you already, I can't see either of your futures anymore. For all I know, this is all part of Estella's plan."

"Fine," Chelsie said, "So how do we get *out* of it?"

He sighed. "I don't know."

"That's a lot of 'I don't knows' for an all-knowing seer," Chelsie growled.

"Well, I don't think that's odd considering the last time a seer weapon of this sort was used was nine thousand years *before I was born*," Bob said testily. "I see the future, not the past. But if I had to make an educated guess, I'd say the only way to beat an absolute weapon is with another absolute weapon."

"You mean go get chains of our own?" Julius asked quickly, eager to break the tension. "Can we do that?"

"If Estella can, I don't see why we couldn't," Bob replied.

"But we can't get there," Marci pointed out. "Even if Amelia made a portal, we don't have a Kosmolabe."

"Don't write us off yet," Bob said. "I might have gotten my teeth kicked in this round, but I'm not *completely* without resources. It just so happens I've already sent help on that score."

"The portal or the Kosmolabe?" Marci asked at the same time as Chelsie snapped, "And you didn't tell us this *earlier*?"

"I didn't want to interrupt the exposition," Bob said innocently. "And 'help' in this case refers to the Kosmolabe. Amelia's ability to make portals should have already come back."

Everyone turned to stare at Amelia, who turned up her nose. "Of course. Why else did you think I was sitting around doing nothing but eating and boozing?"

"I don't know," Chelsie said. "Sounds like a pretty normal Amelia day to me."

"I was *recovering*," Amelia snapped. "Some of us didn't just fall over for Estella, you know."

Chelsie bared her teeth, and Julius jumped in before it came to blows. "So you can make portals again! That's great. But what about the Kosmolabe? When is it coming?"

"You should already have it," Bob said.

Everyone looked at Julius, who shook his head.

"I dare not say more," the seer said cryptically. "Just think about it."

"Now's not the time, Bob," Chelsie growled.

"Wrong," he said. "It's *exactly* the time. How often do I have to repeat that *decisions make the future?* They're the forks in the stream, the intersections in the road of life, the adventures in the Choose Your Own Adventure!"

Chelsie scoffed. "And you're letting *Julius* pick?"

"He's done an excellent job so far," Bob pointed out. "You're still alive, aren't you?"

Chelsie snapped her mouth shut. Julius didn't know what to say, either. Personally, he was with Chelsie. "But what do I do?"

"I already told you," Bob said, his voice growing serious. "*Be yourself.*"

Julius grit his teeth. This again. "But—"

"Just because I'm a seer doesn't mean I've given up being a dragon," Bob reminded him. "Estella might have stolen my pieces and turned the board sideways, but I'm not out of the game yet. Speaking of, I have to go. I'm about to be late for an appointment."

"Bob!" Chelsie cried. "Don't you *dare* hang up on—"

The phone clicked.

• • •

On the other side of the world, Bob switched off his phone and threw it as hard as he could into the neat rows of rice paddies that covered both sides of the fertile Yangtze River Valley in central China. Like everything over the last two days, ditching his phone was a risk, but as he'd just reminded his brother, being a seer didn't mean he'd forgotten how to be a dragon. Estella's greatest weakness had always been that she trusted the future over everything else, even her own common sense. She'd assumed that he, like her, would be crippled without his sight. But Brohomir was as much the son of the Heartstriker as he was a seer. For all his mother's shortcomings, lack of audacity had never been one of them.

And Estella wasn't the only one who could cheat.

"If you can't change the game, change the rules," he said to his pigeon, who'd ridden the whole way here on his shoulder. "Speaking of, you'd better make yourself scarce. My host is old fashioned. He won't appreciate you like I do."

The bird tilted her head at him, and then she took off, flying up into the clear sky. Bob watched her go until she was a speck in the distance before resuming his climb, vaulting up the ancient stone steps two at a time as he scaled the steep bank to the gate of an elegant country manor that looked like it had been built directly into the hillside before the invention of writing.

Despite its obvious age, the two-story residence was in excellent repair with its paper shutters thrown open to the early fall breeze. Bob was still making his way across the tree-shaded courtyard when the front door slid open, and a young-looking Chinese man with long, braided black hair wearing a silk coat older than most dragons stepped out to greet him.

"Let me guess," Bob said in his best Mandarin. "You were expecting me?"

"Since last month," the Black Reach replied in perfect English, looking him up and down with silver eyes that would never pass for human. "Welcome, Brohomir, Great Seer of the Heartstrikers, Consort to a Nameless End."

It wasn't often Bob heard that last title. Never, actually, before this moment. But it came up often in the future, which was where his host spent most of his time. "May I come in?"

The Black Reach nodded and stepped away from the door. "I've already poured your tea."

Bob didn't see the point. They both already knew why he'd come. But it was never wise to refuse an old dragon's offer of hospitality, and the tea here *was* the best in the world. That was as good a reason as any, so Bob plastered a smile on his face and stepped inside the ancient seer's den, shutting the door firmly behind him.

And down the path, unnoticed, his still ringing phone sank deeper into the muddy water of the rice paddy.

• • •

"I *hate* it when he does that!" Chelsie hissed, dialing Bob's number for what had to be the fiftieth time.

"And I don't see why you're upset," Amelia said, taking a long chug off her whiskey bottle. "You've lived with Bob your whole life. Surely you must be used to riddles and half-truths by now?"

"That doesn't mean I like them," Chelsie snapped, though she did finally put the phone down. "How can you be so calm about this?"

"Easy," Amelia said with a grin. "I'm drunk. You should try it sometime. You clearly need a better coping mechanism."

Chelsie glared daggers at her. "That's the worst advice I've ever heard."

"Never said I was a role model," Amelia replied with a shrug. "Seriously, though, you need to chill. I've known Brohomir since he hatched. He never loses."

"There's a first time for everything," Chelsie reminded her.

"I suppose," she said. "But if you're right, and this *is* Bob's turn to fail, then we're all doomed to be hopelessly chained to Estella's whims. I'm not particularly fond of Brohomir's seer-ish antics either, but I'd rather dance to his tune than resign myself to being Estella the Northern Bore's puppet."

Chelsie didn't seem willing to argue with that. "So what do we do now?"

Everyone turned and looked at Julius, who swallowed. "Why do you think I know?"

"Because you're his chosen one," Chelsie said sarcastically.

"And because you know where the Kosmolabe is," Amelia added, eyes bright. "Is it here? Can I see it?"

"I'm pretty sure it's not here," Marci said, glancing at Julius. "Is it?"

"I don't know!" he cried. "I haven't seen the thing since right after Bixby died. For all I know, Estella grabbed it off the ground in the Pit and—"

He stopped short when he realized what he'd said. "I think I just figured out what Bob meant."

"What?" Chelsie demanded, but Julius was already fumbling for his phone.

"Give me a second," he said, walking over to the corner to give himself the semblance of privacy as he pressed the number near the top of his contacts. It was a long shot, but Julius was desperate enough to try anything at this point. If nothing else, at least he'd get to talk to a friend.

All of this was still swirling through his head as the phone began to ring, and then, almost immediately, the call picked up, and Katya's voice cried, "*Julius!*"

"Hey," he said, feeling suddenly awkward. "Are you okay? Did you make it safely?"

"Well, I'm not captured yet, so yes. I—" She was interrupted by harsh female voice rapidly speaking Russian in the background. Katya answered in kind, her voice tense before she came back to Julius. "Sorry, I'm kind of in the middle of something. I heard my sisters were in the DFZ. Are they still there, or have they already left for the mating flight?"

Julius winced. In all the confusion, he'd completely forgotten that the mating flight between Svena and Ian was scheduled for tomorrow evening. "I haven't seen Svena since yesterday," he said. "But I know Estella was here less than an hour ago. That's why I'm calling, actually. I need to know if you've seen the Kosmolabe."

"The what?"

That was right. Katya had been unconscious through the whole Kosmolabe fiasco last month. "Magical object that lets you find things in planes," he explained. "It looks kind of like a golden ball?"

"Oh!" Katya said. "I might know where that is, yes."

Julius's heart began to pound. "Not with Estella, I hope?"

"No," she said, her voice growing smug. "My sister left a golden ball on the seat when she was dealing with your brother. Since I wasn't feeling particularly charitable toward her at the time, I took it. I thought it might be good leverage for when Estella cornered me. I'll gladly give it to you if you need it, though. It's the least I can do to repay your kindness."

"That would be *amazing*, thank you," he said, turning around to give the others a thumbs-up. "Where are you? Can I come get it?"

"Oh, I don't have it on me," Katya said. "What do you think I am, crazy? I left it in the DFZ."

"That's even better," Julius said. "Where?"

There was a long, sheepish pause.

"About that…"

•••

"I can't believe she did this," Marci growled, hovering over Julius as he carefully pried the mirror off the wall above her bathroom sink. "I thought she was your *friend*."

"She is," Julius said, giving the fixture a stubborn yank. "But she was also under a lot of pressure, and this is actually a huge stroke of luck for us. I'd have thought you'd be happy."

"It's the principle of the thing," she said as the mirror finally popped free. "She hid *my* Kosmolabe in *my* bathroom, and I didn't even know!" She crossed her arms. "Seriously, she got here *naked*. Where was she even hiding it?"

Julius shook his head and set the mirror aside. He didn't know enough to explain the specifics to Marci, but it wouldn't have been hard for a dragon as crafty at Katya to smuggle the Kosmolabe under their noses. Personally, he thought the whole thing was a pretty savvy move on her part. Hiding the Kosmolabe in their house let her put it under Bob's protection without actually giving it to him, which would have been seen as an unforgivable betrayal of her clan. But this situation was the sort of delicate, clan politics tip-toeing that was generally lost on humans, so he let Marci's anger slide, focusing instead on working his arm through the hole in the plaster that the mirror had hidden, groping blindly in the space between the struts until, at last, his fingers closed over something cold, round, and delicate.

He pulled his hand out with a flourish, and then was promptly tackled as Marci rushed to grab the Kosmolabe.

"My beautiful darling!" she cooed, clutching the softball sized, golden orb to her chest. "Mommy missed you so much!"

"Did you find it?"

The shout came from the hall, and then Amelia was suddenly in the doorway, her eyes locked on the shiny ball in Marci's clutches. "You didn't tell me it was a *Persian* Kosmolabe!" she cried. "They're the *best*!"

"I *know!*" Marci said, holding it up for her to see. "Just look at the markings!"

Julius shook his head and turned around, replacing the mirror while he waited for Marci and his sister to finish nerding out. "So what do we do now?" he asked when it was obvious they weren't going to stop on their own. "We have the Kosmolabe, but Bob wasn't exactly clear on the next step."

"Bob's *never* clear," Amelia said without taking her eyes off the Kosmolabe Marci was still cradling in her arms like a kitten. "It's against his nature. That said, I think the plan from here's pretty obvious: open portal, go to ruined home realm of dragons, get our own version of seer weapon, come back, beat Estella at her own game, celebrate."

"Sounds great," Julius said. "Just two problems. First, how are we going to get a seer weapon when we're not seers, and second, how do we know this whole trip isn't playing right into Estella's hands? I mean, we know she put a chain on *you*."

"That she did," Amelia said. "But it doesn't matter whether I'm compromised or not, I *have* to go with you. How do you think you're getting home if I'm not there to open a portal back, huh?"

Julius sighed. "Good point."

"It'll be fine," Amelia assured him, trotting down the stairs. "I don't even think seers can influence planes outside the one they're in. For all we know, my going with you will snap the chain all together and solve the whole problem."

"And what about the weapon?" Julius asked, following her down.

Amelia shrugged. "I'm sure we'll figure it out. Bob wouldn't have set us on this course if it was impossible."

"I worry you might be giving him a skosh too much credit," Marci said, carefully carrying the Kosmolabe down the stairs like it was an over-full glass of the most expensive wine on the planet. "No offense to your brother, but Bob seems to be an ask-the-impossible, hope-it-works-out kind of leader."

"Don't let his front fool you," Amelia said. "Bob plays the fool because it suits him, but never forget that he's the reason Estella's doing all of this. She *had* to do something crazy because Bob backed her into a corner she couldn't get out of any other way. You don't beat a seer three times your age by being an idiot. Trust me, if he told us about this, it'll work."

"No argument there," Julius said. "But again, are we *sure* this is Bob's plan?"

"Pretty sure," his sister said. "I mean, I don't *feel* mind controlled."

"Would you, though?" Marci asked.

"No idea," she confessed. "But I haven't noticed any weird impulses or inexplicable urges. I don't even want to murder my mother any more than I usually do."

Marci paled. "You usually want to murder your mother?"

"Have you *met* Bethesda?" Amelia asked, rolling her eyes. "Murderous rage is the usual reaction. She likes it that way, too. Her motto is: If other dragons don't want to kill you, you're not doing it right."

Julius could only nod at the truth of that, and Marci stopped on the stairs. "Wait," she said. "If you all hate Bethesda so much, why are we putting our lives on the line to save her again? I mean, I know she's your mother, but she doesn't exactly seem like the sort of person who deserves this much loyalty."

Technically, she was asking that question of both of them, but Marci's eyes were on Julius. Unfortunately, the only answer he could give her was, "She's my mother."

"Who cares about that?" Amelia scoffed. "I'd be helping Estella kill her of my own free will if it didn't mean I'd end up stuck as the Heartstriker."

Marci shrugged. "Couldn't you just say no?"

"I wish," Amelia said. "Unfortunately, dragon clans aren't just dysfunctional families. We're magical pyramids. When Bethesda killed her father, she didn't just take his lands. She also stole his fire, the magic our clan built up over generations. That's why she's such a big deal despite being only a century older than myself. But if Estella cuts the head off the Heartstriker, all that magic will automatically revert to me. If I claim it, I get stuck with the world's worst job. If I let it drop, the fire of the Heartstrikers will die, and our whole clan becomes easy pickings for our enemies."

Marci frowned. "I see your problem."

"Normally I'd say screw it and head out to my favorite tropical plane for a beach party," Amelia went on. "Alas, the list of family members I *don't* want to die has gotten too long to ignore, and then there's the part where Bob's made this clan his life's work. I'll screw Bethesda over all day long, but I owe Brohomir more than even he knows. I'd take a bullet for Mother myself before I let all of his hard work go to waste." She paused, thinking that over. "That's probably the biggest sign I'm not under Estella's control, actually. I still want Bob to win. I don't actually know how this chain thing works, but I'm pretty sure that wouldn't be the case if I was Estella's puppet. She hates Bethesda with a passion, but Brohomir's the one she's really out to beat."

Julius nodded. He'd had a feeling that was the case ever since he'd witnessed the two seers' confrontation at the party, and while he was still nervous, his sister's arguments made a lot of sense. "Let's try it, then."

"Obviously," Amelia said, turning to walk down the final flight of stairs to the living room. "I'm already set up and everything."

She was. While they'd been in the bathroom digging up the Kosmolabe, Amelia had cleared out the living room, pushing all the furniture, including the couch where Chelsie was sleeping to recover the magic Marci had taken, into the hallway. Now, the whole room was empty save for the floor lamp in the corner and the stuff that couldn't be moved, like the mantelpiece over the fireplace.

"How big a portal are you planning to make, anyway?" Julius asked, looking around at the impressively large space she'd made.

"Go big or go home," Amelia replied, holding out her hand for the Kosmolabe. Marci handed it over with a grimace, and the dragon quivered with delight. "You lovely thing," she cooed, rolling the golden ball lovingly between her hands as she stepped into the center of the room. "Ready?"

Julius blinked. "What, you mean like right now?"

"No time like the present," his sister replied. "Time moves differently on every plane. If Estella's going to make her move at the mating flight tomorrow, we need to get started as soon as possible in case our destination is running behind. It'd suck to spend a day getting everything together only to come home and discover we're a year too late."

Marci paled. "Will that happen?"

"Won't know until we get there," Amelia said, smiling at the Kosmolabe. "Besides, do you know how many centuries I've been waiting to try one of these things?"

"I just hope she gives it back," Marci whispered to Julius as Amelia peered deep into Kosmolabe's interlocking golden circles.

"I'd settle for getting out of this alive," Julius whispered back. He didn't care how easy his sister made it sound. Going into an unknown, ruined dimension to retrieve an ancient dragon weapon that they didn't understand and might not even recognize was crazy, even for a seer plot. They were in way too deep to turn back now, though, and Bob was counting on them. Julius thought that was a pretty foolish decision on the seer's part, but he was still going to do his best to hold up his end. At this point, it was all he could do.

"I'm going to wake Chelsie up," he whispered when it was clear Amelia was going to be at this for a while. "If we're all going, I don't want her to wake up alone."

"Too late for that."

Julius and Marci both jumped, turning around to see Chelsie standing behind them, her face pale and set in a dour scowl.

"Should you be up?" Julius asked when he'd recovered.

"I'll live," Chelsie said, nodding at their sister, who was staring into the Kosmolabe like it contained the meaning of life. "Is she making the portal right now?"

"I can still hear you, you know," Amelia said without looking up. "And yes. I've already found it, actually, but it's pretty far."

"Does that matter?" Marci asked.

"Only if you want me to do this more than once," Amelia replied, glancing at them over her shoulder. "You might want to brace. I don't have enough juice yet to do this properly, so I'm going to cheat and do a rip job, which means things might get a little uncomfortable."

Julius swallowed. "Uncomfortable how?"

The words were barely out of his mouth when Amelia's magic ripped through the room, and the answer became self-evident. Just standing near his sister was like being surrounded by fire-heated knives. Even Amelia wasn't immune to it. Her whole body began to smoke as the power built, her dark hair smoldering as little fires began to appear in the crooks of her curls. Then, just when Julius was sure she was about to spontaneously combust, Amelia lashed out and split the world open.

Having seen Chelsie cut through space numerous times now, Julius had thought he knew what to expect. As usual, though, the truth was something else entirely. Chelsie's cut had been exactly that: an incision through one place to another. Definitely not something you saw every day, but still easy to understand. This, though, this was watching someone punch a hole in reality itself. Just seeing the air tatter and fall away felt wrong on a fundamental level, and as for what lay beyond…Julius couldn't even wrap his head around it.

On the other side of the giant rip Amelia had made in his living room was black desert lit by a blood-red moon. But while that was comprehensible, if creepy, the feel of the place was utterly and inexplicably *wrong*. It was like the moment in a forced perspective photograph when you realized the seemingly normal-sized car in the background was actually a toy in the foreground, only instead of the three-dimensional perspective, this trick was happening on the fourth. Everything beyond that hole—the fine black sand, the starless sky, the red moon with its alien craters—looked like a diorama frozen forever in a single moment. Still, even *that* wouldn't have been so bad were it not for the black mountain in the distance. The mountain that was *moving*, despite the impossible stillness.

"What *is* that?" Marci whispered, her eyes wide. "And what is *wrong* with it?"

"I'm…not sure, actually," Amelia said, looking a bit pale herself. "I—"

Her voice cut off like a dropped knife. At first, Julius couldn't understand why. The landscape on the other side of the portal hadn't changed. He was wondering if something was wrong with the portal itself when his nose caught the now-familiar scent of sea ice.

After everything that had happened, Julius didn't even bother trying to figure out more than that. He just grabbed Marci and jumped. And it was this paranoid anticipation that saved their lives as the front door exploded in a blast of dragon magic, sending shards of wood flying all the way to the opposite side of the house.

"*Get back!*"

The shout came from Chelsie, who suddenly had her sword in her hands, taking up a defensive position in front of Amelia as the last dragon Julius expected to see stepped through the shattered doorway.

"*Conrad.*"

Chelsie said her brother's name like a curse, smoke curling from between her clenched teeth, but Conrad didn't even seem to notice. He just noted her position and stepped to the side, making way for the dragoness who walked in next.

"Right on time," Estella said, sweeping her ice blue gaze over the room full of dragons. Dragons who should have been attacking her as their enemy, but who weren't reacting at all. They just stood there, frozen as Estella smiled at them like they were statues in her garden before turning to face Julius. "You again? Why am I not surprised?"

After what he'd seen on Chelsie's video, Julius's eyes went straight to her wrist, and the seer laughed with delight. "Finally figured it out, did you?" she asked, raising her bare arm for him to see. "Sorry to disappoint, but I don't waste chains on failures."

She glanced at the tattered portal, which was still hanging in the air in front of Amelia. "You know, part of me actually wants to let you try. I'd love to see Brohomir's face when he realizes the underdog he's invested so much hope and effort in is lost forever in the silent grave of our ancestors. Alas," she sighed dramatically, "I'm not an idiot who allows loose ends." She waved her hand. "Kill them."

Since Conrad was the one who'd blown their door open, he was the one Julius flinched away from, but it was Chelsie, not her brother, who attacked, turning and slashing her Fang at Julius.

Any other day, that would have been it. But Chelsie was far from her peak tonight, and Julius had just spent almost an hour dodging an insanely fast spirit. Alone, either of these factors still wouldn't have made a difference. Together, though, they gave him just enough of an edge to duck, dragging Marci to the floor half a heartbeat before Chelsie's Fang sliced over their heads.

"*Chelsie!*" he shouted, his voice cracking. "What are you doing?"

But he already knew. The dragon standing over him was still his sister, but her face was the face of a stranger when she swung again. This time, though, Julius was ready. He jumped before she even started, rolling himself and Marci across the floor to come up directly beside the tattered portal that was still wavering in the air.

"Such quick little mice," Estella said. "But you *are* looking a bit peakish, Bethesda's Shade." She turned to the towering dragon beside her. "Conrad, help your sister take care of Brohomir's pet. Amelia, close the portal."

Conrad nodded and stepped forward while Amelia lowered her hands. Her scorching magic began to fade from the air at the same time, and the portal faded with it, but it was the motion—the strange, automaton-like movement that was nothing like Amelia's normal dramatic flair—that finally kicked Julius over the edge. Before that moment, he'd felt like a mouse caught on the chaotic battlefield for a clash of giants. Now, the entire world had narrowed down to a single goal: getting away from Estella. There was no more room for worry or second guesses, no room even for consequences, and with no hesitation to hold him back, Julius moved faster than he'd ever moved in his life.

He didn't look. He didn't plan. He didn't even bother trying to sidestep Conrad's incoming attack. He simply grabbed Marci around the waist and jumped sideways through what was left of the hole Amelia had ripped in the air.

For a terrifying second, he was sure they hadn't made it. He could actually see the rips in the air above him closing over, closing them in. Then, like a miracle, they were through, crashing together into the black dust on the other side of the hole in the world. Landing on his back, Julius caught one final glimpse of Estella's face as her smile faded, and then the portal vanished, sealing him and Marci on the other side.

• • •

For the first time since she'd returned, Estella felt a stab of real anger. That was *not* supposed to happen.

"Open it," she snarled, yanking hard on the chain that bound the Planeswalker's future. "Now."

Amelia shuddered as the command hit, but even though Estella's word should have been absolute, nothing happened. "I can't."

"*What do you mean you can't?*" Estella roared. "I don't care if you have to burn yourself out, *make that portal.*"

"I can't," Amelia said again, holding up her hands. Her *empty* hands.

Estella clenched her fists in rage, sending a sheet of ice racing over the floor and up the walls. Then, just as quickly, she forced herself to let it go.

It didn't matter, she reminded herself. So what if they'd taken the Kosmolabe? The mortal couldn't use it, and the little whelp dragon was centuries too young for such magic. Even if they did somehow manage to find their way back, they'd never make it in time. Estella knew that much for a fact. She could see the whole of her life spread out before her like a perfect map, and after this turn, neither Brohomir's pawn nor his surprisingly competent mortal had any part in it ever again.

That thought sent the last of her anger away, and Estella let the ice melt, holding her head high as she marched back to the door. "Leave them," she ordered. "They're as dead there as they would be here. We, on the other hand, have a glorious future to create."

She crooked her finger as she finished, grinning wide as Bethesda's three strongest children followed her like lambs out to the idling limo that would take them to the airport where Svena was already waiting.

And back in the house, hidden in the shadows, a ghostly glowing cat slipped out of Marci's forgotten bag and vanished into thin air.

CHAPTER EIGHTEEN

Julius had never felt so far from home in his life.

He was sitting in an ocean of black dust under a starless sky as flat and matte black as Chelsie's feathers. The only light came from the resentful red glow of the full, blood-colored moon frozen at the sky's zenith. There was no wind. There was no movement. There wasn't even scent. Other than himself and Marci, he couldn't smell a thing. It was like he'd been dropped into a sensory deprivation chamber the size of a city, and there was no—

"Julius!"

He jumped, tearing his eyes away from the alien landscape just in time for Marci to tackle him back to dusty ground. "That was amazing!" she cried, hugging him until his ribs creaked. "I didn't even know you could move that fast! I thought we were dead for sure!"

Julius wasn't sure they weren't. "We're in another dimension."

"That was kind of the idea," Marci said, sitting back up with an odd look. "Are you okay? You look kind of freaked out."

"How are you *not* freaked out?" he said, heart pounding. "We're stranded in an alternate dimension!" A dead dimension. With no one who could make them a portal back out.

Julius sat up in a rush, lifting his dusty, shaking hands to his face. What had he done? Why hadn't he jumped another way? Why hadn't he gone *alone*? Estella probably considered Marci beneath her notice, which meant she might have gotten away. But *no*, he'd panicked and dragged her through the one-way portal to a hidden plane and doomed them both.

"Would you stop it?"

He lowered his hands to see Marci glaring at him. "Honestly," she huffed. "I can *hear* you blaming yourself, and you seriously need to cut it out. I *wanted* to come here, remember?"

"But we weren't going to be trapped then," he reminded her.

"Better trapped here and alive than back there and dead," she said with a shrug. "Besides," her look turned sly. "We're not *necessarily* trapped."

Before he could ask what she meant by that, Marci lifted her hands to show him the glistening, golden orb clutched between her palms.

"The Kosmolabe," he whispered, eyes wide. "But...*how?*"

Marci laughed. "Did you forget who you're talking to here? This little beauty was the most valuable thing in the room *and* the only way to get to where we were supposed to go. I grabbed it the moment Amelia went weird."

Julius could have hugged her. He was pushing down the impulse out of habit when he suddenly remembered he *could*. So he did, grabbing her tight against him. Marci hugged him back just as hard, grinning like there was nowhere else she'd rather be. And that was actually what brought him back to reality, because there *were* places they needed to be right now, and if his impulsive decision to get them both stranded here was going to be anything other than a disaster, they needed to get moving.

"Come on," he said, standing up. "We're burning daylight. Moonlight. Whatever."

"Assuming time even works the same here," Marci reminded him, grabbing the hand he offered and pulling herself up. "For all we know, Estella hasn't even left the house yet back in our world."

"Or she could already be at Heartstriker Mountain." That possibility reminded Julius of his seemingly brainwashed siblings, and his spirits dropped even lower. "I wonder if they're aware?"

"I can't imagine they are," Marci said, squeezing the Kosmolabe into her jacket's inside pocket. "If I understood your brother correctly, the whole point of the chains was to take away someone's ability to make decisions, thus turning them into a mindless cog in your own future, and that certainly looked like what was happening. I mean, can you imagine Amelia taking orders like that normally? She'd choke herself first."

That was true, though Julius wasn't sure if it made their situation better or worse. On the one hand, turning them into puppets would vastly reduce his siblings' abilities since their experience and personalities were a huge part of what made them powerful. On the other, even a reduced Chelsie, Amelia, and Conrad were still a giant threat, and they *still* didn't know what had happened to Justin. Even so. "There's nothing we can do for them now except stick to the plan," Julius said, looking up at the motionless red moon. "We'll just have to cross our fingers and hope that, if there is a time disparity, it's in our favor."

"I bet it is," Marci said with an optimistic smile. "This place doesn't exactly strike me as fast moving. There's no wind or animals." She slid her boot through the black dust. "I don't even think this stuff is sand."

Julius didn't think so, either. The soft black powder looked like a cross between extremely fine sand and old ash. Other than being annoyingly soft to walk in, though, it didn't appear harmful. He was about to suggest they get moving when a sudden flash of light on the ground nearly made him jump out of his skin.

"What the—"

Ghost was sitting at their feet, tail flicking smugly back and forth.

"How did *you* get here?" he cried.

The question was more reactionary than interrogative. For once, though, the spirit actually answered. *I go where she goes.*

Marci gasped. "Even through dimensions?"

Ghost flicked his ears, the cat equivalent of a shrug. *We're bound. If you go, I follow. Doesn't matter where.*

"That is *amazing*!" Marci cried, reaching down to scoop the glowing cat in her arms. "Who's my clever boy?" she cooed, covering his freezing fur in proud kisses. The spirit responded by butting his head against her face, rubbing his cheek against hers while giving Julius a smugly superior look.

Julius crossed his arms. Spirit or no, that was deliberately insulting. But he refused to be jealous of a cat, so he just turned away, scanning the landscape to determine where they needed to go next. Not that it was really a question. Besides strange black sand and sky, there was only one other thing here, and that was the mountain.

The black, scary, *moving* mountain.

"What do you think it is?" Marci asked, following his gaze as she placed Ghost on her shoulders.

"Only one way to find out," he said, reaching back for her hand. To his great relief, she took it without hesitation, and they set off together into the rolling sea of dust.

Julius had never missed his wings so much in his life. Every step sent their feet sinking ankle-deep into the fine, ashy dust. When they yanked themselves out, the disturbance sent clouds of the stuff up into the air where it made a beeline for their mouths, eyes, and noses like metal filings to a magnet. To Julius's relief, it tasted just like it smelled, which was like nothing at all, but the fine grit in his throat made him horribly thirsty, a grim reminder that they were on a real time limit here since they had no food or water and zero chance of finding either.

Being mortal, Marci was probably faring even worse, but she didn't say a word of complaint. She just pulled her shirt up over her mouth and nose to form a makeshift bandanna and trudged behind him, keeping her eyes determinedly on the mountain they didn't seem to be getting any closer to.

The only one who actually seemed to be enjoying the trip was Ghost. He trotted over the landscape like his namesake, vanishing every few minutes only to come back and meow silently at Marci, who translated his findings for Julius. Unfortunately, there was nothing interesting to report. Every time the cat came back from a scouting mission, it was the same: desert and more desert.

The whole thing reminded Julius of those anxiety dreams where you run and run as fast as you can but never get anywhere, but it wasn't like they could turn back. Forward was the only valid direction in this place, so they kept moving, trudging through the mercifully cool, apparently eternal night. And then, just when Julius was certain they'd be walking until they died, the mountain was suddenly there, rising straight up from the desert in front of them like a wall.

"About freaking time," Marci said, running toward the cliff.

"Don't touch it!" Julius cried, hobbling after her.

Marci scoffed. "Wasn't going to. I've seen movies."

She did lean perilously close, though, bending over until her nose was less than an inch from the mountain by the time Julius joined her. "What is this stuff? It's not rock."

He leaned in as well, squinting in the dim, red moonlight. Even with his superior night vision, though, it still took Julius several seconds to understand what he was looking at. And when he did, he almost wished he hadn't. "They're chains," he whispered, stomach sinking as he tilted his head back, looking up, and up, and up.

The mountain in front of them wasn't a mountain at all. It was a pile. A colossal, towering, cylindrical pillar of glistening metal chains just like the one Estella had slapped on Chelsie. Each one was scarcely wider than a string, but they were stacked to the sky, all of them tangled together in a giant knot that seemed to have no end or beginning. They were also all *moving*, the little links expanding and contracting in unison like the breathing of a sleeping animal. Just watching something so horrendously creepy was enough to make Julius's skin crawl. Marci, as usual, was unfazed.

"That's so cooooool," she said, leaning back so far she nearly fell over in her efforts to see the pile's top. "I guess we know where Estella got her chains now. So how do you think these work? Do we just pick one out?"

"No way," Julius said with a shudder. "You saw what happened when one of those things touched Chelsie."

"I wonder if they're all different futures?" Marci said, leaning back in to peer at individual links. "You know, all the different chains of events that could possibly happen?"

"How would that even work?" Julius asked. "We're in another dimension, and didn't Amelia say that seers couldn't see out of their own?"

"It has to work somehow," Marci said. "These are clearly the same chains Estella used, so they obviously function in our world." She frowned. "Maybe it's a dragon thing? This is where you're all from. Maybe part of your future is still here or something?"

That wasn't a bad theory, but just trying to think through all the implications was already making Julius's head ache. Before he could reply, though, the black wall in front of them began to vibrate.

"Perceptive lesser creature."

The words rolled through the ground like shockwaves, making them both jump. "Um," Marci said, moving closer to him. "Did that mountain just backhand compliment me?"

Julius was lifting his shoulders in a bewildered shrug when the mountain's surface began to move, the softly pulsing chains curling like tentacles until they'd formed a wide, arched opening.

"Enter."

Again, the voice shook the ground, but this time Julius was ready for it, listening closely to the words as they rumbled through him. Not surprisingly, given where they were, it sounded like a dragon. A *big* one. Under any other circumstances, that would have filled him with a healthy amount of dread. Now, though, after a full day of crisis, an evening of almost dying, and a night spent walking untold miles across an alien desert, Julius was too excited about the possibility of actually finding someone who might have some answers to be more than mildly apprehensive.

"Come on," he said, pulling out his phone to use as a flashlight, the only usefulness it had left out here. "Let's finish this."

"I just hope it doesn't finish *us*," Marci whispered, nervously eyeing the tunnel of chains. "And I thought we weren't going to touch those?"

"The chains are safe," the voice assured them. *"They sleep until cut. Though I invite you to take your time. We have plenty of that to spare, here."*

It might have been Julius's imagination, but he'd have sworn the strange voice sounded bitter at the end. But while the idea of walking over mind-control chains—sleeping or not—sounded like a very bad one, he was sick of dragging this out. So, with a deep breath of the strange, empty air, Julius closed his eyes and took a big step forward, planting his foot straight down on the tangled chains that made up the tunnel's floor.

It was…not pleasant. In fact, Julius was certain the feeling of thousands of tiny threads pulsing through the bottom of his shoe was going to be nightmare fodder for the rest of his life. But other than that cheery detail, nothing actually bad happened.

"Is it safe?" Marci whispered.

"I think so," he whispered back, placing his other foot on the creepy, breathing floor. "Relatively speaking."

She stepped in beside him with a grimace, her whole body shivering like she'd just jumped in freezing water. "That's a feeling you don't forget," she said, opening her eyes at last as she locked her arm through his. "Let's get this over with."

The two of them set off into the dark, marching side by side down the sloping tunnel of chains. Again, it was impossible to say how long they walked. According to Julius's exhausted legs, it was miles, but the reality was probably closer to a few hundred feet before the tunnel took a sharp turn upwards, expanding into a large, and surprisingly open, space.

From the outside, the pile of chains had looked like a tall, steep, strangely cylindrical mountain. Looking up from the inside, though, Julius realized it was actually shaped more like a very steep volcano, and he and Marci had just entered the caldera. Coiled chains rose in sheer walls around them on all sides, but here in the center, the ground was relatively flat, creating an enormous, circular space open to the moonlit sky above. It actually reminded Julius of standing in the center of a giant nest, which was fitting, because lying in the middle of it all was the largest dragon he'd ever seen.

It was impossible to tell just *how* large, because the dragon's snake-like body was coiled in a circle, looped over and over onto itself like a giant pile of rope. That said, even the small coils were still twice Julius's height and as big around as a school bus. He couldn't begin to imagine how huge the dragon would be if it stretched out, but what really made him stare were its scales.

In addition to its enormous size—or more likely because of it— the dragon's body was covered in *huge* scales. Each one was easily five feet across and arranged in overlapping rows, like a snake's. This wasn't unusual—with the notable exception of feathered serpents like the Heartstrikers, most dragons were scaled—but where normal dragon scales varied in size and coloration, these scales were all bone white and so uniform that they looked like they'd been made in a factory. The only difference between them was the writing.

Every scale on the dragon's body was covered from top to bottom with neat, tightly packed lines of curling black script. Julius couldn't read what they said, but he recognized the symbols from some of his mother's oldest—and therefore most valuable—treasures. But just as he was wondering if they'd stumbled onto some kind of giant monument, the coils began to move, sliding over each other with the sound of clicking stone beads as a square, white-eyed head the size of a tank rose from the dragon's center to look at them.

"Welcome, son of the Heartstriker," it said, its deep voice still booming, but at least not ground-shaking anymore.

Julius swallowed. "You know who I am?"

"I know whatever you bring with you," the dragon said. "which, in your case, is very little." It opened its mouth, showing its bone-white fangs in what Julius hoped was a smile. "I am Dragon Sees the Beginning, and while I'd like to have more than twenty-four years to work with, I welcome you all the same. It is entertaining to have something to look at again."

Julius was trying to think up an appropriate response to that when Marci said, "Is 'Dragon Sees the Beginning' your name or your title?"

The giant dragon rolled its coils. "I don't see the difference. It is what I am, just as you are a perceptive, presumptuous, death-bound creature." The wall of smiling teeth grew wider. "Perhaps that should be *your* name?"

"I'll stick with Marci, thanks," Marci said. "But what is it that you do here? Do you just sit around and stare at chains?"

"Does it always ask this many questions?" the dragon said, turning its milky eyes back to Julius. "I shouldn't have to ask, of course, but your recent memories are highly emotional and disordered, which makes them difficult to interpret."

Julius wasn't sure if that was an insult or just a blunt observation, but taking offense at a dragon hundreds of times his size was pointless in any case, so he just moved on. "Is that how you see the beginning?" he asked. "By reading memories? And how is it you are still here? I thought all the dragons had to flee this plane?"

"They did," the dragon said. "I am merely a magical construct created to preserve the history of this world. All that has happened before this moment is mine to preserve." The toothy smile faded. "Unfortunately, since the collapse, there has been little for me to remember and no one to remember it for."

"We would love to hear your memories," Julius said quickly. "I know nothing about this place or why we left it."

"So I can see," the dragon said with a sigh. "The depth of your ignorance is truly depressing, though not surprising. Our kind doesn't like to remember defeats, and there is no defeat more shameful than the loss of one's homeworld to careless greed and lack of forethought."

"How does lack of forethought cause *that?*" Marci asked, pointing back down the tunnel toward the empty desert.

"It doesn't. The waste you crossed is not the current state of the former draconic plane. It is merely a representation of emptiness, a buffer to protect me and the history I guard from the void that lies beyond worlds." He nodded to the chains rising around them on all sides. "Even this place is nothing but a construct created by the future the two of you brought here with you. Though I must admit I'm impressed. I haven't had a mountain this large to enjoy for a long, long time."

"Wait," Julius said. "Are you saying all these chains are connected to *us*?"

"Who else would they belong to?" the dragon asked. "This is a dead world. There *is* no future in this place save what you bring with you." It raised a massive paw from beneath its coils, running its meter-long claws over the curving wall of chains that surrounded them. "These are your possible futures, every chain of events that could yet happen from the moment you entered this place until the end of time."

"So my future's in there, too?" Marci said, her eyes huge.

"A small portion," the dragon replied. "But not bad, for a mortal."

"What about our pasts?" Julius asked. "Are those here, too?"

Dragon Sees the Beginning smirked. "They are, but they were so minuscule, I'm afraid I already consumed them so we would be able to communicate. An unfortunate but unavoidable consequence of coming to this place at such a young age."

"You *ate* our pasts?" Marci squeaked. "How does that work? And what about the future? Do you eat that, too?"

The dragon looked insulted. "Of course not. The past of all dragons and their servants is mine by right of my station, not to mention my only fuel in this empty place. The future, however, belongs to my brother, Dragon Sees Eternity, but he left here long ago to live with the dragons who survived the collapse in their new home."

"So there's another one of you?" Marci asked, getting excited. "Like, on Earth?"

"Is that not what I just said?" the dragon rumbled, shaking its huge head. "We were created to be a pair, but there's not much for a guardian of the future to do in a world that no longer has one. So he left, and now it's just me."

Julius couldn't believe there could possibly be a dragon this big on Earth without *everyone* knowing. But interesting as all this was, it wasn't why they were here. "I'm sorry you lost your brother," he said as tactfully as he could. "But if he's in charge of the future, then maybe he's the one we need to talk to? You see, we came here because another dragon, a seer named Estella, is using chains like these," he pointed at the tangled chains that made up the ground, "to control several members of my clan. I need to find a way to break them."

"You don't need my brother for *that*," Dragon Sees the Beginning huffed. "What you ask is impossible. Chains from this place can never be broken."

Julius scowled. That couldn't be right. If Estella's chains of control were unbreakable, then why were they here? Why had Bob even mentioned this place? Before he could open his mouth to ask, though, the giant dragon lowered his head down in front of them.

"It seems you are in need of a lesson from history," it said, its voice deeply pleased. "Do you know how the future got chained in the first place?"

Julius shook his head, and the dragon grinned wide, launching gleefully into the story like it had just been waiting for this chance. "Ages ago, back when this was a proper plane, every clan had seers. Not just one, either, but dozens, whole teams working together to shape the future to their liking. But, dragons being dragons, this brought them into constant conflict with other clans who were building different futures, ones where *they* ruled. Naturally, it was always the cleverest seers, the ones who used their knowledge of the future most audaciously, who came out the victors in these skirmishes. But no dragon clan has ever accepted defeat gracefully, and it was only a matter of time before a seer on the verge of losing tried something truly desperate and accidentally figured out a way to turn the future back in his favor *permanently*."

"How did that work?" Marci asked. "I thought the whole point of being a seer was looking into the future and meddling with stuff until you got the outcome you wanted, but nothing's really sure until it actually happens, right?"

The dragon grinned. "Not with this. Despite being grossly out-maneuvered by his enemies, this particular seer was very cunning. He knew he'd already been beaten and that the future he wanted was now so unlikely as to be functionally impossible. So, like any good dragon facing defeat, he changed the game. Since manipulating his own future was no longer an option, he reached further still, twisting the relationship between time, probability, and the nature of dragon magic itself to create a situation that allowed him to *purchase* one future over another."

Julius's breath caught. That was *exactly* what Estella had said, that the future was bought and paid for. But, "How can you *buy* the future?"

"By trading one for another," the dragon replied, its voice taking on a lecturing tone. "When it comes to seer magic, all potential futures are simply matters of probability. Some outcomes—such as what happens when you drop a stone—are so likely as to be practically guaranteed. Drop a stone, and it will fall. Others—such as the rise and fall of one particular dragon clan over another—are more fluid. Traditionally, seers combat this by using their cunning to influence key critical events in a timeline until their desired outcome becomes as unavoidable as that falling stone. But achieving that level of certainty is very difficult when multiple seers are all trying to influence the same events at once. For our wayward seer, it was nigh impossible, and so the question became, how can we create a fixed point? How can we forge a chain of events *so* guaranteed that no decision or stroke of random chance can possibly change or upset it?"

The dragon stopped there, looking down expectantly at Julius and Marci. "Uh," Julius said at last. "I don't—"

"*Potential*," the dragon interrupted with a grin. "Seers draw their power from time, and time is infinite. Unfortunately, that's a very difficult sort of power to leverage since, as your highly perceptive mortal pointed out earlier, time marches at a fixed rate. No matter how far you can see down the line of time, you can't go out and gather it up, because it hasn't happened yet. *But*, until a future event actually does or does not take place, there is always the *potential* for it to occur, and that potential has a certain amount of magical weight when you're talking about two seers fighting over a future."

"You mean, if two seers are fighting over two possible futures, the one who has the timeline with the highest potential will win?" Marci asked.

"Precisely," the dragon said, nodding happily. "But—and here's the trick—that seer with the winning timeline doesn't actually have to cash all that potential *on that specific future*. Strictly speaking, when it comes to seer magic, the magical weight of any given future is interchangeable. It can be applied anywhere, any *when*. And if you gather enough of it together and invest all of it in one specific chain of events, then you can create a future *so* potentially likely that nothing—not other seers, not even the decisions of those involved—can keep it from coming true."

The dragon finished with a proud flourish, but Julius was utterly lost. "I don't get it."

"I think it's like a magical version of potential energy," Marci said, tapping her fingers on her chin. "Like, if you're a seer, and your powers are entirely based around seeing and manipulating the future, then any event that *could* happen carries a magical weight based on its likelihood. Normally, seers increase the potential of a specific future by going around and influencing events in the present, but this one seer found a way to cheat. Rather than trying to influence what will happen by meddling in what's going on right now, he just looked into his own future, grabbed everything that was likely to happen, and then used the massive weight of all those potential events to reinforce the one timeline that he actually wanted until no one else could move it."

"Bra*va*," the dragon said, eyes gleaming. "You *are* a clever mortal, aren't you?"

Marci preened under the dragon's praise, but Julius's mind was whirling. "I think I get it," he said. "But if future events have magical weight based on their potential, and you use that magic to force the future *you* want over all the others, what happens to that potential? It seems to me that, if you're burning something for power, it's going to get used up."

Dragon Sees the Beginning sighed. "And thus we come to how things went wrong," he said darkly. "You are exactly right, young Heartstriker. At its most basic level, what our rogue seer discovered was a way of trading the vast potential of multiple possible futures for one specific chain of events. As you might imagine, it takes an absolutely enormous amount of potential futures to force even a minor guaranteed happening. And the more resistance you need to overcome—either from other seers fighting back or because the timeline you're trying to force was already extremely unlikely—the more power, which is to say the more *future*, you need to expend to push it through."

"So it's a terribly inefficient exchange," Marci said. "You have to slash and burn a ton of the future to get even a minor guaranteed outcome."

"Precisely," the dragon said. "At the time, of course, no one saw a problem with that. After all, there's only ever one actual timeline that comes to pass. That means all other potential futures are destined to be wasted by definition, so why not use them? Also, time is infinite. Who cares if the exchange rate is inefficient when there's literally no end to the power you're exchanging?"

"So how did it go wrong, then?" Julius asked. "I'm assuming all the seers started doing this?"

Dragon Sees the Beginning nodded. "Every single one. It was a revolution. Why scrabble around influencing events in the present when you could just buy an outcome with a potential future you weren't even using? Within a year, every significant event—births, deaths, wars, even the outcomes of races—was determined by chains of events bought in advance by seers and paid for with the future. When two clans clashed, victory no longer belonged to the cleverest or most cunning, but to the seer who was willing to pay the most. This went on for centuries, and then, without warning, the future began to run out."

"Run out?" Marci said. "How is that possible? You just said time is infinite."

"*Time* is infinite," the dragon replied. "But a seer's reach is not." He looked back to Julius. "In their desire to win, your ancestors recklessly burned all of the future they could see until, eventually, there was no immediate future left. Every potential outcome, every possible future where dragons existed that the seers could reach had been grabbed and leveraged until there was nothing left, and when that happened, our world ended."

"Ended," Julius repeated. "You mean, time just stopped? Just like that?"

"Just. Like. That," the dragon growled. "By the time the seers realized what was happening, we had less than an hour left to evacuate. The dragons you know are the descendants of those who escaped, the ones smart enough to run. The rest—the ones who ignored the warnings or who refused to leave their lands and hoards—simply ceased to exist, along with their treasures." Dragon Sees the Beginning turned to gaze up at the blood-red moon. "Of all the futures of our world, only one second remains. As guardian of the past, I stayed behind to stretch out that moment as long as I could. That is the time I exist in when no one else is here, the reason I, too, am not sucked into the void beyond worlds. Everything else—the desert, the sky, the future represented in these chains—you brought in with you, a construct of a lost home taken from your racial memory. When you leave, it will vanish again, and I will return to the frozen stillness where nothing exists but memories. The last figment of our once great home."

The great dragon said this with a sadness Julius felt to his bones. Having been born on Earth, he'd never given much thought to where his ancestors had lived before that. Now, though, despite only seeing a shadow of a fragment pulled from memories he'd never known he had, Julius felt the loss of their home like an ache. But it was the *waste*, the greedy, reckless gall of what had been done here, that made him shake with rage. "I never knew," he said, clenching his fists as he stared up at the giant dragon who wasn't a dragon at all. "How did I not know this!?"

"Because dragons are proud," the guardian said. "They would rather look to the conquest of a new land than remember how they destroyed the old."

"That's not pride," Julius spat. "That's arrogance."

"That's dragon nature."

Dragon Sees the Beginning chuckled as he said this, but Julius didn't think it was funny at all. They'd had a home, a place with no spirits trying to kill them where they could live without displacing anyone else, and they'd burned it to the ground. The story of how his ancestors had destroyed their own future trying to one-up each other was the most entitled, draconic, *stupid* thing Julius had ever heard, and given the way most dragons still acted, he could absolutely see it happening again. It *was* happening again. Right now, Estella had traded who-knew-what to chain his clan to a future of her choosing just so she could beat Bob, and the whole thing was so petty and wasteful and stupid, it made him feel ill. It also gave him an idea.

"You remember everything that's ever happened here, right?"

Dragon Sees the Beginning nodded. "All history is my domain."

"So do you remember a seer named Estella the Northern Star who came here last month?"

The dragon's expression darkened. "I do, but I would not suggest following her example, young Heartstriker."

"I have no intention to," Julius promised. "But is there any way you can tell me what future she bought?"

The dragon lowered its head with a thoughtful growl. "No," it said at last. "As my name would imply, I look backwards, not forwards. But I *can* tell you that, whatever timeline she bought, she traded all of her potential futures to do so."

"*All?*" Julius said, horrified. "How could she trade *all* her futures? Wouldn't that mean she would die at the end?"

"It does," the dragon said. "Though I don't think she considered that an issue."

"How is *dying* not an issue?" Marci asked.

"Because, like the seer who first discovered how to trade away the future, Estella was already beaten," the dragon said sadly. "I read her past just as I read yours. I saw how your brother, Brohomir, had cut her off at every turn, walling off her future piece by piece until only decline was left. When she arrived in this place, her mountain of potential futures was little bigger than a hill. Her hatred, however, was stronger than ever, and being a seer, she knew she had no hope of victory left. Given those circumstances, the exchange of a long but bleak future for certain victory over the enemy who'd trapped her in that situation to begin with seemed like a fair trade, indeed."

That was unexpectedly depressing, and for a moment, Julius actually felt sorry for Estella. But while he was sympathetic to how desperate she must have felt, none of that excused what she'd done to his siblings and Katya. Or to him and Marci, for that matter. "Okay," he said. "If you can't tell us what future she bought, can you at least tell us how many chains she left with?"

"Four," the dragon replied immediately. "She left here with four chains, all of varying lengths. I'm not sure about the shorter ones since, again, the future isn't my domain, but I'm reasonably certain that the longest was for three days."

"Are you serious?" Marci said. "Estella traded her entire future for *three days?*" The dragon nodded, and she whistled. "That's one *bad* exchange rate."

"She's fighting Bob," Julius reminded her. "She probably needed the power." Still, hearing she'd left with only four chains was a relief. That accounted for Chelsie, Conrad, Amelia, and Svena, meaning that Justin—whatever trouble he might be in—at least wasn't bound to Estella's future. "You said the longest chain she bought was three days. Is that twenty-four-hour days?"

"Sun up to sun down is the traditional definition," the dragon said. "So whatever that means for your realm."

Julius scowled, thinking the timing through. Since Svena had been acting strange the longest, she was probably the target of Estella's longest, three-day chain. At the party on Friday night, Bob said Svena's future had vanished that morning, so if the chains lasted from sunrise to sunset, and Friday morning was sunrise number one, then Svena's chain would run out at sunset on Sunday, the same time as Ian and Svena's mating flight.

That timing lined up *way* too well. Other than the party where she'd set all this up, the mating flight was the one time Estella was guaranteed to have Bethesda and her children in one place, which made it the obvious time to strike. That timing would also explain why all the other chains had been shorter. Estella had needed Svena's obedience from the very beginning, but she'd hadn't needed his siblings until right before she was ready to kick her final plan into action. But while Julius was certain all of Estella's schemes would come crashing together at the mating flight, he still had no clue what she was actually trying to accomplish.

"Mother's the obvious target," he said, thinking out loud. "But it doesn't feel like enough. If she just wanted to kill Bethesda, she could have attacked at the party and been done with it. Sure she would have died for it, but we've already established that Estella doesn't care about that, so why go through all this trouble? Why drag everything out for three days and spend her own future to bring Conrad, Chelsie, and Amelia into it?"

"Sounds like business as usual to me," Marci said, rolling her eyes. "From what I've seen of your brother, seers can't go to the bathroom without turning it into a chess game."

"True," Julius agreed. "But this is too twisty even by seer standards." And the more he thought about it, the more the whole thing felt wrong.

He'd always assumed Estella was gunning for Bethesda since the Three Sisters' seer made no bones about wanting to bring down their clan and cutting off the head would be the obvious way to do that. That said, though, when did seers *ever* do what was obvious? He had no doubt that Estella hated Bethesda with a passion, but when you looked at what she'd actually *done* since her return on Friday, all of it had been aimed at Bob. Threatening his clan, taking over the siblings he actually cared about, cheating at his game—they were all stabs at her fellow seer, the only enemy on the board who could actually hurt her.

Thinking about it that way made Julius feel like he actually had a handle on Estella's plans for the first time since she'd crashed his mother's party. If you assumed her target was, and always had been, Bob, then all of this convoluted craziness made a lot more sense. But while he could now see Estella's endgame, he still had to figure out a way to stop it. Normally, he'd say that was impossible, that a dragon like him just didn't have the tools to fight a seer. But his situation at the moment was hardly normal, and as he looked down at the giant, breathing mountain of possibilities that was his own future, a crazy idea started to form in his head.

"Hypothetically speaking," he said, looking up at the giant dragon, who'd sat patiently observing this whole time. "Can anyone pick up one of these chains, or do you have to be a seer?"

"Anyone can trade their future for certainty, yes," the dragon said. "Though, since only seers can actually look inside the chains and see which future is which, you might not be happy with your purchase."

Julius cursed under his breath. There went that plan. Not that he'd been particularly keen to trade his future away, but chains seemed to be all they had to work with around here. He was trying to think of some other, cleverer reason Bob had sent them to this place when Dragon Sees the Beginning added. "*I* might be able to help you, though."

That was the last thing he'd expected the giant dragon to say, and his head popped up like a cork. "You?"

The dragon nodded, and Julius gasped. "*Why?*"

In hindsight, that was not the most politic response. Fortunately, the dragon looked more amused than offended. "I find you interesting," it rumbled, leaning down to lay its massive head on the ground, putting its milky-white eyes level with Julius's own. "You are by far the oddest dragon I've seen in a very, very, *very* long time. I've read through your past several times already over the course of our conversation, but even when I observe your decision making process step by step, I cannot comprehend *why* you make the choices you do. It's a fascinating conundrum you've given me, and as you might imagine given my circumstances, I value new entertainment very highly. So, as a show of my gratitude, I'm going to offer you a deal. You tell me what future you want to purchase, and I'll put it together for you and tell you how much it will cost."

"You can do that?" Marci said, clearly skeptical. "I thought you only dealt in the past? And you said only seers can see into the chains! How will you even know what you're doing?"

"Being a construct with dominion over all that has ever been isn't entirely without its benefits," the dragon said with a sniff. "I might not have my brother's skill with the future, but I can see into the chains well enough, and I've watched seers do this uncountable times." The white eyes went back to Julius. "I'll certainly do a better job than *he* could."

That was definitely true. "Sounds good to me," Julius said. "What are my options?"

"Anything you like," Dragon Sees the Beginning replied, lifting its head back into the sky to get a panoramic view of the mountain of chains around them. "You are quite young. You have an entire lifetime of possible futures ahead of you, and that's not even counting the vast potential that your perceptive, presumptuous companion brings to the table."

Marci crossed her arms with a glare. "I thought you said my future was merely 'good for a mortal.'"

"But I didn't say *how* good," the dragon replied with a cryptic smile. "I'm not entirely sure why—again, this isn't my area—but it seems your mortal's connection to the…whatever it is she has on her shoulders has the potential to completely change the course of magic on her home plane."

Marci's whole face lit up. "You mean Ghost?" she asked excitedly. "How?"

"I don't know," the dragon said. "Nor do I particularly care. I'm just telling you what I see in the chains. Personally, I'm far more intrigued by the fact that young Julius here appears to be intricately linked to the future of the Heartstrikers as a whole."

Julius blinked. "*Me?*"

"Yes, it's quite fascinating," the dragon said, leaning down toward the chains for a closer look. "Brohomir seems to be using you as a sort of linchpin, a fixed point around which the rest of your family's futures, including his own, pivot. I'm not sure what he's hoping to accomplish—again, I'm not a seer—but the configuration he's created gives your future an absolutely *enormous* amount of potential, far more than any single dragon should ever have on his own. If you were to cash all of that in, why, you could be the new dragon king of your world."

"Dragon *king?*" Julius repeated skeptically. "As in king of dragons?"

"As in king of everything," Dragon Sees the Beginning said, turning back toward them with a smile that sent shivers down Julius's spine. "Think about it, young Heartstriker. Between your mortal and Brohomir's machinations, you have enough potential here to buy any future you desire, *without* sacrificing your own. With one chain, you could defeat everyone who's ever looked down on you. All of your problems, the things that bother you, we could make them all go away and give you a lifetime of custom-made paradise in their place. Power, respect, fear, wealth, everything a dragon desires could be yours with the click of a claw, and all for the price of a future." The dragon's smile widened. "What do you say? Would that not be glorious?"

"Maybe," Julius said. "But not at that price." He looked at Marci, who'd gone very pale. "Marci's future isn't mine to trade. Same goes for the ones Bob wrapped around me and anything else you see in there. Even if I could trade my own future for everything you just mentioned, I wouldn't, because it was thinking like that that messed everything up in the first place. Also, I'm not actually interested in all that stuff."

The dragon blinked in surprise. "You're *not*? But you would be a king! Don't you want to see your enemies crushed before you?"

"Not particularly," Julius said. Honestly, he was having a hard time imagining a future he wanted *less* than the one Dragon Sees the Beginning had just described. Sure, being all powerful sounded fun, but Julius had met a lot of dragons with a lot of power, and with the exception of his Mother, whom he *never* wanted to be like, not a one of them had seemed actually happy.

"Thank you for the offer," he said. "But minus the current crisis, I'm actually pretty content with my life as it is. If you could just please find me a chain that will let me stop Estella's, that would be great."

He'd tried to word all of that as politely as possible. Refusing gifts was the fastest way to insult a dragon, and offending the only force who could possibly help him with this was the last thing Julius wanted to do. By the time he finished, though, Dragon Sees the Beginning was looking at him with a strange mix of horror and wonder.

"I knew you were odd from the beginning, but now I think I see why." The dragon smiled its terrifying, toothy smile. "I'm beginning to understand why my brother sent you here, Julius the Nice Dragon."

"I don't believe I've met your brother," Julius said nervously. He'd remember if he'd met another dragon like this.

"Perhaps not yet," Dragon Sees the Beginning said. "But you *will*, and to the dragon of the future, that's the same thing. Besides, no one makes it back to this place without Dragon Sees Eternity pulling the strings in some way. Most of the time the reasoning is obvious, but you were a real puzzle. Now, though, I see. If a dragon can come here and turn down unlimited power, there might be hope for us yet."

The dragon said this like it was a revelation, but Julius had no idea what was going on. "I—"

"Right, right," the dragon said, snaking its huge head back around to the wall of chains. "Now that we've established you don't want to rule the world, what sort of future *are* you looking for? I'm not as good at this as an actual seer, but there's plenty here for me to work with. Given the materials at hand, I'm reasonably certain I can fashion something that will force your plan through." The dragon glanced back. "You *do* have a plan, right?"

Julius did, actually. It was a pretty long shot, but it was the only situation he could think of that defeated Estella's objectives without actually having to go directly against the four chains she'd paid her entire future for. It took a while to explain exactly what he wanted to Dragons Sees the Beginning, but by the time he finished, the guardian was smiling wider than ever.

"It certainly is thinking outside the box," the dragon said. "Not to mention you'll be creating a paradox."

"Is that a problem?" Julius asked.

"Only if you don't enjoy watching seers lose their composure," Dragon Sees the Beginning said with an evil grin. "No, this is exactly the sort of thing I was hoping for when you showed up. I'm only sad I won't be able to see it myself until the next visitor brings it in as part of their past."

Julius let out a relieved breath. "So you'll do it?"

Rather than answer, the dragon lifted a long forearm from deep in its coils, running its massive claws over the piled chains like an astronomer searching a star chart for one particular dot in the night sky. After several minutes, the dragon plunged its claws into the wall to pull out—not a snaking rope like Estella's—but a black nubbin of chain no longer than the top joint of Julius's pinky.

"Um," he said when Dragon Sees the Beginning held it up for them to admire. "Will that be enough?"

"Quite," the dragon assured him. "The links are a measure of time, not power, and unlike Estella, you're buying minutes, not days. That said, this is a *very* unlikely future, and there is still the matter of your payment."

"If you're sure it'll work, I'm happy to pay," Julius said. And then, because he could already see Marci opening her mouth, he added. "Alone."

Marci shot him a glare, which Julius ignored. The dragon, however, seemed to be deep in thought. "The payment for this one will be steep," it said. "As I said, it's quite unlikely, and—as was also aforementioned—the exchange rate of the potential for the definite is quite steep. Further complicating the matter is the fact that neither of us is actually a seer. Put all this together, and I'm afraid I can't actually choose what will be taken."

"So what does that mean?" Julius asked.

The dragon's face grew dour. "It means that neither of us has the control necessary to pick which future you will pay. The trade will be decided arbitrarily at the point of transfer."

"You mean it's just going to randomly take part of his future?" Marci asked, horrified. When the dragon nodded, she whirled to face Julius. "Don't do it."

"I have to," he said. "If I don't do this, and Estella wins, we're probably all dead anyway. And it's not like I'll miss stuff that hasn't even happened."

"But what if it takes something you really want?" she asked. "What if it takes the one future where things are actually good?"

"Then I'll make another," Julius said, smiling at her. "Like Bob is forever saying, the future is made of our decisions, and it's never set."

That's why Bob was always bending over backwards to make sure they understood how seers actually worked. All those seemingly random lectures on seer magic weren't just him bragging, or even making conversation. He'd been *teaching* Julius how the system worked so that, when the time came, he would understand that Estella and Bob didn't actually control his future at all. He did. *He* was the one whose decisions created the path of his future, and the more Julius thought about that, the more confident he became.

"It doesn't matter if I lose some vague potential," he said firmly, reaching out to take Marci's hand. "So long as I've got even one timeline to work with, I can make the choices I need to make it good, because it's my future. Not Bob's and not Estella's. Mine. I can do this. For once, I really believe that. Trust me."

"I do trust you," she grumbled, glaring up at the giant dragon. "I just don't trust *him*. Or the random decisions of *these*."

She stomped her foot on the wiggling chain floor, and Julius chuckled. "That makes two of us," he said, leaning in to rest his forehead against hers. "But we don't have to trust them. If Bob's right, and our decisions make the future, then we just have to trust us."

"You mean 'be yourself'?" Marci replied in a terrifyingly accurate Bob impression.

Julius nodded. "Just don't tell him he was right."

"He's a seer," Marci reminded with a laugh. "He already knows."

That was actually very comforting, and Julius turned back to Dragon Sees the Beginning. "I'll pay it."

"Excellent," the dragon said, flicking its claws. "Catch."

It took all of Julius's discipline not to dodge the tiny black chain flying like a bullet at his chest. But though he saw it hit, he didn't feel a thing. The black links simply vanished into his shirt. There was no pain or trauma like he'd seen Chelsie go through in the video. He didn't even feel like something had been taken. "Um, did it work?"

"Only one way to find out," Dragon Sees the Beginning replied. "It was a true pleasure to meet you, young Heartstriker. Give my regards to my brother when you see him."

Julius had already opened his mouth to ask how soon that would be when the layer of chains cracked opened under his feet, dropping him and Marci into the void.

CHAPTER NINETEEN

The sun was low over Heartstriker Mountain when two dragons—
one enormous with scales white as new snow, the other smaller
and covered in rich, royal blue feathers—shot out of the balcony
that opened into Bethesda the Heartstriker's throne room. They
circled each other in the cloudless desert sky, shining like jewels
in the evening light, and then the white dragoness put on a sudden burst of speed, shooting toward the horizon. The smaller male
matched her immediately, folding his wings like a fighter jet as he
set off in hot pursuit.

He would never catch her.

Estella took a deep breath, watched the flash of her sister's
frosted wings until she vanished into the distance. Only when she
was sure Svena was safely away from what was about to happen did
the Northern Star finally turn to face her host.

As always, Bethesda the Heartstriker was dressed like a gaudy
mess. Where Estella looked regal and elegant in a simple, sleeveless
white dress, Bethesda looked like she'd spent the last hour rolling
in her treasury. Her indecently low-cut, golden gown was little more
than a backdrop for the giant, tacky clusters of jewelry she wore
at her neck, ears, arms, wrists, fingers, ankles, and feet. But even
though the Heartstriker was displaying her wealth so hard Estella
was surprised she could still move, the clan head *still* fell short. The
only piece of real value in the whole gaudy display was her headdress: a solid gold Aztec crown commissioned for her by her father
back when she'd been the Quetzalcoatl's spoiled princess. *That* was

actually lovely, but the rest of it reeked of someone who'd spent her whole life trying too hard. But then, "trying too hard" was Bethesda in a nutshell, as the trashy snake proved yet again when she turned to address Estella as an equal.

"They'll be out until midnight at least," she said, her crimson lips curling into a smug smile. "Ian always does things *properly*."

The blatant suggestion in her voice turned Estella's stomach. It was not quite time yet, though, so she hid her disgust, though no force in the world could make her smile as she followed the Heartstriker back into her throne room to the banquet table that had been set up beneath the Quetzalcoatl's suspended skull.

That sight was enough to turn her stomach again, and Estella's jaw clenched. The God of Hurricanes deserved so much better than *this*, reduced to a mere decoration, his teeth stolen so his murderous daughter could have weapons for her spawn. He only had two fangs left at this point: the long one that usually belonged to Bethesda's baby knight, and the one that none of the Heartstriker whelps had yet managed to yank from his head. Neither Fang would ever be used again after tonight, of course, but Estella was still sorely tempted to break them both, if only to see the Heartstriker's face when her treasured weapons were reduced to splinters. She was still enjoying that mental image when Bethesda's smarmy voice interrupted her.

"Champagne?" she asked, holding up a gold-foiled bottle. "I had a case flown in from my son Evan's vineyard in France just for this occasion."

"No."

Bethesda's eyebrows shot up. "Are you sure? It's the best in the world, the private reserve of a winery that had been run by the same family since the seventeen hundreds before we forced them out of the business."

"No," Estella said again, not even bothering to hide her disgust at the blatant name dropping. As always, though, the censure rolled right off the Heartstriker's back. She just shrugged and popped the cork to help herself.

"Now that we're alone," Bethesda said, filling a tall flute with golden, bubbly champagne. "I think it's time we dropped the act and discussed the terms of your surrender."

"I wouldn't discuss that with anyone," Estella said coldly. "Least of all you."

"Come now," the Heartstriker laughed. "Your arrogance is legendary, Northern Star, but surely you've comprehended your situation by now. This room, my mountain, and all the airspace for a mile in every direction is entirely under my control. I have wards set down by my best mages, mortal and dragon, specifically constructed to prevent that little teleportation trick you used to crash my party last time. Fifty of my most talented children are already waiting in the wings. All I have to do is think the order, and they'll rush in to tear off your head so I can add it to my collection. You are completely surrounded in every meaning of the word. At this point, the only choice you have left is whether you enter my service as a slave or a trophy."

By the time she finished, Bethesda's voice was so smug it could have curdled milk. Normally, that would have made Estella furious, but not this time. *This* time, she savored it, letting the silence stretch until even the Heartstriker's victorious grin faltered.

"Nothing to say to that?" she asked, taking a sip of champagne. "Have I rendered the Seer of the Three Sisters speechless at last?"

"Not at all," Estella replied with a smile of her own. "I was simply enjoying the moment before your fall."

"*My* fall?" Bethesda laughed. "I see you've finally gone senile. *I* won't be the one who…"

Her voice trailed off as magic began to build in the air. Not Estella's magic, either, but a power Bethesda knew perfectly well, as evidenced by the pleasingly ashy pallor of fear that washed over her face. "Frieda!" she barked, dropping her glass as she jumped back. "Now!"

Nothing happened.

"*Now!*" Bethesda yelled again, her green eyes wide as they went to the throne room doors. Doors that weren't opening.

"They can't hear you," Estella said slowly, enjoying every moment of the Heartstriker's fear as Amelia's building magic reached a crescendo. "No one can."

Bethesda turned with a hiss, making a break for the hidden door behind her throne, but she was miles too late. The portal was already opening in the air beside her, creating a perfect doorway through space as Chelsie, Conrad, and Amelia stepped into the room.

"Chelsie!" Bethesda screamed, the name sharp with magic as the Heartstriker stabbed her finger at Estella. "Kill her!"

But whatever power was behind that order, it didn't work, because when Chelsie drew her Fang, she pointed it straight at her mother. Conrad followed suit, drawing his massive sword as he moved to block off any escape through the balcony. But despite the swords pointed her direction, Bethesda had eyes only for eldest daughter.

Amelia, of course, ignored her. She simply walked to Estella's side and lifted her hands, filling the room with magic once again as she covered the wards Bethesda had been boasting about only seconds before with an even stronger barrier of her own.

"There," Estella said, looking down on her cornered prey. "That should prevent any interruptions."

Bethesda's green eyes flicked to the various exits, and then she straightened to her full height. "It won't work," she said haughtily, like she was still the one with power. "I don't know what you've done to achieve this compliance, but these are *my* children. My dragons in every way."

Estella smiled, letting her true hatred show on her face for the first time since she'd arrived. "Not any more."

Chelsie stepped closer as she said this, and Bethesda's confident sneer began to waver. "You're bluffing," she snapped as her hand crept behind her back. "Did you think that *I*, of *all* dragons, would not have safeguards in place against treason?"

"Quite the contrary," Estella said, enjoying this to the hilt. "I'm counting on it. Let's put them to the test. Conrad?"

The Heartstriker Champion stepped forward, raising his sword in a smooth sweep. He was about to bring it down on her head when Bethesda's arm, the one she'd snuck behind her back, shot out again, and Conrad's sword went flying, clattering away across the throne room's stone floor before sliding to a stop inches from the balcony's sheer edge.

"What did I tell you?" the Heartstriker crowed, lifting her hand to show Estella the bone-colored sword clutched in her fingers.

Estella arched a pale eyebrow. Even with her seer's perception, she had no idea how Bethesda had hidden a *sword* in that flimsy excuse for a dress, but there was no question that the weapon in her hand was a Fang of the Heartstriker. "I should have guessed you'd keep one for yourself."

"Of course," the dragon scoffed. "Who do you think I am? The Fangs of the Heartstriker are the teeth of my clan. Who else should hold the strongest one but me?"

"But *I*," Estella corrected with a smile, enjoying the dragon's confusion at her lack of fear.

Why should she be afraid? Bethesda's supposed trump card actually made her life a great deal easier. Even for a seer, the Fangs of the Heartstriker were difficult to pin down. This was partially because, as body parts of a dead dragon with no future, they didn't follow the normal rules, and partially because Brohomir had taken enormous pains to hide them. It was common knowledge that one belonged to the clan's Champion, one to the Enforcer, and one, the Fifth Blade, to whatever idiot Bethesda conned into being her knight. But even counting the sixth Fang that had never actually been pulled from the Quetzalcoatl's head, that still left two Fangs of the Heartstriker unaccounted for even with Estella's now perfect knowledge of the future. Now that Bethesda had revealed her hand at last, though, total victory over the Heartstriker had just become one Fang simpler.

"What's the matter, white snake?" Bethesda taunted. "Can't you see the future? Because you wouldn't be smiling like that if you could."

"It's precisely because I can see that I'm smiling," Estella replied, shaking her head. "A sword in your hand makes no difference, Broodmare. You're still outnumbered."

"It makes *all* the difference," the Heartstriker snarled, lifting her blade high.

The moment her arm was fully extended, Chelsie gasped in pain, dropping her own sword, which immediately flew to Bethesda. Conrad's Fang did the same, flying from where it had fallen moments before. By the time Bethesda lowered her sword again, both of her children's Fangs were floating behind her like familiars, their tips pointed directly at Estella's heart.

"Didn't see that one coming, did you, seer?" Bethesda crowed, her face split in a triumphant grin as she held up her sword for Estella to see. "Every Fang of the Heartstriker has its own abilities, but mine is the First Fang that controls them all. Now, you're going to feel their bite. *All* of them."

She raised her blade to her lips as she finished, and the room flooded with magic as Bethesda began to change. Behind her, the swords she'd taken from her children pulled closer, the blades already sparking with her father's green fire. If Estella hadn't been prepared, the display would have been truly terrifying. Bethesda alone was nothing, but three Fangs of the Heartstriker were no laughing matter. But while Estella hadn't foreseen this specific bit about the swords, Bethesda's plan to change into her true form would have been obvious even without her knowledge of the future, and the counter she'd arranged was probably Estella's favorite part of the night.

"Amelia," she said sweetly, stepping back to avoid the green flames licking at Bethesda's feet. "Now."

The Planeswalker obeyed instantly. Bethesda didn't even have time to react before her daughter's hand shot out, launching a wave of fire that sent the Heartstriker, and all her swords, flying.

With the perfect irony that only came from properly executed seer work, Bethesda landed on her throne, crashing into the stone chair so hard it cracked. She was still pushing herself up from the wreckage when Estella climbed up to join her. "Tell me again, Heartstriker," she cooed. "Why should I be afraid?"

Bethesda's only reply was a challenging growl as she tensed. A growl that faded to a whimper when nothing happened.

"*What?*" she roared, staring down at her hands. Her still *human* hands. "Why am I not a dragon? *What did you do?*"

"Don't you recognize it?" Estella asked, her eyes wide with feigned innocence. "I got the idea from you."

Bethesda's fury turned to horror as the truth finally dawned. "You *sealed* me!"

Her scream was music to Estella's ears. "I told you the sword wouldn't do any good," she said, turning to Conrad, who'd just climbed up the short set of stairs that surrounded the throne's raised dais to join them. "Restrain her."

"*No!*" Bethesda cried, fighting like a wildcat as her massive son grabbed her. "I am your clan head! Your *mother*! *You can't do this!*"

Again, magic pounded through the orders, and again, her children ignored her completely. Not that it stopped Bethesda from trying. She screamed the whole way down, fighting like a wild animal, but it did no good. Now that Amelia had sealed her dragon, she was little stronger than the human she appeared to be. Conrad handled her with ease, dragging her back down the steps and forcing her onto her knees on the ground at Estella's feet.

"Now *this* is a sight I've always wanted to see," Estella said, yanking Bethesda's head up by her long, perfect, ink-black hair. "I was contemplating plucking out those famous eyes, but after seeing your collection in the hall, I think I'll leave them in. They'll be so striking when I turn *your* head into a taxidermy trophy."

"Try it and see," Bethesda snarled. "I won't go down like this. You can't kill me so easily."

"Please," Estella scoffed, letting her go. "If I'd just wanted to *kill* you, I could have done that at any time. But I didn't trade my future for something as cheap and tawdry as your life. Even now, killing you is just a means to an end. One more step in a long plan.

Though, of course," her lips curled in a bloodthirsty grin, "that doesn't mean I can't enjoy it."

The Heartstriker began to shake, though to her credit, it was with fury, not fear. "Do it, then," she snarled, baring her white teeth. "*If* you can. I have a seer, too, remember."

"I never forget my true audience," Estella replied, stepping back. "That's why I've arranged for your death to have a little pageantry." She clapped her hands, and a new figure appeared on the other side of Amelia's portal. A tall, angry dragon with eyes like green embers and a sword made of ice. He didn't say a word as he stepped into his mother's throne room, but by the time he reached Estella's side, Bethesda looked truly afraid for the first time.

"Justin?" she said, her voice wavering. "Darling? What are you doing?"

"Isn't it obvious?" Estella said, draping her arms over Justin's shoulders. "Brohomir does *so* love his ironic twists, and what could be more ironic than the great Bethesda struck down by her most loyal son? Not that anyone could blame him. Being left to die at the hands of your greatest enemy because your mother is too proud and spiteful to say the one word that would spare your life *does* tend to shift your world view." She glanced at Justin. "Don't you agree?"

The young dragon said nothing. He just stood there, gripping his new sword in his white-knuckled hands and glaring down at his mother with such focused fury that even the shameless Bethesda cringed.

"I had to do it, sweetheart," she said, her voice all innocence. "It cut me to the core to leave you there. I cried all night, but I had no choice."

"It was one word," Justin growled. "You didn't even have to mean it."

"It was lowering myself!" Bethesda growled back, dropping the hurt mother act as easily as she'd dropped him. "You don't know what Algonquin's like. If I'd given her an inch, she'd have taken the whole clan. I did what I had to do to keep us out of the mess *you* made, and you have the gall to be angry?"

"Typical narcissistic personality," Estella murmured in Justin's ear. "Trying to make her failings sound like your fault. This is exactly the sort of faulty reasoning you'd expect from someone who'd rather throw away their greatest weapon than even lie about saying *please*."

"Don't listen to her!" Bethesda cried, lifting her head as high as she could while still on her knees. "Justin Heartstriker, you are my son, a knight of the mountain! Don't you dare fall for her lies."

"But she's not lying, is she?" Justin said, lifting his sword as he moved in to loom over her. "You're right. I *am* a knight of the mountain, a guardian of what's best for our clan, and that's what I'm going to do."

Bethesda's eyes went wide. "Justin, love, don't do this," she warned, her eyes on the icy blade as he lined the razor sharp edge up with her neck. "Not to me. Not to your mother."

"Don't worry," Justin said, bracing for the strike. "I won't."

He stabbed as he finished, plunging the icy sword, not into his mother, but backwards at the seer behind him.

The seer who was no longer there.

Justin stumbled as his attack found nothing. He rebalanced at once, spinning around to try again, but he hadn't even made it halfway before Chelsie tackled him to the ground. She had him disarmed a second later, sitting on his back with her knee stabbed into his neck as Estella stepped back into range.

"I wish I could say I didn't see that coming," she said, reaching down to retrieve the ice sword from the ground. "But we all know that would be a lie. Still, I have to admit I'm disappointed in you, Justin. The only reason I went through the bother of saving you was to give Brohomir a piece on the board through which to watch my inevitable victory. You were here to give him the chance at a final move, and *that* is all you can manage?"

Justin glowered, and she shook her head. "So disappointing. Where's the grandeur? Where's the drama? I even gave you my best sword in the hopes I'd see something worthy of the dragon who *claims* to be the best seer ever born, but alas. All I get is a sneak attack, and not even a clever one."

"You think I care," Justin growled, fighting ineffectually against Chelsie's hold with everything he had. "The fact that you knew I'd turn on you even after you saved me from Algonquin just proves what I've been saying all along. I am Justin Heartstriker, Knight of the Mountain, the Fifth Blade of Bethesda, and I would rather die with my fangs in your foot than ever betray my clan."

"Is that so?" Estella said, her voice bored. "Then by all means, let's get it over with. Conrad?"

With no more emotion than he'd show a weighted training dummy, Conrad grabbed Justin out from under their sister and threw him clear across the throne room into the wall on the other side. The dragon hit the inlaid stone like a cannonball, cracking the gold and ceramic mosaic depicting Bethesda in all her glory from floor to ceiling. Before he could fall to the ground, Conrad was on top of him, punching him back into the stone wall so hard, his ribs cracked. Justin screamed in pain, but Conrad just kept going, pummeling the younger dragon like he was working a punching bag until Estella said, "Stop."

Conrad stopped instantly, and Justin collapsed on the floor. When it was obvious he wasn't going to be getting up again, the seer turned back to Bethesda, whose face was now as pale as the granite dust hanging in the air.

"There it is," she whispered, reaching down to grab Bethesda's head between her hands. "There's the comprehension." The dragon tried to turn away, but Estella wrenched her right back. "Look at him," she ordered. "That is your most loyal dragon. That is your hope lying beaten on the ground, Heartstriker. That was your final chance. *That* is the difference between your power and mine."

She released the dragon's head, and Bethesda jerked away, her chest heaving like a frightened animal as Estella raised the icy sword she'd taken from Justin.

"I couldn't kill you until I knew you understood," she explained, taking careful aim at the Heartstriker's neck. "I've paid too much for this to accept mere death. I had to see you break, just like your death is going to break your clan, just like I'm going to break everything Brohomir has ever touched. That's what I went to our dead world to purchase. *That* is what I paid for. Not your death or the deaths of your children, but Brohomir's utter defeat. I will smash his dreams to dust and grind his ambition under my feet, and when I am done, I will die satisfied at last, because I will have *won.*"

By the time she finished, Bethesda was shaking. "You are mad," she whispered.

"And you are dead," Estella replied, bringing her sword down.

But then, just as Estella began the strike that would cut the head off of the Heartstriker clan and begin the irreversible downfall of her most hated enemy, something landed on her hand. It was less than nothing, a tiny spattering of black, sandy dust, but it still made Estella freeze, because here, in the moment where every move was planned down to the smallest detail, the dust was a *surprise.* She was trying to decide if it was a significant one when the ceiling opened up, dropping a dragon and his human directly on her head.

• • •

After so long falling through the dark, the sudden burst of light hit Julius like a punch. But while it was instantly obvious he and Marci were finally back in some kind of world and no longer falling through…whatever it was Dragon Sees the Beginning had dropped them into, it took him an embarrassingly long time to actually recognize the huge, golden space as his mother's throne room lit up by the evening sun. That was as far as he got before they crashed down on top of something wiry and wiggling that smelled like an icy sea.

"*Get off me!*"

Julius hadn't even finished landing before the wiggly something threw them off again, launching them both across the room. Julius landed on his feet by pure habit, and then scrambled to catch Marci, who hadn't had his training. When they were both safely on the ground, he finally looked around to see where, and also when, they had landed.

The answer wasn't what he'd hoped. They were, indeed, in his mother's throne room, but the Heartstriker wasn't on her throne. She was on her knees, held there by Chelsie. Amelia was there too, as was Conrad, and, surprisingly, Justin, though he didn't look good at all lying on the floor in front of the cratered wall that he'd obviously been thrown into. But worse than all of that by miles was Estella.

Julius swallowed. Apparently, *she* was the wiry thing they'd landed on, and she looked furious about it, glaring at Julius with murder in her eyes.

"You," she snarled, her pale fingers curling into fists. "It's always *you*! Why am I even surprised?"

Julius glanced at Marci, who shrugged.

"You're *always* in his plans," Estella went on. "Not that I know why. You are literally the lowest of your clan, the bottom of the bottom! If Brohomir wasn't so obsessed with you, I wouldn't even know you existed." She bared her teeth. "What is it he thinks you're going to do here? Talk me to death?"

"It's not too late," Julius said quickly, stealing a quick glance through the balcony at the sun, which was only inches away from the horizon. "We can still come to a mutual—"

"You must be *joking*," Estella scoffed, flinging her hand out. "Kill them!"

The second she barked the order, Chelsie, Conrad, and Amelia turned on Julius and Marci as one. "Oh boy," Marci said, sticking close to Julius as he backed them away. "Not good."

"No," he agreed, edging back as Chelsie and Conrad both leaned down to pick up the Fangs that, for some reason, they hadn't been holding. "Any brilliant ideas?"

"*Me?*" Marci hissed. "You're the one who just sold his future for a solution!"

That he had, but the solution he'd paid for was more of a big picture kind of thing, and he didn't see how it was going to help them now with his three scariest siblings bearing down on them. "I think we should try to separate them," he whispered. "Remember, we don't need to win, just survive."

"Staying alive is always a good plan," Marci said, reaching up to put her hand on Ghost, who was still clinging to her shoulders. "I'll take Amelia, you get the other two. Ready?"

"No," he said, just as Marci yelled, "*Break!*"

She darted sideways, hands flaring as she yanked down her magic and circled to flank Amelia, who was the farthest away. This left Julius alone in the middle of the room with Conrad and Chelsie. He was wondering if he could survive a jump off the balcony when he saw Justin stirring out of the corner of his eye.

That gave him an idea, and he flicked his eyes up toward the massive skull hanging from the throne room's ceiling. Specifically, he looked at the skull's left fang, the one that had been Justin's.

Under normal circumstances, this should have meant Julius wouldn't have a chance of getting it out since Fangs could only be pulled by the hand they accepted, and any sword that preferred Justin would *never* take Julius. But these weren't normal circumstances. This was the timeline leading up to the moment in the future Julius had purchased, the one where he was guaranteed to still be alive, and if Estella could leverage the chain's absolute certainty to make the impossible happen, then so could Julius. He had to do *something* in any case, because while he'd been thinking, Chelsie and Conrad had gotten almost within sword's reach. So, with nothing to lose but his life, Julius put his faith in the future and jumped as high as he could, hands reaching up to grab his grandfather's deadly, curving fang.

He'd never actually touched a dragon bone before this moment. Not surprisingly, it was warm as stone in the desert. It was also stuck fast, and for a terrifying second, Julius was sure he'd just turned himself into a hanging target. But then, right before Chelsie swung to cut him down, an old, terrifying magic bit into his hand, and Julius looked up to see that he was no longer clinging to a tooth. He was holding a sword, the huge, familiar Fifth Blade of Bethesda.

He was also falling.

Big as Justin's sword was, it was still much smaller than the tooth it had been. This size difference meant the sword was no longer connected to the skull, an unexpected consequence that turned up in his favor as Julius plummeted to the ground just in time for Chelsie's attack to slice through the air where he'd been. He landed on his back, rolling when he hit to come up running. That still shouldn't have made a difference given who was after him, but Estella's control must have made Chelsie and Conrad sluggish, because Julius made it all the way across the room without getting snagged, jumping for his downed brother like he was sliding into home plate.

"Justin!"

Justin's eyes popped open. He was lying on his back in a pile of rubble, his face and chest battered like he'd been beaten. "Julius?" he said softly, squinting like he wasn't yet convinced this wasn't a hallucination. "What are you doing here?"

"That's not important," Julius said, holding out his brother's Fang. "I know you're hurt, but do you think you can pull it together long enough to help me save our clan?"

The moment he saw his sword, Justin had eyes for nothing else. "With that, I can do anything," he growled, reaching up to grab the Fang's black-wrapped handle. The second he touched it, Julius felt a much stronger surge of the old magic from earlier, and his brother closed his eyes with a satisfied sigh. Then, like just touching the thing had filled him with new vigor, Justin rolled to his feet, shaking the dust off his body like a dog.

"You've got a lot of explaining to do," he said, glaring at Chelsie and Conrad, who'd spread out to flank them. "But it can wait. I'll take Conrad. You get Chelsie."

"Why do I have to get Chelsie?!" Julius cried, but it was too late. His brother was already swinging, his magic surging as sharp as his Fang as he sliced his enormous sword up, throwing a slash of razor sharp dragon magic across the throne room and into Conrad, who barely dodged in time.

Well, Julius thought, at least Justin was back in fighting form. Guaranteed future or no, he was far less optimistic about own his chances as Chelsie rapidly closed in. "Chelsie," he said quickly, putting up his hands. "Stop. It's me. I don't want to fight—"

She cut him off with a stab at his head. She was so fast, Julius didn't even see her move until the sword was right in front of his nose. But while that should have been the end of him with a sword through the eye, something odd happened. The moment before Chelsie's attack hit, one of the bits of rubble under Julius's feet rolled, making him tilt sideways in just the right way to avoid getting skewered. It was pure, blind luck, the sort of one in a million chance that only happened when you weren't expecting it.

Or when you'd traded your future to buy another where it was guaranteed you didn't die.

That thought gave Julius the oddest burst of confidence he'd ever had, and he turned back to his sister, who was already swinging for him again. This time, though, she was the one who stepped wrong, wobbling at precisely the right moment to send her sword, which had been aimed at Julius's neck, slicing into his shoulder instead.

"Ow!" he cried, grabbing the wound as he jumped backwards. Apparently, not getting killed didn't mean not getting hurt. But though the cut stung like crazy, he could still move, and he did, pumping both arms frantically as he sprinted away from Chelsie as fast as he could.

Think, he had to think. The incredible luck he'd had up until now had convinced him that the future he'd bought was indeed working. But while Julius was confident he'd arrive at the end result he'd asked Dragon Sees the Beginning to arrange, he wasn't a seer, which meant he couldn't look ahead and see how he got there. That left a lot more up to blind faith than he was comfortable with, but at least he wouldn't have to hold out much longer. He could see the sun setting through his mother's balcony, getting closer to the horizon by the second. All he had to do was keep it together a little—

A familiar scream shot through the air, turning his blood to ice. He skidded to a stop, whirling around just in time to see Marci fly through the air to crash into the throne room doors.

Julius had never run so fast in his life. He wasn't sure his feet actually touched the ground until he was beside her. "Marci!" he shouted, dropping to his knees as he grabbed her cold hands. "*Marci!*"

Her eyes popped open with a gasp, and she sat up. "Whoa," she whispered, reaching up touch the trickle of blood coming out of her nose. "*That* didn't work."

"What didn't work?" he asked frantically, running his hands over her arms, legs, and torso to make sure nothing was broken. "What did you do?"

Marci nodded across the room at Amelia, who looked pissed even through Estella's mind control. "Turns out it's a lot harder to suck magic out of dragons when they're not volunteering."

The blood drained from Julius's face. "You tried to suck out Amelia's magic?"

"You know a quicker way of taking a dragon down?" she asked, pushing herself back up with a wince. "Time for Plan B."

"What's Plan B?"

"You don't want to know, and I don't have time to tell you," Marci growled, never taking her eyes off Amelia as she put out her hands just in time for Ghost to appear between them. "We got this. Go."

"Wait!" he cried, but it was too late. Marci had already pushed him off the step.

Julius fell with a string of expletives, most of them surprised. He was the first to admit he wasn't exactly the most hardy dragon, but there should have been no way a mortal like Marci could possibly have knocked him over like that. She must have pushed him just right to knock him off balance, he realized as he hit the ground. And as soon as he looked up again, he understood why.

Chelsie was now standing next to Marci with her Fang wedged in the wooden throne room door exactly where Julius's head had been a second earlier. Marci, being smart, was already scrambling away, looking over her shoulder just long enough to mouth *Sorry!* at him before she turned all her attention back to Amelia. As much as Julius wanted to help her, though, he had his own problems. In the time between when he'd looked at Marci and now, Chelsie had already yanked her sword out of the door, which meant it was time to run again.

Wounded shoulder burning, Julius shoved himself back to his feet, looking around frantically for somewhere he could either hide or that would force his sister into a position where she couldn't attack. Surely in a place as huge as his mother's throne room there'd be somewhere he could use, but with so many different fights going on, all he saw was conflict. The left half of the room was completely taken up by Justin and Conrad's epic duel. A fight that, to his amazement, seemed to be stalemated. He wasn't sure if Conrad was being handicapped by Estella's control or if Justin was getting a boost from finally reuniting with his sword after a full month of rage, but his brother was doing better than Julius had ever seen, taking Conrad on blow for blow.

Unfortunately, since they were both using Fangs, this also meant their half of the throne room was instant death for anyone without one. When Julius turned to check the balcony side of the room, though, Marci and Amelia had taken that over as well. They didn't actually seem to be doing anything, but the smell of both their magic was thick enough that Julius wasn't about to risk stepping between them. That left the middle of the room, but that was also where Estella was, sitting on the Heartstriker's broken throne and watching the fights below like a Roman empress at the Coliseum while she held Bethesda hostage.

No guarantee of survival was good enough to make Julius go near *that*, but he had to go somewhere. Already, Chelsie was right on his heels, and from the glare on her face, she was done playing around. So, with every other path blocked, Julius fled to the only place he had left. He jumped, launching himself straight up into the air and onto the Quetzalcoatl's bus-sized skull.

It swung alarmingly when he landed, the chains creaking where they'd been anchored in the stone ceiling. Both of these only got worse when Chelsie jumped up after him, landing on the hard bone ridge that had once supported their grandfather's crowning mane of feathers.

"Chelsie, stop," Julius said firmly, grabbing hold of a chain to keep from falling off. "Estella's controlling you. You don't want to do this. You've been bending over backwards trying *not* to kill me, remember?"

Her answer to that was to attack, but her lunge sent the skull swaying wildly, and she missed again, cutting through the chain Julius was holding instead of through her brother. But while this miraculous twist of fate spared his life yet again, it also sent Julius into free fall.

He toppled sideways, hands scrambling desperately over the age-smoothed bone for a handhold. His luck must have suddenly reversed, though, because his desperate fingers didn't find a thing. He just slid right off, plummeting straight down the side of the giant skull toward the ground directly in front of Bethesda's throne where Estella was already waiting, her icy sword ready to chop him out of the air.

The fall had gotten his blood moving, but the sight of Estella waiting for him was what sent Julius into real survival mode. The chain he'd bought might protect him from everyone else, but he had no idea how it would stand against a seer with nothing left to lose. He could not, *could not* get anywhere near Estella, and that knowledge let him reach farther than he'd ever thought possible, nearly popping his shoulder out of joint as his hand shot up to grab the tip of the Quetzalcoatl's last remaining fang.

But even though he'd made it, even though he'd grabbed on, his fall didn't stop. He was still plummeting straight toward Estella, because when he'd closed his fingers around the tooth, it had ceased to be a tooth and turned into a sword. A naked, bone-white Fang of the Heartstriker even sharper than Chelsie's.

That was all Julius had time to take in before the magic bit down.

CHAPTER TWENTY

Dragon magic surged down his arm and into his body. It was a bit like what he'd felt when he'd pulled out Justin's sword, only multiplied by millions. But while the sensation was overwhelming and uncomfortable, it didn't actually hurt until the magic hit his seal.

Now Julius doubled over, crying out in pain. It was similar to when the giant lamprey had spit a blue fireball at him a month ago, but while that magic had simply hammered his mother's magic, this cut straight through it like teeth through fresh meat. He could actually feel the sword's edge slicing Bethesda's magic to ribbons until, at last, there was nothing left to cut. In a matter of seconds, the seal his mother had placed at the root of his magic had been sundered completely, and as the shredded remains fell away, everything Julius had lost came rushing back in.

It was like gaining an entirely new body. He felt stronger, faster, more in touch with the magic around him. He could see better, smell better, hear better. He hadn't even realized how much he'd lost until it all slammed back into place. He could actually feel his wings again, itching under the skin of his back, but what Julius felt most of all was the fire in his throat.

He'd never liked his fire. He'd never been particularly good at controlling it, and even when he did manage a decent blast, the inherent risks of having something so dangerous that near to his body kept him from enjoying it. Now, though, the heat in his belly felt good. Natural. *Powerful.* Most important of all, though, it felt under his control, and he blew out a line of smoke just for the joy of feeling it curl through his teeth.

His no longer human teeth.

Julius blinked in alarm. He didn't remember making the decision to change, he couldn't even remember hitting the ground, but when he opened his eyes, he was standing on the floor looking *down* on his mother's throne room for the first time in…ever, actually. He was still small compared to the huge space, but apparently being sealed had actually been good for him, because he was definitely bigger than he'd been when his mother had kicked him out. His claws, tail, and wings were all larger than he remembered, though that might have just been because Julius was stretching them to their limit in an effort to work out all the kinks after being transformed for so long. Even his feathers looked bigger and brighter, shifting from their usual dark blue across the tips of his wings to an electric bright cobalt across his chest and torso. The real kicker, though, was the weight on his head.

When his brother Justin transformed, his Fang went to the front of his mouth, covering his teeth with a second, larger set of jaws. Up until now, Julius had thought that's how all the Fangs worked, but the sword he'd pulled must have been even more different than he'd thought, because this Fang—*his* Fang, he realized with a start—didn't do that at all. It didn't lock into his mouth or his claws or anything that you'd expect from a weapon meant for dragons. Instead, it sat on Julius's head like a crown, pushing back the mane of longer feathers that grew from the top of his head until they felt more like a headdress than things that were actually attached to him. It was a singularly odd feeling, and Julius was trying to get used to it when he realized just how still the room had gotten.

In the confusion of falling and apparently pulling out the one Fang no one else in his family had ever managed to work free, Julius had completely forgotten about the fights. When he looked up now, though, every Heartstriker in the room was frozen in place like someone had hit a universal pause button. Justin and Conrad were actually stopped with their swords locked together mid-clash, and Chelsie looked like she'd been paused mid-leap, clinging to the skull only by her fingertips. Even Bethesda was still, frozen on her knees beneath her throne. The only ones who didn't seem affected by the strange stillness were Marci, who was gawking like a young dragon seeing her first pile of gold, and Estella, who was staring at him with a hate deeper and older than anything Julius had ever known.

"It's not possible," she growled, her pale face going even paler in her fury as she dropped her sword and shoved the immobile Bethesda out of her way. "It doesn't happen this way!" She stomped down the stairs from the throne dais, freezing smoke pouring from her lips. "I knew it could happen. The moment you vanished through that portal, I knew there was a chance you'd find the chains, but it shouldn't have mattered. It is *not possible* that you—*you*, the failure of Heartstriker, the slacker with no potential at all—could buy a future stronger than mine!"

She was screaming by the time she finished, reaching out to grab a handful of the cobalt blue feathers that covered Julius's chest. "How much did you pay, whelp? What did it cost you to buy a future that would trump mine?!"

"Not as much as it cost you," Julius said calmly, looking down at her without blinking until she finally released his feathers. "I know what you did, Estella. I even think I can understand why, but it doesn't have to be this way."

"Doesn't have to—" The seer's face transformed into a mask pure, murderous rage. "I paid for your deaths with mine! This is *my* victory, bought and paid for! *You will not take it from me!*"

She was still screaming when her human body burst into freezing white flames. The change was over in a heartbeat, but Julius couldn't catch more than a fleeting glimpse of massive size and snow-white scales before Estella attacked.

"*You will not steal what I have worked for!*" she roared, slamming him to the ground with a single beat of her much larger wings. Another swipe had him on his back, and then she leaped on him like a tiger with her curving claws at his throat and her blue eyes staring down at him with blind hatred.

But though it was hard to do anything but panic when a dragon five times your size had you pinned to the floor, the next few minutes were too precious to waste on fear. Outside the balcony, the sun was already touching the horizon. Soon, it would vanish altogether. Julius just had to make it until then, and so he took a deep breath and lay back, exposing his throat in surrender.

"I'm not trying to take your victory," he said softly. "I know you're angry and cornered. There's no other reason you'd trade your entire future just to beat my clan. But what good is victory that you won't be around to enjoy and that doesn't make life better for those who will?"

"What would you know of that?" Estella growled, pressing her superior weight down on him until he could barely breathe. "You're just a failure whose only skill in life is convincing better dragons that you deserve to keep living. But I'm not a sentimental fool like Katya, and I have no patience for *nice*. The only reason I haven't sliced you open yet is because you're Brohomir's little puppet. I *know* he put you up to this. Now," her claws dug into his feathered throat, "tell me what your chain does, or I'll pop your head off and we'll see what happens from there."

"If I tell you," Julius choked out. "Will you not kill me?"

Estella growled deep in her throat. Not the answer Julius was hoping for, but his chain had kept him alive against all odds this far. There was no reason not to think it wouldn't last a little longer.

"Fine," he said, lifting his head to look at her. "I bought you a future."

Estella's sea-ice blue eyes narrowed in confusion. "What?"

"I bought you a future," Julius said again. "I met Dragon Sees the Beginning. I know you paid everything you had to buy what happened tonight. I also know that all of that was only enough to buy you control until sunset tonight, after which all your futures will run out, and you will cease to exist."

"I know what I paid," the dragon growled. "But what does that matter to *you*?"

"Because I wanted to stop you," Julius said. "But buying a future that could counteract yours would have cost me far too much. So, instead, I bought the five minutes that comes after your sunset deadline. In those five minutes, you and me and Marci and Bethesda and all the rest of my family are all *still alive*. So you see, I didn't have to buy a future stronger than yours. I just had to look further ahead."

By the time he finished, Estella was staring at him like the world had just stopped making sense, and then she turned away with a sneer. "I don't believe you."

"It's true," Julius said. "How else do you think I could have survived this long against Chelsie? I mean—"

"I don't care about your personal problems," she snapped. "And I don't believe that's the future you bought because it makes no sense. Your own survival I could see, but why would you buy *mine*? My fate is already fixed. If you know enough to buy the future in the first place, why not just let me die?"

"Because I don't do that," Julius said.

"He really doesn't," Marci piped in. "He can't even bring himself to kill a—"

Estella whipped her tail, whacking Marci across the room. Julius tried to go after her, but the seer still had him pinned, and all he managed was a truncated wiggle. All he could do was keep reminding himself that he'd already guaranteed that they'd get out of this alive as he watched her land hard on the stone floor. That was cold comfort when she didn't get up, but Estella had already grabbed his head, forcing his attention back to her.

"You wasted your future," she growled. "I still have five minutes before the sun sets, and *nothing* is going to stop me. I don't know what you did to freeze all my Heartstrikers, but that just makes them easier to kill. You, however, will die first. A fitting punishment for the whelp who spoiled my final victory."

Her claws dug tighter into his throat with every word. By the time she finished, spots were dancing across Julius's vision, but no matter how he struggled, he couldn't push her off. She was simply too big, too old, too strong. He was starting to think that Dragon Sees the Beginning had lied to him about being able to put chains together despite not being a seer when an enormous crash echoed through the throne room.

Estella's head snapped up and swiveled toward the throne room's front doors. "No," she snarled. "Not yet. It doesn't happen yet."

But whatever "it" she was talking about didn't seem to be listening, because another crash came right on the heels of the first, echoing through the throne room like a thunder clap. Estella's grip on Julius's throat had loosened when she'd looked up, letting him gasp air back into his lungs. When his vision cleared again, he saw why she was upset.

Something was banging into the massive wooden doors of the throne room like a battering ram. Each hit sent waves of magic crackling over the ward Julius could now see super-imposed like a glowing box over the throne room's interior, making Amelia jerk against whatever force it was that kept her frozen. But just as Julius was starting to get really worried about his sister, the throne room doors exploded open with enough force to blow Estella off him completely. She was still rolling back to her feet when a tall figure walked out of the rapidly clearing smoke, strolling into the ruined throne room like he owned it.

"Beating up whelps, Estella?" said a familiar voice. "That's not very sporting."

Julius sagged into the floor. The relief he felt at hearing Bob's voice was so strong it was painful. From Estella's glare, she felt the same, though not from relief. "Well, well," she growled. "The puppet master graces us with his presence at—"

Her voice cut off with a hiss as she recoiled, dropping defensively to her haunches. Considering Bob was still in his human form, Julius had no idea what could have scared Estella into such a threatened position, and then he saw the second figure step out of the blasted doorway behind his brother.

That cheered Julius up enormously. Backup, finally! But his excitement quickly turned to confusion, because the figure who walked up to join Bob wasn't one of Bethesda's security team. He wasn't even a Heartstriker. He was, however, most *definitely* a dragon.

His clothing and features in his human guise suggested one of the Chinese clans. That didn't exactly narrow it down—there were a *lot* of Chinese dragons—but he didn't smell like any of the families Julius had met. He was handsome, of course, like all dragons, but there was something about him that didn't quite fit. After a thousand years of being forced to live in them, most dragons wore their human bodies like a second skin, but this dragon's moved like a puppet, standing unnaturally still and stiff beside Bob like he was a statue someone had just now breathed life into. But strange as all that was, none of it explained how his presence could spook a dragon seer as old and dangerous as Estella. But while she was clearly trying to hide it, there was no disguising that Estella was, in fact, terrified, her eyes locked on the new dragon like he was death himself.

There were few things in the world more dangerous than a terrified, trapped dragon. As such, Estella should have been Bob's first concern, but after his initial greeting, he didn't even acknowledge her. Instead, the seer turned to Julius, looking him up and down with a radiant smile. "Look at you!" he cried. "All grown up! You actually look like a dragon now. If I didn't know better, I *might* be afraid."

He paused there, obviously waiting for an answer, but Julius didn't know what to say.

"How rude of me," Bob said, turning to the strange dragon beside him, the one who had yet to look away from Estella. "Allow me to introduce the Black Reach. Estella already knows him, of course since he was…how did she phrase it? Oh yes, 'orchestrating the downfall of empires before her mothers were even born.'" He finished with a wide smile, but it wasn't a pleasant one when he finally turned to face Estella. "See? I warned you that gloating only leads to ironic quotation."

Julius curled into a protective crouch. It seemed suicidally stupid to taunt Estella in her current condition, but even though Bob was openly mocking her, the white dragon didn't seem to hear him. She was still staring at the Black Reach, and the longer she stared, the more betrayed she look.

"Him," she said at last. "Of all dragons, you come to me with *him?*"

"I do not play favorites, Northern Star," the Black Reach replied in a voice that sounded far too deep for his human body. "And I already warned you what would happen when we met again."

"You think I care?" Estella snarled, showing a wall of sharp, white teeth. "I knew what was coming, and I *chose* to die here in victory rather than wither away in eternal defeat. I have paid the price for my own future, and even you won't stop me."

"I don't have to stop you," the Black Reach said sadly, nodding toward the balcony. "You've already done that yourself."

Estella's head whipped around, and her blue eyes went wide. "No."

Outside, the last sliver of the sun was disappearing below the horizon. As the light vanished, Chelsie, Amelia, and Conrad all began to move again, looking at the throne room like they had no idea how they'd gotten there. Only Bethesda remained frozen, but Julius didn't have time to think about why that was. His eyes were glued to Estella as the ancient seer finally broke.

"*NO!*" she wailed, clawing her way across the throne room until she was hanging off the balcony's sheer edge, staring at the place where the sun had been like she could make it rise again through will alone. "It was not for nothing. *It cannot be for nothing!*"

"It was *not* for nothing," the Black Reach said, pointing at Julius. "He bought back the future you threw away, Estella. In this moment, thanks to him, you are still alive, which means you still have a choice. You are a seer. You know better than any that the future is never set. It's not yet too late to let go."

"It's *far* too late," she growled, smoke pouring from her mouth as she turned back around. "My fate was sealed the moment I picked up the Kosmolabe, but if it's my time to go," her blue eyes flicked to Bob, who was still standing beside Julius, "*he's* going with me."

The words were still echoing when Estella opened her mouth, whiting out the whole room with her fire. Like all of her magic, it was freezing cold, an icy flame that consumed everything it touched, including Bob, who was standing right at its center, and Julius who'd gotten caught in the blast behind him. But then, just when Julius was certain he was dead and just hadn't realized it yet, he noticed that, despite the blinding white fire blazing all around him, he wasn't actually in pain. Likewise, Bob was still there, whole and unburned, standing in front of him with a pigeon on his shoulder and a Fang of the Heartstriker in his hands.

For the rest of his life, Julius was never able to say where Bob's sword came from. His blade was even bigger than Justin's, a massive wall of curving, bone-colored power. Even accounting for the fact that Fangs of the Heartstriker had a flexible relationship with physical reality—changing shape and size seemingly at will—there was still a limit, and Bob definitely hadn't been carrying a sword when he'd walked in. For all Julius knew, the pigeon had coughed it up. Wherever it had come from, though, the sword was in Bob's hands now, and he was using it to split Estella's fire like a rock against the tide until, after what had to be a solid minute, Estella's fire finally sputtered out.

She collapsed on the balcony, panting and glaring in pure hatred as Bob lowered his sword. "Always a trick," she spat, forcing herself back to her feet. "Always a way out."

"Of course," Bob replied, stabbing his sword into the stone floor and leaning on it like the Fang of his grandfather was a hitching post. "That's what clever dragons do, Estella. We keep finding ways to win even when older, wiser dragons tell us winning is impossible."

"You can't be clever forever," she snapped. "I'll never stop, Brohomir, and now, thanks to your soft whelp of a brother, I don't have to." She sat up with a smirk. "He bought me a new future. He actually *gave up* his future to buy back what I'd traded away to crush you. Now, thanks to his soft-hearted idiocy, I don't have to stop. I am free to hunt you until the end of time, until the moment finally comes when your cleverness isn't enough. And then, Great Seer of the Heartstrikers, I'll see you fall at last."

She finished with a snap of her teeth, but Bob just heaved a sad sigh. "Flattering as it is to be the target of such unwavering obsession, I'm afraid that won't happen, Estella."

He pushed himself up off his sword, walking toward the exhausted white dragon. "You're right. My uncommonly kind brother did, in fact, buy back a portion of the future you squandered. In doing so, however, he actually bought far more than he knows. You see, by spending his own future to buy your survival, he created a paradox, a five-minute fragment within which you both cannot and *must* exist. But in these five minutes which you were never supposed to have, your decisions have sparked a whole new spectrum of possibilities, creating new potential and possibility." He spread his arms wide. "The river of your future is literally being reborn as I speak. That is a *miracle*, Estella, and the greatest tragedy of tonight is that you've already squandered it."

"How?" Estella scoffed. "By refusing to abandon my fight and gracefully accept my decline?"

"No," Bob said, shaking his head. "Though refusing to even acknowledge your second chance is *very* sad, the particular misstep I was referring to is tactical, not philosophical."

Estella rolled her eyes. "This is why we could never get along. There's nothing worse than a *clever* dragon who doesn't know when to shut up."

"You're entitled to your opinion," Bob said, his voice turning hard as he stepped sideways, motioning behind his back for Julius to move with him. "Personally, though, I think it's *far* worse to be an old dragon who lets someone else's talking distract her while she's sitting in enemy territory."

The superior look fell off Estella's face. She whirled around, her head snapping up to search the sky above the mountain, but before she could even finish turning, something large and white shot through the open balcony and crashed into her like a rocket. It moved so fast, Julius couldn't make out more than a vaguely dragon-shaped streak before both it and Estella went flying, tumbling into the throne room in a ball of white fire and flashing claws that rolled right past where Bob and Julius had been standing.

In the chaos of the rolling fight, neither opponent seemed to have the advantage. When they crashed into the far wall, though, the new dragon ended up on top, and she used it to her full advantage, darting down to wrap her jaws around Estella's neck before the seer could even lift her head.

Exhausted from the fire she'd used on Brohomir and taken completely by surprise, Estella never had a chance. It didn't matter if you were older or stronger or even if you could see the future, when a dragon's fangs closed around your exposed throat, there was nothing you could do. She didn't even seem to have fully realized what was happening before the dragon bit down, snapping her jaws shut like a trap.

The *crunch* that followed was a sound Julius knew he'd hear in his nightmares forever. Estella jerked in pain, her whole body spasming, but the white dragon on top of her just bit down harder, clamping down on the seer's neck with her jaws until, at last, Estella fell still, her blue eyes fading. Only when it was obvious that the seer wasn't ever getting up again did the dragon unlock her jaw and let Estella's head fall to the ground.

Until this point, Julius had actually had a hard time figuring out who the new dragon was. She was obviously a daughter of the Three Sisters—no other dragon clan had those pure white scales—but figuring out *which* daughter was impossible while she and Estella were tangled on the floor. Given the ferocity of the sneak attack, his money was on Svena. She certainly had every right to be murderously angry after what Estella had done. But when the dragoness finally untangled herself from the dead seer, the bloody face that turned toward the gaping Heartstrikers *wasn't* Svena's.

It was Katya's.

"Hear me!" she roared, spreading her frosted wings wide. "To save our clan and to preserve what remains of our good relations with Heartstriker, I have killed Estella the Northern Star! Now, by right of combat, I claim her place as head of the Daughters of the Three Sisters."

Her voice boomed through the stunned silence of the throne room. But while Julius was extremely impressed, he didn't understand why Katya was saying all of this to *them.* As the echo of her announcement faded, though, he became aware of a new sound behind him. It sounded like wings. Lots of them.

He turned around in a rush, eyes going wide. In the time between Katya's sneak attack on Estella and now, an entire flight of snow-white dragons had appeared in the air outside his mother's balcony. One of them landed as he watched, transforming instantly into a severe woman whose hair—which was an even paler blond than Svena's—fell all the way to the floor, covering her naked body like a waterfall. From the way she held herself, though, she might as well have been wearing full armor as she marched stiffly across the throne room to Estella's body, leaning down to close the seer's dull eyes with a business-like brush of her fingers.

"It is over," she announced, rising back to her feet. "I, Ysolde the Frost Caller, Fifth Born, stand as witness that Estella the Northern Star, Seer of the Three Sisters, First Born of us all, is dead. By right of combat, I now recognize Katya, Last Born, as head of the Daughters of the Three Sisters. Any who would challenge her, challenge me."

Up until that last part, she spoke with the calm, formal cadence of ritual. By the end, though, Ysolde the Frost Caller was growling, her teeth bared in anticipation. But while she looked more than ready to make good on that threat, none of the other white dragons seemed to want to take her up on it. Every one of them instantly bowed their heads in submission, lowering their eyes before Katya, who looked prouder than Julius had ever seen.

"Hello again," she said, flashing him a bloody grin as she looked him up and down. "Not quite the plan we discussed, I know, but how was *that* for backup?"

"Amazing," he got out at last. "You saved us."

"I *told* you I would repay you," Katya said. "And now that we're officially even, would you like me to ask my sister to look at your human? Ysolde's cold even for us, but she's a miracle worker when it comes to healing, and I know how much you value your mage."

Julius's stomach dropped. How could he have forgotten about Marci? He spun around, frantically scanning the room until he finally spotted her on the ground, lying on her back with Ghost pacing nervously next to her head. "Please," he begged, not even caring how desperate he sounded. "I'll pay anything if you help her."

"No payment needed," Katya replied with a warm smile. "We are friends, are we not?"

If Julius hadn't been so worried about Marci, that would have made him feel warm all over. But it was hard to feel good when he couldn't even see Marci breathing. As it was, he barely managed a thank you before he rushed to her side. "*Marci!*"

She twitched at his voice, and then her eyes fluttered open, staring up at him in wonder. "Hey," she said softly, reaching up to touch his feathered nose. "You're a dragon."

"I think we've established this," he replied, breathing deep. Now that he was unsealed, it was like a mask had been removed from his nose, giving him back his full range. But while he could definitely smell Marci's pain, he didn't smell her blood, which helped calm him down.

"So," she said, tilting her head to look at Katya, who was still standing tall over her sister's body. "I guess we won?"

"We did," Julius said. "Katya came in with the cavalry and took out Estella. One of her sisters is on her way now to help take care of you."

"You mean like dragon healing magic?" Marci asked excitedly. "Cool! How does that work?"

Julius couldn't help but grin at that. Leave it to Marci to be more excited about the magical part of her magical first aid than the actual aid. "You'll have to ask her," he said, nodding at Ysolde, who'd gotten her orders from Katya and was now walking toward them at a stately pace.

It didn't seem possible, but Marci looked even more excited than before. "Eeeee! Is that one of the Daughters of the Three Sisters?! She looks like a freaking Valkyrie! This was *totally* worth getting smacked into a wall for!"

She said this like it was the best thing ever, but Julius's grin faded. "I'm sorry you got hit," he said, lowering his head until the soft feathers of his nose pressed against her cheek. "I didn't want you to get hurt."

"Hey, you run with dragons, you've got to be willing to take your lumps," she said, reaching up to touch his feathers again. "I'm not upset at all. I'm mostly happy that I finally get to see what you really look like."

Julius froze, instantly bashful. "Do I live up to the hype?" he asked at last.

"Way better," she assured him. "Blue's my favorite color, you know."

He gave her a skeptical look. "I thought your favorite color was purple?"

Marci grinned. "Not anymore."

If Julius had been human, that would have turned him red from his head to his toes. Fortunately for his dignity, feathers hid blushes. He was sure he still looked stupidly, goofily happy, but Julius couldn't really bring himself to care. Marci was alive, he was a dragon again, and except for Estella, everyone had lived, which meant they'd *won*. Against all odds, they'd pulled it off, all of it. If he couldn't be happy after that, when could he?

He was still smiling like an idiot when Ysolde finally reached them. Marci started bombarding her with questions immediately, completely immune to the dragon's scornful looks. Julius was trying to find a spot where he wouldn't be in the way when someone tapped him on the tail.

When he looked over his shoulder, Bob was standing behind him with an uncharacteristically serious look on his face. "If you're not busy," he said. "We need to borrow you for a moment."

Julius glanced back at Marci, but she was still happily grilling Ysolde. Satisfied he wouldn't be abandoning her, he turned back to his brother, keeping his head as low as possible so he wouldn't have to look down on the Great Seer of the Heartstrikers. "What's going on?"

"Nothing much," Bob replied with a shrug. "But now that all this Estella business is wrapped up, there's one last piece of family drama we need to settle."

He looked back over his shoulder as he finished, drawing Julius's attention back to the cracked throne in the center of the room where all the other Heartstrikers were now gathered in a circle around their mother, who was still frozen on her knees.

At the sight of Bethesda, Julius began to shake. It didn't matter that he was currently five times her size, or that she was still bound by magic he didn't understand. The fear of his mother was too deeply ingrained to be pushed away by minor details. "Do I have to?"

"Yes," Bob said with a sharp look. "This is a once in a lifetime opportunity, Julius, which is saying something for a dragon. It took a great deal of effort to arrange this situation. If we don't take it now, we might never get another chance."

Julius's eyes went wide. "Arrange?" he said. "You mean, *you*—"

Bob pressed a finger to his lips, and Julius snapped his mouth shut. When it was clear he wasn't going to interrupt again, Bob continued.

"Sometimes you have to smash things to rebuild them," he said, his eyes getting that faraway look they always had when he was peering into the future. "When I was your age, our grandfather told me that just as there are opportunities that only reveal themselves in defeat, there are victories that can't be won through force. Being a properly ruthless dragon, I never really understood what that meant. Now, though, I'm beginning to understand."

"I don't," Julius said.

"You will," Bob promised. "Or, at least, you'd better, because if you don't, I've just lost us the farm."

He started walking away after that. When Julius hesitated to follow, Bob looked over his shoulder. "Come on, Julius," he said with a cryptic smile. "Don't you have anything you want to say to our mother?"

Julius had plenty he wanted to say to Bethesda, and his brother was right about at least one thing. This *was* a once in a lifetime opportunity, because, for the time being at least, Bethesda was still frozen on her knees. That made now the perfect time to talk since the only way his mother would ever *actually* listen to him was if she was physically unable to do anything else.

"Okay," he said, starting after his brother. "Let's go."

"Fantastic," Bob said. "Go change first."

Julius looked down at his feathered body in alarm. "But I just got this back!"

"If *you're* a dragon, *everyone's* going to want to be a dragon," his brother pointed out. "And I'd rather not have Justin easily able to breathe fire for this conversation. Now." He turned and pointed at the door behind the throne that led to Bethesda's private apartments. "I had someone stash your clothes in there yesterday. Go change and join us as soon as you're done."

Julius still didn't want to go back to being human yet, and he *definitely* didn't want to set foot in his mother's private lair alone, but there was no point in arguing. Bob was already walking away, spinning his sword like a baton as he climbed up the dais steps to rejoin the others. So, with a final stretch of his wings, he turned and started toward the door to go change back into his usual self.

CHAPTER TWENTY—ONE

Julius had never been in his mother's personal lair before. Not surprisingly, it looked exactly like what you'd expect from Bethesda's apartments: a dragon-sized maze of gilded rooms packed to the rafters with gold, jewels, designer clothes, and mounds of exceedingly expensive, over-designed furniture that somehow managed to be both ugly as sin and uncomfortable.

As Bob had promised, Julius found clothes waiting on the gold and glass coffee table in the front room. How the seer had managed *that*, Julius was past trying to guess. He just focused on changing as quickly as possible and trying not to get crushed by his new Fang in the process.

Five minutes later, he reemerged dressed in a plain black turtleneck, jeans, and a pair of flip flops. The Fang, which had thankfully returned to the usual sword-shape as soon as he'd finished shifting back, he carried in his hands, mostly because he had no idea what else to do with it. It hadn't come with a sheath, and Bob hadn't given him a belt in any case. But while walking around with a naked blade felt wrong, just leaving the thing in Bethesda's apartment felt worse. In the end, Julius made the best of it, carrying the sword tight against his side in an attempt to look like he knew what he was doing as he climbed up the dais steps to join the rest of his family gathered in a tight knot on top around his mother's cracked throne.

Given that they were in Heartstriker Mountain, Julius had expected a lot more dragons by this point. Bob must have given an order of some sort, though, because the only Heartstrikers in the throne room were the ones who'd been there the whole time: Chelsie, Conrad, Amelia, Justin, himself, and Bob. With the exception of Amelia, everyone had a Fang of the Heartstriker, including, Julius realized with a start, his mother.

"Now this is a momentous occasion," Bob said brightly as Julius joined them. "All six Fangs of the Heartstriker, together again for the first time since they were in our grandfather's mouth! Quite fitting, too, since we're here to discuss Heartstriker's future."

"There will be no discussion," Bethesda hissed through her locked jaw, her green eyes dropping to her own sword, which someone had placed on the floor in front of her. "The moment that blade is back in my hands, all of your swords will be mine again, and then we'll see how *you* like being on your knees."

"I'm afraid that's impossible," Bob said. "You see, so long as Julius has *his* sword out, none of us can so much as contemplate violence against the others without ending up like you."

Bethesda growled deep in her throat, but Julius looked up in surprise. "What?"

Bob flashed him a grin. "Haven't you figured it out yet? That's what the sixth Fang does. Just like the others, it has its own special trick, but where Chelsie's can cut to any of us, and Mother's controls all the others, *your* Fang freezes any Heartstriker with killing intent the moment you draw it. Think of it as a localized family 'Time Out' button."

"You're kidding," Julius said. When Bob shook his head, he looked down at his sword in astonishment. "I thought these things were supposed to be the ultimate dragon weapons! How is *peace* a power of a Fang of the Heartstriker? "

"Because before they became Fangs of the Heartstriker, they were the *actual* fangs of the Quetzalcoatl," Bob explained. "And despite being long dead, some of his magic lives in them still. That's why they have to choose their wielders instead of simply going to whomever Bethesda chooses, because, ultimately they're not hers to give. Each Fang follows its own judgment according to our grandfather's values: strength, wisdom, control, all that Elements of Harmony stuff." He leaned in closer. "Coincidentally, that's also why it took over a thousand years to find someone who could pull the blade in your hands. *Your* Fang contains our grandfather's diplomatic, compassionate side, and a compassionate dragon is a rare bird, indeed."

That made sense, Julius supposed. A sword that radiated an anti-violence aura definitely wasn't the kind of tool you normally found in a dragon arsenal. That said, it still didn't sound like the sort of thing that should belong to *him*, especially since he had no idea how it actually worked. "Is there any way to turn it off?"

"Who knows?" Bob said with a shrug. "But so long as it's on, you are the only one here who can raise a weapon, which means *you*, Julius, are currently the most powerful Heartstriker."

The implication of those words hit Julius like a freight train. From the sudden horror in his mother's eyes, Bethesda grasped it, too. "Julius, baby," she said in a voice so sweet and innocent, he barely recognized it as hers. "I know things have been a little tense between us recently, but—"

"*Tense?*" he growled. "You sealed me and then used that to make me do whatever you wanted! You've done nothing but abuse and bully me since I hatched!"

"It was for your own good," Bethesda said defensively. "I'm your mother. It's my job to be hard on you so you'll grow into a strong dragon, and it was more painful for me than it was for—"

"Stop."

Bethesda's green eyes flashed. If she'd been able to move, she probably would have slapped him across the room for interrupting, but she couldn't. So long as his Fang was doing its thing, she couldn't move a muscle. That meant Julius was the one with the power, and for once in his life, his mother was going to listen to *him*.

"You always do this," he said, moving forward until he was standing right in front of her. "You *always* say you're hurting us for our own good, but you're not. It's for *your* own good. All my life, I thought that if I could just live up to your expectations and be a good dragon, I'd be happy, but that's a lie. *No one* in this family is happy, because even the dragons you value, you abuse and manipulate!"

"Of course," his mother growled. "Because I'm running a *dragon clan*, not a happy home. The soft don't survive in this world, Julius. You stand there whining that I hurt your feelings and made your childhood hard, but you don't even stop to consider I'm the reason you got to grow up inside the shelter of the greatest dragon clan in the world. Heartstriker rose to the top because *I* was willing to do what other clans wouldn't, and if you're too soft to appreciate that, then you don't understand what it means to be a dragon."

"No!" Julius yelled. "It's *you* who doesn't understand! You think I don't know what dragons do? I've been to our old home, the original plane where all dragons came from, and do you know what's there? *Nothing.* The whole place is a motionless, timeless desert of ash because *dragons* made it that way!"

He could see it again as he spoke, the endless black desert under the frozen sky. That waste—not even a real place, but a construct taken from a racial memory—was all that was left of their only real home. And the more he thought about that, the angrier Julius got.

"Vann Jeger was right," he said bitterly. "Dragons *do* destroy everything they touch. We didn't come to this plane as conquerors. We came here because we had *nowhere else to go*. We'd already ruined everything we were given, literally sold our own future out from under us, and do you know why? Because dragons like *you* were willing to do anything for power. It was that sort of selfish, victory-at-any-cost thinking that destroyed our old home and nearly took out our entire species, and you want me to respect you for it? To try and be like you?"

"Big words from a timid little whelp," Bethesda snarled. "But you're the one with the sword now. If I'm so terrible, use it. Kill me, if you've got the guts."

She was obviously taunting him, and Julius was about to tell her to knock it off when Chelsie said, "Do it."

Justin began to growl, but Conrad grabbed the knight's shoulder, pinning him in place. For her part, Chelsie didn't even glance in Justin's direction. She was fixated on their mother, staring at the beautiful old dragon with so much hate, it made Julius's blood run cold.

"Do you know what she's done to us?" his sister said softly. "What she's made us do? You were just a failure to be used and thrown away, but we were the ones who did her dirty work." She glanced at Julius. "If you're really the compassionate dragon, then end this. Kill her now, and set us all free."

By the time she finished, Bethesda's eyes were as wide as they could go, but Julius shook his head. "No."

"Are you stupid?" Chelsie snarled, stabbing her finger at their mother. "She's ordered your death twice, used you countless times, demanded you sell out Amelia to save Justin, and that's just this month. We're not even counting the last *eleven hundred years*. Every one of us would be better off without her, and you know it. Kill her."

"No," Julius said again.

"Why not?" Chelsie demanded.

"*Because I'm not like her!*" he yelled, clutching his sword tight. "I don't care how awful they are, I *don't* kill my family! I don't kill *anyone*, period, and I will never throw someone away just to make my life easier!"

"So you're just going to let her stay in charge?" Chelsie yelled back. "You can't keep her frozen forever!" She turned to glare at Bethesda. "If you don't do something, she'll just get her power back, and then she'll grind us all into the dirt."

"I'll do much worse than that," their mother said. "When I get free—"

"Shut up!" Chelsie snarled, turning back to Julius. "If you won't kill her, I will."

"You can't," Conrad said calmly. "You are bound."

Chelsie clutched her sword. "I can still *try*."

"No," Julius said, grabbing his sister's arm. "No one is killing her, because no matter how horrible she's been or what she's done, she's *still our mother*, and if you keep going, you're acting just like her."

That got Chelsie's attention. She stopped cold, and Julius saw his chance. "Don't you see what's happening here?" he said, letting her go. "We're just repeating the same mistakes over and over again. We act like violence and ruthlessness are the only tools we have, but that's just not true."

He pointed down the stairs where the white dragons were waiting silently, not even pretending like they weren't listening. "Look at me and Katya. She, a daughter of our oldest enemies, came to help us tonight because she loved her sister and because she was my friend. If you listen to *her*," he pointed back at Bethesda, "she'd call that weakness, but anyone with eyes can see it's not weakness at all. All you need are muscles to swing a sword, but it takes *actual* courage to lower your weapon and hold out your hand in friendship."

His sister rolled her eyes. "So we should forgive and forget? Cuddle up to Mommy until she stabs us in the back again?"

Julius shook his head. "Just because I don't want to kill her doesn't mean I want to keep her as my clan head."

"So you're saying we should dethrone her and make Amelia the Heartstriker?" Conrad said. "Sounds good to me. I've been saying as much for years."

"And you can keep saying it," Amelia said, crossing her arms over her chest. "I refuse. I'm not touching this crazy bin with a ten-foot pole. Go find another chump."

Conrad opened his mouth to argue, but Julius beat him to it. "That's not what I'm saying at all."

All the dragons looked at him, and he bit his lip, trying to think of how best to explain this. "The Heartstrikers are one of the most hated clans in the world," he said at last. "Mother claims that's because we're strong and the other clans envy us, but she's wrong. We have enemies because *she* made them, and if we're strong, it's in spite of that. But has it ever occurred to any of you how much stronger we could be if we stopped making enemies and started making alliances?"

"Impossible," Chelsie scoffed. "No one would respect a clan head who did nothing but roll over."

"Working together isn't the same as rolling over," Julius reminded her. "But you're partially right. The other clans *wouldn't* respect a dragon who didn't follow the apex predator script. But if we changed the game on them entirely? What if we didn't have a clan head at all?"

Now the others just looked confused. "How would *that* work?" Justin growled.

"Pretty well, I bet," Julius said. "Think about it. What if, instead of a single-dragon dictatorship, we actually talked about what *we* want this clan to be and then *worked together* to get there?"

He finished with a hopeful smile, but his siblings were staring at him like he'd just suggested they adopt the tutu as their clan uniform.

"Julius," Amelia said at last. "Have you *met* our siblings? 'Working together' isn't part of their vocabulary."

"Amelia's right," Chelsie said. "Without a bigger dragon keeping them in line, Heartstriker would tear itself apart."

"Maybe as we are," Julius said firmly. "But that's because, as things stand now, the only way up the ladder is through another dragon. That kind of violence and infighting is inherently wasteful, and if there's anything ambitious dragons love, it's a better way to get to the top. I'm not saying it would be easy, but if we came up with a new clan structure, something that let all of us pool our efforts and resources together instead of wasting them on cutting each other down, I think you'd be surprised how fast Heartstriker would come around. I mean, we're already the biggest dragon clan in recorded history. If we stopped fighting for a clan head's favor and put all that energy toward actually getting what we want instead, we could rule the world."

Julius wasn't actually terribly interested in ruling the world, but he knew the idea would appeal to everyone else. And so far, it seemed to be working. Justin certainly seemed to like the idea of Heartstriker ruling the world, and even Chelsie didn't look as blatantly skeptical anymore. "*If* we agreed to this nonsense," she said, crossing her arms over her chest. "How would it work? If a clan doesn't have a head, how does it even run?"

"We could form a council," Julius said. "Humans do it all the time. It might not be as efficient as a clan head, but if we had a group that we could elect and replace, we'd at least guarantee that Heartstriker is run according to what *we* actually want instead of according to the whims of a single dragon."

"How very egalitarian of you," Amelia said. "But seriously, have you ever tried to get a group of dragons to come to a consensus? I'd call it herding cats, but cats usually don't try to kill you when they don't get their way."

"It can't be any worse than being used as pawns by our mother," Julius countered. "At least with a council, if someone wants to throw one of us away for power, there'll have to be a discussion about it, first. That's miles better than what we've got now, so why not try? Unless *you* want to be Heartstriker."

Amelia grimaced. "Point taken."

"Well, I think it's a stupid idea," Justin said, crossing his arms over his chest. "We'd be the only clan in the world without a clan head. Any proper dragon family would see us as a bunch of leaderless animals wasting time before we collapse into anarchy. We'd never be taken seriously again. Why, without Bethesda, we wouldn't even be Heartstrikers."

Bethesda flashed her favorite son a warm smile, but Julius refused to back down. "So long as this is our clan, we'll always be Heartstrikers," he said. "And if the others don't take us seriously at first, they'll learn to when they realize that we're *not* leaderless. We're an entire clan acting together as one. That's way more powerful than any single dragon could ever be, and if there's anything the dragon clans respect, it's power. That said, though, I actually think that Bethesda should be the first member of our council."

"Doesn't that defeat the purpose?" Chelsie growled.

"Just the opposite," Julius said. "Having a powerful, established dragon like her on board would give our new council legitimacy.

Besides, Justin's right. She *is* the Heartstriker, and while I don't want her ruling me with an iron claw anymore, I do think she deserves a seat at the table in deciding the fate of her own clan."

"As if I'd take it," Bethesda sneered. "Share my power with my own ungrateful children? Be forced to *vote* on decisions that should be mine by right?" She turned up her nose. "I'd rather die."

"That can still be arranged."

Julius jumped. Bob had been so quiet through all of this, Julius had actually forgotten the seer was there. Now, though, Bob pushed his way forward, taking Julius's place in front of their mother with a smile every bit as ruthless as anything the Heartstriker had worn.

"Showing your true colors at last, I see," Bethesda said, glaring up at her oldest surviving son. "I always suspected Julius, but I never thought *you* would betray me, Brohomir."

"And that's the only reason it worked," Bob replied. "You were a useful tool, Mother, but the world is changing, and the old ways are no longer enough. You took us as far as you could, but if Heartstriker is to become the power I need it to be, we all have to adapt. Even you."

"You can't be serious," she growled. "You can't actually think *I* would give up my clan, the title I killed for, to become a passenger in this idiot's plot?"

Her eyes darted to Julius, who shifted uncomfortably, but Bob laid a hand on his shoulder. "I do," Bob said. "Because our clan is no longer yours to lose."

She looked appalled by that, but Bob just kept going. "Tonight, my littlest brother saved your life twice over. Once from Estella, and once, just now, from your own children. But even though you live, you've lost. You are on your knees, defeated and sealed, watching helpless as your children divvy up your clan." His eyes narrowed. "You know how this ends, Bethesda. You know, because you were once in our position yourself. This clan will march on with or without you, so unless you want me to carry on the family tradition and show you the same courtesy you showed your father, I suggest you accept what Julius has so generously offered. A seat on his council might not be the future you wanted, but at this point, it's the only one you're going to get. So what will it be, Mother? Will you die for your pride? Or will you act like a real dragon and take your power where you find it?"

Bethesda took a shuddering breath, her frozen body straining against the magic of Julius's Fang that held her in place. And then, slowly, the fight drained out of her. With his hand wrapped tight around the hilt of his sword, Julius could actually feel the moment his mother gave up. The Fang's magic released her a few seconds later, and she slumped forward, landing on her hands. She rested there for a moment, and then she rose to her feet, reaching up to straighten her skewed golden headdress.

"I never was one to take nothing over something," she said with as much dignity as she could manage. "I accept your compromise."

"Excellent!" Bob said, his voice bright and cheery again as he pulled an elaborately folded square of expensive looking paper out of his pocket. "Council it is, then! I've got the paperwork all drawn up."

"Wait," Julius said, almost too shocked to speak. "How is that even possible? I only came up with the idea a few minutes ago. We haven't even discussed what a Heartstriker Council would look like yet. How can you *possibly* have paperwork already?"

"Because I am the handsome, powerful, charismatic, and all-knowing seer of the Heartstrikers," Bob reminded him with curt look. "Honestly, Julius, you act like Estella was the only one with an end game on the board. As you just pointed out, this entire thing was your idea, and have I not *continually* said that your future was the only one I could always see?"

"Oh," Julius said, his face heating. "Right."

"Now this is just the initial agreement," Bob said, unfolding the paper to reveal a beautifully handwritten contract the size of a movie poster. "Parameters for the transference of Bethesda's power, how the council will be formed, and so forth. There's a lot more details to hammer out, but I only had one piece of paper with me, so I figured we'd figure the rest out later when we had a council to argue about it."

Chelsie arched an eyebrow at the giant, densely written contract that fell from Bob's fingers all the way to the floor. "*That's* your start?"

"I was *trying* to be thorough," Bob said, pouting. "Though I do admit the calligraphy is a bit much, but it was a *very* long flight from the DFZ to China, and I wanted to make sure everything was perfect. It's not every day we get to completely redefine the idea of what a dragon clan is."

He spread the unfurled contract out over the cracked seat of Bethesda's throne, and all the Heartstrikers crowded in to read. But while Bob hadn't been kidding about going overboard on the calligraphic flourishes, the contract itself, while extremely overwritten, boiled down to three key points. First, it destroyed the position of clan head, preventing Bethesda or any other Heartstriker from seizing absolute control of the clan ever again. This, by extension, also removed Amelia's position as heir, which made her very happy. Second, Bob's contract outlined the formation of a council with an unspecified odd number of voting seats (to prevent deadlocks) that would take over all the responsibilities and powers that had previously belonged to Bethesda, including declaring war, forming alliances with other clans, creating and enforcing rules for acceptable behavior within the family, and so forth. Thirdly, it ordered that, with the exception of Bethesda herself, the council seats should be equally divided between Heartstrikers with Fangs and Heartstrikers without, both to be decided by a clan vote.

"I like the voting part," Julius said. "But why divide things by Fangs?"

"Because we need them," Bob replied, patting his own sword. "The Fangs have always been symbols of Heartstriker's power. A council that didn't include them wouldn't be respected within the family, let alone by outsiders, but a council that was nothing *but* Fangs would be seen as Bethesda's puppets. A fifty-fifty split felt like a good compromise. That way, we always guarantee there will be at least one heavy hitter and one seat open to the ambitions of the clan at large. By dividing the power in half, we ensure that we have two sides who can both work together to gang up on Bethesda."

This observation raised a growl from their mother, which everyone ignored.

"I also set a term limit of five years on elected seats," Bob went on, pointing at a particularly florid paragraph toward the bottom. "That way, there's never more than a half decade's wait between chances to seize power, which is vital if you want to avoid assassinations."

"And we definitely want to do that," Julius said, reading the paragraph Bob had indicated. "But, not counting Mother's, there are only five Fangs total. If there's a five year term limit, then only two dragons who have Fangs can sit on the council at any given time without being in violation. Add that to what you just said about the fifty-fifty split, and we've only got five Heartstrikers on the council— two with Fangs, two without, and Mother."

Bob shrugged. "How is that a problem? Small councils make faster decisions."

"You can go ahead and count me out," Chelsie said, crossing her arms.

"Why?" Julius asked, alarmed. "Don't you like the idea of a council?"

"I like it fine," Chelsie said. "But I'm bound to Bethesda, remember? If I sit on that thing, all I'm going to do there is give her another vote, and I refuse."

"Thank you for that, *dear*," Bethesda snarled. "I'll be sure to keep your opinion in mind later."

There was a world of implied consequences in those words, but they seemed to roll off Chelsie's back. Julius, on the other hand, was starting to get nervous.

"Okay," he said, turning to Amelia. "What about you? I know the contract says Fangs, but I don't think anyone would object to—"

"No thanks," Amelia said, cutting him off. "Now that I can stay on this plane without worrying about my mother constantly trying to kill me, my schedule is full. Don't get me wrong, I wish you crazy kids all the luck in the world with your alternative forms of government, but I've got much bigger targets on my radar than Heartstriker."

"Count me out as well," Conrad said. "I'm a knight, not a bureaucrat. I want the clan to be strong and secure. Other than that, I have no interest in how it's run."

"If Conrad's out, then so am I," Justin said, puffing out his chest. "I'm a knight, too. I'm supposed to be out there fighting duels and expanding our reputation, not sitting around in meetings listening to Julius *talk*."

"Oh come *on*!" Julius cried. "You can't leave all of this to me and Bob!"

"Actually, I'm afraid I have to bow out as well," Bob said apologetically.

Julius whirled around to face him. "*Why?*"

Bob arched an eyebrow. "Because I'm the Great Seer of the Heartstrikers. I've already seen how I'd do on the council, and, trust me, it's a hot mess. Everyone will be constantly accusing me of manipulating the votes—which of course I *will* be whether I'm on the council or not—but that's a kettle of seers we do not *want* to open. No, I've seen how this shakes out, and we're all far better off when I stay behind the curtain. Plus, Justin's right. Meetings *are* boring."

Julius couldn't believe this was happening. "You can't all refuse! That just leaves me." Alone. On a council with Bethesda and one other Heartstriker, making decisions that would decide the entire clan's fate. "No," he said. "Absolutely not. I'm not doing it."

"But you have to do it," Bob said, wrapping an arm around his shoulders. "This was your idea, Julius. If you refuse, then your council will fizzle before it begins."

Julius shot a terrified look at Bethesda, who was already eying him like he was a lost lamb. "I'm *not* sitting alone on a council with Mother," he hissed at Bob. "My heart can't take it."

"You give your heart too little credit," Bob said. "Remember, you hold the current family record for standing up to Bethesda.

The rest of us were smart and learned our lessons the first time, but you've done it *twice*! That's the sort of borderline self-destructive dedication we need if we're going to make this thing work."

"You're not making me feel better," Julius said, shoulders slumping.

"I wasn't trying to," Bob said sternly. "I'm here to tell you the truth, not coddle you, and the truth is that you're the only one who can do this. We're about to attempt reforming an entire dragon clan. Changes like that don't stick with the same-old, same-old in power. If we're *really* going to make this thing work, we need a dragon who doesn't think like a dragon. Someone who can handle Bethesda and the rest of us without resorting to the kind of power games that got us into this mess. Someone who's seen the consequences of the path we're on and actually wants to change it. We need *you*." He grinned. "We always have. I keep telling you I didn't pick you at random. This moment is the result of years of work. You can't throw all that away now. And besides, it's not like you'll be alone with Mother. According to the rules, you'll have at least one other, non-Fang-holding member of the family to help you along."

Julius did not consider a random member of his family to be a "help," especially not one ambitious enough to get chosen as the final member on a three dragon council. But while he was still terrified and more than a little furious about having all of this dumped on him, Bob was right. This *was* his idea, and he desperately wanted it to work. He'd hated the way dragon clans worked his whole life. He and Katya and Chelsie and Justin and pretty much every dragon he called friend had all suffered in one way or another under the system that let clan heads like Bethesda and Estella be tyrants. Now, he had a chance to change all of that for the Heartstrikers, bloodlessly, with the help and support of the top members of his family. That really was a once in a dragon lifetime opportunity, and certain as Julius was that this was going to suck *epically* for him for years to come, he couldn't let that pass him by.

"Okay," he said with a sigh. "I'll do it."

"I knew you would," Bob replied, producing an old-fashioned inkwell and a suspiciously large, painfully beautiful, peacock blue feather quill from somewhere in his pockets before turning to their mother. "You first."

Bethesda shot him a dirty look, but she didn't argue. She just reached up and jabbed one of her sharp nails into the soft flesh of her inner arm, holding it out so Bob could collect the bright red blood in the inkwell. When they had collected enough, Bethesda took the feather, which Julius strongly suspected was one of Bob's own, and dipped the tip of the quill into the blood, tapping the excess off neatly before leaning down to sign her name in a recalcitrant scrawl.

"There," she growled, tossing the feather back at Bob. "It's done. Now," her murderous glare shifted to Amelia. "Unseal me."

Amelia's lips curled into a cruel smile, but before she could say any of the cutting, painfully appropriate comebacks that were clearly on the tip of her tongue, Bob beat her to it.

"We'll leave that for the council to decide," he said cheerfully. "We just got it! It'd be a shame not to use it."

"You would have me stay like *this*?" Bethesda roared, gesturing down at the magical seal which Julius—now that his own seal had been broken—could clearly see shimmering over her magic. "Impossible! You might as well hang a sign on my back that says 'stab here.'" Her eyes narrowed to glowing slits. "Not that that would be a change of pace after tonight."

"I'm sorry," Bob said, rubbing his ear. "I couldn't hear that last bit over all the times we've saved your life tonight."

Bethesda's glare turned surly, and Brohomir stopped smiling. "You will be unsealed when the council is complete and decides to do so. You'll have a vote, but you do not give orders here anymore, Bethesda. This is a new era, and as you once said to *me*, if we're going to ensure your full participation, we need as much of your skin in this game as possible."

Julius had never heard his mother say that specifically, but he knew someone's words being thrown back in their face when he saw it. But though their mother definitely looked killing mad, she didn't say anything else. She simply drew herself up like the queen she no longer was and left, her high heels clicking angrily on the cracked stone as she stormed down the dais steps and into her apartments, slamming the door with an echoing *bam*.

"She's going to claw her way back to power the first chance she gets," Chelsie said quietly.

"The more things change, the more they stay the same," Bob said with a bright smile. "Welcome to the new Heartstriker!"

His sister glared at him, but Bob was too busy nicking his hand on his sword to notice, using the welling blood to sign his own name on the contract as a witness before turning to offer the paper—and the bloody quill—to Julius.

● ● ●

After that, it was all over surprisingly quickly. Despite the inherent queasiness involved with signing his first blood contract, Julius managed to get it done without making a fool of himself. They still needed the signature of whichever Heartstriker became the third vote on the council before they could actually do anything, but with Bethesda's name already down, she was no longer Queen of Heartstriker. It also meant Julius was now officially one of the three voices running the biggest dragon clan in the world, which, now that his siblings had gone to inform the rest of the clan of the new way of things, was actually making him feel a little ill.

"I still can't believe you talked them into a council," Katya said, shaking her head. "The other clans will go insane when they hear."

She was back in human form, cleaned up and wearing a shift dress made of unmelting snow that one of her sisters had conjured for her. They were sitting together on the steps of his mother's throne, watching the human cleaning staff go to pieces over the wreckage in the throne room. Estella's body, thankfully, had already been quietly burned while the Heartstrikers had been deciding what to do with their clan, though Julius wasn't sure if the quick funeral was a family tradition, or if the Daughters of the Three Sisters just couldn't wait to be rid of her.

"Bethesda's the one I'm worried about," he said, glancing over his shoulder at the closed door to Bethesda's private apartments. "She's…upset." And almost certainly planning his downfall.

"She's probably just in there hiding her treasures from the revolutionaries," Katya said with a shrug. "Old dragons don't take kindly to change, and tonight has been nothing but."

With regime changes for two of the most powerful dragon clans in the world *and* the death of one of the three dragon seers, that was putting it mildly. "She's not going to roll over on this. Bob forced her into signing today. He's holding the seal over her head to keep her in line, but we have to unseal her sometime, and there's no way she's going to keep playing along after that. The moment we sit down on that council, she's going to start trying to take over again."

"Naturally," Katya said. "You took away her power. Of course she's going to do everything she can to take it back. You'll just have to make sure that you and whichever Heartstriker gets the final council spot can work together well enough to stop her."

That was exactly what Julius was afraid of. "So," he said, changing the subject to something less terrifying. "Have you found Svena yet?"

"No," Katya said, her face falling. "We came here hoping to reinstate Svena as clan head. We weren't actually planning to kill Estella, but when I saw my chance, I took it."

He arched an eyebrow. "And the whole 'I am Katya, bow before me!' part was also spontaneous?"

"If I do the work, I'm not going to refuse the reward," she said primly. "Who do you think I am? You?"

Julius made a face, and she laughed. "Honestly, though, satisfying as it was to finally see Estella fall, I'm handing this mess off to Svena as soon as possible. I've spent my whole life running from my sisters. I have no idea how to lead them. Svena was always the one who did all the work."

She glanced over at the balcony, where the moon was already rising over the desert. "I've already told my sisters I'm abdicating to Svena, and they're fine with it. I think they'd take anyone sane at this point. But no matter how hard we look, we can't find our sister anywhere. All our spells turn up nothing. It's like she and Ian both just vanished."

Knowing Ian, Julius had his own ideas about that. He didn't think Katya would find them comforting, though, so he kept his mouth shut. One of her sisters, he couldn't tell which at this point, was already coming over to ask her more questions anyway, so he wished Katya good luck and made himself scarce. He was about to head downstairs in search of where the staff had stashed Marci when Bob shouted his name.

That was a surprise. The last he'd seen, the seer had taken the contract and his pigeon and vanished into his hoarded warehouse of a room. But apparently he was now back, running across the throne room toward Julius with Black Reach following behind him at a stately pace. "Julius!" he cried, panting. "Good, I found you. You have to meet my guest before he leaves."

That struck him as a little odd, but it wasn't every day you got to meet one of the three dragon seers, so Julius put out his hand. "It's an honor to meet you, Black Reach."

The dragon peered down at the offered handshake like he wasn't sure what he was looking at.

"The Black Reach agreed to help us as payment for a favor I'm going to do him in the future," Bob explained as Julius awkwardly lowered his hand. "He's about to go home, but he wanted to talk to you first."

"Sure," Julius said, trying not to sound as nervous as he felt. "What about?"

"Nothing in particular," the old dragon replied in his strange, too deep voice. "Just that I am pleased with the path your clan has chosen today. It is nice to finally find a dragon who isn't bent on repeating the mistakes of the past." He smiled, which somehow only made him look more intimidating. "I see why my brother helped you."

In the space of those seven words, Julius's stomach shrank to the size of a marble. "T-thank you," he stuttered at last. "I'll try to keep it that way."

The Black Reach inclined his head a fraction before turning back to Bob. "We shall meet three more times, Seer of the Heartstrikers. See that you don't waste them."

Bob smiled wide like this was a perfectly normal thing to say, waving goodbye and calling out well-wishes as the dragon turned and walked out of the room. Julius, on the other hand, was barely keeping himself together. "Bob," he whispered as soon as the old seer reached the throne room doors. "Do you know—"

"I know," Bob said through his plastered-on grin. "Shut up. He can still hear you."

Julius clamped his mouth shut, but that didn't stop him from fidgeting nervously the whole ten minutes it took the Black Reach to walk down the hallway and into the elevator at the end. When the elevator doors closed, though, he couldn't hold it any longer. "That's Dragon Sees Eternity!" he blurted out. "The guardian of the future!"

"I am well aware," Bob said, dropping his fake smile at last. "Trust me, I didn't want to involve him, but he was the only thing in the world big enough to scare Estella into wasting her time."

Julius cringed. "Did she know what he was?"

"Probably," Bob said with a shrug. "We all figure it out in time. There are only ever three dragon seers alive at any one time: a male, a female, and the Black Reach. That should make things pretty cramped—the future's not a big place when you're dealing with competing seers—but whenever we look into what could be, the Black Reach's hand is nowhere to be seen"

That didn't make sense to Julius. "So is he not a seer then?"

"Quite the opposite," Bob replied. "He's the greatest of us all. It's taken me centuries just to learn how to spot his movements, and even when I do, I still can't see why. He's clearly operating on a completely different level from the rest of us, and once you add in a basic knowledge of dragon history, it's not that hard to guess the Black Reach isn't your usual grumpy old dragon." He fell silent after that, and then, almost like an afterthought, he added. "He's also the first seer we see."

"What does that mean?" Julius asked.

"The first vision of the future any seer sees is their own death. As you might imagine, it's a traumatic experience for a young dragon, definitely not the sort of thing you talk about. But even if you tell no one, the Black Reach always shows up the next day. That's his test. If you recognize him, that means you're a true seer."

Julius frowned. "But why would you recognize him? You'd only had one vision at that point, right?"

Bob's face grew somber. "Because he's there. He's always in that first vision, because the Black Reach is present at the death of every seer. I've seen him at *my* death, so when he says, 'three more times,' I tend to take him at his word."

He sounded so sad by the time he finished, Julius's heart went out to him. "Is there anything I can do?"

Bob laughed. "Yes," he said, clapping him on the shoulders. "Keep being yourself. You've been an absolutely delightful tool, Julius Heartstriker. Without you as my unlikely hero, none of this would have been possible. But now at last, thanks to you, I've broken through Estella's block. Without her constantly nipping at my heels, the future is wide open for the first time in my life, which means the real game can begin."

Julius didn't like the way he said 'real game,' but before he could ask what that meant, all the white dragons in the room cried out as one.

"And there it goes," Bob said. "Right on schedule."

"*Bob!*" Julius yelled, running across the room to help Katya, who'd collapsed on the ground. "What happened?" he asked, falling to his knees beside her.

She looked up at him with wide, terrified eyes. "They're coming," she whispered. "Oh, Julius, they're *angry*."

"Who's angry?" he asked, but she'd already curled into a ball, covering her head with her arms like she was bracing for impact. He was trying to get her to at least look at him when he heard it.

OUR STAR!

The magic in the words hit him like a blow across the shoulders, sending him sprawling to the ground beside Katya.

OUR DAUGHTER, TREASURE, GONE! WHO HAS DONE THIS?

Julius reached up frantically, clutching his ears in a desperate attempt to shut out the voice. Voices, he corrected, because though they spoke in perfect unison, there were definitely more than one. It was impossible to say how many exactly, but given the way Katya and her sisters were shaking in terror, Julius's bet was on three.

"Seems the events of tonight haven't gone unnoticed," Bob said, strolling over to squat beside him. "The mommies are awake at last."

Julius had guessed as much already. "The Three Sisters," he whispered, his whole body shaking. The three oldest, most magical dragons left alive had finally woken from their thousand-year slumber, and from the sound of it, they were not happy about Estella's death.

"What should we do?" he asked Bob frantically, scrambling back to his feet. "Aren't they like gods or something? Should we evacuate?"

"Their anger just knocked us all down from halfway across the world," Bob reminded him. "I don't think running a few more feet is going to do us any good."

"Then what are we supposed to do?" Julius cried. "I didn't stick my neck out to reorder our entire clan just to lose it thirty minutes later!"

Rather than answer, his brother pulled a phone out of his pocket. Not his usual one, either, but a new, cheap model that looked like it had come from one of those pre-paid airport vending machines. "Don't worry," he said at last, turning on the cheap screen. "They're not coming for us."

Julius stopped. "They're not?"

Rather than explain, Bob turned the phone around to show Julius the glaring emergency broadcast alert on his screen. A few seconds later, the message vanished, and a woman's face appeared.

At first glance, she looked like a handsome older Native American woman in a navy-blue power suit with braided, steel-gray hair and blue eyes. On the second, it became obvious that her features were too regular to be real, and her flat eyes definitely had an Uncanny Valley quality to them. Most telling of all, though, was that her face refused to be still. Even though she wasn't moving, her image flickered and rippled on the screen, despite the crystal clear video quality of the rest of the shot. But then again, what else could you expect from the public face of the Lady of the Lakes?

"I don't understand," Julius said. "Why are we watching Algonquin's—"

"Shh!" Bob said, waving at him to be quiet as the spirit began to speak.

"This is a message for the newly awakened Three Sisters," Algonquin said, her voice as musical and light as falling water. "Simultaneously broadcast on all frequencies, all over the world. To the dragons currently disrupting the flow of magic worldwide, I understand you are upset over the loss of your daughter, the infamous Northern Star, and that you are even now searching for her killer. Well, search no longer."

She lifted her hand up to the camera, showing off a long, white mass of something clutched in her wavering fingers. A few seconds later, Julius realized it was *hair*. Very familiar, white hair cut to a length that perfectly matched what Estella had been missing earlier this evening.

"That's right," Algonquin said proudly, brandishing the tangled hair like a hunting trophy. "*I* killed Estella the Northern Star, just as I kill any dragon who is found trespassing on my property. If you want to do something about that, I invite you to stop wailing and come to my lakes in the Americas, where we will settle this once and for all."

As soon as she finished, the shot switched to a live, night sky-line feed of the DFZ from across the river. It was a classic postcard angle that showed off both the Upper and Lower cities as well as Algonquin's white tower lit up like a spotlight in the distance. What Julius didn't understand, though, was, *why*.

"What is she doing?" he whispered, glancing at his brother. "Is she *trying* to get her city burned to the ground?"

"Keep watching," Bob said, reaching up to pet the pigeon who'd just fluttered down to land on his shoulder. "Here it comes."

Julius turned back to the screen in time to see the camera shake, and then the whole city rocked as three enormous shapes appeared in the sky above the DFZ with a thunderclap as big as an earthquake. They were so large, Julius didn't even recognize them as dragons at first. Even with the DFZ's superscrapers for scale, it was hard to comprehend a living thing *that* big, let alone three of them. But when spotlights came on all over the city to illuminate the monsters in the sky, he wasn't surprised at all to see that their scales were white as snow.

YOU WILL PAY, WATER SPRITE, the Three Sisters roared in unison, their voices twined together like a braid as they flew toward Algonquin's tower in the center of Lake St. Clair. *YOU AND YOUR CITY.*

White fire was glowing in all three throats by the time they finished. It looked just like Estella's, but on a city-destroying scale. And then, just as Julius was saying goodbye to the crazy town that had become more of a home to him than anywhere else, a new light appeared in the sky, rising from the darkness that marked Reclamation Land.

It flew up like a firework, sparkling in the night like sunlight on water. For a long heartbeat, it hung there in the air, a silver thread connecting the dark land and the starry sky. Then, as suddenly as it had appeared, the thread of light exploded outward in a perfect halo, shooting across the sky like a scythe to cut through all three dragons.

The blast was so bright, it whited out the screen. In the split second it took the cameras to adjust and bring the picture back, the enormous dragons were already falling, crashing out of the sky in a cascade of snow-white and shimmering red down into the lake surrounding Algonquin's Tower. The impact when they hit sent water flying almost to the tower's peak, and then the cameras cut back to Algonquin's triumphant smile.

"Mortals of this world," she said proudly. "You have nothing to fear. We Spirits of the Land have ever been your protectors. You have known my anger once before. Now, you see it again, cutting down the vipers who would enslave you all."

That must have been the PR part of the message, because after it was done, Algonquin's watery voice lost all trace of humanity. "And to the dragons watching this—the snakes who think they can kill my spirits and infest my land—consider this your first and *only* warning. With one shot, I have killed the three most powerful of your kind left on Earth. Now, I declare war on the rest. *Any* dragon who enters the DFZ, or any other nation which requests my protection, will meet the same end. You have now become *my* prey, and the hunt will continue until the current dragon infestation is entirely eliminated." Her flickering lips curled in a smile. "See you in Detroit."

The video cut out after that, taking them back to the emergency broadcast message, but all Julius could do was stare.

"Well," Bob said, slipping the phone back into his pocket. "*That* escalated quickly."

Julius couldn't even form a reply. He just sank silently to the floor, landing beside the equally shell-shocked Katya as Marci came bursting into the room to ask if they'd seen what'd just happened on TV.

EPILOGUE

A few time zones away, in a heavily warded basement beneath the United Nations headquarters in New York City, a woman of indeterminate age wearing a very expensive suit was cursing under her breath. In front of her, a three-foot-deep nest of layered AR projections showed what had just happened in Detroit on constant loop: the version Algonquin had broadcast, footage from their own cameras, and selected clips from the thousands of independent witnesses that were now flooding video sharing sites. No matter how many angles she watched it from, though, the story was always the same. Algonquin had shot down the three most feared dragons in the world within minutes of their awakening, which meant they were *all* in a great deal of trouble.

"Ma'am!"

The woman didn't move, just glanced at her side camera to see one of her aides slipping through the heavily reinforced door into her darkened room with a black folder in his hands. "*Please* tell me that's the sit rep from the DFZ office. I want a full report of where she got the magic for *that*," she pointed at the looped footage of the giant white dragons falling from the sky, "and I want it now."

"No, ma'am," the young man said, his face pale. "This is the confirmation from Stanford University's Thaumaturgy Department you ordered this morning. They're reporting the same results as yesterday. We've also gotten readings in from our offices in Jerusalem, Mumbai, Tokyo, and London, all positive."

The woman sighed and leaned back in her leather chair, turn-ing to glare at the large raven sitting on his custom perch beside her. "I thought you said we had fifty years before we had to worry about this?"

"I did," the raven replied, turning its head to look at her with each of its beady eyes. "But I've been mistaken before."

"A Merlin rising *five decades* before he's supposed to is a pretty big mistake," the woman snapped, glancing back at the falling drag-ons that were still playing on loop across all her projected screens. "Though I suppose this could help explain why Algonquin chose tonight to play her hand."

"Ma'am?" the aide said, glancing nervously at the perch which, to him, most likely appeared empty. "Are you talking to me?"

"I am now," the woman said, standing up in a fluid motion. "Pack me a bag with the usual, and have someone dig Myron out of his labyrinth."

Now the aide looked terrified. "The Under Secretary of Magic?" he said, voice trembling. "I can try. But forgive me for asking, shouldn't we be getting someone from the Office for Spirit Affairs for this?"

The woman laughed. "With Algonquin taking over every video feed in the world to show off a triple-dragon kill? I'm sure the OSA is already at maximum panic, which is to say, useless." She put out her arm for the raven to hop onto her wrist. "If we're going to have any hope of getting control of this situation, we need to come at the problem from a different angle, which means I need Myron and a flight to New Mexico."

At the mention of New Mexico, the aide cringed. "Yes, ma'am," he said, pulling out his phone. "But...are you certain you want to handle this personally? The last agent we sent didn't fare so well."

"True," she said with a smile. "But I'm a lot tougher than he was, and haven't you ever heard that the enemy of my enemy is my friend?"

"Yes, ma'am," the aide said, backing into the hall with a defeated sigh. "I'll go pack your bag."

"And make sure they get Myron specifically!" she yelled after him. "Don't waste my time with anyone else!"

The door slammed shut before he could answer. It didn't matter, though. The woman was already in motion, stripping off her suit jacket as she walked to the weapons wall—a massive display that took up the entire rear half of the room—and started loading up.

THANK YOU FOR READING!

Thank you for reading *One Good Dragon Deserves Another*! If you enjoyed the story, or even if you didn't, I hope you'll consider leaving a review. Reviews, good and bad, are vital to any author's career, and I would be extremely thankful and appreciative if you'd consider writing one for me.

Want to know when my next novel is available? Visit **www.rachelaaron. net** to see all my books and to sign up for my new release mailing list! You can also follow me on Twitter @Rachel_Aaron or like my Facebook page, facebook.com/RachelAaronAuthor, for up-to-date information on all of my releases.

The third Heartstriker novel, ***No Good Dragon Goes Unpunished***, should be coming out in 2016! If that's too long to wait, I hope you'll check out one of my other, completed series. Simply visit **www. rachelaaron.net** to see all of my books complete with their beautiful covers, links to reviews, and free sample chapters!

Thank you again for reading, and I hope you'll be back soon!

Yours sincerely,
Rachel Aaron

WANT MORE BOOKS BY RACHEL AARON? CHECK OUT THESE COMPLETED SERIES!

THE LEGEND OF ELI MONPRESS

The Spirit Thief
The Spirit Rebellion
The Spirit Eater
The Legend of Eli Monpress (omnibus
edition of the first three books)
The Spirit War
Spirit's End

"Fast and fun, *The Spirit Thief* introduces a fascinating new world and a complex magical system based on cooperation with the spirits who reside in all living objects. Aaron's characters are fully fleshed and possess complex personalities, motivations, and backstories that are only gradually revealed. Fans of Scott Lynch's *Lies of Locke Lamora* (2006) will be thrilled with Eli Monpress. Highly recommended for all fantasy readers." - **Booklist, Starred Review PARADOX**
(written as Rachel Bach)

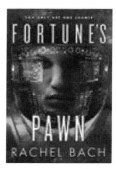

PARADOX
(written as Rachel Bach)

Fortune's Pawn
Honor's Knight
Heaven's Queen

"*Firefly*-esque in its concept of a rogue-ish spaceship family...
The narrative never quite goes where you expect it to, in a
good way...Devi is a badass with a heart."—**Locus Magazine**

"If you liked *Star Wars*, if you like our books, and if
you are waiting for *Guardians of the Galaxy* to hit the
theaters, this is your book."- **Ilona Andrews**

"I JUST LOVED IT! Perfect light sci-fi. If you like
space stuff that isn't that complicated but highly entertaining, I give two thumbs up!" - **Felicia Day**

**To find out more about Rachel and read
samples of all her books, visit
www.rachelaaron.net!**

ABOUT THE AUTHOR

Rachel Aaron is the author of eleven novels as well as the bestselling nonfiction writing book, *2k to 10k: Writing Faster, Writing Better, and Writing More of What You Love,* which has helped thousands of authors double their daily word counts. When she's not holed up in her writing cave, Rachel lives a nerdy, bookish life in Athens, GA, with her perpetual motion son, long suffering husband, and obese wiener dog. To learn more about me, my work, or to find a complete list of my interviews and podcasts, please visit my author page at rachelaaron.net!

Finally, a very special thank you to my incredible Beta Readers: Michele Fry, Jodie Martin, Eva Bunge, Beth Bisgaard, Hisham El-Far, Robert Aaron, Judith Smith, Sarah Nutt, Elizabeth Poole, Kevin Swearingen, and the ever amazing Lali. I couldn't do this without you. Thank you all SO MUCH!

Made in the USA
Columbia, SC
26 November 2022

72115467R00265